The
Espionage
of the
Saints

By the same author

Political studies

Communism and the French Intellectuals
The Left in Europe since 1789
Fanon
The Fellow-Travellers: a Postscript to the
    Enlightenment
The Great Fear: the Anti-Communist Campaign
    under Truman and Eisenhower
Under the Skin: the Death of White Rhodesia

Novels

At Fever Pitch
Comrade Jacob
The Decline of the West
The Occupation
The K-Factor

Other works

The Demonstration (play)
The Illusion: an Essay on Politics, Theatre and
    the Novel
Collisions: Essays and Reviews
Cuba, Yes?

THE ESPIONAGE OF THE SAINTS

Two Essays on Silence and the State

David Caute

HAMISH HAMILTON
LONDON

First published in Great Britain 1986
by Hamish Hamilton Ltd
Garden House 57–59 Long Acre London WC2E 9JZ

British Library Cataloguing in Publication Data

Caute, David
   The espionage of the saints: two essays on
   silence and the state.
   1. Freedom of information
   I. Title
   323.44′5   JC597

   ISBN 0–241–11750–X

Phototypeset by Input Typesetting Ltd, London
Printed in Great Britain by
St Edmundsbury Press, Bury St Edmunds, Suffolk

Contents

Acknowledgments

Grateful acknowledgment is made to the following for permission to print or reprint passages contained in 'Marechera and the Colonel': to Dambudzo Marechera, for 'The Black Insider' and 'Portrait of a Black Artist in London'; to Heinemann Educational Books, for *House of Hunger* and *Black Sunlight*; to College Press, Harare, for *Mindblast*; to the William Morris Agency for Athol Fugard's *Sizwe Bansi is Dead*.

Introduction

This book contains two reports. Both describe the punitive measures taken against citizens who, in the year 1984, committed word-crime. The dishonourable disclosure which children call 'telling' occurs when one boy reports another to 'them' – to authority. Word-crime is the same act of verbal disloyalty in reverse: a member of the staff common room comes out into the playground to reveal to the children what the teachers have been saying and plotting. It's a form of rebellion involving neither guns nor barricades, merely words, knowledge, information. But these are formidable weapons which tap deep fears. For private citizens and corporations as well as governments, security in an adversarial, threatening climate lies in prudent silence; under challenge, this silence is codified by clan oaths as secrecy. The Zimbabwean state, like the British, insists that certain types of knowledge, and certain critical perspectives, must not be communicated to 'unauthorised' persons – which invariably means the population at large. When the code is broken, the silencers respond with punitive measures.

Two British civil servants, Sarah Tisdall and Clive Ponting, were charged under section 2 of the Official Secrets Act; more or less concurrently, the Zimbabwean writer Dambudzo Marechera was thrown into a police cell in Harare under emergency powers derived from the old British colonial administration of Southern Rhodesia. In both London and Harare the culprits were accused of disloyalty to their government and therefore to their country: a significant equation. In terms of library catalogues the essay 'Marechera and the Colonel' belongs to 'Africa/Zimbabwe/writers/arrests' whereas 'The Espionage of the Saints' belongs to 'UK/civil servants/Official Secrets Act/prosecution'. To my mind they are separate motions in a single choreography that I observed in the year associated with Orwell. The convergences far outweigh the divergences.

Sarah Tisdall and Clive Ponting are both well-balanced, decently modest people rooted in solid, middle-class England and in time-honoured traditions of service and loyalty. Neither of them would toss saucers at chandeliers, as Marechera did when awarded a literary prize in London, nor would they write lewdly and disparagingly of their parents. Marechera's anarchism is of a sort more familiar among European artists. In breaking the law, or their professional code of conduct, Tisdall and Ponting hesitated, winding themselves up, against the grain, to a single act of defiance unlikely to be repeated. Marechera is a law unto himself, though the alleycat has a sharp nose for danger. When Clive Ponting faced detection his main thought was to leave the Ministry of Defence with a sound letter of reference (a dominant preoccupation for the majority of professionals). Only the devil would write Marechera a reference. His life is a model of bad behaviour but his intelligence is acute and his fiction is among the most arresting (if the pun may be excused) in contemporary Africa. He loathes the state and he distrusts anyone touched by politics and power.

Unlike Tisdall and Ponting, Marechera acknowledges no debts and duties, other than to himself and his vision of a free writer's licence. He's a vagrant, in and out of the cells both in Zimbabwe and England. Had he been singled out for his precocious brilliance by an enlightened eighteenth-century English patron, put in wig and satin breeches and taught Latin (which Marechera himself sees as a symbol of civilisation), he would have repaid the debt by laying milord's daughter in the summer house before taking off with a clutch of rare volumes and being whipped in a slave-hold all the way from Bristol (Clive Ponting's native city) to the West Indies. On arrival he would have despised the creoles and made fitful attempts to teach them Latin for a keg of rum.

The two English civil servants do, however, share certain qualities with Marechera, most obviously an intense dislike of the humbug and mendacity lurking behind the mumbo-jumbo of official secrecy. But their protest is securely bonded by the real; Marechera's extends to the surreal. Neither Tisdall nor Ponting wish to explore the subconscious, the province in which Marechera is most at home.

Tisdall and Ponting enjoyed the support and sympathy of powerful pressure groups. The Leader of the Opposition denounced Sarah Tisdall's prison sentence. She was a political issue, polarising clan loyalties. MPs visited her in prison, women demonstrated outside Holloway gaol. Ponting's defence campaign was endorsed by all three Opposition leaders and by the country's two leading liberal newspapers. No Zimbabwean lawyer will touch Marechera; when Ponting came to trial, the Government was made to bleed to the point of haemorrhage. Neither Marechera's publishers nor his fellow-writers thought it prudent to raise a whisper on his behalf.

The police apparatus in Zimbabwe is more capricious than in England – at least on the surface. A young writer who wants to play the Fool will be treated like one: blows first and never mind 'due process'. The very respectability of Tisdall and Ponting ensured that they were regarded as prisoners of conscience, but Marechera's disreputable life-style offers Zimbabwean society the pretext for washing its hands of him: 'He's his own worst enemy.' Could he exist and write without the stimulus of repression? Most certainly: his most penetrating insights reach beyond forms of government to illuminate the cancer of conformism which outlives particular constitutions.

The extent to which Tisdall and Ponting polarised opinion, became symbolic protagonists in a long-running drama, brings us to the vital distinction between politics and principle. If we judge their actions, and the countervailing response of the state, only in terms of our political allegiances, we miss every important moral dilemma. Double standards cost nothing. When I refer to Tisdall and Ponting as 'saints' I do not imply that their proper resting place is a stained-glass window; I point only to a peculiar moral quality in their actions. As far as one can tell neither of them wished to be detected. Civil servants who believe in freedom of information do not necessarily apply the doctrine rigorously to their own behaviour and motivations. There are shaded areas which I have tried to explore. How deep is our attachment to secrecy can be seen from the behaviour of the *Guardian* newspaper after its editor virtually ensured Sarah Tisdall's arrest by complying with a court order and handing back to the Government one of the two documents she had leaked. This chain of events releases a full flight of defecating pigeons and one purpose of 'The Espionage of the Saints' is to see where the droppings may fall.

In working on the two reports more or less concurrently I have cut the cloth to fit the characters. The Tisdall-Ponting cases involve a dense quantity of documentary material, a constant sifting of evidence, the sort of digging we associate with 'investigative' journalism. But Marechera's province is that of the imagination and I have allowed my own to make a parallel journey, the result being that 'Marechera and the Colonel' moves back and forth across the hazy frontier between fact and fiction, between a writer's life and his art. The Colonel himself, whether real or mythical, black or white, Zimbabwean or British, stands astride that frontier, making short work of justice. The Colonel is not merely an emblem of authority but also a facet of the loyal, outraged tribesman in each of us.

MARECHERA AND THE COLONEL

– a Zimbabwean writer and the claims of the
state

'I had been expelled from the University of Central Africa for throwing a paving stone at a fascist professor of medicine whose black bullet head I missed by a breath. A sudden crackdown on the campus by the secret police had forced me to decamp clear out of the country and I found myself awarded an Oxford scholarship. . . .'

'I had hitchhiked down from Wales where I had spent three months in prison for possessing cannabis. . . .'

'It's the ruin not the original which moves men; our Zimbabwe ruins must have looked really shit and hideous when they were brandnew.'

Dambudzo Marechera—'The Black Insider' (an unpublished novel)

ONE

Marechera had been arrested. No one at the Book Fair seemed to know why, or to care. It was rumoured (correctly) that he was still held in Harare Central Police Station, an imposing colonial structure commanding the corner of Inez Terrace and the old Railway Avenue, now renamed after the President of Zambia, Kenneth Kaunda, the Christian humanist whose trademark is a silk neckscarf and a handkerchief fluttering from his left hand. Clearly Marechera's fate was of little concern to the Zimbabwean writers, academics and politicians lazily circulating among the book stands, exchanging greetings prefaced by the triple revolutionary handshake: thumb-palm-thumb. An urgent clasp already grown lethargic and decadent with ritual use.

Foreign visitors, whether London publishers on expense accounts or representatives of liberation movements still thirsting for justice – Namibia, Palestine and the Western Sahara – were not keen to spoil their journeys by raising the matter of Dambudzo Marechera. Marx, Engels and Lenin were also on display, but they too were in no hurry to complicate their message with ill-informed protests about a writer of dubious reputation. It was, after all, an 'internal matter'; to intervene might be mistaken for neo-colonialism.

Marechera in trouble again? Hadn't that vagabond barfly done his best to disrupt the previous year's Book Fair, heedless of the wound to a new nation craving for respect, for recognition as anglophone Africa's leading 'book centre'? An original talent, of course, if you can stomach the stream of obscenity, the dung heaped upon Shona culture and 'Zimbabwe in Transition', but don't squander your sympathy. No one is arrested without good reason. Probably pissed out of his mind. Zimbabwe needs patriots, not flamboyant exhibitionists. Sheer brilliance had won him a scholarship to Oxford, the dream of every Zimbabwean youth, and how did he repay the honour? By trying to burn down New College. Or maybe that's apocryphal, but it would be typical anyway:

The black girls of Oxford, whether African, West Indian or

American – despised those of us who came from Rhodesia. After all, we still haven't won our independence. After all, the papers say we are always quarrelling among ourselves . . . We had become – indeed we are – the Jews of Africa, and nobody wanted us.[1]

Television defines the climate. It's controlled by those who make the weather. Shortly before Marechera's arrest the nightly TV bulletins had been crammed with foreign dignitaries arriving at Harare airport for the ruling party's long-awaited congress: Nyerere of Tanzania, Machel of Mozambique, Kaunda with his hanky, Arafat of Palestine – diplomats, dignitaries, the King of Swaziland, fraternal delegations from Eastern Europe – all of them offering the triple handshake, all congregating on the VIP platform to applaud Robert Mugabe.

And how did Marechera celebrate the party congress, the first since Independence? With a sober poem of praise, with stirring lines dedicated to the future of his country? No, he chose the moment to publish a work defaming the Great Stone House, which is what Zimbabwe means in Shona. That he has talent, no one at the Book Fair would deny; but if a writer launches his literary career by denigrating his parents, then loyalty is clearly foreign to his nature:

I knew my father as the character who occasionally screwed mother and who paid the rent, beat me up, and was cuckolded on the sly by various persons. He drove huge cargo lorries, transporting ground nut oil to Zambia and Zaire and Malawi. I knew that he was despised because of mother, and because he always wore khaki overalls, even on Sundays.[2]

Visitors to the Book Fair paused cautiously at the North Korean stand, where inscrutable gentlemen wearing stone-age lapel buttons impassively stood guard beside the heaped works of Kim Il Sung, pastel-tinted Father of his People. It was North Korean advisers who had settled in the Inyanga hills to train the Fifth Brigade and the Presidential Guard in such martial arts as brick-breaking, later displayed, with Kung Fu grunts and Bruce Lee yells, to ecstatic crowds in Rufaro Stadium. From ceremonial brick-breaking to the real thing, neck-breaking in Matabeleland, had been a short (and necessary) step – and just as visitors to the Book Fair were disinclined to discuss Marechera's arrest, so also the publications on display offered no hint of the stricken villages and shallow graves

[1]Marechera, *The House of Hunger*.
[2]Ibid.

round Kezi, Antelope Mine and Nyamandhlovu. The North Korean 'editors' stood motionless by Father Kim Il Sung, their short jet-black hair polished across their unbroken skulls. But enter Hatchard's in Piccadilly and the excremental cells of H-Block also seem far away.

Marechera, like Matabeleland, was giving Zimbabwe a 'bad name'. The phrase is often used. At the height of the guerrilla war, a Rhodesian farmer's wife complained, over dinner in a heavily fortified homestead, that the death of Steve Biko had been used by the Western press 'to give South Africa a bad name'. Silence is the safest guardian of reputation; the safest guarantee of silence is to wipe the mind.

One learns a lot about people by merely studying what they do not want to know. Everybody doesn't want to know something or other.[1]

Zimbabwe is not a totalitarian country. Marechera had been temporarily removed but he had not 'been disappeared' or declared a non-person. Piled high at the central counter of the Book Fair were copies of his new book, *Mindblast*, an orange-coloured paperback with a surrealist design involving a humanised cat and a black in a space helmet.

I approached the woman in charge of the commercial side of the Fair.

'It's the kind of publicity we don't need,' she said. She also asked me to keep my voice down. Only yesterday a couple of Western journalists had been making inquiries about Marechera – 'like vultures'. Then she said, 'I've no comment to make.'

Enquiring at the College Press stand about the fate of their author, I encountered only murmurs and pumping adam's apples: please go away. An effusive white executive of College Press bestrode the aisle, wringing visiting hands – a huge wind of extrovert energy that could not be stilled.

Outside Kingston's bookstore, venue of the Book Fair, lies Cecil Square, framed and shadowed by exotic trees and plants imported by the old, colonial municipality. It was here that Marechera, slowly spooning his breakfast of sour milk or yoghurt, had squatted with the swivelling saucer eyes of an alleycat, observing the passage of the 'shefs', the new, post-colonial elite:

The neatly pressed safari suits of the shefs bludgeoned his senses, gouged his eyes . . . . They passed by in their stinkingly

[1]Ibid.

5

expensive safari suits and briefcases. Passed you with a contemptuous curiosity and fear in their eyes. After all, they did not know – what with so many demobilised combatants around – whether you were just an insane tramp or a 'dissident'.[1]

Later he wrote:

The Harare I was living in was someone else's creation. I could not encompass it.[2]

Finally I approached the Director of the Book Fair, whose photograph had that morning appeared on the front page of the *Herald* in the company of the Minister of Information and the Director: he white, they black. For years a correspondent of the London *Observer*, David Martin had settled in Zimbabwe after Independence, set up his own publishing house, cultivated his contacts within Zanu-PF, the ruling party, and seized the expanding textbook market with such entrepreneurial energy that the older firms could only glower in sullen envy. Martin and his colleague Phyllis Johnson had launched their Zimbabwe Publishing House with a big and important book of their own, *The Struggle for Zimbabwe*, a history of Zanu's long and bitter campaign in exile. The work of a dedicated *compagnon de route*, it ruthlessly took the losing parties, Muzorewa and Nkomo, the Kadets and Mensheviks, off the great throughroad of national liberation. Blessed with a preface written by Robert Mugabe himself – the ultimate *imprimatur* – the book sold like hot cakes.

Unable to compete with so calculating a business intelligence lacquered by long devotion to Zanu-PF, the established firms which had done business within Ian Smith's Rhodesia could not afford to boycott David Martin's prestigious brainchild, the Zimbabwe Book Fair, dear to the hearts of ministers.

We greeted each other with the effusiveness of rival assassins caught in open concourse, under too bright a light. He was kind enough to praise a book of my own.

'I haven't met a politician here who doesn't like it.'

I reminded him that he had published a local edition of Marechera's first, prize-winning book, *The House of Hunger*. Indeed this book was heavily on display.

The Director's mouth tightened. Marechera's behaviour, he explained, had been inexcusable, a constant provocation which

[1]Marechera, *Mindblast*.
[2]Ibid.

6

could no longer be tolerated. Having done his best to wreck last year's Book Fair, the writer had tried to repeat the performance this year by confronting the Minister of Information and accusing him of keeping his new book out of the shops. As Director of the Book Fair, David Martin had been obliged to intervene rapidly to protect the minister.

'Was that why he was arrested?'

'Not at all.'

'Then why?'

'I've made enquiries, that's all I can say.'

TWO

Africa is not short of morality tales about how young men took to the bush and hills to raise rebellion against their oppressors; how Grandma got her revenge when her cow was stolen; how young girls in the towns get into trouble; and how virtue is sometimes rewarded but not always. Marechera hates the bush and Grandma as well. As for the virtue of young girls,

> Miss Piggy squealed with
> Exquisite pain
> When love thy neighbour
> Went against the grain.[1]

His writing blisters every totem pole. At the heart of his new volume, *Mindblast*, piled high at the Book Fair but without the author's autograph, a one-act play called *Blitzkrieg* carries the surrealist onslaught – the tradition of Jarry, Artaud and Ionesco – to Zimbabwe's new ruling elite. The party, disturbed by mounting charges of corruption, had responded with its own 'leadership code', a blueprint for socialist purity. Marechera is not convinced; what distinguishes him from most of his fellow-citizens is that he says so.

Marechera's extravaganza, *Blitzkrieg*, is set in the home of a rich

---

[1]Marechera, 'Portrait of a Black Artist in London' (unpublished).

7

and cynical white entrepreneur living in Harare, Mr Norman Drake, who has thrown a lavish, multi-racial party:

> Throughout the play people of all shades are queueing up to use the loo. Men, women and children. The action and dialogue is therefore periodically punctuated by the flushing of the toilet which, because it is not working, gives a weird, mind-jamming gaga flush.[1]

Enter now DRAKE himself, politely shaking off a lustful black lady, MRS NZUZU. She, it emerges, is the wife of a leading member of the Government – and here comes her husband, the minister himself, the Rt Hon. COMRADE NZUZU. Despite Drake's attraction for his simpering wife, NZUZU readily accepts from the white businessman two envelopes stuffed with dollars as well as the keys to DRAKE's silver Rolls Royce. Clearly the Code of Conduct is not quite operational. MRS NZUZU, meanwhile, drags DRAKE off to a bedroom while babbling about her husband's past trials and tribulations, 'the Struggle, detentions, banning orders, humiliations, imprisonment'. All very boring to MR DRAKE, who had no doubt fully supported the régime which inflicted the said tribulations.

Marechera now stirs the pot by introducing ALFIE, a radical proletarian recently returned from England with a white wife whom he met at a CND rally. His opinion of the new Zimbabwe?

> ALFIE: . . . It's still the same old ox-wagon of the rich getting richer and the poor getting poorer . . . You say you're getting hungry and the shef peers over his three chins down at you and says Comrade, you're the backbone of the Revolution . . . . And before you even finish what you're saying he's got the CIO and the police and you are being marched at gunpoint to the interrogation barracks.

Marechera, as we shall see, knows well the Central Intelligence Organisation; heir to the old Rhodesian Special Branch, one of its wings operates (as in Smith's day) under the direct control of the Prime Minister's office.

But wait: radical ALFIE will not have all the best lines. Enter now the beautiful, tempestuous ARABELLA AKA BIBI to engage him in a deadly duel about sex and politics. Indeed she loses no time in drawing a gun on him:

ARABELLA: Don't move, Shona bastard. (*She gestures towards the*

---

[1]*Blitzkrieg.*

toilet.) Get in there. Lock the door. Well, mister, it's goodnight from the Western Zimbabwe Liberation Front. (*She aims and fires three shots through the thin plywood door.*)

The Western Zimbabwe Liberation Front is a fiction – Marechera's way of formalising the armed dissident movement in Matabeleland which, as we have seen, had provoked the Fifth Brigade, with their North Korean karate chops, to embark on the pacification of Zimbabwe's Ndebele province. But why does Arabella shoot Alfie? Because she divines his real identity; despite the class-war pose, Alfie is another secret policeman. In short, politics is filth from top to bottom: trust no one.

Marechera now diverts his attention to the whites who have broad-mindedly stayed on in Zimbabwe to help shoulder the great national enterprise known as 'Reconciliation'. The dramatist offers us no less than six WHITE MEN angrily lined up outside the locked toilet door.

3rd MAN: We are queueing for cooking oil, we're queueing for matches, we're queueing for bread, and NOW WE ARE QUEUEING FOR LAVATORIES. And for what?
5th MAN: To shit decently, of course.

A bit bored with this, Marechera launches from within the toilet not the body of the assassinated ALFIE but Drake's mysterious employee, SHOGUN.

5th MAN: Hiroshima didn't finish off slit-eyed Banzai.

A furious punch-up ensues. The six WHITE MEN are subdued by SHOGUN, who then offers an inscrutable joke about the toilet.

SHOGUN: Me make joke on you? Me, no. Toilet yes.
DRAKE (*unconsciously talking like Shogun*): Toilet make joke on Comrade Drake?
SHOGUN (*suddenly laughing hysterically*): Yes? Yes. Toilet make joke on whole country!

At which the curtain comes down. Later in this essay we shall learn more about Marechera and violent toilets, though we may remain uncertain as to whether his life owes more to his art than the reverse.

Now, gathered round the heaped copies of *Mindblast* at the Book Fair, were a group of concerned north Europeans, handsome people carrying leather shoulder bags, heavy (at a guess) with Nikons, light meters and spools of precious film. They were knotted in animated, low-voiced discussion, as if debating whether they were confronted by a major international scandal (is not freedom indivisible?) or merely one of those little local happenings, wrapped in cultural misunderstanding, that it would be imprudent to penetrate. Had they perhaps planned to make a film of Marechera's *Black Sunlight*, a work initially banned in Zimbabwe, in the dramatic heat of the Zambezi Valley – beautiful footage of elephant roaming among the giant baobabs, long shots of Tonga boatmen crossing the great river in their dug-outs, fair-skinned actresses blistering in the black sunlight, the making of the film in forty Celsius providing wonderful hype for the film festival journalists (if not for the juries)? Had they applied for the requisite permissions at the Ministry of Information, only to meet with baffling delays, bureaucratic obstructions, angry remonstrances – 'Why choose Marechera, he's the least typical Zimbabwean writer!'? Was a large and expensive crew of cameramen, sound recordists and continuity girls kicking its heels round the hotel swimming pool while the director and script writer searched in vain for the wayward genius himself, visiting with Scandinavian thoroughness every one of Marechera's reported hideouts and watering places, peering in dark, smoky bars and illicit township shebeens for a glimpse of the soft, baby face with its catlike saucer eyes?

> From all around I hear dark
> Dread:
>   'You think you are a poet
>   You are black and buggered.'[1]

And now the disconcerted film unit had discovered he was in a police cell. Quite sensational but no one seemed to care! Rather sullenly they thumbed through his latest publication, and by nightfall might have laid plans to incorporate in the film a vast, stone-age toilet in the middle of Zimbabwe, a 'shit and hideous' (Marechera's very words) historical monument to art as defecation. It would be an adventure as well a stunning film, something to reminisce about at the end of the year, in the months of centrally heated editing, vodka and good cheese, seated in elegant Scandinavian furniture and exchanging notes about 'their' tribes, their Shona, Hausa, Kikuyu and Xhosa. But in the short term the problem was to make the film; they had been warned against greasing palms in an acutely sensitive revolutionary climate, but perhaps they had been too inhibited, perhaps they had overlooked human nature. . . .

[1]'Throne of Bayonets' in *Mindblast*.

10

THREE

Two years had passed since Marechera's infamous 'lecture' at the University of Zimbabwe. Returning from England in October 1981 after a long exile, he was greeted by the news that the Censorship Board had banned his new novel, *Black Sunlight*, as obscene. The ban was lifted under the protests of fellow-writers, but Marechera was – and never is – in any mood to be mollified. The university hall was packed for his lecture: Marechera is the only Zimbabwean writer capable of turning furniture into trees.

Our Zimbabwe ruins must have looked really shit and hideous when they were brandnew.[1]

The sacred pile of stones over whose ethnic origins the archaeologists had fought a long war, a coded duel about race and cultural authority, was casually trashcanned by a writer who visualised Great Zimbabwe as a fifteenth-century Holiday Inn. Anticipating more in this vein, academics and students crowded the lecture hall like German intellectuals expecting Brecht or Toller to piss on both the Kaiser and the Weimar Republic. Besides, *The House of Hunger* was already an optional text in the literature faculty: no student could afford not to sift the poet's crap for usable gems.

Like any self-respecting writer, Marechera intended to bite the hand that fed him. Small and pretty like a cat, with the sort of pout that excites anal inspections at immigration points, he was led onto the platform by guardians who had been trying, all afternoon, to keep him from the bottle. The poet sat down but soon stood up again and began to walk about the platform, laying sticks of dynamite while tapping his pockets for matches.

'In Zimbabwe,' he declared, 'we have these two great indigenous languages, ChiShona and Sindebele.' Marechera reached for something in his hair: a louse, perhaps, or a thought. 'Who wants us to keep writing these ShitShona and ShitNdebele languages, this missionary chickenshit? Who else but the imperialists?'

Cautiously the academics cleared their throats. It was now official

[1] 'The Black Insider'.

11

policy to encourage vernacular literature. One could as well discuss the Queen's menstrual cycle in *The Times* as admit in Harare that the Shonas had been without a written vernacular until the missionaries compiled one.

Seated near the front of the audience, listening intently but with a studiedly non-committal expression, was a neat, dapper man wearing a sharply pressed safari suit in the Mugabe mode, his beard trim, his hands slowly folding and unfolding in his lap. A rising star in the Literature Faculty, an authority on African poetry in the light of Karl Marx, he was also a gifted administrator marked out for promotion. A particular burden of his life nowadays was travelling abroad, attending conferences and seminars from Nairobi to Oslo, lecturing on 'Literature, Ideology and Africanisation'. He had learned a few tricks. When questioned (inevitably) about Marechera in sub-zero capitals by bohemians in anoraks, their pale faces washed in sincerity, he invariably replied:

'I cannot really answer in my official capacity. There are in fact members of our Faculty in Harare who specialise in Marechera's work. To be honest, we have as our urgent national task the development of a new literature which will achieve for our people what Gorky's *The Mother* achieved for the Russian working masses.'

Allowing his gaze to wander from Marechera – who was now sulking around the platform, fiddling with an empty wine glass which had somehow popped out of his pocket, the comrade academic glanced obliquely towards the vice-chancellor and his wife seated in the front row. Ambition hammered in him like a second heart.

Marechera seemed to be saying that to a poet, an artist, the glass in his hand was a beautiful woman; whereas to ordinary philistines like those he was addressing, the only question was 'how much water can it hold?'

The comrade academic adjusted his creased legs and refolded his 14-carat hands. It would probably not be sensible to lock Marechera away – yet. Fund-raising in the Scandinavian countries might suffer. In Copenhagen he had recently addressed a conference, courtesy of SAS, on 'Literature and Change in Southern Africa: New Perspectives', despatching in advance a short abstract in which he argued, most originally, that 'the form and content of literature change in proportion to the development of national consciousness.' No one in Copenhagen had challenged this insight. The comrade academic had been emboldened to call for a materialist, non-metaphysical poetry of combat, full of concrete images

Marechera was now likening the wine glass to a white arse and sticking his finger in. This kept some members of the audience wide awake, while others slipped into private trances, their new quarter-acre real-estate plots (or 'stands') pushing back into the space temporarily vacated for a crazed poet. Like the sea seeping into the shallow trench round a sand-castle. We go to lectures and are always disappointed. The comrade academic, often bored while adjusting the simultaneous translation on his earphones in Oslo and Copenhagen, normally relieved the tedium by improvising travelling expenses with a silver pen.

The worst enemy of art, Marechera announced, is the educated philistine who has girded his loins for the encounter. He drowns the flame in a surfeit of tolerance and studiedly situates himself beyond shock or outrage; show him the presidents of the OAU masturbating, or master-baiting, in the toilet of Great Zimbabwe, and he winks knowingly at his wife. Good play, eh? Are you enjoying it, Susie? You'd better enjoy it, Susie! This is Real Art, you bush-woman! Our ideal man of culture is inoculated by the knowledge that art is only art.

'Impossible for a writer to stay alive in Zimbabwe,' Marechera said. And waited. 'There are no magazines, no journals – unless you write government shit.'

The vice-chancellor was studying his shoe laces.

Something stirred in the comrade academic. Tucking his silver pen in his pen pocket, he checked his Seiko quartz watch (duty free, Singapore, a trip sponsored by Auckland Friends of Africa). How dare this filthy little unwashed pornographer imagine that he could – ?

'I wanted to talk to the "boys",' Marechera announced, abruptly changing tack, 'but no one is interested in the freedom fighters anymore, no one cares about the squatters either: not the Government, not the shefs here today. We have this shit and hideous monument, Heroes' Acre, but half the Heroes have been buried alive!'

A growl ran through the hall: he had gone too far. Where had *he* been during the liberation struggle? Glad to have overstepped the mark, Marechera pouted, walking about the platform in diminishing circles and muttering 'Oh God oh fuck, it's impossible to work here, impossible!'

'Then why don't you leave?' a student shouted.

Marechera was halted. 'I'm leaving! Tonight! Now.'

'Where will you go?' (Laughter.)

'Who will have you?' (Laughter.)

Marechera sulked. He looked shifty. Had he been paid yet for the lecture? But suddenly, as if in tribute to Chaplin, he was in possession of a large, dilapidated cardboard suitcase which he dragged from the auditorium together with his baby typewriter

13

straight into a Rixi taxi, screaming abuse, demanding payment, threatening legal action.

Smiling indulgently, the shefs drove home in Mazdas, Datsuns and Renaults to houses newly acquired, with the aid of the Beverly Building Society, in the once-white suburbs: Mount Pleasant, Avondale, Belgravia, Greendale. Arriving at the airport entirely alone, Marechera displayed a temporary British travel document and demanded for himself the status of Permanent Exile Scum. They shook their heads and laughed: no Zimbabwean passport, no exit. But we'll search you all the same – behind that screen, please, hope your rectum's clean. He fought, raged, then borrowed a coin to telephone Knottenbelt, much-loved Christian and Warden of Manfred Hodson Hall, Marechera's hall of residence ten years earlier, before his flight to England.

'Hullo, Charlie,' Knottenbelt said, for he knew the boy by his real name.

'Knotty, I've burnt my boats I don't have a friend in the world except you nowhere to go shall I sleep on the airport roof and be buggered by maintenance mechanics all night?'

'Will you behave yourself, Charlie? No late nights? You know we're getting old, can't take it any more.'

'I promise, Knotty. I'll be good.'

Once installed in the Knottenbelts' Christian home, Marechera stayed out drinking every night, rousing the old couple from their beds at one, two, three in the morning.

FOUR

Later that evening I was driven by a friend to the television centre, ZBC, where personnel and ideology have radically changed since 1980 but not, unaccountably, the perky chimes which introduce the 7.45 p.m. news bulletin, leading one to expect a blonde speakerine with a plum-jam accent announcing the day's casualty figures: 'Combined Operations report the death within the past twenty-four hours of Trooper Albert du Plooy, married with one son, of Salisbury. Combined Operations also report that security forces have

14

killed nine terrorists, four terrorist collaborators, five women running with terrorists and three civilians caught in crossfire.'

Outside the ZBC studios our car was halted at a barrier manned by soldiers – most of them the 'terrorists' previously denounced from the same television mast.

Caught in crossfire. Unfortunately crossfire is not a thing of the past and ministers who were also 'terrorists' not long ago resort to the euphemism as readily as their white predecessors. Explains the Security Minister to protesting Zapu MPs in the House of Assembly: 'We always regret the death of innocent civilians in crossfire. The blame lies entirely with the armed dissidents and those who harbour them.'

My friend dimmed his lights as the soldier approached us. He peered into the car, in no hurry to be convinced that one of us was scheduled to appear on television. Across the world, time is a measure of authority.

This soldier was not long ago a Zanla guerrilla, a peasant boy from Mrewa or Mtoko who crossed the border into Mozambique, survived semi-starvation, rats, bilharzia and the lacerating scream of diving Hawker Hunters, the snarl of Canberra bombers flattening out – of the Air Force supplied to Salisbury by London when the Central African Federation was wound up. Probably this soldier adopted a Chimurenga name: James Bond, Male Goat, Zex Zacharia, Gun Fighter, Ugly Shiri, Bomber reZimbabwe, Dzungu Boy, Never Chimurenga, Kid Colt, Jehova, Jesus Christ, or Drama-Joe Brown. He may have helped to dig the mass graves at Chimoio and Nyadzonia, tipping in dead children whose petrified faces were stained with tears. It cannot be easy for him to peer into a darkened car and search the complacent white faces about to appear on his television.

He knows all about the Western press. The Minister of Information keeps him informed. Near Rusape (where Marechera was born) they are digging up more of the Smith regime's mass graves, and the Minister is photographed standing beside heaps of skulls and bones: another 'heroes' acre'. Tomorrow he will hold a press conference to denounce the Western journalists who persist in reporting imaginary graves of more recent vintage in Matabeleland.

I was to appear on the weekly programme whose hostess is a plump, maternal woman who quickly puts one at ease. To start tossing Marechera at her (as I had been plotting to do) might, on reflection, seem churlish – and (as friends have advised) counter-productive as well:

'David, you'll only force the police and Government to justify his arrest. If you challenge them publicly they'll concoct charges.

15

Almost certainly Dambudzo will be free as soon as the Book Fair closes. Besides, they're paranoid about criticism from visitors.'

We are not far from the Limpopo where the elephant child acquired its trunk and learned wisdom in the jaws of the crocodile. The white liberals who have remained in Zimbabwe since Independence, making money and complying with the new laws protecting domestic servants, have one message though various voices: 'Don't make trouble.' And the one-party state? 'In my opinion, the sooner the better – if that's what they want.' Making trouble and grumbling about civil liberties is now, rather paradoxically, the preserve of 'old Smithy' and his dwindling band of diehards; the man who incarcerated half a million Zimbabweans, mainly women and children, in 'protected villages', has at last discovered habeas corpus and the folly of offering 'military solutions to political problems'. Meanwhile the white liberals, calculating their dividends and scattering chemicals across their swimming pools to combat algae, have embraced silence.

As Marechera puts it, everyone doesn't want to say something.

Placing us under bright lights and before two cameras, my hostess begins by referring to the opening sequence of my book, an encounter with Zipra guerrillas operating west of Shabani in May 1979. But she does not say 'Zipra'. The Zimbabwe People's Revolutionary Army had been the military wing of Joshua Nkomo's party, Zapu. As late as 1982 you could say 'Zipra' but today it is mentioned only in a furtive whisper. The list of fallen heroes published by the Prime Minister's office contains not a single Zipra freedom fighter. Zipra's two leading military commanders, Generals Dumiso Dabengwa and Lookout Masuku, languish in prison, probably Chikurubi, though acquitted of treason charges in the High Court.

'Yes,' I say, 'I did meet the Zipra "boys".'

The interview is recorded, not live. Farewell interview? As it turned out, I was wrong. It was broadcast, uncut.

Leaving the studios, I try to convince myself that saying 'Zipra' was an adequate substitute for saying 'Marechera'. And how is he faring in the police cells tonight, without a drink? Climbing into bed after a hot bath and a couple of whiskies (£17 a bottle), I open *Mindblast*:

> Political ideologies were quietly sneering at the back of my mind. I turned to them only to find them equally shit. Talk of organising human beings always reminds me of jail. I turned to friendships – and discovered the covert and overt betrayal that underlines all relationships.

16

FIVE

What do we know about Marechera's life in England? Clearly his expulsion from New College, Oxford, was the crucial event. It was self-willed, whether regarded as delinquency or as a decisive break with opportunism, with the glittering ladders of the 'shefs'. Marechera does not tell us much about being booted out of Oxford; the dons who sent him down are neither named nor characterised.

'I slept three nights on the roof of the English Faculty Library.' His reaction to personal misfortune is typically one of surreal humour; he was comforted to discover that Shelley had also been sent down for his part in a pamphlet called 'The Necessity of Atheism'. In later years Marechera became affected by the same bitterness towards philistine critics that afflicted other poets who dared to turn the world upside down. Shelley complained:

> Persecution, contumely, and calumny have been heaped upon me in profuse measure; and domestic conspiracy and legal oppression have violated in my person the most sacred rights of nature and humanity. The bigot will say it was the recompense of my errors; the man of the world will call it the result of my imprudence . . . .

The sharing of an honourable fate with so great a spirit touched in the African writer a vein of sentiment normally alien to him. In the unpublished (and possibly forgotten) manuscript, *The Black Insider*, he quotes four lines, unattributed, which belong to Edward Fitzgerald:

> A book of verses underneath the bough
> A jug of wine, a loaf of bread - and thou
>   Beside me singing in the wilderness –
> Oh, Wilderness were Paradise enow!

Putting Oxford behind him, bumming between squats and prison cells, the writer Marechera forged his own style:

17

I woke up dead in Southall
There were policemen investigating themselves
There was the Queen admiring a pig at the Sussex
                                        Agricultural Show
    Miss Piggy squealed with
    Exquisite pain
    When love thy neighbour
    Went against the grain.[1]

The lines point to the age: the revival of racism, the alarming growth of the National Front, the birth of the Anti-Nazi League, the suspicion that the Metropolitan Police hated blacks. 'Who killed Blair Peach?' howled the placards. For Marechera the chief skinhead lurking between the Leicester Square fruit machines and the Palace of Westminster was Enoch Powell. But there were others:

    Who's that at the end of the bar
    Looks like Martin Webster breathing tar[2]

Marechera's ally Shelley had walked these roads before him:

    I met Murder on the way –
    He had a mask like Castlereagh –
    Very smooth he looked, yet grim;
    Seven blood-hounds followed him:

Yet we miss Marechera entirely if we take out on his behalf a subscription to any Jacobin Club or dissenting Corresponding Society. One hundred and thirty years after Shelley died at sea, off Leghorn, Charles Marechera was born to a poor truck driver in the middle of Africa. Because he was very clever he was offered Shelley at school; wept out of love for this kindred spirit; but could never himself write out of such fantastic illusion:

    Last came Anarchy: he rode
    On a white horse, splashed with
      blood;
    He was pale even to the lips,
    Like Death in the Apocalypse.

Africans do not turn pale. Though drunk and drugged, Marechera could live without sentiments served up to pre-Raphaelite beauticians:

---

[1]'Portrait of a Black Artist in London' (unpublished).
[2]Ibid.

The Eumenides are not behind the curtains but are the spots of dirt on my spectacle lenses . . . Steve Biko died while I was drunk and disorderly in London . . . Soweto burned while I was sunk deep in thought about an editor's rejection slip.[1]

He was discovering, too, the cynicism of 'literary London'. Books are talked about, not read. In the television age an evening's solid reading is an achievement, like not smoking. A pretty black writer will be fed and watered like a butterfly destined for net, pin and nature book. A woman don bears down on him with a huge, devouring smile:

'Are you angry and polemic or are you grim and nocturnal or are you realistic and quavering or are you indifferent and European?'[2]

He had spent three months in Cardiff prison, convicted of possessing cannabis. Forbidden to import his typewriter, he had passed the time 'twiddling my thumbs in a Welsh jail full of magi and addicts'. Released, he came to London, high on the news that Heinemann African Library had agreed to publish *The House of Hunger*. But he had nowhere to stay. He was a shelterless vagabond:

I don't know how many times I stared at the pictures in the National Art Gallery. Or at the pigeons shitting on Nelson's head . . . . Then a black policeman stopped me one morning in St James's Park. He demanded to search the rucksack . . . throwing my things out onto the ground and the increasing flow of tourists and sightseers gave us a wide berth . . . . My dirty socks and underpants. My books and manuscripts. The typewriter and my thick-lensed spectacles. Next he searched me, feeling up from my ankles up to my crotch and then around my hips up to the armpits. He was not satisfied. There was the question of identification. I told him I had come to London from Oxford to sign the contract for my book . . . . He looked at my jeans and waistcoat and T-shirt; they were filthy beyond belief from sleeping on the ground in the rain. . . . He demanded to see my letters from Heinemann. I gave them to him. He smiled a sort of Kojak wry smile and said sternly, 'Keep out of trouble'.[3]

[1]'The Black Insider' (unpublished).
[2]Ibid.
[3]Ibid.

SIX

Saturday morning. The servant brings my breakfast: paw paw with lemon, bacon and egg, coffee, toast. Winter is ending, swimming pools will soon be bearable, 17 or 18 Celsius, if only drought regulations permitted their replenishment. The morning paper reports, at the foot of an inside page, that Dambudzo Marechera remains in Harare Central Police Station. I remind my children that lavatories are to be flushed only in certain conditions and take them up to North Avenue to watch the hockey. The irrigation of the posh pitches continues despite the drought, sprinklers rotating, the turf a soft English green.

Harare Schoolgirls are playing Zambia. Four years have passed since 'Zimbabwe' won the Olympic hockey final in Moscow without the help of a single black player. Today the Zambian team includes five black players; Harare Schoolgirls, none.

I surrender to memory, the sun hot on my back. It was here, at the old Salisbury Sports Club, that I watched an hour of the last Currie Cup cricket match between Rhodesia and a South African provincial side. The end of an era. Mugabe had just announced his first Cabinet. The new Minister of Sport in this super-white, super-macho, T-bone society was to be a twenty-four-year-old black woman terrorist by the name of Teurai Ropa (Spill Blood) Nhongo.

I had once interviewed her. Today she is the only woman in the Cabinet, the only woman in the Politburo. Why not telephone her on Marechera's behalf?

Hard to imagine any two Zimbabweans with less in common. She, the tough, bush-hardened guerrilla fighter, weapon-trained in Zambia, who had transcended the customary frontiers of age and sex to command thousands of refugees when only nineteen years of age; he drying out in Cardiff gaol. She with little more than primary schooling behind her (only when she became a Minister occupying a posh office on the top floor of the Earl Grey Building did she begin to study for her 'O' levels); he the Oxford scholarship boy. She brimming with patriotism and loyalty (at the climax of the party congress in August 1984 she fell on her knees before Mugabe); he defaming his mother's memory and everything sacred. She pure of mouth, he foul; she motherhood and duty; he stains on the

20

sheet. She, transported in a Mercedes, flanked by bodyguards and secretaries; he, spooning sour milk in Cecil Square and sleeping off a hangover on an empty bench outside her office.

Teurai Ropa had married the deputy commander of Zanla, Rex Nhongo. She began having babies but remained at her post as the Rhodesian air attacks on Mozambique achieved their furious climax in the last months of 1979, during the Lancaster House conference in London. The *Guardian* newspaper chose that moment to award its fiction prize to an unknown Zimbabwean writer. To show his appreciation Marechera threw quiche lorraine across the room, broke plates, drank everything in sight, and accused his hosts of smug and patronising posturing.

It was a season of odd parties, but Mrs Nhongo attended none of them. At the Arts Club in Dover Street a London publisher launched a new book about Rhodesia with a flourish, audaciously inviting both the Trojan Hectors and the Greek Achilles, even though the Rhodesian Air Force was concurrently destroying bridges along the Limpopo Valley, which produces eighty per cent of Mozambique's rice crop, while Rhobabwe's Prime Minister Muzorewa took time off from London's flashier tailors and two-tone shoe makers to order a blockade on Zambia's desperately needed imports of maize. These diversions notwithstanding, Greeks and Trojans moved easily around the Arts Club, nonchalantly pumping hands and squeezing arms, black detainees and their erstwhile gaolers plucking wine and canapes from the silver trays, swapping jokes. Laughter veneered onto the furniture of war. Gliding among the guests, the well greased information secretary of successive Rhodesian Prime Ministers, Mr Costa Pafitis, greeted journalists whose expulsion from Rhodesia he had either engineered or serviced. The Minister of Justice, Mr Chris Andersen, had taken time off from hanging terrorists to attend Lancaster House as a member of Ian Smith's delegation; now he chatted with the comrades of those he hanged. (And today he serves in Mugabe's Cabinet – no use telephoning *him* on Marechera's behalf.)

Good old Smithy didn't attend this glittering party. Not his style. Granted immunity from prosecution for his rebellion against the Crown, he was sped under police escort to Twickenham where the All Blacks were playing England. To ram the point home, he appeared as London Weekend Television's guest of honour at a soccer match.

Teurai Ropa Nhongo preferred, or chose, life in the front line. A robust peasant girl, she had cut short her own schooling when she heard voices not unlike those which spoke to Joan of Arc. She recalls the grim existence in the Mozambican bush:

'Because of the political orientation I was giving them, people

21

could stand the hardships. Really we had problems of medicines. We hadn't anything even to cure a headache. And we had no clothes to give the comrades so they could go with their, you know, buttocks being seen, and sometimes we could have one meal a day and without any relish to go with, and we couldn't even get meat, really we had since forgotten about breakfast nor, you know, having soap to bath with . . . .'

Like all Zanla guerrillas, she feared, hated and despised the treacherous internal settlement between Smith and Muzorewa. 'Those puppets,' she says. Unknown to Teurai Ropa Nhongo, a frail and effete poet living in London squats had nailed the Salisbury Agreement with a few well-chosen lines. Enter now the BISHOP, accompanied by MAROTA (clearly modelled on Byron Hove, the only black minister in the Transitional Government to have taken a principled stand, thus incurring the immediate wrath of Smith, General Peter Walls and the black lackeys – who promptly dismissed him.)

Here MAROTA speaks of Smith:

MAROTA: He has made jokes of us.
BISHOP: I'll laugh while it lasts.[1]

MAROTA complains that the Patriotic Front guerrillas are beating at the door, at the windows, and on the roof – yet the Smith-Muzorewa coalition can think of nothing more persuasive than bombing Zambia while keeping nationalists in detention and the peasantry in the hated 'protected villages'. The BISHOP, unmoved, struts about the stage:

BISHOP: I am the masses. Did I not rout Pearce? And with placards too. Have I not engineered the first black and white government without a Congo or an Angola . . .? Africa in its long sweltering breath has always cried out for the heartbroken.
(Enter now SMITH, casting an evil glance at MAROTA.)
SMITH: He reads too much. He is a great observer, and he looks quite through the deeds of men . . . . Come on my right hand, Bishop, for this ear is deaf, and tell me truly what you think of him for I don't want him in my cabinet – I mean, our cabinet.[2]

The Shakespearean metaphor also occurred to 'Marota' himself. When I called on Byron Hove in his chambers in the Temple,

1"The Black Insider'.
2Ibid.

22

following his hasty departure from Rhodesia, he described how he had broken with the Bishop, quoting Macbeth in the process:

> . . . I am in blood
> Stepped in so far, that, should I wade no more,
> Returning were as tedious as go o'er.

Despite the Mercedes and the entourage, Teurai Ropa Nhongo is foreign to cynicism. She is St Joan without Jesus and without virginity:

'And then, you know, during this period I wasn't married, I was still a spinster and that's when my husband proposed love with me . . . really I was hesitating to be a mother and at the same time carrying out all these military duties. But really in 1977, I then was finally married to Rex Nhongo, who's my husband. And in 1978 I gave birth to my first daughter called Kumbirai Rungano' (roughly: 'an answer to the people's prayers').

Today Mrs Nhongo is party to the arm-twisting of Zanu PF's opponents and rivals. She is in and of the machine. Her innocence has diminished: the peasantry have not been given the land promised to them but she does not protest. By contrast the cynical and worldly Marechera has gained in innocence. It is he who now hears the voices.

Naturally Marechera can never survive the purity tests fashioned in the pulpit; by any Christian standard he is filthy beyond redemption:

Whenever mother took away my sheets to wash them she would make me explain every single stain on them. Since they were invariably stained with semen she would contemptuously give me a long sermon about how girls are 'easy' and 'why don't you get on with laying one or two?' . . . 'There is nothing to it,' she said. 'You stick it in the hole between the water and the earth, it's easy . . . . You strike like a fire and she'll take you and your balls all in. Right? Up to your neck.'[1]

Marechera is invariably up to his neck in the lower depths:

The subject of women has tantalised me all my life; possibly because mother – so soon after father's death – became a prostitute to keep the family going. I felt it keenly and was all of eleven years old . . . . It was then that I hated all notions of

[1] *Mindblast.*

23

family, of extended family, of tribe, of nation, of the human race. There was also within me an active sexuality directed at my little sister who a few months ago payed me back in brutal coin.[1]

Yet by comparison with the respectable Greeks, Trojans and Romans smoothly circulating in the reception room of the Arts Club in Dover Street, Marechera's semen-soaked soul is unstained. Drifting away from the publisher's hospitality and the wearying obligation to pump the hand of the enemy, a group of journalists gathered across the road in the Albemarle: among them, a black reporter whose name I had first encountered when reading the *Rand Daily Mail*, which carried his syndicated column reporting the war against terrorism in Rhodesia. But then, abruptly and mysteriously, he had vanished; not only his column but his stout, Rand-swollen personage as well. Three months elapsed before he re-emerged in Maputo and was paraded before the press by Zanu to announce his conversion. He had been kidnapped near his farm and force-marched across Rhodesia, a converting experience. Now, in the Albemarle, he recalled how *we* had founded Zanu in 1963; how *he* had been Bishop Muzorewa's closest adviser from 1969 to 1975; how *he* had counselled the Bishop to quit politics; how he had been right about this, that and the other.

We discussed the question of war reporting. Would not *ZANU News*, published in Maputo, gain in credibility if it documented Zanla's casualties as well as the enemy's? And might not some of the more inflated, Falstaffian, claims – 25 Fascist planes shot down, 1,750 white settler mercenaries killed – be cut down to plausible proportions to aid the digestion?

Eyes swivelling in a motionless head, the born-again journalist nodded, his voice dropping into satin confidentiality: 'I have mentioned it, David. But one has to be very careful, one could be misunderstood.' He repeated this phrase: 'One could be misunderstood.' Clearly he took care not to be misunderstood, for two months later he was reincarnated in Harare as Mugabe's press secretary, following the Zanu leader's return from exile. Besieged by the foreign press for interviews, he used to stand in Meikles, brusque in his fat power, saying, 'Call me again this afternoon.' But when, and where?

Five years have passed and the Trojan who became a Greek is now a Trojan again, his glassy eyes mirroring long corridors and calculations of advantage too byzantine for the foreigner to grasp. He still guffaws, chuckles and makes irreverent jokes on planes

[1]Ibid.

24

crossing the Atlantic, but at home, seated behind banks of microphones and flanked by acolytes, staring straight through reporters he slaps on the back in London, he denounces the imperialist media for fabricating atrocity stories in Matabeleland, easily shifting into automatic newspeak when servicing awkward questions. He does not defame his father, call his mother a whore, or profess unnatural feelings for his sister; but compared to Marechera, he is a spirit bent beyond redemption.

Marechera had not been invited to the publisher's party, having recently established a rather singular reputation in that regard. The *Guardian* fiction prize for 1979 was shared between an Irish writer and a Zimbabwean. The former spoke sensibly, and briefly, of the two nations' shared experience of British colonialism; Marechera spoke insensibly, and interminably, of no one knew what, and it soon became apparent to the guests assembled in a splendid room over the old Drury Lane Theatre that there was no reason at all why he should ever stop. In desperation, the literary editor of the *Guardian* began to clap when Marechera drew breath and everyone joined in the terminal applause. Twenty minutes later there was a commotion; Marechera was tossing saucers with great dexterity either side of a precious chandelier – one of his party turns. Among those who tenderly moved to restrain him was Lord Longford, scarecrow champion of hopeless causes, but not long afterwards the saucers were again raining up and down. Marechera's reputation was secured. Flaubert wanted the novelist to disappear behind his novel, but the modern publicity machine ensures the opposite.

In those days I was responsible for the literary pages of the *New Statesman* and called Marechera to ask for an unpublished short story. The answering voice was soft and accommodating, indeed he spoke as if we were old friends and he had been waiting for my call. He would bring a story into Great Turnstile on the morrow, without fail. But he didn't.

SEVEN

Saturday afternoon and Marechera was still detained in Harare Central Police station. President Julius Nyerere had been invited to open the Agricultural Show. The white farmers and fertiliser salesmen had applauded politely, then gone home to roar with laughter over their sundowners – what greater shambles in Africa than Tanzania's aborted socialist agriculture? But if Mugabe wanted them to applaud Mwalimu (the Teacher), then they would applaud Mwalimu, or ujaama, or ju ju – anything to please. It did not greatly disturb them that among Zimbabwe's new development-ologists were men schooled in the radical 'discourse' of the University of Dar es Salaam and thus poised to launch a three-pronged assault on imperialism, the national bourgeoisie and the rising petty bourgeoisie. Such rhetoric counted for little against the surplus of maize, tobacco and beef which only the commercial farmers could guarantee.

The old enemy converged on the Harare show grounds to display its prize bulls, sows, rams and combine harvesters. The old enemy is in remarkably good shape: ninety-five per cent of top jobs in senior and middle management (with the partial exception of mining) are still occupied by middle-aged white males. Cultural skirmishes deplete no bank balance. Let them rename the towns and streets while guaranteeing a healthy subsidy on farm produce. Mugabe understands – even if elements in his party do not – that a prudent pragmatism is the price of a viable socialism, a delicate balance best achieved by applying the pragmatism to policy and the socialism to speeches.

During the first euphoric weeks after independence the white community had suffered a bad bout of nerves. Statues of Cecil Rhodes were pulled down and television viewers were bombarded by films denouncing colonialism. Culture shock frightened away the more antediluvian settlers and the more rapid white apprentices, but those wise enough to hang on had been rewarded. Even if their 'houseboy' or 'cookboy' was local Zanu chairman or their farm foreman was secretary of the workers' committee, he still turned up at seven in the morning clothed in traditional deference.

The black bourgeoisie were also content. They no longer looked to Muzorewa for salvation from Marxist communism. A stone's throw from the hot and fetid cell where Marechera is incarcerated huge crowds throng the bus station, some packing into the long, maroon-and-cream coaches returning to the black townships, Mbare, Tafara and Highfield; others heading for destinations and family homes further afield. Zimbabweans are great travellers. Theirs is a country of buses, all of them owned by rags-to-riches black entrepreneurs like Ben Mucheche, the first African business-man to be appointed a director of the Reserve Bank under the Smith régime.

I had visited him at his bus depot in Craster Road, Southerton, during the unreal interlude of the 'internal settlement'. A Muzorewa man, Mucheche explained that Britain was run, disastrously, by its trade unions. No, he didn't want minimum wage legislation in Zimbabwe, what he wanted was free competition, a 'democratic business dictatorship' such as prevailed in Kenya. Occasionally Mucheche glanced out of the window at the constant activity in the depot and repair shops where his thirty-seven buses were serviced, but it was a casual, confident glance: he had appointed only the best supervisors and mechanics.

'And if they're white, they're white. If they live in a suburb where I'm still not allowed to live . . . .' His hands clasped and unclasped in controlled anger as he leaned across the desk. 'I tell you this: the Bishop will have no alternative but to eliminate the guerrillas. They've served their function, you understand? They have won the war so now they should surrender, understand?' Today Mucheche is a Mugabe man.

Saturday afternoon at the Agricultural Show. How Marechera would enjoy the festivity! How he would gaze at the splendid white women astride well-bred mounts with saucily flouncing tails. I recall how these same ladies, or their sisters, had resolutely made the journey to the show grounds during the guerrilla war, Land Rovers and horseboxes braving the ambushes, their bodies sheathed in black velvet, their faces caked in makeup as if the sun were studio lights in a commercial. Does not Marechera deserve to witness all this and imagine, beneath the tight jodhpurs, the silky pubic hair?

On the first page of *Black Sunlight*, the photographer-narrator is projected into the court of a savage chief, a tyrant 'as black as human beginnings', who has only just received his first report of the existence of white people. This news gives the chief an instant erection. He orders the captive photographer to suck his cock. The victim begs for mercy – anything but that! – the 'pitlatrine' would be a lesser punishment. Beguiled by the photographer's tales of distant voyages, the chief relents:

'My years of exile in the wide world, even across the seas to the land where these white people live. Their hair is long and shiny even between their thighs . . . . Some of their women are of great beauty and if you have them from behind for the first time the sky will come down.'
'You have experience in it yourself?'
'Well,' I said. 'Yes and no.'

Marechera once turned up at Heinemann Educational Books, dressed in riding jacket and jodhpurs, to beg the fare to Oxford.

When advised to hitch-hike he became indignant: 'What! dressed like this?'

A writer must have a sense of occasion. The hot afternoon offers so many delights to those at liberty: the prize bulls (Brahmans, Santa Gertudis), pigs and rams brought by the fathers of the girls on horseback – observe this proud ram huffily kicking as lifted into the van, his forelegs clamped in the farmer's hand, then instantly docile once inside, the huddle and scent of fleeces evaporating his anomie. And the Agricultural Show also has another spectacle to offer.

I cannot guess Marechera's reaction to this display – almost certainly highly favourable, unless he should judge it to be insufficiently degrading. Gathered in their thousands on the terraces of the stadium are the revolutionary proletariat, stacked shoulder-to-shoulder to admire a pageant performed by long-legged drum majorettes, peach-skinned jacaranda queens whose cleverly synchronised uniforms (tight bodices and short, flared skirts) have been harlequined to provide a kaleidoscope of shifting colours and delights as the beauties whirl and stamp to the music of the Police Band. Four-fifths of them are white. Only one 'platoon' is mixed.

It's certainly an unusual combination. The Zimbabwe Republic Police Band has inherited its high professional standards from its predecessor, the British South Africa Police, so-named because the white Pioneers who penetrated Mashonaland in 1890, bringing white sunlight to a people reportedly terrorised by Lobengula's Ndebele *impis*, did so in the name of, and under the financial auspices of, Cecil John Rhodes's British South Africa Company. The explorer Frederick Courtney Selous acted as guide to the Pioneer Column, for a fee; in Kimberley they show you the place where the wagons assembled for the historic, civilising mission, not far from the Big Hole where prospectors stacked themselves like bees in their quest for diamonds.

As the drum majorettes execute their seductive routine, the Police bandsmen toil and sweat beneath pith helmets worthy of Dr Dolittle (now, alas, condemned by the Action Group against Racism and Sexism in Books – as if literature were a form of hygiene).

More is to come: military displays, waltzing helicopters, tango-ing parachutists, Hawker Hunters belching candy-pink smoke – very probably the same planes that used to dive-bomb Chimoio in Mozambique and Freedom Camp in Zambia. The same pilots, perhaps? Along the way, in July 1982, Zimbabwe lost half its strike capacity when thirteen planes exploded in rapid succession at Thornhill airbase, Gweru. Subsequently half-a-dozen white Air Force officers, including an Air Vice-Marshal, were tortured with electric shocks, acquitted by a black judge, re-detained, then finally released under strong pressure from Mrs Thatcher. For a few months reconciliation, the linchpin and coping stone of the Government's racial policy, was under severe stress.

One can hardly quarrel with the wisdom of keeping the poet out of sight during the Prime Minister's carefully scheduled surprise visit to the Book Fair this Saturday morning. Mugabe takes no chances. Two hundred yards of best avenues are curfewed from dusk to dawn every day because they pass the residences of Prime Minister Mugabe and President Banana. When Smith lived there the house was called Independence; when Muzorewa moved in it became Dzimbabwe and they installed in his front hall the sort of metal detection device you walk through in airports. During press conferences the Bishop used to perch on the edge of his chair, his two-tone shoes dangling above the floor as he denounced communism and 'cheeky' journalists who wanted to know why a black leader should bomb Zambia. I saw him sprint round the running track of Sakubva stadium, Umtali, dressed like the joker in a pack of cards, engulfed by photographers, his tiny arms raised like 'The Winner!' he was.

Would Marechera really dare to try anything with the Prime Minister? Better be safe than sorry. There is of course no firm evidence that André Breton fired a pistol at President Raymond Poincaré; that Dada tried to plant a bomb at the Versailles Conference in 1919; that Brecht was involved in a plot to kill Hitler, or Mayakovsky in one to rub out Stalin. It's almost certainly untrue that Dylan Thomas was rude to Clem Attlee in a pub near Merthyr; that Wole Soyinka tipped a glass of palm wine over the head of General Gowon; that Ngugi wa Thiong'o had a go at the senile Kenyatta; or that Allen Ginsberg was involved in the assassination of John F. Kennedy.

Even so, Marechera might have said something unsayable. Much wiser to ensure that the *Sunday Mail* should be spared painful headlines. On their day of rest citizens deserve anodyne newsprint – like the following report of the Prime Minister's appearance at the Book Fair:

'Cde Mothobi Muloatse of the Skotaville Publishers, which is a cooperative of black South African writers, was overawed by the surprise visit.

' "I am still overawed by the whole thing. This is really incredible. He is down to earth and this is unbelievable. He is interested in books and this is not just an impression he was trying to create." '

The display concluded, the crowds pour out of the Show Ground Stadium. Some of the whites you see here are of the new variety, the potato-pale fellow travellers of de-colonisation, hurrying out to teach, to drill bore holes, to staff rural clinics, to get laid. Gone now

29

(almost) are the embittered 'Rhodies', the soft-vowelled, hard-eyed artisans from the Mashaba Mine and the Trojan Nickel Mine, patrons of the Queen of Sheba massage parlour in Rotten Row. They have gone because, as they put it, the country has gone. We was betrayed, man, the bloody Brits sold us out. They took the gap, carrying their artisan certificates and their doctor's certificates, their rugby trophies and their memories of 'super' times at Oriel Boys', Peterhouse and Mabelreign. Taking with them bitter-sweet memories of the bush war, of shorts cut to the crotch, of biltong and *shumbas* (Lion lagers), of trampoline marathons in suburban gardens to raise money for the Terrorist Victims' Relief Fund, of 'revving' the terrs, of T-shirts announcing 'Terrorism Stops Here'.

Of taking on the whole world.

All gone.

Arriving home, I make a phone call. No, Marechera has not been released. My informant is shocked. She had expected him to emerge from the police cell moments after Mugabe's wailing cavalcade sped away from the Book Fair. (How awesome his elevation when one recalls the relaxed, virtually unguarded figure casually bantering with journalists and providing Maputo telephone numbers from his diary in the lobby of a London hotel in April 1978 – a sharp-nosed, razor-keen grey-black man with a metal voice and a metal mind. Now his name is known to every schoolboy in Africa and his waxwork features are in Madame Tussaud's.)

'Maybe you should have said something on television, David.'

'But you advised against it! You said it would be counter-productive. You told me that a lawyer had advised you that – '

EIGHT

The following day we attended a beautiful lunch party. Drinks on the lawn, bloody marys, then a local wine called Vat 10. Lunch was served by two black girls. A diplomat talked about his plans to take his family camping at Mana Pools on the Zambezi, where the night reverberates with the most ominous grunts and you may even wake up dead in your camp bed.

Someone told a story about Mana Pools. Three white gays from

England had arrived at the river and almost immediately discovered a new-born hippo, still attached to its bloody umbilical, floating abandoned downstream, forty-five pounds of tender steak observed by a huge crocodile in the process of slithering into the water from a mud flat. Knowing as they did that for many of God's creatures the moment of birth is also the moment of death, they bravely plucked the baby hippo out of the water and adopted it. But what should they feed it? They decided to make a fruit salad – pineapple, orange, guava, melon, delicious. No sooner was the job done and the fruit floating in its aromatic syrup than who should walk out from between the trees and start flapping his enormous ears? The three gays bolted for the nearest baobab and watched, horrified, as the elephant consumed the fruit salad, releasing huge turds as he ambled away, his bowels nicely lubricated by this gay laxative.

'Of course it served them right,' said one of the lunch guests, a sculptor. 'It serves us all right. You won't catch a native writing letters to *The Times* warning that lion, or tigers, or leopards may soon be extinct. "Good riddance!" he says. The native fears and hates the wild animal: the hippo that ravages whole bean plots by night, the baboons that devastate the mealies, the leopard that snatches the goat, the calf and the chickens; the snake you can never trust, the crocodiles which take more than sixty human beings a year in Zimbabwe's rivers; the elephant that can destroy the livelihood of an entire village. So the tiger was an endangered species, eh? Good news in Bengal! To keep a single tiger alive by expanding the protected reserves has cost the Indian Government $10,000 a year in administrative costs and lost farming revenues. Bloody waste of money. Why not spend it on starving kids?'

The sculptor had drunk too much Vat 10. His belligerence fore-stalled criticism; on another day he might have adopted the opposite line of argument, cursing the natives for endangering wildlife throughout Africa.

Someone mentioned Marechera.

'I hear he was sodden drunk again,' a woman said, 'so they took him inside to dry out.'

I said no.

My hostess asked me why, then, Marechera had been arrested. She was gentle and I was wearing my anger like a turban. I told them all why, exactly why, fundamentally why – I'd had four bloody marys before lunch and was affected by the story of the elephant and the gay fruit salad:

The flies from a respectful distance scanned every mouthful as did the skinny dog from next door. I was eating sadza and trying to make one piece of meat last. I was reading James

31

Hadley Chase's *No Orchids for Miss Blandish* . . . . From the other door, firmly shut, came the noise and din of bedsprings being punished again and again. Susan was in there with another client. We were eating the proceeds from her last but one client.[1]

The following day I met a friend for lunch, a university lecturer. He was waiting for me in Meikles and lifted a hand in diffident greeting. Since his servant regularly cooks him a proper dinner in the evening, we settled for beer and a toasted sandwich.

'You heard about Marechera, I suppose?' He began, and I relaxed into the deep leather chair, glad to be in the company of a friend with shared values.

'Yes. But tell me everything you know.'

With mock caution, he swivelled to scan the neighbouring tables.

'Why – are you seriously interested?'

'Is the arrest of poets a specialised academic sub-discipline, like Early Middle English or the adventures of the hexameter?'

'I hadn't suspected that Marechera was your kind of writer. Not very *engagé*, to say the least.'

Someone should write the history of Meikles Hotel. Only two decades ago the manager refused to house a conference of Catholic bishops on the ground that one or two of the visiting prelates would be black. In the course of a heated debate in the House of Commons, when the young and not unself-confident Foreign Secretary, Dr David Owen, was defending his refusal to recognise the Rhodesian internal settlement which Ian Smith had signed with the Three Stooges – and rather enjoying the barracking from the Tory benches – Mr Austin Mitchell rose from the Labour benches to describe the black politicians of the internal settlement as the sort one found lounging in the bar of Meikles. This provoked howls and much laughter, for more of the assembled MPs had in their time seen the inside of Salisbury's most famous hotel than would ever cross the threshold of the Dorchester or Connaught.

Was Dr Owen right to insist that no settlement of the long-running Rhodesian crisis was viable without the participation of the Patriotic Front – or part of it? Did he understand history better than his Tory critics, or might history itself have taken a different turn had diplomatic recognition been granted to the new régime in Salisbury?

Those who study contemporary history (which might be defined as the period through which we have lived) know well how personalities, initiatives and dramas which loom large at one juncture may

---

[1] *Black Sunlight*.

within a few years recede into such pallid obscurity that even the names of the protagonists are half-forgotten. Who, now, can spell the Reverend Sithole's first name: Ndabaningi?

In 1978-9, in the time of the Transitional Government, when Marechera was composing his satire in London and the Conservative Party, supported by the most influential leader writers, was calling for a settlement which would exclude the 'Marxist terrorists', few could have spoken with genuine confidence about the ultimate victory of the Patriotic Front. The guerrillas were killing white farmers and imposing an increasing strain on the stretched European population, but they were also (it's easy to forget) being mopped up by the Rhodesian airforce and the RLI fireforce like exhausted flies on a hot window pane. They were the grumbling appendix. It needed only the advent of a Thatcher Government – the Rhodesians referred to her as the Great White Hope – and that would be curtains for the chilling black Robespierre, Robert Gabriel Mugabe, even if his uncertain ally, the wily old bear Nkomo, was lured into a broadened coalition of 'Zimbabwe Rhodesia'.

It did not turn out like that. What promised to become one of history's main, and 'moderate', highways, faltered and then vanished – just another muddy diversion rapidly overgrown with weeds. As for dat bushtrack terr Mooghabey, he now de main road!

Do we therefore conclude that the majority of British leader writers in 1979 were poor historians confusing the wish for the reality? The common response, surely, would be to expel future projections from the science of history as mere guesswork vulnerable to a thousand contingent factors. According to one school of historiography, contingency, accident, Cleopatra's nose, explains far more about the past (let alone the unknowable future) than the 'determinists' and 'historicists', with their linear programmes, allow. Robert Mugabe might have been ousted by his own faction-riven central committee; might have expired in a plane crash (General Tongogara died in a motor accident); Zanu might have fallen apart. Similarly, had Mrs Thatcher's first Commonwealth Conference been held in a non-African capital, rather than Lusaka, she might have proved less accommodating towards Kaunda, Nyerere and the Nigerians. Any observer familiar with the hairy twelve weeks between the arrival of Lord Soames in December 1980, as British Governor of a re-legalised Rhodesia, and the announcement of Mugabe's electoral victory, must know how many factors might have intervened to thwart it: the stuttering shoot-outs round the guerrilla assembly points, the frustration of the trigger-happy Rhodesians, the bombs and assassination attempts, the possibility of a military coup, the pressure on the Governor to ban Zanu-PF regionally if not

33

nationally. So many contingent factors were rapping their claims on the big kettle drum of history.

It may be that the whole notion of 'history', as we commonly deploy it, is based on a fallacy. Even if we reject the teleology of pre-charted, pre-engineered historical highways, even if we accept that the path is hacked out, step by uncertain step, from impenetrable jungle, we are still left with the seminal idea of highways and paths. Most historians, even those devoted to Cleopatra's nose, tend to assume that history is a journey whose destination – securely sited on our retrospective map – sorts out the highways from the forgotten diversionary footpaths. Yet we make no such assumption when we consider our own lives. We no longer regard childhood as merely the apprenticeship of an imperfect, half-grown being for adult life. Childhood is not a rehearsal; whatever we may learn in the process of growing, each moment is as full and valid and self-contained an experience as the one that follows it. The boy or girl who dies in childhood is not of the same order as the abandoned foundations of a building.

Of course many historians are involved in re-creating the lived experience, viewed as an *en soi* rather than as a link in a chain, of some distant city state or peasant community. Such acts of empathy involve disposing of a certain amount of contemporary cargo. But when we come to consider the idea of 'history', almost invariably we revert to the image of links in a chain whose very meaning and purpose is known only to us, to posterity. A minor but not trivial reflection of this image is found in the sentimental phrase, heard at cenotaphs: 'They died that we might live in freedom.' We like to imagine those who fell on their faces in the poppy fields of Flanders resting easier in their graves because their sacrifice made the world safe for democracy. This is a mistake. Whenever a person dies history shatters, terminates. History is no more than a single person's lived experience.

But the living drive on, the fat cigar of 'History' between their teeth, handing down merit awards to posterity for its gallant spadework. At any single moment contemporary society is enthralled by the sense of being 'it' – the epicentre of all patterning and interpretation. When we visit the museums and gaze at the skulls of 'primitive' man, do we not view them as imperfect prototypes for our own craniums? When we inspect the simple tools of the Iron Age, don't we treat them as pathetic, if noble, attempts to forge steel bridges and link the world by satellite? In this respect we are all 'historicists', even if we reject the heavy metal of Marxian determinism.

The notion of material and technological 'progress' (which is undeniable), of each generation building on the advances of its predecessor, is probably the key to modern historicism. It was generally absent before the industrial revolution. Admittedly medieval painters depicted Jesus and his contemporaries in medieval costume, but that error was due more to ignorance, to lack of perspective, than to the assumption that the year 1300 AD explained the year 13 AD. Modern man, bloated on the hubris of material progress, gradually extended the twin notions of progress and history to the political sphere as well, viewing the resistance of the Pyms, Hampdens and Cromwells to royal tyranny as England's apprenticeship for 19th- or 20th-century parliamentary democracy: the real thing. 'Robespierre would have joined the French Communist Party' announced a poster of the Popular Front era. Our view of development leads us to regard human history as Aristotle explained the seed's teleological destiny in the fully grown plant.

One notices how our sense of progress and development, our confidence in ourselves as the proper reference point for the entire human experience, falters when we discuss music or literature. No one regards Shakespeare as a rehearsal for Bernard Shaw (except Shaw, and he was joking). No one treats Mozart as a warm-up for Mahler. Indeed each poem, play, painting and symphony – whatever its derivations – reminds us (as if freezing our onrushing sense of history) that every moment in time, every incident and experience, is a complete picture framed fore and aft.

In September 1978 it seemed, very reasonably, to Mr Austin Mitchell, MP, that the black politicians of the Smith-Muzorewa internal settlement were the sort you'd find lounging behind their paunches in Meikles Hotel. It is no reflection on his sense of history to point out that as my friend and I talked about Marechera in the same hotel, six years later, we were very much in the company of Zimbabwe's new élite, revolutionary politicians and former freedom fighters (those not selling matches on street corners), who had been suffering from hunger, thirst and bilharzia in the Mozambique bush when Mr Mitchell spoke up for them.

Not that their initial entry into Meikles had been smooth. A hotel which refuses to entertain black Catholic bishops in 1960 may not be accommodating to black Marxist terrorists in 1980. Waiting for General Rex Nhongo and his 'gooks' were the embittered remnants of Smith's security forces, tough troopies with Jesus haircuts and St Christophers dangling on their bared chests, all convinced that they had 'knocked the living daylights' out of Zanla and Zipra before the Brits, specialists in betraying their kith and kin worldwide, their tongues black with Nigerian oil, had sold them out. So things were not easy in Meikles and the police were often called as each army, schooled to hate the other, refused to yield up the phantom Helen of victory.

My friend had other things on his mind besides Marechera. His brothers were still operating the family farms in Matabeleland, despite the murder of more than sixty whites by Ndebele dissidents since Independence. The white farmers, he reported, had lost all confidence in the police and army: one might as well bay at the moon as call for help on the agric-alert radio alarm. My friend, who had both detested the Smith regime and quietly dreaded its alternative, was in a state of despondency. On her deathbed his mother had enjoined him to look after her dog and hang on to his shares in the Rhodesian Printing Corporation. He had obeyed and the shares were now practically valueless following the nationalis-ation of Zimbabwe's newspapers.

He was also weary of official rhetoric, of the heralded utopia of the one-party state, and of 'Marxists who know very little about literature but a great deal about the "three laws of dialectics".' Shona literature was all very well – but not as an obligatory subject for every student in the department. As Marechera's character, Grimknife, puts it:

> My field anyhow is now quite hopeless. I am a specialist in Latin and Greek but who wants to learn Latin and Greek these days? They are shouting for Shona and they have got it. Their inalienable right to their authentic culture.[1]

'Tell me about Marechera's arrest. I've been trying to find out what happened.'

'I'm leaving for South Africa,' my friend said. He lit a cigarette but could not support my silence. 'Perhaps you've already heard?'

'I heard a rumour.'

'But were too polite to say anything? Please don't imagine that I look forward to South Africa with anything but horror. To begin with, I don't know a soul. And secondly I don't like apartheid. Perhaps you don't believe me. Or you do, but attach supreme importance to a man's actions.'

I said: 'I'm not at all sure it's the duty of white progressives not to live in South Africa.'

I am not at all sure. The arguments are complex, both pragmatic and existential – one respects the call for an absolute boycott, a stand of absolute physical dissociation, yet would one wish that Athol Fugard had exiled himself from the world he depicts so brilliantly? Or Gordimer; or Coetzee? Should events in South Africa go unreported by foreign journalists because for the period of their assignment they must assume the legal privileges of the master race?

I had recently paid my first visit to Cape Town, its sky in

[1] *Mindblast.*

permanent watercolour, the peninsula greened by the abundance of rain so desperately needed across thousands of miles of veld and bush to the north, from Kimberley to Lusaka. The Coloureds and Indians had delivered an emphatic 'No' to Botha's new, cosmetic constitution – much less seduced, I had to admit, than Rhodesia's blacks had been in 1979, when Smith and Muzorewa offered them 'black mask, white power'. Had Marechera accompanied me he would have been allowed to share neither my accommodation nor the Nie Blankes compartment of the train. On the other hand we could have stepped into the public library together to scrutinise Jacobsen's Index of Banned Books – which contains all of his titles but only half of mine (the others residing mysteriously on the open shelves). The Index itself is amusing as well as sinister. A title is often sufficient to generate the spot with which the censor damns the book. *Black Sunlight* would stand no chance even if it were an astronomer's treatise. But Dambudzo Marechera entertains no expectations of immortality south of the Limpopo; his concern is with censorship this side of that grey and greasy water:

> His poems were, they said, capitalist trash.
> 'We want poems that will uplift the people,' they said.
> 'But. . . . '
> 'Know what's wrong with you?' they said.
> He shook his head but in his semiology meaning that he did know.
> 'Your education,' they said . . . .
>
> Or the police sneering at his poems, or the army officer saying with a leer, 'We can make you disappear,' clicking his fingers. 'Just like *that*. See?'[1]

On 22 June 1984 the Zimbabwe Government Gazette reported that the Minister of Home Affairs had issued an order prohibiting the publication of the play *Pulse* by Alem Mezgebe (an East African), which had recently been produced in Harare by Comrade Albert Chimedza. The order, issued under section 60 of the Emergency Powers Regulations, followed a performance sponsored by the National Arts Foundation. According to a subsequent newspaper report, the play traces the murderous career of a crude, uneducated and somewhat demented young army officer who assumes power through a military coup. The banning order, which was upheld following a visit to a later performance by the Secretary of the Ministry of Home Affairs, the Secretary of Information, and a senior

[1]Ibid.

police officer – no reason was given – drew protests from a number of Zimbabwean writers, including the secretary of the writers' union, Musa Zimunya (who had been active in opposing the ban on *Black Sunlight*), and the novelist Stanley Nyamfukudza, the editor at College Press without whose support *Mindblast* might never have been published.

But had Dambudzo Marechera protested?

My friend glanced apologetically at his watch. We had not discussed Marechera's arrest, or the role of the two Dutch radio journalists who had been picked up with the poet and had subsequently interviewed my friend, the better to understand the literary history of this faintly alarming country. He gave me their names. They were presently staying at the Monomotapa. 'Quite unusually attractive,' he said.

We parted sadly, stuttering out clichés: 'Next time you're in London, do please. . . .' I know his dread of London, the streets, the latent violence, the tubes at night. He once left his umbrella at my house and wouldn't come to collect it because of the journey.

'Do write,' I said.

'I probably won't. I've destroyed several friendships through my inability to write letters.'

We dithered on the steps of Meikles, searching for a perforated line, a clean parting. Later I learned that he had been refused an entry visa to South Africa.

NINE

I drove to the Monomotapa.

Miss Myrle Tjoeng was staying in room 1414. I phoned from the lobby. Yes, she would see me. I took the lift to the fourteenth floor – why must this spacious continent engage in these ugly, prestigious enterprises? The woman who opened the door cautiously – recent experiences had not been reassuring – was of Indonesian appearance and beautiful. Her colleague, Miss Marka Kaess, was a blonde of cheerful disposition.

During the internal election of 1979 the Monomotapa housed a team of observers from the African Freedom Foundation. (Both the

US President and Congress had boycotted the elections, in line with the policy of the Labour Government in Britain.) The leader of the Freedom Foundation's delegation was Bayard Rustin, formerly an aide to Martin Luther King and now a cold warrior predisposed towards a 'moderate experiment in inter-racial partnership' such as Smith and Muzorewa were attempting to sell to a hostile world. Rustin insisted that Martin Luther King would have taken the same view (just as Eduard Bernstein claimed to be a better Marxist than Kautsky or Lenin when advocating an end to class struggle; later, in 1984, when South Africa enfranchised its Indian community, both the boycotters and the participationists claimed Gandhi's inheritance). It was clear that Bayard Rustin enjoyed the VIP treatment he was accorded in Rhobabwe by Smith's desperate officials and Muzorewa's muppets. He also knew very little about the country. 'The Ndebele, who are they?' he asked me in Bulawayo. Putting the case for the Patriotic Front over dinner in the Monom-otapa, I had made no headway.

All of this was unknown terrain to Myrle Tjoeng, an editor of literary and cultural programmes for NCRV, Hilversum. An ideal witness, clear, sincere and straightforward, she recounted how she and Miss Kaess had run into Marechera on the first day of the Book Fair, finding him understandably incensed about College Press's failure to produce copies of *Mindblast* for display and sale. The Dutch women had then begun a tape-recorded interview which was soon interrupted, though Marechera was clearly very content in their company. All three took the short walk from Kingston's book store to Meikles, where the Noma Award for Literature was to be presented. They may have known that prize-givings do not noticeably tranquillise Marechera: he will as readily disrupt a ceremony in his own honour as one in which he is merely a spec-tator. Walking along Stanley Avenue, past the importuning flower sellers, they passed Cecil Square, latterly his workshop:

> My days were simple. I would dust myself up from whatever alley I had been sleeping. I would think of where my next meal was going to come or not come from . . . food. That must always come first. I trudged into a Greek-owned grocery store, bought myself a pack of sour milk and three buns and headed for Cecil Square to sit, eat and type this story.[1]

Passing the long ranks of Rixi taxis (the same journey never costs the same in any two of them), the poet was almost certainly

[1]Ibid.

pondering where the interview with Dutch radio might lead. Was he only hours away from another Continental night of fire?

> Dagmar was two days of sheer fire in my life. West Berlin leapt up in flames, the anguish and terrifying beauty of our chance meeting. There, a bare twenty metres from us, was the Berlin wall.[1]

Marechera's British publisher recalls that the writer bluffed his way to West Berlin, through several cordons of East German Volkspolizei, without a valid passport, the only one he possessed having been issued by Ian Smith. A visit to a London post office had been in vain, for the poet lacked a birth certificate and indeed loathed the very fact of his own birth to parents such as his. Thus his mother breaks the news of his father's death:

> 'The old man's dead,' she said.
> It sounded both cryptic and ridiculous. I laughed long and loud.
> But she regarded me without the slightest interest.
> 'He was hit by the train at the rail-crossing,' she said. 'There was nothing left but stains.'
> That hoarse bass voice of hers had not always been like that. She blamed it on the way she had 'come down in the world'; which was merely a euphemism about her excessive drinking.[2]

Later she used to strike him for talking to her in English. She had saved the money to send him to the best secondary school, then to university, and he resented his indebtednes to the point of scorning her sacrifice.

In all probability Marechera behaved impeccably throughout the 1984 Noma Award ceremony because soothed by the company of two pretty ladies from Holland, and because the evening ahead now shimmered with prospects even more tangible than literary acclaim. The poet's love of white flesh irradiates his writings – I was later to observe the simplicity of its *modus operandi*.

With a white lady there are fewer complications. A 'complication' is not necessarily, as might be assumed, an unwanted baby; a Shona complication is the girl's father. European fathers have long since abandoned their horsewhips, even if prepared to embark on a trek

---

[1]Ibid.
[2]*The House of Hunger.*

of 6,000 miles, nor can they sue in the customary, or tribal, courts for damages. The truly dedicated Zimbabwean 'seducer' (as he is called) may well have two or three concurrent court cases against him pending, each of them involving half a year's wages. The reason for this is that a Zimbabwean marriage, even among men and women educated abroad, must involve a deal – *lobola*, or *roora* – which is traditionally negotiated between the bridegroom's uncles and the bride's on behalf of their respective fathers. Lobola is the Western dowry in reverse: the bride fetches her price in *mombes*, cash or – not unknown in the towns – crates of Castle lager. But the seal on the deal is the young lady intact. Discovering otherwise, the indignant husband can reject his new wife while his angry relatives demand the return of the *lobola*.

It happened that during the month we are describing Chief Justice Enoch Dumbutshena handed down a judgment which provoked demonstrations across the country, from Mutumbura to Beitbridge, and brought letters flooding into the newspapers. Chivhu district court had ordered Mr John Katwekwe to pay the sum of $800 to Mr Mhondoro Muchabaiwa, whose daughter he had seduced in May 1983. But in Chief Justice Dumbutshena's view the new Age of Majority Act, recently passed by Parliament, deprived fathers of the right to seek damages for the seduction of daughters over the age of eighteen, such right henceforward being invested in the adult daughters themselves.

Even the Prime Minister was disconcerted by the ruling. He told a laughing House of Assembly that this was no laughing matter; and that if his sister (Mugabe has no surviving children) wanted to be married he would demand *roora*, or bride price, from the prospective husband. If the latter thereupon quoted the judgment of Justice Dumbutshena, namely that adult women are free to regulate their own relationships, the Prime Minister would send back the message: 'Do you want to marry my sister or don't you?'

It's reported that even Mr Smith laughed from his obscure corner of the Chamber where he sits like a one-and-a-half-eyed owl, brooding upon civil liberties.

The Prime Minister's attitude is not, of course, inspired by cupidity but by a wisdom older than any social order. It seems that on this subject even Marechera shares a Venn diagram with Mugabe:

Marriages based on beauty and amorous desires are soon blitzed out of existence; and, as Juvenal says, 'verses have their own fingers to excite,' producing a mood more amorous than

41

love itself, so much so that each time I saw Tsitsi I was, with Virgil, 'athirst to take the member and hide it deep'.[1]

This covers a great deal of ground – perhaps it would be wiser to leave the Prime Minister out of the diagram. Who is Tsitsi, who is she? To my knowledge she appears only in this unpublished work, bursting upon the narrative as the poet's wife, but soon vanishing 'with the children' to Hollywood or somewhere. Her brother Owen, we are told, was the friend whom Marechera most loved and admired, a fellow-poet of kindred disposition. The three of them used to make films in the Salisbury townships, Tsitsi the actress, Marechera the scriptwriter, Owen the director.

> Our detractors said we had become not black writers but mirrors of the fashionable or eccentric movements in Europe and Russa . . . . Owen had been one of those brilliant students whom our country nourishes solely in order to break their spirit on the anvil of crude racial antagonism. He and I enjoyed the common and sordid freedom of being born in the slums and hacking our way out of it by the skin of scholarships . . . . But whereas I fled the country, he remained and fought for the survival of his sanity among those whom he knew he could neither love nor trust.

This passage may owe more to literature than to life, yet it seems that at some stage Owen did leave Zimbabwe for London, where he began painting murals in a flat they shared while dreaming 'about puting LSD into South Africa's drinking water'. Then Owen died – suicide perhaps. By that time Tsitsi had sent a telegram from Zimbabwe demanding a divorce and custody of 'the children'; this followed (shades of Shelley) a savage attack on Marechera's stories by a local critic.

Flanked by two enchanting versions of Dutch radio, Marechera was no doubt again 'athirst to take the member and hide it deep', as he passed within yards of the flagpole where the bullet heads, the short-back-and-sides, the Churchill-would-turn-in-his-grave veterans of Arnhem and Alamein used to parade in formations of rectangular atavism, 'dressing' by the right, refugees from Mr Attlee's England. In declaring Rhodesia independent they had printed new postage stamps showing the old bulldog, haloed by a helmet (the upturned soup plate worn uniquely by Brit and Commonwealth forces), his resolute jaw silhouetted against a searchlight-raked night sky. In 1978 Churchill's grandson resigned

[1]'The Black Insider'.

as a shadow minister in protest against Mrs Thatcher's vacillating failure to vote for the immediate removal of all sanctions against Rhodesia. The Labour Government, he said, was 'leading the pack in holding down the peoples of Rhodesia so that the surrogates of the Soviets may more speedily slit their throats . . . .' Later, when this diabolical plot had come to fruition, Dambudzo Marechera began to encounter 'the surrogates of the Soviets' around Harare:

He had been in 'the Struggle' and seen death at close quarters. There are a lot like him around. Youngsters who have tasted death and who will not flinch from firing it at you if they think you are an enemy. I hope I am not an enemy.[1]

While hoping, and typing his book in Cecil Square, he had noticed a derelict white woman slumped on a park bench in a 'muddied flowery dress'. Barefoot, she carried a cardboard box around like a handbag, a bottle of spirits trailing from her other claw. One day he observed that her eye was black and her cheek bruised; a thin trickle of blood ran down from her clumsily painted mouth. She plucked up courage – at last – to approach him:

'Still at it,' she said – her accent was Cambridge.

She told him she had been robbed of five dollars by a friend. She wept in the telling. Her boyfriend, a teacher, had been killed during the guerrilla war. 'One of your people shot him . . . . ' The woman said she was twenty-eight but she looked sixty. Marechera's cat's eyes told him she was telling the truth. She confessed to hunger: one could always get a decent plate of sadza for fifty cents at the Railway Hotel and did he have fifty cents? She offered herself.
He said he had work to do.

I felt her humanity but – is it macho – despised her female vulnerability. Her White European female vulnerability. Feeling shit even as I felt this. Feeling in some gruesome way I was betraying the very source of all writing, spurning and rejecting her this way.[2]

It put him in communion with de Sade. 'I had read all of de Sade.' The world's persistent sadism excited his quivering political antennae:

[1] *Mindblast.*
[2] Ibid.

South Africa fucking Maseru. Or the Israelis sodomizing the Palestinians in Beirut. Or the Nazis screwing the shit out of the rest of Europe.

Or Mr Shoichi Noma, founder of the Japanese publishing firm Kodansha, creating an annual prize of $3000 open to African writers whose work is published on the continent of Africa – but not giving the money to Marechera. Hence (perhaps) MR NORMAN DRAKE's crazed Japanese assistant, SHOGUN. And so Marechera entered Meikles Hotel for the second annual Noma Award, in the company of Miss Tjoeng and Miss Kaess, heading for arrest and imprisonment. Though he was without a formal invitation (having disrupted the proceedings the previous year), no check was made at the door and he entered the Stewart conference room unchallenged. When Marechera is on his best behaviour his baby features are wrapped in the most exquisite innocence. The Colonel, however, had not found that infant countenance so appealing. Who is the Colonel?

As Marechera took his seat in the Stewart Room there were smiles and sniggers from the assembled shefs. A year earlier he had been roughed up by two of the Minister of Justice's bodyguards while attempting to burst in on a writers' seminar which had barred him because he was bound to disrupt it. That same evening he had leapt to his feet during the Noma ceremony to warn the academics, publishers, diplomats, journalists, foreign dignitaries and ministers that he, Marechera, Zimbabwean poet, novelist and playwright, was about to be dragged away by municipal police in blue uniforms. The prediction was self-fulfilling: it happened immediately.

Marechera had screamed: 'This is the last time you'll hear me! This is the last time you'll see me!'

Everyone had laughed. Even his London publisher had laughed. Why? 'Because it was all so predictable. I suppose I've witnessed too many of Dambudzo's performances over the years. He used to come here, to Bedford Square, in search of royalties, loans, tips, fights. Often he turned up in a beard or dressed as an old woman. The girls at reception were both fascinated and alarmed. They were under instructions to call me as soon as he showed up.'

TEN

On the fourteenth floor of the Monomotapa Hotel, an S-shaped monster dominating the western reaches of Harare, Miss Kaess engagingly refolds her legs across the brocade bedspread.

'Did Marechera make another scene at this year's ceremony?'

'Why should he?' Miss Tjoeng looks indignant.

Cowering beneath the Monomotapa, with its transnational grammar of modern comfort, like a cartoon mouse awaiting the pleasure of a Disney cat, is the small Presbyterian church which had been bombed in Feburary 1980 by – screamed the headlines – 'the Marxists'. The election campaign was approaching its violent climax and Bishop Muzorewa had warned that 'the Marxists' were poised to abolish Christmas, Easter, the Family, and Property. The truth was a great deal worse: 'the Marxists' had penetrated Rhodesian Combined Operations; the bombing of four Salisbury churches was the work of an officer in the Selous Scouts, Lt Edward Piringondo, Silver Cross of Rhodesia for conspicuous gallantry in the war against terrorism. No black man was commissioned in the Rhodesian security forces until the year 1977; Piringondo had been one of the first – the sort of splendid askari who used to appear, resplendent in their imperial uniforms, their tulip-bright cummer-bunds, on Wills' cigarette cards. Before the night was out Piringondo, aided by a certain Sergeant Moyo, had also bombed two other churches before blowing himself and his colleague to fragments so small that they had to be swept up with dustpan and brush. Just a 'stain', as Marechera would say.

'Marxists Bomb Churches!' But this didn't last long. Mugabe had walked into a press conference holding the registration document of Piringondo's devastated car.

And that was the end of the old colonels. Within a year General Walls had been given the boot and the 'terrorists' had assumed most of the key positions in Zimbabwe's armed forces. A new breed of colonels emerged, the guerrilla commanders. Their primary duty, by 1982, was the pacification of Matabeleland, but those remaining on duty in the barracks ringing Harare had casual energy to spare for beating the shit out of pansy poets defaming their country. Enter soon the Colonel.

45

Far from disrupting the Noma ceremony, recalls Myrle Tjoeng, Marechera had been in high spirits, darkened only by the failure of College Press to get copies of *Mindblast* to the Book Fair on the opening day. Not once had he heckled as the 1984 award was divided between Simakahle Ndebele, a young professor at the University of Lesotho, and a sixty-three-year-old veteran of Mau Mau, Gakaara wa Wanju, author of patriotic songs in Gikuyu and Swahili as yet untranslated into English. Gakaara had spent seven years in a British detention camp. Despite his flamboyant iconoclasm, Marechera is not without respect for such men.

The ingathering of literary talent for the Noma Award had also brought Marechera's first meeting with another Kenyan writer whom he regards with awe, though one would be surprised if the sentiment were reciprocated. Ngugi wa Thiong'o had flown in to deliver a lecture urging African writers to reach out to their own people via the indigenous languages. Ngugi is the Sholokhov of the Equator, a fiercely committed socialist realist and now an exile from his native Kenya. Although his novels do not enjoy huge general sales, the key to commercial success in Africa is invariably the educational curriculum: Ngugi's novel *The River Between* is an 'O'-level set book while *A Grain of Wheat* is required reading for the 'A'-level literature syllabus. Marechera does not enjoy royalties on that scale, although *The House of Hunger* is an optional text at the University of Zimbabwe – mere pin money, insufficient to keep a writer in beer let alone pay the rent. Marechera's rent is paid by a woman of singular generosity, the only friend to have visited the poet in Harare Central Police Station after his incarceration.

This brings us to the circumstances of Marechera's arrest. The Noma Awards concluded, Miss Tjoeng and Miss Kaess had found a quiet spot in Meikles to resume their interview. But had the poet been shouting, as reported; was he drunk? Was the literary editor of the *Herald* correct when he assured me that Marechera had been making the usual exhibition of himself when arrested?

'No, no, not at all.' Myrle Tjoeng's swallow eyes do not lie. 'He spoke with passion, but quietly. He didn't shout, as people are saying. Dambudzo was not making a disturbance.'

Indeed, as she pointed out, the proof of this resided in the tapes later confiscated by the police. But each time she had called at the police station to recover her tapes she had been told to return at a later date.

What had Marechera talked about?

'About his work and his ideas. He also told us how he had been beaten up some weeks ago, when the first review of *Mindblast* appeared in a magazine.'

'Beaten?'

46

'In the toilet of the Holiday Inn. By a Colonel of the Zimbabwean Army. The Colonel cursed him for writing filth that would defame the reputation of Zimbabwe and its Government.'

When Marechera was nine he offended his father, the truck driver who was later to die at a level crossing, by destroying a school exercise book:

A chair, drawn back, creaked. I tensed. I stared stonily at the floor, at the books. The blow knocked my front teeth out . . . . He was rubbing his knuckles thoughtfully and looking down at me as though I was a cockroach in a delicatessen.[1]

And then?

Tjoeng: 'Then a man was standing over us. He said, "Marechera, are you all right? I'm very concerned." '

And the poet's response?

'He said, "Who the hell are you?" '

Was there an answer?

'The man introduced himself as the designer of the Book Fair.'

Odd?

'We thought so.' She glanced at Miss Kaess for confirmation. 'Marechera demanded that this man identify himself. The man did show him a card. Marechera said, "You're CIO." '

Did the man deny it?

'He said, "No, Marechera, I'm not police at all." '

And then?

'Marechera said, "Piss off." '

I had to admire Myrle Tjoeng's unhesitating elocution of these words – clearly she was familiar with the literary scene. But had she kept her tape recorder running through this interrogation?

'No, it was an interruption.'

Here is the difference between a true journalist and a literary editor. A writer would recognise that the interval is the play, the sub-plot is the main plot. I asked this patient and beautiful lady to continue.

Two other silencers had now arrived, demanding to speak to the poet 'in private'. Marechera had become agitated. He kept saying, 'You see, these are the conditions under which I have to work, what kind of a régime is this, we were only talking about books.'

But that wasn't quite the case – he had also spoken of the Colonel in the toilet of the Holiday Inn?

'Yes.'

Miss Tjoeng seemed to be reassessing me.

[1] *The House of Hunger*.

47

She said, 'We protested: Why didn't these men say whatever they had to say in the open?'

And then?

'They flashed cards at us – with photos: CIO.'

It was now about eight in the evening. At this juncture a friend of Marechera's, a well-known poet and university lecturer, intervened, protesting that such interviews were perfectly legal.

People passed by, assessed the situation with a glance, did not stop – rather like the crowds in St James's Park when the unwashed vagabond Marechera was stopped and searched by a black constable of the Met. It is in the lives of delinquents that history most insistently repeats itself.

One of the CIO officers went off to make a phone call. Marechera and the two women began to retreat upstairs to the lounge, looking for a way out of this slow-motion nightmare, but another CIO man pursued them. 'You're not collaborating with the Zimbabwe police,' he warned. Marechera suddenly blew his top, a violent rage, took the CIO man's name and stormed off in search of a phone to check his credentials.

'The policeman did not prevent him. He just laughed. And then suddenly there were a whole lot more of them, new ones, surrounding us on the stairs. There was a fat one who was in charge. He said, "I'm a real policeman," and laughed. He kept laughing. Then he demanded to see our press accreditation.'

The focus of the attack suddenly shifted to the Dutch women. It's illegal to practice journalism in Zimbabwe without a twenty-nine-day permit from the Department of Information. Due to a bureaucratic cock-up, Tjoeng and Kaess were still without the requisite permits. Twice that day they had called at Linquenda House, in Baker Avenue, and twice they had been told to return later because no one competent to issue a permit could be found.

You enter Linquenda House through a shopping arcade. In its long, antiseptic corridors, journalists used to apply for 'facility trips' to the war zones and 'protected villages', in-and-out-in-a-day by Dakota and helicopter, courtesy of South Africa's Defence Forces. While they waited helpful officials handed out gruesome reports of atrocities printed on cheap, greyish paper from the Umtali mills. The most famous was 'Massacre of the Innocents', which carried on its cover a photograph of a cherubic, chortling white baby who had been bayoneted to death by terrorists on the step of her home in Chipinga. Dedicated enemies of Communist terrorism though these white officials were, not a few of them later revealed admirable elasticity by staying on to serve the terrorist Government.

Tjoeng and Kaess had failed to acquire the journalist's permits. Now the CIO pounced in Meikles.

'Fat One roared at us, "You're lying! You're lying!" '

Tjoeng turned to Kaess in puzzled remembrance and spoke a few words in Dutch. 'They kept saying that,' she murmured, 'over and over: "You're lying! You're lying!" '

An official from the Ministry of Information then showed up. The women had scarcely begun to repeat their explanation when he, too, became frenzied: 'You're lying! You're lying!'

Tjoeng's swallow-tailed eyes settle on me. 'We were quite frightened.'

So it goes: an arrest is a form of accident, the hurt and surprise and outrage of it is always one step ahead of the victim's dazed reflexes. But now, listening fascinated to Tjoeng's measured, soft-spoken account, I began to understand.

Innocent and unsuspecting, Tjoeng and Kaess, Indonesian and north European, had been projected into the hysteria of Zimbabwean sexual politics. Had NCRV happened to send a pair of ugly males to soak up Zimcult, none of this, in all probability, would have happened. The barflies and hotel lounge lizards of the CIO resent Marechera's effortless success with white women; it galls them, maddens them to violence, the suspicion that before the night was out he would be 'in deep', screwing 'like a circular saw' – one of his recurring images. Sexual psychosis was sweeping the country. A bizarre crackdown on 'prostitutes' had resulted in the arrest of hundreds of women, black and white, young and old, as excited police, soldiers and militiamen raced through the streets, plunged into bars, raided cinemas, halted stage performances, seizing all 'unaccompanied women' (even when accompanied), demanding to inspect their marriage certificates, slapping them for answering back, filling the cells with weeping females, then transporting many of them, without legal warrant, hundreds of kilometres to a tsetse-fly infested 'rehabilitation centre' in the Zambezi Valley. Where, to this day, some of them still languish. Even white women found themselves seized in cinemas and bars; the powerful historical taboo protecting the 'meddems' and 'missus' had at last been ruptured by the revolutionary vigilantes. The Red Guards had come to Zimbabwe.

'You're lying! You're lying!' yelled Fat One.

'You're lying, you're lying!' shouted the Ministry of Information Official.

They meant: why will you go with him, this baby-faced little prick, this skinny, eight-stone weakling – and why not with us? Aren't we the real men? Didn't we fight the bush war?

Marechera himself sheds light on the nature of the Zimbabwean sexual trauma, the constant equation of sex and violence, sex and self-assertion, sex and revenge. Here he describes the frequent displays of wife-beating he witnessed as a boy:

> The most lively of them ended with the husband actually fucking – raping – his wife right there in the thick of the excited crowd. He was cursing all women to hell as he did so. And he seemed to screw her forever – he went on and on and on until she looked like death. When at last – the crowd licked its lips and swallowed – when at last he pulled his penis out of her raw thing and stuffed it back into his trousers, I think she seemed to move a finger, which made us all wonder how she could have survived such a determined assault.[1]

Confirmed in their suspicion that Tjoeng and Kaess lacked proper press passes, the CIO no doubt concluded that these two attractive foreign women were – like all attractive foreign women – prostitutes. But the CIO men dared not bring this charge:

'You're lying!'

Stunned, protesting feebly about the confiscation of their tapes and recorder, they found themselves in the back of a police car with Fat One at the wheel and the incensed Information official beside him.

And Marechera?

'They dragged him into another car. He was shouting to us, "Don't let them separate us, they're going to beat me!" '

Did they beat him?

'We didn't see it.'

One thing she remembers clearly, as they were led out of Meikles: the distinguished poet and university lecturer, the one who had intervened on Marechera's behalf upstairs, was watching from a discreet distance: 'Rather slyly, keeping out of trouble,' comments Marja Kaess, breaking her silence.

The narrow angles we hastily draw round ourselves. Perhaps literature is a serious business, after all.

From Meikles to Harare Central Police Station is not far, three minutes' drive at the most. Fat One was now insisting that the two women divulge what, exactly, Marechera had said during the interview. 'You'd better tell the truth,' he warned. Tjoeng reminded him that it was all on the tape now in his possession. But no one showed any inclination, then or later, to listen to the tape.

'We asked to telephone the Dutch embassy. The Fat One refused. "No phone calls," he said.'

[1] Ibid.

50

The room into which they were led was small, very crowded, oppressive.

'They were all shouting at us. We were never allowed to finish a sentence. We begged them to ask their questions one at a time, but they just went on shouting at us, "Answer our questions, yes or no!" '

Then Fat One eased off, loosening his collar, letting the sweat drain down his sirloin neck.

' "Why interview Marechera, of all people?" he said. When I attempted to reply, to explain, he leaned over me: "Are you being harassed?" '

Mother said: 'Now you're late jerking off into some bitch . . . . It must be those stupid books you're reading – what do you want to read books for when you've finished with the university?'[1]

Marechera had been held in the same small, cramped, hysterical room as the Dutch women. Tjoeng recalled him repeatedly demanding to know why he had been arrested.

'Fat One said, "Because you're drunk." Then he said: "If you'd been driving a car I'd have locked you up." '

Marechera's reply?

' "I'm not in a car. I can't even drive." Fat One then told him he was under arrest for subversive activities.'

Fat One refused to specify the charge.

He had been arrested many times and each time they would not tell him the nature of his crime. They would merely mock his poetry and sneer at his 'Ambition' and casually – by the seat of his trousers – throw him into a dark, stinking cell.[2]

The hours passed, the interrogators' cigarette stubs littered the floor, the twisted stems crushed under heel after a couple of angry inhalations. Tired, clapped out, the CIO men became self-pitying, post-coital.

'We're only doing our job, please leave now.'

Tjoeng and Kaess were driven back to the Monomotapa, without their tapes or passports. One CIO man had wanted to confiscate their recorder as well, but a colleague advised that this would be against regulations.

Of the six confiscated tapes, only two had actually been used.

[1]Ibid.
[2]*Mindblast.*

51

One of these carried an interview with the Chairman of the Noma Award Committee, Professor Eldred Jones, the Principal of Fourah Bay College, Sierra Leone. A *faux pas*, perhaps? A blunder which might call into question Zimbabwe's capacity to stage an international book fair? No, no: who cares so long as business is done? It's not Marechera's arrest, or the confiscation of Miss Tjoeng's tapes, that vexes the foreign publishers in town, it's the local exchange control regulations which prevent the importation of their books in commercial quantities.

Tjoeng and Kaess returned to Harare Central early next morning, as instructed. No one knew anything about anything. Fat One and his squad had gone to their shebeens and towngirls, to familiar embraces and compliant sighs, then fallen into the sleep of the damned, of those who will never know what Marechera knows. Fat bums and scarred legs. At least they had deprived that baby snake of his catch.

Not much poetry out of him tonight!

There was not even a bucket or hole for him to shit. So his faeces would mount up, growing, stifling him, stinking him in his poetry. Reminding him of an army officer who had once sneered at him, saying, 'You're a mental case. You still expect us to pay for the sins of our fathers.'[1]

That army officer again, that Colonel. 'We can make you disappear.'

Returning yet again to Harare Central Police Station at three in the afternoon, accompanied by an official from the Dutch Embassy, Tjoeng and Kaess did recover their passports, but not their tapes. Those, a white police officer explained, would have to be referred to a higher authority. He was cautiously apologetic, one white to another: Fat One and his colleagues of the previous night's work may have gone 'slightly over the top'.

'Did you enquire about Marechera?'

'The Embassy warned us not to mention him.'

Two hundred and eighty kilometres from Marechera's cell, high in the hills along the eastern border, lies the poet's old school, St Augustine's. In dormitories crowded with iron beds Zimbabwe's next generation of doctors, lawyers, academics and politicians sleep; among them the son of the head of the country's Central Intelligence

[1] Ibid.

Organisation. And beside him snores (let us imagine) another boy, as clever, opinionated and egotistical as Charles Marechera had been when St Augustine's most detested student. We can only guess this new prodigy's fate: will he, like Charles, re-christen himself Dambudzo, which means affliction, hardship, a curse? Will the one boy imprison the other?

It is morning. The school rises for breakfast and chapel. In Harare Marechera wakes to police boots, the report of iron bolts, a tin bowl of cold sadza tossed through the door. The thwarted Scandinavian film crew, pursuing the poet's ghost, stretch their tanned limbs in the comfort of Mutare's Manica Hotel, once called the Cecil. St Augustine's is their destination but it hasn't been easy: a hired Toyota with worn tyres, dirt tracks strewn with boulders, their corn hair caked in red dust, the bones of cattle in dried-up river beds, and beyond every hill and horizon more hill, more horizon. At one moment of despair they had been forced to a halt by an old man standing motionless in the middle of the track, like an anthill sculpted out of the red-brown earth. Flies clustered round the pus oozing from his eyes; at his feet lay a pile of rotting watermelons.

The film crew bought the pile and found the phrasebook.

'*Mangwanani, Baba. Tinoda kuenda kuSt Augustine's*'

The old man thought about this. 'Ten dollar,' he said.

They went on, lost, despairing at each unsignposted fork in the track until, ascending a steep mountain path in heavily wooded border country, searching for the twin church towers of St Augustine's, they found their approach covered by a white man with a shotgun and several labradors.

'Thought you might be Gumbo,' the landowner said. 'Comrade Gumbo of the Ministry of Lands. Comes here every six months to tell me I'm a fascist. Meet any of "my" squatters, did you? You were lucky. Law's on my side, of course, but who cares? Certainly not Comrade Gumbo. The Minister came here when there were only six of them on my land – now I've got five hundred squatters spread over 2,000 acres and I'm down to four hundred head of cattle and no ways am I going to re-stock, man, no ways. Know something? This country has gone. During the war you could count on your neighbour – now I haven't got a neighbour for twenty miles, unless you count the comrade squatters. They all took the gap: I was the fool.'

'Sir, could you kindly direct us to St Augustine's mission?'

The landowner took a notebook and pen from the lapel pocket of his shirt. Carefully he drew a map, sketching in landmarks, distances, signs. He glanced only once, shyly, at the pretty women in the film crew.

He said: 'The sun will be down in less than an hour. Round here only a *houtie* is out after dark. Ten to one you'll get lost again. Don't count on the police. They make themselves scarce. The party rules round here and the party won't lift a finger against the comrade squatters. Some of them are former terrs, you see, gooks – our new national heroes. If you're prepared to rough it, I can put you up for the night.'

The film crew conferred uneasily in Swedish. One continuity girl belonged to a Maoist cell in Stockholm. 'This man is a fascist settler,' she whispered.

The film director turned to the landowner. 'Perhaps we could reach Mutare tonight, eh?'

The landowner drew them another meticulous map.

'Don't say I didn't warn you.' He turned and vanished into the dense trees, the dogs bounding after him.

Two hours after nightfall the film crew saw the lights of Mutare spread across the floor of a valley ringed by mountains. They were glad not to have accepted the landowner's hospitality but equally glad to have had his two white fascist maps.

ELEVEN

I drive to the airport to meet my family, who have spent the day at Victoria Falls. Six years have passed since I watched a goods train creeping out from the Zambian shore until it came to rest, hissing, exactly halfway across the suspension bridge linking two countries virtually at war. After a prudent pause a Rhodesian locomotive ventured out to couple with the wagons. In the majestic folly of politicians, Smith, Vorster and Kaunda had once conferred in a train parked on the same bridge, their carriage windows filmed in spray from the frothing chasm of the mile-wide Falls.

Had they read Robert Early's *Time of Madness*, a political thriller of a sort familiar south of the Zambezi, the statesmen gathered in fruitless negotiation on the bridge might have paused to watch the titanic struggle being fought on a tiny island only inches from the rim of that terrible precipice known to local tribesmen as Mosi-oa-Tunya, the smoke that thunders. In our corner the hero, an officer of the Rhodesian Special Branch; representing Satan, a Moscow-trained baby butcherer set on subverting every human decency. Kaunda, Vorster and Smith would have heard the villain's ghastly howl as he slid over the 350-foot drop while being simultaneously dismembered by a crocodile – nothing in the Kremlin's manual could save him now.

Admiring the baobabs ('the lofty baobabs, to whom the comings and goings of the seasons meant nothing,' as the Senegalese novelist Sembene Ousmane put it), I had fallen in with the deputy editor of a London daily paper (rather as a tick falls in with an elephant). He had come to inspect the internal settlement after an 'extraordinarily successful' visit to South Africa where he had interviewed Botha, van der Bergh (head of BOSS, as it was then called), and the magnate of magnates, Harry Oppenheimer, Chairman of Anglo-American. His admiration for this 'very great man' had been deepened by a small incident. During lunch the industrialist happened to drop his napkin; as the waiters hurried forward, Oppenheimer insisted on bending down to retrieve it himself.

'That's typical of the man,' said the deputy editor.

The conversation turned to the prospects for Rhodesia. A veteran of many campaigns round the world, in peace and war, this sagacious, weather-beaten, chain-smoking old journalist advised me that the 'Marxists' enjoyed little support among the peasantry and got their way purely through intimidation. No, he hadn't visited the tribal trust lands himself, but had 'taken soundings' and dined in Meikles – Meikles again! – with middle-class blacks who wanted to 'make a go' of the internal settlement. He'd also been granted interviews with Prime Minister Smith and General Peter Walls, both of whom had informed him that 'Rhodesians of all races are tired of being pushed around'.

Approaching Kandahar Island, our United Tourist Company cruise boat sounded its horn in salute as a slim patrol boat crewed by macho lads sporting FN rifles sped past – but prudently distant from the Zambian shore.

The tourists from Indiana and Bavaria lifted their stetsons to cheer, the latter sporting '*Ich liebe Strauss*' badges on their nylon shirts, cameras and binoculars at the ready. They all knew and repeated interminably the standard joke about it being perfectly safe so long as the 'terrs' were aiming at you. Both the Germans and the Americans had adopted this word: 'turrrss'.

Those were the days. The fortified, mine-defended Zambezi had then been the frontier of civilisation, the frontier with black Africa, with what Ian Smith called 'chaos, corruption and Kaunda'. It was *Daily Telegraph* country and now it's 'gone'.

When the chips were down, the *Telegraph* columnist Peregrine

Worsthorne flew into the Falls and shared supper with the crew of a police patrol boat. 'It's not black rule we're fighting,' they explained, 'it's black misrule.' He liked the distinction. But how, the young warriors asked, 'can we be expected to surrender to terrorism, which is evil whatever the colour of its face?' Worldly and widely experienced, Worsthorne nevertheless chose to be deeply moved by this avowal. Watching the patrol boat chug upstream into the darkness, he reflected: 'What can one do but take their side? It is impossible under such circumstances not to feel the pulls of kith and kinship.'

'Good luck!' he called.

But to no avail – even Mrs Thatcher let him down.

Driving to Harare airport, passing under Independence arch, I try to re-examine not only the manner of Marechera's arrest but also the balance sheet of four years of black government in Zimbabwe. The *Telegraph*'s columnists had greeted the brutal repression in Matabeleland with cries of joy thinly disguised as yells of rage. Told you so! Worsthorne himself commented: 'The principle of national self-determination, exported to Africa by the West, was and is a recipe for tyranny and anarchy.' A further remark shed light on what he had meant, six years earlier, by 'the pulls of kith and kinship.' Independent Africa, he said, had been 'a marvellous tonic so far as white pride is concerned.' His colleague Richard West, meanwhile, offered the stockbroker belt the snarl it craves:

'One cannot imagine that, had Zimbabwe once belonged to France, the Fifth Brigade of Robert Mugabe would get away with the massacre of the Matabeles.' The French President would have promptly sent in the paras. As for Mrs Thatcher, West quoted an anonymous Ndebele: 'She created this monster Mugabe. She must get rid of him.'

If a *mea culpa* is to be offered, clearly it cannot be into the lap of such lunacy. The myth that Western intellectuals imposed independence on black Africa is a hoary one – the ferocious revolt of Shonas and Ndebeles in 1896 against white rule was not inspired by the *New Statesman*, yet unborn, or by the BBC, ditto, or by the works of Karl Marx. It was precipitated by white conquest and white rapacity, by the wholesale theft of land and cattle; and by the massive affront to the dignity of the tribesmen. Listen to the voice of a typical 'Pioneer', W. A. Jarvis:

'There are about 5,500 niggers in this district and our plan of campaign will probably be to proceed against the lot and wipe them out, then move on towards Bulawayo wiping out every nigger and every kraal we can find.'

But there was an overwhelming objection to that particular final solution – no niggers, no cheap labour.

Self-determination is taken, not given.

In Worsthorne's view, Africans 'really are politically inferior; that is to say, less able than other peoples to benefit from liberal prescriptions.' Let us not waste time computing the bloody dictatorships, the military coups, the torture chambers which Europeans, and men of European stock (as in Latin America) have added to the annals of human misery in this century. What does worry me is the propensity of many white liberals, keen champions of black Africa, to subscribe – tacitly, implicitly, out of friendship rather than derision – to an outlook not so different from Worsthorne's: that liberal democracy, or social democracy, is alien to African tradition and African psychology.

Arriving in Harare for the second national congress of the ruling party, Zanu-PF, a great occasion, indeed a state occasion in everything but name – the Ministry of Information and ZBC serviced the congress without any pretence to political neutrality – I was struck by a change of atmosphere since my last visit two years earlier. Mugabe's long campaign preparing the ground for a one-party state, the denigration of pluralistic democracy as a colonial legacy ('the shackles of Lancaster House'), the local party recruiting drives (including an assault by militiamen on disabled ex-combatants at Vukuzenzele cooperative farm), the relentless fire directed against Nkomo and his associates in the press – all this had brought Zimbabwe a long step closer to the familiar symptoms of a People's Republic: hushed voices and furtive conversations, the automatic glance over the shoulder, the precautionary retreat to the shade of a msasa tree.

And the slogans:

'Let us all defend Cde R. G. Mugabe with our lives. Youth League.'

'We love you, our consistent and authentic leader.'

These were only two of the banners draped hugely over the grandstand at Borrowdale racecourse where six thousand delegates gathered for the party congress – a congress which allowed no open debate of critical motions from the provinces, no censure of the Government's failure to give the people their promised land, barely a mention of the 300,000 rural squatters, nothing of genuine substance, just ritual speeches from the 'fraternal delegates' of Eastern Europe with their shop-worn phrases and mechanical eyes and singed sideburns. As for Zanu-PF's internal elections, Mugabe outwitted even Lenin by choosing his own Politburo and a fair slice of the central committee too.

No doubt currents of inner-party democracy still flowed, though along carefully carved channels. The popularity surrounding Edgar Tekere, once general secretary of the party and now chairman for Manicaland, was one example; the sceptical attitude of some provinces towards Simon Muzenda, vice-president of the party, was another; but in the event almost every issue, including that of corruption, was manipulated to the leader's advantage. As for the one-party state, it became clear that he could turn it on or off like a tap: with falling urban incomes and so much land hunger generating cynicism and resentment, Mugabe needs Baloo the bear, needs Super Zapu, needs the occasional assassination of his own local officials, needs a constant hullabaloo, a recurring Nkomobaloo, as a means of rallying support, cementing loyalty and diverting attention from the 'real' issues. Did not Mrs Thatcher, so unpopular in the opinion polls, so inept in her handling of the economy, need the Falklands war? Did not the Brighton hotel bomb blast of October 1984 send her party's ratings in the polls shooting up? Had Mondale pressed Reagan closer in the presidential race, Nicaragua might well have been invaded.

Let me keep my promise to toss a brick or two at the white liberals whose friendship for black Africa leads them to stand liberty on its head. Down at Wedza the most intelligent of white farmers assured me that there is no alternative to the one-party state and quoted Denis Norman, the Minister of Agriculture: the sooner the better.

'We love you, our consistent and authentic leader.'

I had thought about this while driving across the Wedza and Chiduku reserves, slow going, long sections of the dirt road reduced to the texture of corrugated iron, the closely spaced ridges causing the frame of the car to shudder and judder until one imagined the yellow-red dust strewn with rivets. Progress was punctuated by heart-stopping bangs as the under-belly of the car struck protruding boulders or scraped the walls of small ravines (one feared for the tank and shock absorbers) – a process of demolition cheerfully observed by knots of dusty boys idling beside their emaciated *mombes* in a Hieronymus Bosch landscape of soaring kopjes and flat-topped hills dropped out of beach buckets.

The road meanders on and on: there is always more of Africa. Far away in London a group of concerned liberals will shortly gather to hear the Speaker of the Zimbabwean House of Assembly, the Rt Hon. Didymus Mutasa. It is a middle-aged audience, some elderly, with gentle faces whose perpendicular creases carry a life-time's concern for black Africa. Comrade Mutasa is explaining the virtue and necessity of the one-party state.

Twelve years ago some of these same concerned people occupied a corner of the Foreign Office to protest the imprisonment of Garfield Todd and his daughter Judith in Rhodesia. We bluffed our way in duffle coats past reception, honking in the best accents, then squatted patiently, peacefully, on an ornate marble staircase – churchmen, missionaries, professors, playwrights, an actress – while mandarins hurried past, pretending not to notice, like bit-players in an Ealing Studios farce. It was an hour before the police consented to carry us out.

Now, in 1984, the concerned liberals listen respectfully to Comrade the Rt Hon. Mutasa, a leading member of the Zimbabwean administration which regularly resorts to emergency powers similar to those used against Garfield and Judith Todd. It being 1984, Madame Tussaud's has on display a wax replica not only of Robert Mugabe but also of George Orwell, haggard but upright behind his tiny black typewriter, his desk bare of anything but tobacco, paper and a built-in propensity to call a cat a cat, whatever its colour. It was Orwell who rapped the fellow-travellers of Soviet tyranny in the 1930s, the Webbs and Laskis who explained how suitable to Russian conditions and traditions was Stalin's version of democracy. But do we ever learn?

Mr Mutasa patiently explains that the pluralistic version of freedom is really confusion, and not freedom at all; whereas by eliminating all parties but one you restore to the people genuine freedom of choice. 'We must get rid of factionalism, sectarianism, and personal ambition,' he declares – and his audience applauds. 'Our people, you see, have traditionally obeyed a single monarch, a single leader: it's natural.'

Then he speaks of stability. 'What we need, ladies and gentlemen, is stability. As in Zambia, Tanzania and Kenya.'

Two weeks before Comrade Mutasa's lunchtime lecture in London, and two weeks after the arrest of Dambudzo Marechera in Harare, President Moi returned from Addis Ababa to his thoroughly stabilised Kenya. He said:

'I call on all ministers, assistant ministers and every other person to sing like parrots. During Mzee Kenyatta's period I persistently sang the Kenyatta tune until people said: This fellow has nothing to say except to sing for Kenyatta. I say: I didn't have ideas of my own. Who was I to have my own ideas? I was in Kenyatta's shoes and therefore I had to sing whatever Kenyatta wanted. If I had sung another song, do you think Kenyatta would have left me alone? Therefore you ought to sing the song I sing. If I put a full stop you should also put a full stop.'

Vigorous applause, no doubt.

The applause in Nairobi is partly fear-induced: sweating hands. But we applaud in London because we feel guilty about our colonial past, about foisting the Westminster model on Africa; because we want to remain 'friends of Zimbabwe' (or wherever); because some of us have been intimately associated with that country's new rulers, have shared their trials and tribulations, and would not wish, now, to jeopardise that friendship. I fear the same considerations applied to the British life-peer who appeared on the platform at Zanu's party congress to bring greetings 'from the Labour Party' and to say not a word about pacification, detention without trial or the one-party state – all, one might have thought, somewhat alien to the democratic traditions of the Labour Party. His name is Lord (John) Hatch. In a moment of confusion Mugabe introduced him as 'my old friend, Lord Hailsham'. The following week Hatch was reincarnated in Harare as one of five British parliamentarians visiting Zimbabwe under the auspices of the Commonwealth Parliamentary Association. Their host was none other than our friend Comrade Didymus Mutasa, Speaker of the House of Assembly.

The leader of the delegation, Guy Barnett, MP, was impressed by the case for a one-party state, provided it was done by 'persuasion and consent' – an odd position for a British parliamentarian, perhaps, but one shared by Lord Hatch, who later reported in the *New Statesman* that Mugabe had explained to him that he sought a one-party state on the Yugoslav rather than the Soviet or Chinese models. Paradoxically, it was a Conservative member of the delegation, Peter Bottomley, MP (now a junior minister), who had the temerity to inform Comrade Mutasa that a one-party state and detention without trial were not the goals which had led him to oppose the Smith régime. Mr Barnett did not raise the question of detention without trial during his interview with the Prime Minister because, as he told me, 'I know what Mugabe would have answered: he would have said things were better now than when he was in prison.'

Though a socialist, Mr Barnett did not enquire about the slow pace of land reform in Zimbabwe. On the contrary, he considered the retention of white skills to be supremely important: 'One must not frighten off the wealth-producing classes' (i.e. the colonial landlords). What a wretched bunch are the Labour MPs of Meikles Hotel, so flattered by the three-gun salute of a semi-diplomatic reception, so quick to swallow their tongues in the presence of presidents and prime ministers. As Donald Anderson, Labour's deputy spokesman for foreign affairs, put it after his return from Namibia, the issue of repression and civil liberty in black Africa is 'a less sexy subject' than resistance to apartheid and South African rule in Namibia. Twenty years ago John Hatch wrote: 'Sycophancy is false friendship. And those who fought colonialism did so not only because they preferred to see black rather than white faces behind ministerial desks . . . the replacement of arbitrary colonial administrations by equally arbitrary African oligarchies.'

Zimbabwe is not run by an arbitrary oligarchy, but Hatch's

performance at Zanu's party congress – playing to the crowd – does lead one to wonder about the 'sycophancy' he once rejected; what also leads one to wonder is Hatch's assertion, in the *New Statesman* of 4 January 1985, that the Zimbabwean Government 'has always honoured' the verdicts of an independent judiciary. Dumiso Dabengwa and Lookout Masuku, Zipra's leading generals during the guerrilla war against Smith, might take a different view. Despite their acquittal in the High Court, they have spent the last three years in prison. And Hatch, a specialist on Africa, knows this perfectly well, just as he knows that the case of Dabengwa and Masuku is by no means unique.

Of course multi-party democracy in Africa does prevent a certain type of 'consensus' and 'stability'. But what are the empirically verifiable results of 'one-party democracy'? Nkrumah introduced his version in Ghana in 1960 – though in theory not until the farcical referendum of 1964, when 2.8 million voted Yes and 2,452 voted No! Between 1960 and 1965 about 1,360 Ghanaians were detained, not excluding ministers of Nkrumah's own CPP. In 1965 the President broadcast to the nation announcing whom he had selected as MPs and what constituencies they would 'represent'. His francophone radical ally, Sekou Touré of Guinée, who made his own PDG the sole legal party two months after the country opted for independence from France, then ruled for twenty-six years, forcing an estimated million Guineans into exile, executing or murdering seventeen Cabinet ministers, sentencing eighteen more to life imprisonment, and starving a former general secretary of the OAU, Diallo Telli, to death. If Nyerere of Tanzania has presided over a more restrained one-party state, this might remind us that civil liberties ought not to depend on the character or whim of a single man.

What one-party rule invariably provides is mounting leader worship, sycophancy, the 'Life President' (Osagyefo, Mwalimu, Mzee, Kumuzu, Mobutu Sese Seko Kuku Ngbendu Wa Za Banga) syndrome; the erosion of the rule of law and the independence of the judiciary; a servile press and radio;[1] an arrogant and arbitrary police force (Fat One's Field Day); a stifling of debate about fundamentals; the apotheosis of His Excellency Mercedes waBenzi.

---

[1]Also threatening to 'consensus' and 'stability' are free trade unions, a free press, free universities. The closing down of the university altogether is a measure frequently taken in Africa; alternatively, dissenting students and faculty members may be thrown into prison, as in Kenya, one of Mr Mutasa's models. Among Kenyan academics presently imprisoned are: Kamoji Wachiira, senior lecturer in the department of geography; Al-Amin Mazrui, lecturer in linguistics; Willie Matunga, senior lecturer in commercial law; Mukaru Ng'ang'a, lecturer in the Institute of African Studies; and Maina Kinyatti, senior lecturer in history.

TWELVE

Marechera had been released.

I expected not to find him. He was reported to be living in a block of flats on Rhodes Avenue but you would not find Beckett at home, even if he was, or Genet (in certain respects a kindred spirit to Marechera: both prison graduates, both savage mockers of the good people, the shefs, both writing books designed to be read with one hand). For both Genet and Marechera their own lives and erections are the torch of history; and both are addicted to the back passage – Genet's drag queen, Divine, carried 'a bank between his buttocks'.

Rhodes Avenue is not a bad part of town. Until 1979 no African was legally entitled to live there, but today there are more blacks than whites in the block of flats where Marechera lives. Not the *povo*, of course: a worker earning $150 or $200 a month cannot afford to pay a rent of $66. The working class lives elsewhere, in the townships which encircle the city, in Highfield, Mbare, Chitungwiza, Tafara, Mufakose – 'high-density suburbs' as they are now called.

Few people would choose to live in the matchbox townships if they had an option and Marechera is no exception. It's a mistake to imagine that the inhabitants are accustomed to these characterless, monotonous, parade-ground rows of uniform dwellings, grim rectangular grids of stored labour power lit at night by huge floodlight towers. To go in search of someone living there is a bad business; the local expression reflects the inhabitants' feelings about the physical monotony of their streets: *mudhadhadha*.

The townships of southern Africa are, historically, extensions of the mine compound dormitories, reservoirs of black labour; in colonial days rarely was the worker permitted to bring his family to share these utilitarian dwellings. Today that solution obtains in South Africa whose black inhabitants are governed by pass laws designed to separate the labourer from his family and thus abort any permanent claim to abide in the Republic. When Athol Fugard's play, *Sizwe Bansi is Dead*, was first performed in the Port Elizabeth township of New Brighton – a grim, squalid, refuse-littered square mile of embittered humanity – one particular scene stopped the performance. And I will admit that the main flaw in Marechera's writing to date, the great lack, is a scene of comparable power, empathy, involvement to Fugard's.

The character Sizwe Bansi ardently desires to remain in Port Elizabeth and look for work, but he cannot obtain the required permit. Then one night, in the company of a friend, he stumbles across the body of a dead man whose passbook contains the necessary endorsements. Sizwe Bansi need only swap his identity with that of the cadaver:

SIZWE: I don't want to lose my name, Buntu –
BUNTU: You mean you don't want to lose your bloody pass-book! You love it, hey?
SIZWE: Buntu, I cannot lose my name.
BUNTU: All right . . . start walking, friend. King William's Town. Hundred and fifty miles. And don't waste my time. You've got to be there by yesterday . . . .

So involved did the New Brighton audience become in Sizwe's cruel dilemma that a Xhosa voice cried out from the back of the hall: 'Don't do it, brother. You'll land in trouble. They'll catch you!'

But another voice replied: 'To hell with it! Go ahead and try. They haven't caught *me* yet.'

The performance continued, climaxing in the entire audience rising to sing the Xhosa version of the universal African anthem, '*Inkosi Sikilele Africa*'. A comparable emotion may beset audiences leaving Brecht's *Mother Courage* or Ngugu wa Thiong'o's *The Trial of Dedan Kimathi* – but not, surely, Marechera's scatological drama, *Blitzkrieg*. Is Zimbabwe's Minister of Information justified in calling for a new, 'positive', progressive, morally uplifting literature – a call which Marechera sees as a sinister edict, filling him with dread? Should one urge this taut, cat-like poet to leap out of his own skin, to spread his talents more generously?

His apartment block stands in an area of broad, clean, well paved streets seasonally adorned by vast splashes of colour, pinks, scarlets, orange and yellow, by bougainvillaea, jacarandas and flame trees. Four years have passed since the revolution swept away the old white-dominated city council, but the surface texture of Harare has changed very little. Standards have been maintained: no hawkers, no women roasting maize cobs at street corners, no piles of garbage, no fat dripping from spare ribs, no fruit peel scattered across the sidewalks. Moving into the white suburbs, taking possession of the swimming pools and avocado trees, the stoeps and floodlit tennis courts of Highlands, Greendale and Mount Pleasant, the shefs insist that urban squatters be removed by the police, carted away, out of sight, dumped in the far country.

I parked. The street was quiet.

A young man was observing me through the parted curtains of a ground-floor window: a baby face lazily spooning yoghurt from a large carton. His front door being jammed, unusable, he indicated in mime that I should walk round the flats to the back entrance. I walked round. He stood in the back entrance, still spooning yoghurt, a small, boyish figure, very thin and delicate, assessing his visitor. I noticed tufts of reddish wool lodged in his hair.

He said come in. Sorry about the mess. I noticed the posters on his wall, and an Afro comb lying beside a small, salmon-pink typewriter.

How was he?

'Fine.'

Happy to be at liberty?

'Incredible. I never thought they'd release me.'

We had bought a decorative Afro comb in a Lusaka market. The girl had laughed because we had the wrong kind of hair. She made very little effort to sell it. The traders of southern Africa do not pursue customers, do not hustle, peddle or haggle. When we came to the glistening silver heaps of dried fish, piled on old copies of the *Zambia Daily Mail*, the cheerful boys did try out their English – 'You like?' – but not insistently. Very different from an Arab bazaar and quite different from a West African market. The settler state of the south chained and corralled the native, taught him his place, his corner, broke his spirit. A cheeky kaffir got and deserved the sjambok; the missionaries completed the job.

Soon after Marechera was born I spent a year in the Gold Coast as a subaltern. The photos I took invariably showed people coming towards me, gesturing, calling, sometimes mocking; but in all the pictures I have taken in southern Africa what emerges is a negative print, a withdrawn, wary quality, expecting the worst.

In Lagos and Accra the young man plays bold, hailing you loudly, honking his taxi horn to attract your attention, tossing language at you, grinning as he dodges away through the market stalls and 'mammy wagons', your wallet in his hand. Pidgin, wholly absent from southern Africa, is any language spoken among peoples none of whom are native speakers of it – only when so assimilated that it supplants the original language does pidgin become a creole. In West Africa pidgin injects intercourse with a fast, sharp, cosmopolitan quality, a cunning cultural response which both consoles and cons the white overlord, dipping into his pocket, then baffling him with agile mutations of familiar words. On discovering he is carrying a visitor proud of his diplomas, the taxi driver delivers insults the victim cannot grasp: 'Na him make I no de want carry you book people. To too know na him de worry una.'

Pidgin, like creole, is the language of the melting pot, usually found in colonised islands or along commercially penetrated seaboards. Southern Africa is big, landlocked, static; the devotion to standard English is a measure of deference. In Lusaka's Cairo Road the bakeries are closed but the General Post Office maintains the best British bureaucratic standards, each counter assigned a clearly marked function, including the 'Philatelic Section'. Despite the traffic, no one honks; in central Baghdad it's impossible to sleep at any hour of the night.

Marechera no longer wears his Rasta locks. His hair is cut short, tight and wiry. African hair seems to be genetically paramount; however pale the offspring of a mixed marriage, the hair is invariably negroid. Marechera politely removed some clothes and magazines from the chair and perched himself on the bed, with the strawberry yoghurt.

'Will you please excuse me? My breakfast.'

'I apologise for calling so early. I thought I might miss you otherwise. Indeed I didn't really expect to find you.'

'I live here now.'

Having bought the Afro comb, we encountered Dr Zulu, who occupies a shaded corner of this Lusaka market. He is a witch-doctor, but not a naked one: his clothes look as if they originated in the OK Bazaar; his address is not Heart of Darkness but PO Box 34538. According to his painted sign, he is 'The Healer with a difference. Dr Zulu is here to solve your problems. Fits. VD. Evil spirits. TB. Asthima (so spelt). At Home. Marriage. And also Jobless Problems.'

Would he mind if I copied all this down? No, not at all.

I asked Dr Zulu what he meant by 'At Home' problems. He responded cautiously, his old rheumy eyes registering the presence of my wife and daughters: he was sure I didn't have any At Home problems. Born in Malawi, he was by now bored with witch-doctoring a decreasingly superstitious urban population. He preferred to talk of the 'shortages.' Everyone in Lusaka uses this English word. At the airport an official had even advised me against visiting his country:

'Too many pickpockets. Too many shortages.'

I told Marechera that his taped interview with Dutch radio was still in police custody. He said, 'Oh fuck,' but casually, as if he had already put the episode from his mind. Then he remembered something:

'Do you know what they said to me when I was released?'

'What did they say?'

'They said, "Next time you open your mouth to a journalist, we'll get you".' He gestured towards his desk. 'They came in here, broke in, looking for incriminating documents.'

'Did they find any?'

He laughed. 'Honestly, I don't even know what's an incriminating document.'

I asked him to sign my copy of *Mindblast* and he looked pleased. He wrote in it: 'With best wishes from Dambudzo Marechera (Harare 4th Sept. –84).' He avoided inscribing my name, no doubt still uncertain who his visitor was, though he frequently inserted my first name when talking, sugaring his sentences in colonial fashion – it's like touching someone's arm when talking to them. If we were less anal and repressed we would most probably rub noses and massage each other's genitals in the course of normal conversation or when negotiating a contract. I noticed that his legs were stick-thin under his unwashed blue cotton trousers.

In London he had worn dreadlocks and played around with Rastas. Marechera is familiar with the many faces of the black man and knows that to the West Indian or street-wise black Cockney flogging electronic hardware in the Tottenham Court Road, those Africans with their short hair and 'best behaviour' are helplessly square. Not winners at all. Who was this bloke Biko anyway? Not Brixton, not ours. Césaire and Fanon had bridged the Atlantic with ideology, Senghor the Mediterranean with negritude and black Orpheus, but the postwar Sartrean era of *Les Temps Modernes* is gone and Africans are once more on their own.

The posters on Marechera's wall constitute a cry against this isolation. He has caught sight of one world and wants to belong to it.

He had studied all over Europe under some of the best modern European sculptors. His work was totally cosmopolitan, nothing to do with any particular tradition. After the revolution he had returned to find his sculpture denounced by critics left and right. His work, they said, was incomprehensible . . . . And the tourists and dealers of course only wanted to buy 'genuine' Shona pieces.[1]

The posters on his wall were not what one might expect: not pink-rimmed vaginas, Douanier Rousseau, Dada, Magritte. One poster advertised the Zimbabwe Book Fair; two others promoted the works of Ngugu wa Thiong'o; a fourth was not really a poster but the book jacket of Peter Abrahams's *Tell Freedom*.

[1] *Mindblast*.

66

'You admire Ngugi?'

'I admire that man. He has been an inspiration. I was totally delighted to meet him, to be introduced, at the Book Fair. Before my arrest.'

He had finished the yoghurt. Delicately he put down the carton and spoon, re-crossing his spindle legs.

Marechera's admiration for Ngugi puzzled me: could any two black writers have less in common, the highly political socialist realist composing Zola-esque, wide-angled epics of oppression and resistance; and the self-absorbed, perverse, brilliant miniaturist who knows that writers are neither doctors nor priests? Some weeks later I came across a passage in Marechera's unpublished novel, 'The Black Insider', in which he expresses his regard for the major writers of the African continent. But notice how the light drains from his prose as the shadow of the academy falls across his desk:

The forces that gave rise to the black renaissance in letters were the specific and immediate demands for independence and historical parity. Such forces were peculiarly fertile in the fashioning out of the epic style of novel such as Achebe's *Things Fall Apart* and Ngugi's *A Grain of Wheat*. I must confess that I grew up on Peter Abrahams's *A Wreath for Udomo*, in which the roots of our history and the possibility of an African image were explored . . . . At the same time the seeds of disillusion were sown: Okonkwo's alienation from his shadow and his subsequent suicide; Ngugi's awareness of the betrayal of Uhuru; and Abrahams's prophetic insight into the sort of corrupt expedience which an African front-line state can get into. But there was one weakness in all this. History is not something outside and apart from us; it is human beings – us . . . . Kwei Armah in his *The Beautiful Ones are not yet Born* not only stripped the African image of its clothes but also forced it to undergo a baptism of shit . . . our roots have become so many banners in the wind with no meaningful connection with the deepseated voice within us.

'Tell me about the Colonel.'

He jumped up, threading a passage between the bed and my legs. 'Ah, you heard about that.'

'I heard a story, yes.'

He was eager to tell me. The Colonel had happened several weeks earlier. Always alert for free booze, Marechera had cadged an invitation to the PTA Conference reception at the new Holiday Inn and –

'Wait. What's the PTA?'

He looked shocked. 'The Preferential Trade Agreement.'

'Ah.'

'I was really very happy that day. The first review of my new book had just appeared and I was showing it to everyone in the Snuff Box Bar. "Look, you're all saying Marechera is just a bum who's stopped writing, now here's proof I've been working, here it is." '

From his desk he extracted a magazine which he put into my hand. It was open at the last page, page 46, which carried a review of *Mindblast*. The page was covered in rusty blobs of blood.

'That's my blood, David.'

The review looked friendly enough – certainly not the kind of hammering that causes an author's nose to bleed. I noticed the byline: 'Oliver Nyika', a name unknown to me.

'Quite a promising writer,' Marechera said, reading my thoughts. Arriving at the Holiday Inn, he had circulated among the shefs, indigenous and foreign, the civil servants who fly from capital to capital, from conference to conference, burning up enough funds to furnish a whole drought-stricken region with boreholes, a radiant Marechera brimming with whisky, brandishing his magazine, the evidence that the flame of his talent still burned. God knows what he said, what remarks he uttered, in his euphoria, in his boyish desire to be accepted, recognised by the shefs he satirised.

Trotting to the toilet, he had been followed by a big, confident, smartly dressed man who seized him, forced him up against the wall, and informed him that he was a louse whose filthy writings defamed his country and his government.

'He started beating me. I was clutching this magazine as if it were my life. He hit me here and here' – indicating the hollow on either side of the nose, the sinus cavity – 'again and again, with savage, expert blows. It was a professional job.'

Another man, another shef, had then entered the toilet. Marechera knew him and cried out for help.

I'm taking notes, trying to record each detail. Ngugi is pinned to the wall behind Marechera's sulky features, the broad-shouldered future Nobel Prize-winner presiding like a guardian of African values while the boy stares at his own rusted blood, his spotted review.

'It was Abishai Zvogbo. I cried out to him for help. Abishai protested to the man who was beating me up: "Shef, what are you doing, that's Marechera you're beating." '

'They knew each other, then?'

'They did.'

'Who is Abishai Zvobgo?'

68

'He's a state prosecutor and a brother of Eddison Zvobgo'.[1]
'Did your assailant desist?'
'He told Abishai to fuck off. Which he did.'
The beating had continued.
'David, I was bleeding profusely. My blood was everywhere, on the walls, the floor, this magazine. I thought he would kill me. Then the old toilet cleaner came in with his bucket and mop, you know, and I cried out to him, "This man's killing me, get help!" The old fellow rushed out. Only then did my thrashing come to an end. He straightened his tie, washed his hands, and walked out calmly, with dignity.'

Marechera had granted the Colonel some of the grace and favour normally accorded to fictional creations. But the magazine *Mahogany* in my hand was real, and the review, and the blood. Marechera's prose writings are saturated with blood, frenzied violence, his father knocking his teeth out with a single blow when the boy was nine, his father beating his mother, the men of the village fucking their wives in public, and, always, the violence of an elder brother:

I slid my knife back into my coat and walked upstairs, leaving Philip to smash the boy into a stain. Stains! Love or even hate or the desire for revenge are just so many stains on my sheet, on a wall, *on a page even*.[2]

At the University of Rhodesia, Marechera is attacked by a mob of racists who find him with a white girl:

I tore into them. They were tiring me out. I scratched, mauled, flailed, and threshed into these too many white faces. But they hammered into me until I had lost so much blood that I wondered I was still alive.[3]

But even without physical violence his own ('Buddy's' own) blood flows. The psychic violence of the new class of 'socialist' shefs who reject his poetry is enough:

The Man had then sternly nodded him out of the office. Buddy left for his park bench. There he tried to write but started coughing horribly, raucously; he coughed blood. It trickled

[1]Eddison Zvobgo: lawyer, poet and wit, Minister of Justice and Constitutional Affairs. Former Minister of Local Government. Detained for seven years under Smith. Later taught in the USA. Was not elected to the Politburo in 1984: a major surprise.
[2]*The House of Hunger*; the present author's italics.
[3]Ibid.

down his chin and onto his dirty heat-thinned-out shirt. He looked at the blood with wonder.[1]

THIRTEEN

Before Dambudzo resumes his report and we follow his attempts to identify his assailant, it may be useful to pause and return to the ugly episode at the University of Rhodesia in the early 1970s, a time of searing tension between black and white students.

Acutely as he suffered from the humiliating arrogance of the master race – when arriving at Salisbury airport you turned your watch back twenty years – Marechera's rebellion never fitted the nationalist mould. He could not subsume his personality in a cause. His own blazing quest for singularity, common enough among boys of imaginative capacity, inevitably separated him from the comrades. He was not popular. He wanted to be neither black nor white. He detested the tribe. In re-inventing his early years onto paper he both repudiated and abolished all family ties.

One day in London, lingering outside Dillon's bookshop, too poor to buy books, longing for a fag, he met a fellow-Zimbabwean who had also been expelled from the riot-torn University of Rhodesia five years earlier. Marechera begged a cigarette. He was so short of smokes that the first drag caused him to sway from dizziness. Embracing, the two of them headed for the Africa Centre in King's Street, Covent Garden, but after a beer or two his friend became belligerent:

I know you through and through. Your brother was right about you. You're unbelievably selfish and vain and fucking shit . . . . You hate being black . . . . All these five years you never wrote back home. Do you know your uncle died a few months ago in a car crash? They told me how at a party in Hertford College the people there said how sorry they were and you didn't even know what they were talking about!

[1] *Mindblast.*

You're shit. All you think about is yourself and using black people as material for your disgusting stories.

This anecdote is recounted in Marechera's unpublished work, 'The Black Insider'. Against such charges he does not attempt to defend himself; he stands helpless. When his angry friend threw a mug of beer over him in the bar of the Africa Centre, Marechera offered to buy him another.

Consider again the violent scene at the University of Rhodesia when a mob of white students beset him and his white girlfriend, Patricia. 'Patricia is five feet two. Green eyes. Light sandy hair piled loosely down to her waist.' Clearly she was an unconventional girl – according to Marechera she had allowed herself to be filmed 'in the throes of rather violent intercourse' with the poet. Following the traumatic campus beating, Patricia, near-sighted and club-footed, vanished. A private detective hired by her parents tracked her down to a shanty town near Cape Town, where she had exhibited her paintings and been charged with subversion of morals by the police. Again she disappeared; surfaced in a Chinese opium den; escaped; and finally turned up in Salisbury, feverish, half-blind, her voice gone. She was admitted to a whites-only hospital (presumably the Andrew Fleming) where Marechera was not permitted to visit her.

They managed to save her sight. But she would never be able to talk again.[1]

How awful! Five years passed, by my reckoning. The poet had already written the sentence quoted above, and had signed a contract to publish it along with many other sentences, when, emerging from three months in Cardiff gaol, he made a beeline for the speechless Patricia – by now teaching at the University of Aberystwyth. Welcoming him warmly, she produced hash and marijuana, threw out her resident man, informed Marechera that he was a 'wreck', and took him to her, talking all the time. The episode is vividly portrayed in the unpublished 'The Black Insider'.

Another white woman, well known to me and entirely reliable, reported that in the late seventies she had been introduced to Marechera by a mutual friend. They met in a smart pub in SW5. The poet arrived more than an hour late. His appearance made a vivid impression on her. It was high summer and he showed up in a singlet, 'minuscule' shorts, and 'covered in bandages, an awful sight'. Given the upper-crust quality of the pub's clientele, and the

[1] *The House of Hunger.*

71

routine prejudice against half-naked black vagabonds swathed in bandages, it was fortunate that the three of them were able to sit at a table on the pavement outside.

Closing time was not thirty minutes away. Marechera therefore asked the mutual friend to order him several pints of beer and several tots of whisky: simultaneous delivery. This done, he turned to the woman:

'I've heard so much about you. I've always wanted to meet you.'

But why, she asked, the bandages? Oh that. Oh shit. He'd been thrown out of the Africa Centre. Incensed, he'd returned in dead of night and shattered the Centre's plate-glass window by hurling himself at, and through, it.

'How awful,' she said.

'I would like to come home with you,' Marechera said, his saucer eyes glowing.

She said no, quite impossible – his reputation runs ahead of him. But the plan had lodged in his head and, like any great lover, he wouldn't take no for an answer. When she got up to leave he at once rose and followed, forcing her to come back and sit down again. This happened twice. He was inexorable, as if on stretched elastic. Finally she signalled to their mutual friend, a man of some size, to grab the poet while she made a dash for it.

'I could see his eyes watching me, so I turned the wrong way and later doubled back.'

Some months later she met Marechera in Harare. He shook her hand warmly: 'I've heard so much about you. I've always wanted to meet you.' Marechera's memory is a strobe light. No doubt he could have recalled the encounter in a London pub had it suited his purpose, but only to his typewriter does he confide.

His pursuit of white women is nevertheless not charted in his writing with complete candour. Hidden behind the predatory alley cat is the cuddly kitten rubbing against the legs of middle-class women blessed with comfortable homes, begging a saucer of milk before a warm fire. A saucer becomes a season. Marechera installs himself. If he doesn't get his way there are scenes, outrageous accusations, nagging phone calls throughout the night – households fall apart under the strain. He craves security and acceptance. He wants a woman who will be mother, sister and mistress to him, not merely because he needs these varieties of comfort but also because he yearns to bust them. To fuck your mother is to send an ironic message, a victory signal, back to the womb. To fuck your sister is to have the last laugh on taboo, on the years of stifled childhood longing:

The bible was my first porn book. I remember being very

excited by the passage in Kings where the girl Tamar is raped by her brother. I used to masturbate while reading that over and over.[1]

The super-clever child who transcends a hostile environment is a mystery, a source of awe. How can we, born to the tongue we shall unthinkingly employ throughout our lives, imagine the extravagant leap of mind and spirit of the wriggling, spitting Shona boy who clawed his way from Rusape to the *Guardian* fiction prize:

> I was mesmerised by books at a very early age. I obtained my first one – Arthur Mee's *Children's Encyclopaedia* – in the local rubbish dump where the garbage from the white side of town was dumped everyday except Sundays. . . . One brilliant blue morning I found what I thought was a rather large doll but on touching it discovered it has [was?] a half-caste baby, dead, rotting. I fled as fast as I could back to the safety and razorfights of the ghetto.[2]

Marechera fashioned his own landscape out of the dun-coloured plasticine of rural Africa. But probably he exaggerates the crippling philistinism of his family. At least his parents recognised that education was the only means to advancement. Not only he but his brother as well attended the best black secondary school in the country and his sister works as a civil servant in Harare. She is said to regard her brother's writings and lifestyle with ironic detachment.

But what of Tamar, whose rape, so arousing to the young Marechera, actually occurs in Samuel, not Kings? She was the daughter of David, brother of Absalom, and half-brother of Amnon. 'Now Absalom, David's son, had a beautiful sister, whose name was Tamar; and after a time Amnon, David's son, loved her. And Amnon was so tormented that he made himself ill because of his sister Tamar; for she was a virgin and it seemed impossible to Amnon to do anything to her.' So he, on a cunning friend's advice, pretended to be be ill and asked his father to send Tamar to him with cakes.

Which she did. Whereupon he dismissed his attendants and commanded her: 'Come, lie with me, my sister.' Tamar refused, 'for such a thing is not done in Israel; do not do this wanton folly. As for me, where could I carry my shame?'

[1]'The Black Insider'.
[2]*Mindblast*.

But Amnon would not listen, 'and being stronger than she, he forced her, and lay with her'.

Having had her, Amnon immediately rejected her: 'Then Amnon hated her with very great hatred . . . . ' He told her to 'Arise, and be gone'. But she clung to him. 'No, my brother; for this wrong in sending me away is greater than the other which you did to me.' The ruthless half-brother commands his servant: 'Put this woman out of my presence, and bolt the door after her.'[1]

The incensed Absalom bides his time, then has Amnon murdered, bringing about tragic divisions in David's household.

This episode works as erotic literature only if violation, rape, is found arousing. Tamar's hymen is broken but not the incest taboo itself. Indeed the sister's horror is immediately transmitted to the brother after the deed. There are, by contrast, many stories and dramas which depict illicit mutual love between brother and sister: overt, defiant, as in John Ford's *'Tis a Pity She's a Whore*; masked and sublimated as in Melville's novel, *Pierre*; tormented and guilt-ridden, as in Sartre's *Altona*. But these works were presumably not available to pupils of St Augustine's Mission, Penhalonga.

FOURTEEN

'And what did you do?'

Covered in blood, Marechera had stumbled to the reception desk of the Holiday Inn.

'I said to them, "Call the police. I've been beaten up." '

But he was surrounded by shefs, important men attending the PTA conference and reception: among them, as ever, the CIO. Who now intervened.

'They told the duty manager not to call the police. They said I was drunk, that I'd fallen down.'

Calling the police is not, of course, the gesture of the authentic anarchist. '*Descendez les flics, copains*,' wrote Aragon, '*descendez les flics*' – for which he was given a suspended sentence. Such nihilism belongs, in Zimbabwe, to the dissidents of Matabeleland and certain

[1] II Samuel 13 (Revised Standard Version).

criminal elements – but Marechera knows nothing of guns. In his experience the uniformed officers of the Zimbabwe Republic Police are his only protection against the CIO.

One of the hotel staff, a man known to him, did recognise the seriousness of Marechera's physical condition and called the police. When they arrived the CIO moved to intervene, insisting that the poet was fantasising, concocting an 'incident' to sabotage the conference and Zimbabwe's image abroad. But the ZRP officer 'politely but firmly' insisted on doing his duty and produced a notebook from his starched tunic. The aggrieved writer made his deposition.

'But the man who beat you up – you couldn't identify him?'

Later Marechera called on state prosecutor Abishai Zvobgo, explained that he had recorded a complaint with the police, and required his testimony as a witness.

'You were beaten by Colonel Nyika from King George VI Barracks,' Zvobgo informed him.

Marechera later typed out his notes on the affair, including the Colonel's name, on a sheet of notepaper letter-headed 'Preferential Trade Agreement' (which had somehow found its way into his possession). Later (he says) the CIO broke into his flat – hence the jammed front door – and spirited away this sheet of paper.

'I know they did this because when I was later arrested and taken to Harare Central Police Station, the CIO men waved it under my nose, leering, and threatened to take me up to King George VI Barracks "to meet the Colonel".'

I nodded. 'Colonel Nyika, you say?'

'Yes.'

The reader of this narrative may be more observant than I was; it was only later, in London, perusing my notes, that I discovered that the critic who had reviewed *Mindblast* in the magazine *Mahogany* had the same surname as the Colonel who had spilt the poet's blood over the review. However, Marechera has subsequently confirmed the coincidence.

'Can you tell me about your arrest in Meikles?'

'Of course. Actually I was very happy that day. I'd been introduced to Ngugi and I was, you know, really quite sober. I'd more or less been picked up by these two Dutch journalists but didn't anticipate that giving an interview about my work would pitch me into the shit.'

I asked him about the distinguished poet and university lecturer who, according to Miss Tjoeng, had at one stage intervened in Marechera's support, before withdrawing to a safer vantage point. But Marechera looked blank. Like a true artist he was already re-composing the sequence of events, eliminating the inessentials, the supporting cast – possibly the Dutch girls would not survive the second draft.

'What happened after you arrived at the police station?'

'The uniformed police there treated me well. They told the CIO that they couldn't detain me unless I was charged. But the CIO don't care about the law. They are beyond rules and regulations. The one who'd arrested me insisted that I was being charged with subversion. The uniformed officers said the charge had to be more specific. Finally after an hour of argument the fat one just yelled, "Lock him up! That's an order!" '

When the CIO had finally departed at about 2 a.m., the uniformed officers on duty pointed to a telephone. If Marechera cared to make a call – and swore to say nothing about it to the CIO – they would turn a blind eye. If the CIO later turned nasty about news of his arrest having got out, he was to blame the Dutch women, who by that time, as we know, were back in the Monomotapa. Marechera telephoned a white journalist he knew well.

'Then I begged to be released. But the duty officer shook his head, very apologetic. So I begged not to be put in a cell with violent criminals who would beat me up.'

He's small, frail, pretty. I had my own vision of 'rape' among 'men', a make-believe pastoral, in the year of his birth (1952, though his book jackets say 1955) and the year after, memories of panting pursuit, sometimes predator, sometimes prey, through frosted Berkshire woods, the hunting-down of peach-bottomed 'fags', the squealing tussles in wet leaves and bracken, bare legs mauve with winter, the treble-alto protests of the ravished: Ow, Murdoch, ow! It was the time of Churchill's second Government. We were training to be Marechera's District Officers: the ones who counted the cattle and levied the tax, never believing what the natives told us. Sweets were no longer rationed; in the tuck shop the boys had cheered when Attlee's Government fell on the wireless. I got no further south than the Gold Coast, a subaltern. My 'boy' (batman) looked a bit like Dambudzo but was not bright. I habitually lost my temper with him. He used to scorch my uniform with the charcoal iron. His name was Seidu but I called him Sulley in my novel.

My homosexuality did not extend beyond the routine 'paper chase' through the Berkshire bracken, but my fictional imagination pretended otherwise, and when I went to All Souls the three leading old queers, indulgent about the novel as seducers are, advised me (separately, each foraging for himself) not to fight 'my nature'. One even promised me an imminent change in the law: I think he was on the relevant commission.

'They found you a friendly cell?' I asked.

Marechera smiled radiantly. 'They put me in with a gang of con men who reckon they've pulled off the perfect fraud. The money has never been recovered and they spend all their days planning what to do with it when they get out. In six days with them I learned more about making money than in the rest of my life!'

'What did they think of you?'

'They laughed at me – that a person of my respectability should be in gaol! A writer! And don't forget I was arrested wearing my Book Fair suit.'

He lit a cigarette. 'Do you smoke, David?'

'No.'

'As a matter of fact, this gang they called me a "balance".'

'Meaning?'

'It comes from the Shona '*baranzi*', meaning a straight guy, a fool who always obeys the law and keeps his nose clean. If I tried to sleep during the day they'd say, "Hey, look, Half-past-Four wants to sleep, hush hush." '

'Meaning?'

'A Half-past-Four is someone who works a regular day and stops work on the dot of half-past-four.'

He laughed merrily. It was a pleasure to watch him break from his own cocoon and take delight in other men.

'David, have you noticed the red wool in my hair?'

The first thing I'd noticed, yes.

'The prison blankets are red, you see.'

He studied his watch anxiously. Each morning he taught 'A'-level English at the People's College in Rezende Street, under the benevolent eye of Mr Saddiqi. He was not always punctual but now excused himself, he must put on better clothes.

'Unfortunately standards at the College are not all they might be. It worries me.'

Decorously he carried his cleaner clothes into the toilet and half-closed the door. From within he talked about censorship: did I realise that most Zimbabwean writers were censoring themselves so strenuously that the Censorship Board was in danger of having nothing to do?

'And now our Minister of Information is telling us what to write. Every working day I must take my work-load from the front page of the *Herald*!'

When he emerged it was in cleaner drainpipe jeans, though he was clearly in no hurry to comb the tufts of red wool from his hair. In our age casual dress is almost obligatory for the artist, but it was not always thus in bohemia. Observe Henri Matisse at work on a nude, dressed in stiff collar and tie, the neat beard of a *père de famille*. Those demonic practitioners of art-as-outrage, the dadaists and surrealists, terrorists of the subconscious, intent on vandalising the *bien pensant* culture, nevertheless appear in photographs as if about to take Sunday lunch with their Catholic grandparents. No doubt Wedekind wore a tie and sock suspenders while writing *Lulu*, and maybe while loving her too. Here, in this frame, artists and writers who consider themselves outlaws gather to denounce War: Eluard, Arp, Tanguy, Tzara, Breton, Dali, Ernst and Ray – each incendiary immaculately turned out in collar, tie and jacket. Out of doors, a hat.

We left by the serviceable door.

'When I was released the warder opened the cell door and shook my hand. "Are you the one who was in England and writes books?" he asked. My gang of forgers cheered and shook my hand, too. "Good luck, Half-past-Four," they called.'

The sun was hot now, winter yielding to spring.

He hesitated. 'David, I hear you put me into your last novel.'

'No. Next time.'

'To be frank,' he said, 'the most dangerous period for me is always waiting for a book to be published. I just can't get down to anything else.'

'Pure hell,' I agreed.

We drove down Second Street towards the city centre. I've never felt happy in Harare; like Basingstoke, it could have been dropped, ready-made, pre-assembled, by parachute onto the flattest available plain.

Marechera said various publishers owed him money.

I told him how on my first visit to his old school, at the height of the war, when boys were burning their 'O'-level certificates and crossing the border into Mozambique by night, I had talked to the fourth form about the life of a professional writer. When I'd finished explaining the system of royalty payments a boy stuck up his hand and asked how an author knew whether the 'publishman' was telling the truth about the number of copies sold to the shops 'when he sends you this royal thing'.

The class had roared at the mistake but – we were now driving past the House of Assembly on the north side of Cecil Square – the fourth-form boy had instantly plucked down an over-ripe truth never glimmered by many authors in a lifetime of gullible toil.

We passed the flagstaff. Here *Mindblast* was written. Here the veterans of Arnhem had paraded. Here ladies in Wimbledon hats had annually celebrated treason against the Crown. Here, in 1890, the Pioneers had made a display of marching about, watched by a crowd of incredulous tribesmen who dubbed these strange, bearded strangers '*varume vasina mabvi*' – 'men without knees'.

Marechera was brooding. 'I went to give a lecture at St Augustine's recently. Did you hear?'

'No?'

'When I'd finished, the Principal said to me: "Get out and never come back again".'

'Father Prosser said that!'

'That's what he said to me, David.'

'Were you . . . had you been drinking?'

'You see, David, there had been these various faction fights at the school, political in nature, of which I was completely unaware.'

Marechera, of course, is not a loyal alumnus, and no great Christian either:

The first six years were thickly buttered by the Christian religion instilled in me by the monks and nuns who taught me up to university level. Belief in Christ and illusions of pure love were heavily underlined by the after-lights-out horrorshow of brutally detailed and demonstrated sex scenarios in the dormitories. Masturbation and confession in the church alternated with extreme regularity. Thoughts and prayers centred on Christ; the imagination and dream emissions continually subverted all faith.[1]

We arranged to meet again, two days hence. I was to find him in one of the bars of the International Hotel at the corner of Baker Avenue and Fourth Street – he would be drinking there all afternoon so it wouldn't make any difference if I arrived a bit late.

'Just ask the doorman. He'll know where to find me.'

FIFTEEN

Writers are desperate people. Whatever their scorn for fame and fortune, for hype and hypocrisy, when the telephone rings they lift the receiver. A film of *The House of Hunger* could only be a travesty of the original because Marechera's passionate nihilism, his

[1]*Mindblast.*

extravagant war with the human condition, withers and dies once cut loose from written language. Interviewed, he is just words, pouts and cigarette smoke; filmed – the same. And that goes for most of us.

But a tele-film of his first, prize-winning book! – how could he say no? So here he is, little Dambudzo, walking briskly, for no apparent reason, through the deserted streets of an East End dawn, pursuing his muse between tall warehouses and tenements rising to an alien sky. 'Just be natural, be yourself,' the director must be urging.

The film crew climbs up into his cramped squat where Marechera obligingly sits cross-legged on the bare boards, his only prop an ashtray. How he talks to the camera! on and on, to the steady click of TV sets changing channel. But now comes, at last, a nice joke. Thrown into prison he'd been required to name his next-of-kin.

'None,' he told them.

'If you die, someone must bury you.'

'In that case – I name Heinemann, my publishers. Imagine being buried by Heinemann!'

So tempestuous had been his recent quarrels with his publishers that they had finally forbidden him to enter the premises. On one occasion they called the police.

It was the film that paid his air fare back to Zimbabwe after an absence of (perhaps) eight years. The master-plan was to 'shoot' him in London, then film dramatised sequences from *The House of Hunger* in Zimbabwe, and finally persuade the author to revisit the mother, family and home which he had publicly likened to hell. It may be a tribute to Marechera's moral sense that the plan aborted. But he was Brechtian enough to accept the airline ticket before throwing a scene and pulling the plugs in the Park Lane Hotel, Harare. Embittered by the banning of his second book, *Black Sunlight*, over-wrought, disoriented, stoned and rarely sober, he screamed obscenities at the film director and insulted a former freedom fighter attached to the unit. Desperate to salvage something from the débâcle, the director kept the camera turning while engaged in a shouting match with the poet.

Like the proverbial drunken actor, Marechera became known in publishing as an untouchable. 'He drew a knife on our receptionist. We told him never to darken our doors again.' Down he went, destitute, into the obscurity which hovers behind the shoulder of every new, firecracker talent. There are always other fuses to light. Even the commissioning editors now occupy seats resembling electric chairs.

* * *

Why do we love Africa? Why do we hover, vulture-like, above the jungles, grasslands, veld and karoo, enchanted by the tom-toms below, the twang of mbiras, tenderly running a comb through the untidy heads of the thatched huts? We hover, beady-eyed, talons outstretched, poised to seize what is beautiful as the British officers once carried away the golden treasures of Benin.

The General sent Malraux on a mission to the Antilles and Guiana. This voyage was to be the final motion in a vast choreography, a grand design to bind black people to France while setting them free. Reaching Guadeloupe, Malraux disembarked at Pointe à Pitre. Trumpets greeted the emissary of the Republic, then the Marseillaise. At that moment the famous writer smelt Africa, a delicious odour like an over-ripe cheese soaked in rum and set alight by a voodoo more potent than the ju-ju of the Niger basin or the enfeebled magic dished up by Zimbabwe's spirit mediums. They garlanded him in flowers and cried out his name as if he were a god: 'Merr-lo Merr-lo!' He in turn laid flowers at the foot of the bust of the Republic and some more for Schoelcher, the enemy of slavery. Emancipation, a mystical notion, was in the air: the mood on the island that day was ecstatic.

Malraux was greeted by a famous poet and statesman, Aimé Césaire, the apostle of black Africa and revolutionary negritude. Mayor of Fort de France and loved throughout the Antilles, Césaire led Malraux up the steps of the *mairie* and declared:

'I salute in your person the great French nation to which we remain passionately attached.' Not the fawning imprecation of the colonised subject, but the bold utterance of a free man. Now the crowd, in an unforgettable gesture of concord, tilted back its single head, opened its rum-lined throat, and cried: 'Viv'-de-Gol! Viv'-Cézer! Viv'-Merr-lo!'

Malraux gazed in awe at the unfurling of the '*videh*', the millenarian festival in which humanity is delivered from its own bondage and from its own skin. He knew himself to be in communion with the eternal black *jacquerie* of the greatest of black Jacobins, Toussaint Louverture.

Later, in Guyana, the Prefect received de Gaulle's emissary in a Cadillac *de grand luxe*. Malraux himself noted this down – a man of acute intelligence, just as you and I, Marechera, take note of the white Mercedes purring around Africa. We turn these cars into words and feel we have done something useful.

SIXTEEN

When I showed up at the International Hotel two days later, at 5.15, there was no sign of Marechera. I searched a maze of smoke-filled bars packed with punters laying money against the bank of daylight sobriety. I peered in corners like a policeman, apologising, searching for a chameleon in drag, an invisible Pan laughing at me from under my armpit. The doorman was adamant:

'Dambudzo is not being here today.'

I drove to his flat. The curtains were drawn. The broken front door yielded but would not open. Four hours later he dragged me from my bourgeois lethargy. The voice on the telephone sounded aggrieved. Apparently I had left the International only moments before he arrived – the doorman was his witness. And more: Marechera had taken the trouble to bring along his editor at College Press, Stanley Nyamfukudza, who had broken into an afternoon's work to meet me.

Five years had passed since I phoned Marechera at his squat near Euston station to ask for a short story for the December double-issue of the *New Statesman*. Our staff had awaited his arrival biting their nails and clutching their chairs. The beast did not surface. Wanting a story from Zimbabwe, I contacted Nyamfukudza, who duly came up from Essex, where he was working in a furniture factory. I had no idea that the two writers were friends. Marechera himself says that the two of them used to criticise each other's poems and stories 'with that sincere insincerity of two people who know each other only deeply enough to wound'. Both had sat out the war in England: in this respect the Zimbabwean intelligentsia followed the Kenyan model.

I found Marechera in the Park Lane Hotel, one of his favourite haunts and also the scene of the final débâcle during the filming of *The House of Hunger*. In its time the Park Lane was a watering hole for the Fireforce commandos of the RLI, pissing drunk, and for French mercenaries with neat, pencil moustaches, veterans of Algeria and Indo China (if you believed them and discounted their age), weekend heroes fresh from culling gooks in the Hurricane operational zone to the north of Bindura. From Monday to Friday the villages burned and the helicopters wheeled like kites above the stricken kraals. This was the killing season – and, as Anatole France remarked, 'All armies are the finest in the world.'

Most of them have gone now. They have scattered: to South Africa, to Australia, to the oil rigs of the North Sea, to vacant plots in Bolivia. Marechera would not have lasted five minutes in that company. Racial tension hummed like a generator during the disco dances, the white suburban girls mincing on high heels across the lobby to the ladies', the bronzed warriors striding to the adjoining facility. But now they are gone and largely forgotten. A school-teacher told me how she played my radio drama, *The Zimbabwe Tapes*, to her class of seventeen-year-olds in the Harare township of Highfield, a tough and often violent place. She was apprehensive lest the first twenty minutes of the play should offend these black kids, depicting as it does the phobias of white Rhodesians convinced that the British Foreign Office, obedient to the Kremlin as always, was working hand-in-glove with the 'kaffirs', 'munts', 'coons' and 'terrs'. But no, she said:

> To my surprise the students had been most interested in the first twenty minutes [of the play] which consists mainly of interaction between the white characters. They explained to me that although they recognised the accents and were familiar with some of the attitudes expressed, they had never listened to Rhodesians speaking together . . . . They were very interested in the tobacco auctions, the young trooper and the searching of the bus. They were also excited by the scene in which Dick Clark [the central character, a white farmer] is captured by the guerrillas and made to say Pamberi ne Mugabe. The character of Commander Victory aroused their interest and they disputed among themselves whether the actor playing the part was Zimbabwean or South African . . . . They were also fascinated by the conflict between Clark and Commander Victory and there was a fair amount of sympathy for the older white man who was seen as someone whom time had left behind. They debated Victory's point that he could have gone overseas to study rather than taking part in the war.

Here she reported something which ought to provoke thought among Zimbabwe's captains of culture: despite several filmed documentaries shown on television,

> they . . . said it was the only drama they had heard or seen about the liberation struggle . . . . Three short African plays from the BBC World Service have been broadcast recently but

83

the subject matter of these plays has been removed from the students' experiences. I was asked if I had 'anything else about Zimbabwe'. It is widely reported in the Zimbabwean press that Western media coverage of Zimbabwe is unjust and the students were delighted to hear something which, in their view, gave a fair impression of the liberation struggle.[1]

The obstacle lies in a single notion: 'Reconciliation'. From the time of Independence, white Zimbabweans have protested about 'propaganda' on television and radio – usually films depicting the freedom fighters as heroes serving a just cause. But such films never portray white Rhodesians, either in fact or fiction; their villainy remains implied, offstage. A play exploring the collision of the races at the height of the war – the kidnapping of a white farmer by Zanla guerrillas and his subsequent exposure to the reality of the camps in Mozambique – would not assist 'Reconciliation'. No one, neither the socialist Government of Zimbabwe, nor the International Monetary Fund, nor the British Foreign Office which administers modest grants for land reform, wants the erstwhile 'fascist' farmers, 6000 of whom held half the viable agricultural land in Rhodesia, to leave. Only Zimbabwe's 300,000 rural squatters and twice that number of land-hungry peasant farmers want them to vacate the 15 million fertile hectares appropriated to Europeans by the Land Apportionment Act of 1930 – an Act signed on the nod by the distinguished Fabian Colonial Secretary, Sidney Webb, 'to protect the African'.

Marechera, finally found in the Park Lane Hotel, hails me, very cheerfully, my delinquency forgiven. He is not alone. Slumped beside him on the plastic mini-sofa is a young woman, long-haired, plastered, very floppy. Her face is puffy with love. Her neck can no longer service her head, which keeps collapsing on the poet's shoulder – she resembles an uncomfortable passenger trying to sleep, and not to sleep, in a jolting train.

'This is Emma.'

My few polite questions are wasted on her. She does not want me there. She murmurs erotic imprecations (I think) in his ear; sometimes her face is clenched like a baby's, so intense is her need. The poet talks to me of literature, man to man, explaining that

[1] The 'three short African plays' she mentions were part of a series of six which the World Service offered, on tape, to African broadcasting corporations. One of these, *Welcome to Zimbabwe*, was an abbreviated version of the ninety-minute play my friend played to the students of Highfield High School. In July 1984 the Minister of Information wrote to me asking that tapes of one or both versions of my play be sent to him. This was done. Over a year later I have heard no more – nor, it seems have the many Zimbabweans possessing radios.

there are really two species of African writer: those committed to radical change and those who adorn the status quo.

'Among the radicals you have Ngugi, Soyinka and myself.'

In my mind's eye I see Ngugi, short, tough and stocky, climbing on a fragile chair to address an *ad hoc* gathering of friends and admirers. He grins: 'I'm afraid of heights.' He speaks of the need to give back to the African peoples their stolen sense of themselves.

I order two beers: Emma's glass is half-full and she needs no more. Does Marechera intend in future to write less about himself and more about working people? – a grim, seminarian question. No, he says, he disposed of the proletariat in *The House of Hunger*, did with them for good. His next book would focus on Zimbabwe's new class of shefs, the civil servants, junior managers and smart boys in sharp suits.

I nod.

'That's why they arrested me.'

A man is standing over us, stout and important. Reluctantly I glance up. He is leering at Marechera. His presence finally forces us into silence.

'I hope I'm not disturbing you, Dambudzo.'

Is he auditioning for a role in *Blitzkrieg*?

'Yes you are,' Marechera says. His eyes have dulled.

The secret policeman grins and spreads his arms like a ham villain. 'But Damb-udz-o . . . I'm an admirer of your poetry, I really am.'

Marechera rises. 'David, will you excuse me a moment?'

Together he and the stout secret policeman walk towards, then into, the toilet! But I'm mistaken if I imagine that my friend walks as the dismissed batsman 'walks', even before the umpire has raised his finger; or walks as the thirteen-year-old fag caught flicking butter at Murdoch walks when the latter summons him, ten minutes after lights out, to the penal bathroom. I am wrong because the CIO man, like the Colonel before him – or is he the Colonel? – is at this moment being swallowed, ingested, by an insatiable literary imagination. Another beating, another chapter.

I focus on the girlfriend. 'Tell me about yourself.'

She struggles to focus. Her blond hair splays across the back of the plastic sofa. 'Just . . . .' She reaches for a cigarette. 'Just . . . you know.'

'Things aren't always easy here.'

'Who are you?'

'I'm a writer.

'I said who are you?' She lifts her beer glass then flops it down, a rag doll.

85

'Have you known Marechera long?' I ask.

'Dambudzo? All my fucking life. You didn't say who you are . . . . Oh yes, the writer. I was in the Playboy Club and Dambudzo rescued me, he was bloody decent. Are you bloody decent? – the writer. You don't look at all bloody decent.'

My attention is held by the entrance to the men's toilet. Ought I not to burst in there on behalf of Amnesty International? What kind of moron sips beer while history repeats itself? But Emma has roused herself to an effort at conversation:

'I've been teaching in Buhera.'

'Buhera! Teaching what?'

'Bricklaying.'

I flew into Buhera during the war – by that time it was totally inaccessible by road. Zanla had chewed up the dirt tracks, setting the *povo* to work with spades. The District Commissioner, wearing a sky-blue safari suit, reported that his telephone lines had been cut for the past four months. 'Not much fun when you've got kids in boarding school.' On the wall over his desk he'd fixed a luminous sticker: 'I'm staying to make it work.' Outside his office brown-shirted Pfumo reVanhu (Bishop Muzorewa's 'auxiliaries') slouched with their FNs and G3s, waiting to murder and be murdered.

Emma nods, half-asleep. 'You Rhodesian, then?' she murmurs.

Marechera is returning alone and undamaged, like a fleet-footed cat who has just seen off a large hound.

'Who was it?'

'CIO'.

Emma starts to lick his ear and neck, mumbling her love. The poet lights a cigarette.

'The Zimbabwean writers have shown no conscience or solidarity over my arrest, none at all.'

Is he a member of the writers' union?

He shrugs dismissively. In England, he says, writers form proper unions like the NUJ, real unions, and they understand the need for solidarity. But not here: just shit selfish. He drains his glass. I raise a hand for the waiter. Loathing the effort of conversing in noisy restaurants and hotels, the brassy laughter, the need to shout above the piped mufax, I feel myself grow weary and censorious.

'If you set such store by solidarity, why haven't you joined the Writers' Union here?'

'I stood for general secretary, David. I lost by only four votes.'

'But then you refused to join, because you lost?'

A small motion of his hands; he is perfectly at home with the indignation of old men and shefs. 'They're all conformists here,' he says.[1]

Emma flops on to his lap like a pink blancmange. A whispered conversation ensues. Dambudzo's saucer eyes swivel slowly like the twin dishes of a satellite station – the girl can no longer be denied but he is loth to abandon a night's drinking. He leans forward, as between men:

'David, maybe I can contact you later tonight? Will you be around? Where can I find you?'

'In bed.'

Ten minutes later I drop Dambudzo and his Emma off at the corner of Rhodes Avenue (whose name remains mysteriously unchanged although someone has removed all the street signs). In my driving mirror I watch them crossing the intersection, she the taller and heavier, leaning on him, forcing him to zig-zag like a midnight Chaplin. Will he, two minutes hence, turn Miss Piggy upside down and inside out, forcing her to squeal with delicious pain/When love thy neighbour went against the grain? Is she Tamar? Will the sky come down?

SEVENTEEN

From time to time Dambudzo Marechera is invited to address schools and colleges around the country. There are always admirers incautious enough to brave the man who is custodian of the talent. One such mission school lies in the flat, drought-stricken bush beyond Masvingo, a fine place run by Catholic priests totally dedicated to their students and their wider flock. I make regular visits.

The road south is straight, the passage swift. Rhodesia's roads were legendary and Zimbabweans boast about them, but the

[1]Five months later a correspondent wrote to me from Hararae: 'I went to a meeting of the Zimbabwe Writers' Union, a very sedate, dull affair. The only interesting event was that Dambudzo Marechera turned up and heckled throughout the evening . . . . Dambudzo kept asking why the writers didn't protest when he was detained, and of course he failed to get an answer. Unfortunately, very few of the Zimbabwean writers I know have any sympathy for him but this is because they see him as a nuisance and refuse to look at the wider issues.'

question to ask is why they pass exclusively across European farming land while leaving peasant farmers in the communal reserves to the mercies of rutted, sometimes impassable, dirt tracks. A young woman from the Ivory Coast, studying at a French university, asked me a different question about these straight roads. Her project was a *'doctorat de 3e cycle d'études Anglo-Saxonnes'*, and her chosen subject, *'Les Romans Africains de David Caute'*. Visiting me during the summer of 1983, she carried the third and most recent of the species, *The K-Factor*, a novel set in Rhodesia at the moment of apocalypse. Why – she demanded to know – had I written the following?

Charles Laslet had travelled the four hundred kilometres from Salisbury in less than four hours, spurning the armed convoys and burning up the straight, empty roads laid down by a superior civilization.

What exactly was meant by these radio-active words, 'a superior civilization?' My interlocutor is a woman of great beauty, her hair enchantingly braided across her skull, and we had got on well until this moment. But now her chin was set. I told her that the straight roads were real and that it was my fictional character, Mr Laslet, a white farmer of reactionary disposition, who held them to be proof of European superiority – not that he needed proof.

'But you don't say so in the book.'

'You might call it indirect attribution.'

She looked suspicious.

I said: 'As a matter of fact, I rather agree with Charles Laslet. But the passage you quote belongs to his head, not mine.'

She did not lower her eyes from mine. I was unmasked, my progressive pretensions punctured. I had been caught hiding behind my own fictional characters.

'In my view,' I explained, 'civilization is not strictly a moral category. The Roman civilization was extremely advanced and efficient, yet also cruel, rapacious and corrupt. Civilization is an ordering of things: those who possess the wheel, coins of exchange, staple crops, a written language, sail-driven ships and a well-ordered bureaucracy will build straight roads and aqueducts to dominate the tribes lacking these skills and amenities. . . .'

(I should not have said 'tribes': her eyes blazed.)

' . . . but that in no way implies greater kindness, richer imagination, deeper parental love, closer bonds of kinship, or a more profound religious instinct.'

I splashed hot water round the coffee pot and waited.

She wasn't having any of it. Fully *assimilée* to European culture as she was, fluent in two languages as well as her own, her clothes

88

a brilliant blend of Western fashion and African exoticism, she was nevertheless a walking wound waiting to be reopened under the frosted sky of Europe.

'So you believe yourself superior after all?'

Well damn it! – which legacies of the hated imperialism do Africans in practice incinerate? Do they do away with railways, bridges suspended across wide rivers, water pumps, motor vehicles, the aeroplane, canned and frozen food, a written language – or Charles Laslet's straight, tarred roads? (The latter do sometimes disappear, but inadvertently.) And if Africans hang on to all this colonial detritus, is this not in itself an admission that . . . . By this stage such conversations invariably spill over the dam wall until both parties are locked, tooth and claw, cock and cunt, in a war without survivors.

For the next year I looked forward to the arrival of her final thesis with curiosity and apprehension.

The ironies of time. Only two years had elapsed since, driving along a road like this one, towards Masvingo, I had 'seen' how *The K-Factor*, then verging on completion, must end. In those two years the novel had been completed, set in print, proof-read, published, devoured by the young scholar from the Ivory Coast, and then served up shredded, pulped and fried, in a heavy thesis *présentée* and *soutenue* only days before I returned to the scene of the crime. Invited to attend the *soutenance* at the French university, I had flunked out, excusing myself on account of a hectic schedule. Of course they didn't swallow that – authors don't know what to do with their time.

It was not her duty to spare my feelings and she didn't. My God, why hadn't I forced her to read Marechera, shown her the contours of real damnation, reminded her that a novel is not a laundry, not a church, not a cattle dip, not a health clinic?

I composed a reply: a defence, a self-justification, adopting a dignified, even a magnanimous tone, but that didn't last long – the Gregorian chant soon rose to a protracted wail. She had caught me on the raw.

Her central thesis was simple enough. Here we have a 'progressive' English writer, clearly sympathetic to African self-determination, manifestly opposed to colonial rule, and convincing enough when portraying black nationalist politicians whether good, bad or indifferent. But what do we find lurking beneath this perfectly sincere commitment to African liberation? A tangled knot of racial phobias, racist assumptions, sexual prejudices – in short, a vast superiority complex floating on an abysmal ignorance of African life, African customs, African language.

Masvingo used to be called Fort Victoria. A dull place.

89

Brooding on the state of literary criticism in the Côte d'Ivoire – she had even berated me for resorting to the term 'tribe', which is just fashionable nonsense – I reached my destination, the Catholic mission school near Masvingo, had a hot bath, dined with the Brethren, and heard the following story about Marechera.

An English teacher of English, whom I shall call Robert, eager to bring controversial authors to the school, keen to 'stir things up a bit', and encouraged by his senior pupils' enthusiastic response to late-night readings from *The House of Hunger*, had, with the Head's cautious approval, invited Marechera to talk to the sixth form. Not only did the poet show up on time, he arrived a week early, carrying his typewriter and quite a large suitcase.

The 'week' may have become exaggerated in the telling – but Marechera, like other legends, generates hyperbole. Swallowing their surprise and hastily clearing the baby from the spare room, Robert and his wife Sally spent an invigorating evening with their charming guest, sending emergency calls for more wine to neighbouring teachers as midnight passed and the eastern sky turned pink.

Robert thought there would be no great difficulty in bringing Marechera's talk forward by a few days to suit the writer's itinerary, and was nonplussed to learn that he was in no hurry at all: Marechera announced his intention of residing with Robert and Sally indefinitely, as the school's new 'writer in residence'.

Now Sally, too, is a radical, no less keen than her husband to stir things up. Like many of the women who have been attracted to independent Zimbabwe, she's an idealist and a crusader, poised to tackle every kind of 'problem', from teenage pregnancy and the evils of '*lobola*' to infant malnutrition and endemic Shona male chauvinism. Not only did she establish nutrition classes for young mothers, a mobile 'literary clinic' for local villagers, and classes in women's rights, she also caused uproar in this Catholic community by biting the bullet of contraception. ('Abortion-on-demand is only a matter of time,' confided the Head to his brethren.) The Head was faintly surprised when on the second day of Marechera's visit Sally came up to the Priory to complain.

'It was Robert's idea,' he gently reminded her. On the third evening angry shouts were heard from Sally's house and when the Head strode down past the neo-Romanesque brick chapel in his large, sandalled feet he found her close to hysteria. The poet, squatting on the floor, typing steadily, looked up at him with large, tranquil saucer-eyes, then resumed his work. Robert wasn't in the house and the Head felt like a man admitted to a theatre after the interval. Clearing his throat, he offered Marechera a bed in the Priory for one night.

Marechera leapt up. 'You want to throw me out, you bloody white racist!'

During the war of liberation the Head had twice been taken by the police for questioning about his reported assistance to 'terrorists'; not only his pupils and ex-pupils, but the entire neighbouring community were devoted to him. But now Marechera erupted into the night and soon the black teachers of the school were gathered in angry knots and sending spokesmen to protest against the 'provocative' and 'insulting' treatment accorded to 'one of our Zimbabwean writers' by Sally, Robert and – it was more than hinted – the Head himself.

'Provocative!' screamed Sally. '*Me*, provocative! Then why don't *they* take him in!' The night reverberated with italics and exclamation marks. The divine concordance of the mission was fissured. Two days later the Head drove the poet, his typewriter and his suitcase into Masvingo to put him on the express coach to Harare. Having read *The House of Hunger*, the Head was inclined to believe the story that the authorities at New College, Oxford, had finally given their delinquent Zimbabwean scholar an ultimatum: to enter the Warneford psychiatric hospital or be sent down – though when dining with the Dean at New College high table he had been told, rather drily, that arson had not been involved, merely non-attendance at tutorials in English literature.

Reaching Masvingo, the poet asked to be excused, he must stop off at a hotel to use the toilet. But when he stepped out of the car in the filthiest pair of jeans the Head had ever seen, Marechera unloaded his suitcase and typewriter as well, walked into the hotel without a word, then came back on thin, bouncing legs.

'Actually,' he said, 'I'm short of a drink.' He giggled. 'Of several drinks.'

The Head dug into his pocket. 'You'll miss the bus.'

'Yes, all my life.'

I telephoned Myrle Tjoeng, the day before she left Zimbabwe, to inquire about the fate of the tapes confiscated by the police. All of them, including the interview with the chairman of the Noma Award, had finally been returned to her – except the interview with Marechera. That, she was informed, had been destroyed.

Postscript

When I returned to Zimbabwe I knocked on both doors of his ground-floor flat, back and front, without response. Behind iron

window bars a pane of glass hung open; in an apparently uncon-
scious paradigm of this entire literary endeavour I finally reached
in and drew back the heavy, floor-length curtain. 'Go away!' I
heard from the shadows where the bed lay. 'Go away!' Only then
did I have the wit to announce myself.

Dambudzo came to the window, wrapping the curtain round his
nakedness and peering at the day suspiciously through large, oval
glasses. Half an hour later I came back to collect him for lunch in
the company of a white woman (offering antelope to the lion?) and
found him squatting on the floor with a companion engaged in
running a comb through her copper hair. The four of us walked
down to one of the poet's haunts, the Terraskane (I had rejected
his first two suggestions, the International and the Oasis) where
Dambudzo chose fish and slowly mauled a withering salad between
bottles of beer and cigarettes. The waiters hovered nervously,
muttering to Dambudzo in Shona, until I paid the bill.

'How's your teaching job at People's College?'

'They sacked me. After my arrest the CIO kept coming and
questioning the staff and students to find out what I was saying
about Antony and Cleopatra.'

'And your new novel?'

'College Press have turned it down. Here.' He handed me the
reader's report with a brief, disturbingly non-committal covering
note from Stanley Nyamfukudza. Marechera shrugged philosophically; his response to rejection is never self-pitying – revenge is
exacted in the next text. Stanley, he explained, had fought a battle
to publish *Mindblast* and couldn't risk another; having written a
bold critique of the one-party state for Zimbabwe's only readable
periodical, *Moto*, Nyamfukudza had probably been feeling the heat.
(A few days after *Moto* published interviews with disenchanted,
unemployed ex-freedom fighters the CIO – 'We're from the Prime
Minister's office' – called at the Mambo press in Gweru asking for
the addresses of the malcontents, the better to 'assist' them.)

Marechera ordered more bottles in batches of four and soon I
was pushing half of mine in his direction. The afternoon was far
gone and rain was in the cold wind when Dambudzo engagingly
remarked, 'My God, David, I hope you're on expenses.' I wasn't,
but it was my do and meagre recompense for his generous, uncon-
ditional permission to let me quote extensively from his unpublished
manuscript in an essay I have not allowed him to see.

'And what of the Colonel?'

Marechera began relating the whole story again for the benefit
of my companion and with relief I mentally checked each detail
against the original version. Yes, Prosecutor Abishai Zvobgo had
indeed provided eye-witness evidence for Marechera's complaint to

the police, but Zvobgo was no longer seen in the bars of the International and Marechera had heard that he was no longer a prosecutor – I cannot vouch for this. Nor for the note that Marechera claims to have recently received from the police, announcing that they had detected the 'culprit' (presumably the Colonel) but had called off the investigation because the complainant had withdrawn his charges.

'Why did you do that?'

'I didn't.'

'Do you still have that letter from the police?'

'I tore it up.'

While Marechera paid the first of several visits to the toilet I read through the letter from College Press rejecting his new novel, *The Depths of Diamonds*. It began with a conscientious summary of the characters and, so far as it existed, plot, then hurried into a vast 'No':

> Publication in its present form would be suitable for a small circle of erudite literary figures captivated by the author's undoubted brilliance as a writer. As a novel for the ordinary reader it is unreadable for reasons stated above [dense refeences to Greek mythology, no story-line, etc]. Though not libellous, there is a possibility of the censor having doubts about allowing its publication because the ms. is saturated with four-letter words and lurid descriptions of sexual intercourse . . . . If the author intended this work for the (sic) mass consumption it has to be re-written in the language a man with a reasonable education understands.

Even from the commercial angle, this argument is suspect. Marechera's books have always sold well, both in Harare and London, and he collects periodic royalty cheques for *Mindblast*. The real offence of *The Depths of Diamonds* is its pyrotechnical political iconoclasm; the parallel drawn by Marechera himself – Mayakovsky – is by no means pretentious. He is now without hope, no one to turn to, 'sucked down', and the manuscript, typed in a faint red ribbon on coarse paper, gathers dust as he lies in bed all morning and drowns the rest of the day in beer. The only work currently available to him is worthy of Balzac's *Lost Illusions*: writing book reviews on commission from a certain publisher, who then passes them on, 'under an arrangement' (Marechera laughs slyly), to the literary editor of a leading newspaper. Marechera cheerfully names names.

'I need the money.'

Beer pours through the poet without leaving an ounce of surplus fat; he can weigh barely nine stone and not a line or shadow disturbs the smooth, glowing skin of his cherubic countenance. (He was in fact born in June 1952, though the book jackets all say 1955.) Properly watered, his hands flowing, his voice rising, he launches into a sequence of stories distilled by a surrealist sense of symmetry and galloping malice. Each scene involves a confrontation between the damned poet himself and the two most respected figures in the Zimbabwean literary establishment, Musa Zimunya and Charles Mungoshi.

Scene: the Norfolk bar of the International Hotel. Enter Marechera. Zimunya and Mungoshi hail him. Grudgingly he accepts their company as the price of a drink, or several. Lubricated, he asks Zimunya why he has bothered to plagiarise Marechera's own work in his latest book of poems. 'Surely you don't need to? Surely you are a better poet than I?' Zimunya, a professor at the University, instigator of the legal action which lifted the ban on *Black Sunlight*, and secretary of the Writers' Union (though challenged for the post by Marechera), allegedly seizes a beer bottle and theatens to remove the oft-battered waif's remaining teeth. Mungoshi intervenes, physically restraining his friend. Marechera then nods to his retinue of regular drinking companions and the dean of Zimbabwean letters is tossed out of the Norfolk bar into the street.

Scene two: same venue. Enter Marechera. He is hailed by Zimunya and Mungoshi. Grudgingly he accepts their company as the price of a drink, or several. All forgiven, Zimunya offers him a well-paid afternoon addressing incoming students of literature at the University, plus something else under British Council auspices. Marechera announces loudly that he accepts no favours (apart from beer) from 'literary prostitutes'. Zimunya grabs him by his shirt and shakes him like a rag doll. 'Who are you anyway? You can't even fight.'

(Marechera tells the two white women at our table: 'How do I know if I can fight?')

Again Mungoshi intervenes. (Mungoshi, whose poetry has been translated in *Le Monde*, is the University's current writer-in-residence; Marechera's stories invariably reduce him to the role of dull, worthy peacekeeper, but malice is no enemy of art.) Once more Dambudzo's Norfolk bar pals come to the rescue and Zimunya is yet again hurled out into the street. I suspend disbelief, as if Dylan Thomas was recounting how he was assaulted by T. S. Eliot and had him thrown out of the Museum Tavern.

The third scene takes place at a meeting of the Writers' Union. Marechera arrives late, deliberately, but despatches in advance a German lady, Flora, a keen enough student of Zimbabwean poetry to have accommodated its genius in her home for some months, her mission being to photograph all ensuing incidents. Enter

Marechera. Cat-striding to the front, he squats on the floor and immediately begins heckling the poet Chenjerai Hove, who is reading enthusiastically ('romantically,' grins Marechera) from his own work.

'Why did you do nothing when I was arrested last year?'

Hove turns for help to Zimunya, who shrugs wearily. The heckling continues. Even when it's the turn of Stanley Nyamfukudza to read, Marechera directs the same hectoring accusation at his old friend, the editor of *Mindblast*.

'Stanley came towards me. He was going to beat me up, definitely! But Flora was flashing away with her camera and he thought better of it!'

Marechera leaps up and hurries to the toilet, ordering more beer on the way, his imagination in top gear.

As the empty bottles accumulate, men begin drifting to our table. Some are friends but most are tediously belligerent with drink.

'Marechera!'

He looks up, witheringly. 'I don't know you.'

'But I know you, Marechera! We've met.'

'In which prison?'

'What?'

'I said. "In which prison?" Were you the murderer or the rapist?'

The presence of white women may orchestrate these exchanges. My companion later told me they grew uglier after I took my leave, which I had to do, and wanted to do, as the late afternoon drowned in a wash of head-aching beer. Dambudzo heads for the toilet again and I am tempted to terminate on that characteristic exit, leaving this report swathed in an old literary convention – that of the faceless, rational observer-narrator, the disembodied intelligence, the camera-eye. However, here Marechera returns, clasps me, and hurls me into the narrative:

'David, you owe me money.'

College Press had granted permission to quote passages from *Mindblast*, for a fee of Z$130 (£65), the money to be paid directly to the poet.

'They sent me a copy of their letter to you, David. It said $180 or something.'

'One-hundred-and-thirty. Writing about you is not a way of earning my living, Dambudzo. I'll pay sixty.'

Bastard. Marechera covered in confusion.

'Yes, yes, it's just that I got this letter from College Press, I mean that's just for *Mindblast*, my unpublished work is between you and me . . . .'

I gesture towards the empty beer bottles. 'I'm not on expenses.'

'Oh God. Okay, come on Monday, I'm always at home in the morning . . . . I'll sign a proper receipt.'

On the Monday, my last day, I wore a tie to interview (1) a senior civil servant and (2) Zimbabwe's clandestine legman to South Africa. I also spent forty of the dollars I could have given to Marechera on cheap, gift-shop Shona carvings. Hearing my cold, high voice at the open window, Marechera came out of bed in his underpants and handed me his new novel in a brown envelope. I tossed the sixty dollars through the window bars, like bread to a duck; they slid from the sill to the floor.

'Don't drink it all.'

'No, I won't, really. Wait.'

The curtains closed over the open window. I stood outside under the hot sun that winter sometimes offers at midday. Dambudzo's bare arm thrust through the bars: a receipt for Z$130.

'But I only gave you sixty.'

'Take it, David. If College Press want to know, you've got this to prove you gave me one-hundred-and-thirty.'

On the plane home I began to read his new novel but was distracted by a fat 'shef' in the next seat whose arms spilt over the rests. Downing his twelfth whisky, towards 2.30 in the morning, 39,000 feet above Zaíre, he darkly warned his plastered companion about 'Dube':

'Now the elections are over Dube must be confronted and offered a final ultimatum: renounce Nkomo, renounce Zapu, or be eliminated. Dube's a good man, of course . . . .'

'Brave man.'

'A brave man during the struggle, yes. But he must renounce Nkomo. We don't know what Dube's up to. It's a time to give Dube an ultimatum.'

THE ESPIONAGE OF THE SAINTS

– Tisdall, Ponting and the claims of secrecy

ONE

On 2 January 1984, *The Times* reported a 'buoyant New Year's Message' from the Prime Minister, Mrs Margaret Thatcher. To those students of Orwell who had approached this particular year with foreboding, she offered reassurance: Orwell had been quite wrong. The year ahead – *her* 1984, not Orwell's – would be one of 'hope and liberty'. Less than two weeks later a 23-year-old civil servant called Sarah Tisdall appeared at Bow Street magistrates, court, charged under the Official Secrets Act. Within three months she was in Holloway gaol. A month after she came out of prison another civil servant, Clive Ponting, arrived at Bow Street, charged under the same act.

Both Miss Tisdall and Mr Ponting had put words, forbidden words, restricted words, classified words, in an envelope and delivered it to unauthorised persons. Neither had been propelled by selfish motives.

Mrs Thatcher's 1984 was not many weeks old when she tackled the problem of another place where words are intercepted, received, de-coded, transmitted (to authorised persons, usually). She removed from 9,000 employees at GCHQ Cheltenham, the signals-intelligence centre, the right to belong to independent trade unions. At about this time a prominent investigative journalist, whose expertise about GCHQ had some years earlier resulted in his own conviction under the Official Secrets Act, happened to fall off his bicycle. Found in the panniers of his machine were the tools of his trade, which is to inform the public: a number of documents, his contacts book, and the keys to his home. When Mr Duncan Campbell came out of hospital the Special Branch embarked on a six-hour search of his home, lifting down each volume from his shelves with gloved hands, examining Christmas cards, riffling through his drawers and filing cabinets. His contacts book was returned only after it had been photocopied.

The popular press – and, one may assume, the wider public – seemed not greatly concerned whether this was Orwell's 1984 or Mrs Thatcher's or both. Though Sarah Tisdall's indictment was reported, front-page concern was reserved for Miss Sara Keays, whose emergence from a nursing home holding the baby of a prominent Tory politician coincided with the day of Miss Tisdall's first appearance at Bow Street. 'Sara: it's great being a mother' (*Daily Express*); 'Sara's bundle of joy' (*Sun*).

No joy for Sarah Tisdall, apart from 'Mole Case Girl's Dad Wades into Telly Men'. Bow Street was packed for her second court appearance. After the normal parade of overnight drunks, dossers and drifters shuffling before the magistrate to take their medicine, Sarah Tisdall appeared in the company of smartly dressed gentlemen who asked for her case to be dealt with summarily, without a jury, on a plea of 'Guilty'. The Attorney General, however, withheld his necessary consent: he wanted the full works. The case was accordingly remanded to the Central Criminal Court.

On Bow Street pavement a small group of women were waiting to greet her with daffodils, tulips and a kiss. They also carried a banner: 'Is the future of Britain an official secret?' Everyone, not least the photographers crowding round her taxi under the shadow of the Royal Opera House, understood this banner; the secret documents that Sarah Tisdall had leaked to a newspaper concerned the installation of cruise missiles in Britain.

On 23 March she entered the dock (derived from the Flemish *dok*, meaning a cage) of the Central Criminal Court, a tall woman dressed in a blue suit and red blouse. Across the well of the panelled court she faced an imperially raised dais bearing a row of splendid leather chairs, each embossed in the royal arms. As the judge entered, all rose; an usher in black suspended the great sword of justice above his throne.

Only ninety minutes later, Mr Justice Cantley adjusted his spectacles and said, 'Six months.'

TWO

Heinrich Böll's novel *The Lost Honour of Katharina Blum* tells of a quite ordinary, decent young woman whose reputation was suddenly stripped from her by a tabloid newspaper. She, utterly incensed, shot the journalist who had defamed her.

Ten years later Sarah Tisdall set out from her office in Whitehall at the end of a working day, clutching two classified documents in an envelope. In time she, too, would confess to her crime; like Katharina Blum, it was by courtesy of a single journalist that she went to prison; in her case, the editor of the *Guardian*.

The *Guardian*, of course, is not a gutter tabloid or the sort of paper in which one naturally wraps fish and chips; it is, as its own letterhead points out, 'one of the world's great newspapers'. Nevertheless, its editor capitulated in December 1983 on a vital point of principle – the protection of a source against ignominy and punishment – with the result that another ordinary, decent young woman forfeited both her career and her liberty.

Searching for the *Guardian* building, Sarah Tisdall got lost, confusing Farringdon Road with its southerly extension, Farringdon Street – a bleak, noisy stretch of the City where container trucks hurtle past West Smithfield and the pile of dirty brick called Atlantic House. Little can she have imagined, on that autumn evening two days before the end of summertime, how eight weeks later to the day a man would make the same journey in reverse, holding one of her two leaked documents, climbing the steps to the maroon and gold iron bridge of Holborn Viaduct, his bleak mission to hand it over to the Government's agent in a solicitor's office. This man was the editor of the *Guardian*, Mr Peter Preston.

Let it be admitted that what most readily arouses our indignation is behaviour which excavates our own buried fears about ourselves. If I have become much preoccupied by Mr Preston's betrayal (as I see it) not only of Sarah Tisdall but of his calling, then it's ten-to-one that I am insecure about my own performance in a crisis; my own capacity to put honour before self-preservation. For writers and journalists this is, or ought to be, a fairly constant preoccupation. Those of us who work in the relatively liberal climate of Western Europe must sometimes wonder how we would conduct ourselves under fire in Czechoslovakia, Poland, South Africa or Chile. Would pragmatism deftly seduce its cousin, principle? Would we emerge like those characters who parade their principles in the early scenes of a play by Vaclav Havel, only to fail every test that hurts? We are all, in our weak moments, Peter Preston.

So Mr Preston climbed up to Holborn Viaduct, carrying the document: Who will rid me of this source?[1]

---

[1] The bare elements of Preston's career as given in *Who's Who* are as follows: Born 23 May 1938. Educated at Loughborough Grammar School and St John's College, Oxford. M.A., Eng. Lit. *Liverpool Daily Post*, 1960–63; *Guardian* Political Reporter, 1963–64; Education Correspondent, 1965–66; Diary Editor, 1966–68; Features Editor, 1968–72; Production Editor, 1972–75; Editor since 1975.

Sarah Tisdall had chosen the *Guardian* because, as she later explained, this was the only 'left-of-centre, middle of the road' daily newspaper with national coverage. In one respect her expectations proved accurate: the *Guardian* did indeed turn her two documents to immediate front-page advantage. She knew that a major CND rally was due to assemble on the morrow, a Saturday, and the men on the first floor of 119 Farringdon Road were equally alert to the main chance. But whatever assumptions she may have entertained concerning her own security were false; indeed she would have been less likely to end up in Holloway gaol had she entrusted her documents to any of the Fleet Street tabloid editors knighted by Mrs Thatcher.

Sarah Tisdall had inherited from my own generation (which is also Mr Preston's) a world sewn thick with 50,000 nuclear warheads. She was clearly one of those young people who, by acts of defiance and gestures of witness, refuse to shut their eyes to the danger of nuclear holocaust; and who refuse to accept that our masters, military and political, West and East, can safely be entrusted, *sine die*, never to unleash, by design or accident, this terminal technology. 'Indecent,' she described one of the documents, 'sort of doing it by the back door and I couldn't stomach it. I felt the public had a right to know what was being done to them.'

The following day some 250,000 demonstrators gathered along the Embankment to register their concern and anger; copies of the final edition of the *Guardian* passed from hand to hand, its front page splashed with the fruit of Sarah Tisdall's journey to Farringdon Road: 'Whitehall sets November 1 cruise arrival'.

Since the late 1950s I have been on a number of CND marches, from the age of the duffle coat to the age of the anorak; from Bertrand Russell and Canon Collins to E. P. Thompson and Monsignor Bruce Kent. On this occasion I walked with my son, a student of Sarah Tisdall's generation, and with his friends. We, their parents, have nothing to be proud of, no long-service medals to parade, only the knowledge that we have failed to prevent the nuclear garden triumphantly expanding to obscene proportions in mockery of our intermittent protests.

Sarah Tisdall, the daughter of two Devon doctors, was a twenty-three-year-old clerk working in the private office of the Foreign Secretary, Sir Geoffrey Howe. She had been a civil servant for three years and her service record was impeccable. The two documents she was told to photocopy on 21 October had been written the previous day by the Defence Secretary, Mr Michael Heseltine, and were addressed to the Prime Minister, with copies distributed to six senior members of the Government, including the Foreign Secretary. Reading the documents during a quiet moment in the office, Sarah Tisdall became indignant, made an additional copy of each, and put them in her handbag. At the end of the afternoon she set out from Whitehall, stopped at Ryman's smart, green-painted shop in the Strand to buy an envelope and felt-tipped pen, heavily scored out the official markings on the documents, and addressed the envelope to the 'Political Editor' of the *Guardian*. She then caught a bus heading east down the Strand and Fleet Street.

Meanwhile, another timetable was in full gallop:

17 June 1980: the Defence Secretary Francis Pym had announced that the US would deliver 160 cruise missiles to Britain;

15 May 1983: Geneva Arms-limitation talks had begun;

20 October 1983: Heseltine had written two memoranda to Margaret Thatcher: the first concerned the imminent delivery of cruise missiles to Greenham Common air base in Berkshire, how to gain the best coverage from the media, and how to outwit the Opposition. The second concerned sensitive security arrangements at Greenham Common, including the use of firearms against demonstrators penetrating an unacceptable number of perimeter fences.

Finding the *Guardian*, Sarah Tisdall left her envelope at the reception desk and vanished. The envelope was taken by messenger to the in-tray of the News Desk on the first floor, where it was opened by the reporter on duty. He said 'My God' and took the documents straight to the editor's office. After a considerable delay Preston telephoned his Defence Correspondent, David Fairhall, who in turn checked the accuracy of the information contained in the documents, without disclosing the *Guardian*'s possession of them, by speaking to his contacts in the Ministry of Defence.

Fairhall's 800-word, front-page story was the one which absorbed the demonstrators gathering along the Embankment the following morning. Without referring explicitly to either document, Fairhall's report drew heavily on them both. In view of what was to happen later it is worth stressing that from the outset the *Guardian* crowed about the predictable impact of such a leak on the Government's security plans:

'If the missiles are coming on November 1,' wrote Fairhall, 'and in the light of this report the timetable is almost certain to be called into question again in Whitehall, security at the Berkshire base will be massively strengthened.'

He also anticipated that the British and American Governments would 'hastily review their delivery timetable'. On Monday 24th, Fairhall followed up in a style calculated to provoke the angriest possible Government reaction:

'And the Prime Minister was warned by officials about the *Guardian*'s disclosure before Saturday's edition went on sale and Downing

Street indicated last night that an immediate investigation to find the source of the leak was expected.'

One must bear this noisy euphoria in mind when assessing what the *Guardian* later did to the unknown source of its scoop.

Yet Preston and his senior colleagues hesitated to publish either document in full, even though Greenham Common air base was virtually besieged by demonstrators during the following week and a hundred of them were arrested for cutting through perimeter fencing. Not until 31 October was one document published verbatim on page 2 of the paper; henceforward referred to as the 'published document', it outlined the arrival timetable and Heseltine's self-congratulatory strategy for outwitting the Labour Opposition and the peace movement. But Preston shrank from publishing the second document, which described security arrangements on the ground at Greenham: to publish it, he later explained to me, might have encouraged someone to do something 'foolish'. Indeed the first explicit reference to the second document did not appear in the *Guardian* for a further five months, until 24 March 1984. Even so, it had been used by Fairhall and was to be used again in a report which appeared in the edition of 1 November:

Guard grows for Greenham nuclear core

Mr Michael Heseltine, the Defence Secretary, recently ordered that RAF Regiment personnel should be stationed at this inner cordon, forming the first line of defence, with armed US guards behind them. In the last resort the rules of engagement for both the US and RAF guards allow them to open fire, but such action would be taken first by the British servicemen and not the Americans.

It was this story that precipitated a noisy exchange in the Commons when Labour and Liberal spokesmen challenged Heseltine and the Prime Minister to deny that in the last resort infiltrators at Greenham, most probably women, would be shot. No such denial was forthcoming.

Now came fear and paralysis; instead of promptly destroying the documents, Preston telephoned his solicitors, Lovell, White & King, to ask what he should do if the police arrived. What did eventually arrive was a letter dated 11 November from the Treasury Solicitor, demanding on behalf of Heseltine and the Attorney General the return of the published document: it was Government property. Squandering the moment – an almost unending moment – to destroy the sheets of paper, Preston again telephoned Lovell,

White & King to seek advice. He was advised that it would be an 'offence' to destroy the document. So he didn't.

Here one must distinguish between Peter Preston's actions and those of his legal advisers, whose job is to convey the law to a client in the narrowest terms. It's no use phoning your solicitor to say, 'I'm parking on a double yellow line, can I get away with it?' Preston had already committed an 'offence' under the Official Secrets Act by publishing one classified document and using another; by destroying the document, as virtually any other experienced journalist would have promptly done, he would have scarcely compounded his offence; in any case a letter of request, such as he had received from the Treasury Solicitor, carries no legal force and until a writ was issued there could be no question of contempt of court.

Preston was later to explain his actions in terms of his overriding respect for the law. By 'the law' he meant 'law enforcement', the tramp of heavy feet on the stairs, the warning glint in the judge's eye.

Preston now naïvely informed the Government, through his solicitors, that he did indeed possess the published document which contained markings that 'might disclose or assist in the identification of the source'. Therefore he begged to be allowed to erase the incriminating markings before returning the document. The Treasury Solicitor, no doubt astounded and delighted by the editor's vacillations, declined to make any such concessions: after all, it wasn't the document they wanted, but the source of the leak. On 27 November a writ was issued for the return of the document.

The *Guardian*'s naïvety was compounded by its assumption that the excision of the blacked-out markings on the document would stymie any police inquiry. It is the sheet of paper which under examination reveals the specific photo-copier used – and Sarah Tisdall, as we have seen, had made her duplicates on a Foreign Office machine. Even if Preston or his News Editor, Peter Cole, had audaciously put the document through their own office photocopier, then destroyed the original, the process of detection might have been thwarted. But none of this was done. Cole attempts to explain why, and why not, in his official history of the affair published in the *Guardian* on 24 March 1984: the impression he conveys is that of a belated search by a stoned knitting circle for a ball of wool sitting in the middle of the carpet.

On legal advice the *Guardian* decided to invoke section 10 of the Contempt of Court Act in support of its plea that the markings should be erased before the document was returned:

No court may require a person to disclose, nor is any person guilty of contempt of court for refusing to disclose, the source of information contained in a publication for which he is responsible, unless it be established to the satisfaction of the court that disclosure is necessary in the interests of justice or national security or for the prevention of disorder or crime.

But note the warning phrase: 'in the interests of . . . national security'.

The *Guardian*'s defence was almost certainly doomed from the outset; many of the paper's staff subsequently laid the blame on poor legal advice. But section 10 was the *only* defence available once Preston had (repeatedly) failed to grasp the obvious solution and destroy the document in the office shredder. Ultimately the *Guardian*'s lawyers ended up in court quibbling about copyright over markings and whether a piece of paper enjoys the same immunity under section 10 as the identity of a known source. The whole enterprise was hazardous and probably futile: either you are determined to protect your sources or you are not. On behalf of the fourth estate Preston should have insisted that he owed an overriding debt of honour to the individual whose 'leak' his paper had triumphantly exploited; and also owed an obligation to resist those strategies of Secretary of State Heseltine which are designed to deceive Parliament or keep it in ignorance – something which Mr Clive Ponting was soon to achieve with resounding success.

To embark on such a *political* defence, however, requires the choice of lawyers unimpressed by the grandiose claims of the State and aggressively committed to the defence of civil liberties. The long record over the years of the *Guardian*'s association with Lovell, White & King suggests persistent timidity rather than crusading flair; and now, as counsel, the paper chose to retain a pillar of the Tory establishment, Lord Rawlinson[1] who, one may assume, believes in the right of civil servants to leak classified documents on a point of conscience as ardently as the Ayatollah believes in a woman's right to remove her veil whenever she so chooses. Indeed Rawlinson lost little time, once in court, in condemning the 'betrayal' of trust by the civil servant who had passed the document to the *Guardian* – a very promising start.

That Preston was resolved to present himself as a responsible and patriotic citizen is apparent from his affidavit to the court: 'I

[1]When Conservative Attorney General in 1972, Rawlinson had obtained a High Court injunction restraining the *Sunday Times* from publishing an investigation of the thalidomide tragedy largely based on documents obtained from a source within the Distillers Company. Not until the European Commission on Human Rights ruled that the ban was a violation of free speech was the story finally published on 31 July 1977.

accept that a free press has responsibilities not only to its source but also to the Government.' He also referred to his newspaper's 'anxiety not to act irresponsibly', insisted that the publication of the document had 'no national security implications', and pleaded that 'there was nothing in the memorandum which was published in the *Guardian* which could not easily have been gleaned by any person sitting in the public gallery at the House of Commons.'

Astonishing cant when we remember David Fairhall's original, leak-inspired, article of 22 October: 'However, the fact that the plan has now leaked out must force the Government security services to a hasty review of their delivery timetable in consultation with the US Air Force, particularly since atomic warheads are involved.' And indeed the delivery timetable was subsequently revised.

Preston's affidavit reveals one of the more timid of the *Guardian*'s several souls, as well as the profound ambivalence of Preston and his senior editors towards the Campaign for Nuclear Disarmament – an ambivalence mirrored in Peter Cole's official history of the affair:

> Inevitably there was some considerable discussion of what sort of person the source might be, and there were differing views. The non-coincidence, as it seemed, of the delivery of the document and the Hyde Park CND rally raised uneasy questions. It was certainly not axiomatic that the leaker would have acted out of altruism.

What can this mean? Playing the Soviet game (as Heseltine's campaign of denigration against CND was designed to suggest)? Whatever it was that troubled the gentlemen at the *Guardian* it certainly had not inhibited them from snatching their scoop and running with it all the way to the 250,000 massed on the Embankment and in Hyde Park.

THREE

On 15 December, following an adverse judgment in the High Court, the *Guardian* went in front of the Master of the Rolls, Sir John

Donaldson, and his two colleagues of the Court of Appeal. The resemblance between the political profiles of Donaldson and the *Guardian's* counsel, Lord Rawlinson, was a striking one. Rawlinson had served as Heath's Attorney General from 1971 to 1974, while Donaldson became President of Heath's ill-fated National Industrial Relations Court. Now they were confronted by a memorandum from a Tory Defence Secretary to his Prime Minister concerning an issue – nuclear weapons – about which every strand of Conservatism closes ranks.

That Sir John Donaldson would treat the *Guardian's* leaks with indulgence was rendered no more probable by the fact that the Master of the Rolls himself had recently been the subject of an article in that paper, based on yet another leaked document, describing his political consultations with a senior civil servant on the subject of trade unions and the courts (a subject in which Sir John has displayed an abiding interest); these consultations, moreover, had been set up by the then Chancellor of the Exchequer, Sir Geoffrey Howe – who had served as Solicitor General when Rawlinson was Attorney General and Donaldson President of Heath's National Industrial Relations Court. Such consultations confirm that the ranks remain closed and drive a coach and horses through the notional independence of the judiciary from political influence. The *Guardian's* report provoked an agitated telephone call from Downing Street to the Home Office; the Lord Chancellor, Lord Hailsham, later issued an irritable statement that he expected to be consulted before judges engaged in such activities.

In the United States one would expect in such circumstances a defence challenge as to the judge's impartiality. But not in Britain. Here such a challenge is treated as contempt of court. By local standards no impropriety was involved when Donaldson heard a case the previous September involving a litigating company, Mercury, in which he himself had purchased shares, and a trade union. No British judge, it is well understood, would allow himself to be influenced by such considerations. So when the *Guardian* came before Donaldson on 15 December 1983, the last thing that would have crossed his mind was the mauling he had recently received at the hands of that newspaper, regarding both his political consultations and his Mercury shareholding.

Three legal issues had to be decided:

(1) Did the Crown enjoy proprietorial rights over both the document and the spoiled markings?

(2) Was handing over a document from an unknown source tantamount to revealing a source (i.e. was it covered by the protective provision of section 10 of the 1981 Contempt Act)?

(3) Did national security factors apply in this case, thus nullifying that protective provision?

The latter was the decisive issue. The principal establishment officer at the Ministry of Defence, Mr Richard Hastie-Smith (who will duly reappear in the trial of Clive Ponting) argued in an affidavit that the cruise missile arrival date was 'the subject of high level exchanges between the Government and the NATO allies. This exchange was highly sensitive'. Disclosure might damage the confidence of Britain's allies – an argument which later emerged as central in the prosecution of Sarah Tisdall.

All three Appeal Court judges declared themselves convinced that the national security factor did apply and did preclude a successful defence under section 10. The Appeal Court seemed to be stressing not so much the security damage involved in the publication of the *Guardian*'s document as the future danger to national security if the source of the leak went undetected. Said Donaldson: 'Whether or not any harm has been done on this occasion, the next may be different.'

On 16 December the Court of Appeal confirmed the ruling of the High Court the previous day that the *Guardian* must immediately return the document to the Government – despite the paper's declared intention of appealing to the House of Lords.

Leaving the court, Mr Preston complained that the judges had assumed the culprit would in future 'rob a bank' just because he or she had already 'whipped a tube of Smarties'. But in so saying Preston was privately aware that the same source had leaked two documents, the second being, according to his own criteria, too sensitive to publish verbatim.

This brings us to a crucial question. If Mr Preston knew about the second document could his own legal advisers have possibly remained in ignorance? Hardly; and what then of the actual danger to 'national security' as virtually any conservative lawyer would interpret it? The Government had demanded the return of only one document, the memorandum published in full by the *Guardian* on 31 October. As the Attorney General explained in a written state-ment on 12 April 1984, 'When the *Guardian* published the secret minute . . . it was appreciated for the first time that the paper must have the document, or a copy in its possession.' Clearly no such certainty attached in the Government's mind to the second docu-ment; whatever his suspicions the Attorney General did not care to go fishing in the dark. Indeed the Treasury Solicitor's correspon-dence, and the subsequent writ for recovery, made no mention of the second document.

But why did the Court of Appeal convene with such crashing haste, only hours after the High Court's ruling? Why were they so convinced of an urgent future danger if the source of the leak remained undetected?

A number of journalists who attended a crisis meeting in Preston's office immediately after the Appeal Court's ruling, on 16 December, believed that the truth about the second document had been conveyed through lawyers representing the *Guardian* to lawyer's representing the Government. They explain this as a conscious act of plea-bargaining by the newspaper in an attempt to demonstrate its patriotism, persuade the Crown to drop its demand for the return of the published document, and also to avoid subsequent criminal prosecution under the Official Secrets Act. According to one journalist, 'They told the Government about the second document to prove what good boys they really were'; according to another, 'We told them we hadn't published the second document out of patriotism' (one recalls Preston's affidavit affirming the press's responsibilities to 'the Government'). A third source reported that the newspaper had 'blabbed'; a fourth was confident that the judges had been apprised of this.

It was also reported that Preston had subsequently let it be known that the Government had learned the truth about the second document from the *Guardian*'s counsel, Lord Rawlinson, during the trial. Hugh Stephenson, editor of the *New Statesman* (and perfectly well disposed towards Preston), says this:

> I did have a conversation in a pub at someone's leaving party and the Tisdall case came up. I had been talking about the case to people on the *Guardian*, and I am, therefore, clear that I 'know' that Preston's view is that he had bad legal advice in general and from Rawlinson in particular and that Rawlinson made an 'unforced error' in relation to the second document. I could not say – for I kept no notes – that Preston said all this to me in those terms at the pub meeting. It may be that he said something that confirmed what I already knew from someone else to be the case.

However, we must be cautious about such recollections. Preston has flatly denied that there was any form of collusion, any passing of information about the second document. Here he refers to the crisis meeting held in his office immediately after the Appeal Court judgment:

> On the contrary – and ever since, because there is no other truth – I said that I had formed the view in court, from what Simon Brown, the Treasury Counsel, said tangentially at two

points, that the Government knew (or strongly suspected) that we had had a second document.

Nor, he insists, had he ever put it about that Lord Rawlinson had divulged the truth about the second document by an 'unforced error': 'I confided nothing of the sort to friends or anybody else because none of it bears any relationship to the facts.' There is of course no way of knowing what instructions the *Guardian* management gave to counsel or what advice counsel gave in return.

Naturally lawyers do not divulge what passes between them; in no other profession is the spirit of confidentiality so jealously guarded. In the corridors outside a court a defence lawyer may advise his 'opponent' (his 'learned friend') that his client will confess to charge A if the prosecution drops charges B and C. But if such a deal is rejected then the judge and jury must not be informed of the conversation. I therefore wrote to the various lawyers involved less in expectation of a full and frank disclosure than to cover myself against the obvious challenge: 'Why don't you ask them?'

The *Guardian*'s solicitors, Lovell, White & King, refused to grant me an interview despite a written request and an oral one to the editor himself. The deputy Treasury Solicitor was Mr J. B. Bailey; it was he who received the published document from Preston at about 1.00 p.m. on 16 December and then immediately asked for the second document. Mr Bailey replied to my inquiry and denied having learned anything about that second document from the *Guardian*'s lawyers. Treasury Counsel in the case, Mr Simon D. Brown, wrote to deny that Lord Rawlinson said 'any such thing to me and I shall be very surprised if he suggests the contrary'. Lord Rawlinson himself replied that he could not 'possibly comment – either by way of refutation, admission, rejection, acceptance, elaboration, explanation or what you will'.

The recollections of the principal editors, or 'kitchen cabinet', at the *Guardian* do not coincide. While Preston and Peter Cole deny any exchanges between lawyers concerning the second document, deputy editor David McKie twice told me, once orally and once in writing, that according to his recollection the second document 'had been mentioned in informal discussions between lawyers,' though he insisted that the *Guardian* had not asked Rawlinson to enter into any kind of plea-bargaining with the second document as one of the counters.

I also wrote to the three judges who heard the case in the Court of Appeal. Asked whether the Court, in assessing the national security factor, had knowledge that the same source had in fact passed two documents to the *Guardian*, the Master of the Rolls, Sir John Donaldson, wrote: 'My recollection of the details of the *Guardian*

newspaper case is quite insufficient to answer the question you ask.'
Mr Justice Slade wrote: 'I can do no more than echo what he
says . . . .' Mr Justice Griffith answered that convention prevented
him from commenting.

It may be useful to leap ahead by ten months in order to follow
the judicial process to its conclusion.

In October 1984 the Law Lords rejected the *Guardian*'s appeal
against the Appeal Court's order – long since complied with – to
return the Tisdall document to the Government. The majority was
narrow: three to two. What divided Lords Diplock, Roskill and
Bridge from Lords Fraser and Scarman was whether national
security had indeed been at stake, thus nullifying the protection of
sources afforded by section 10 of the Contempt Act; or whether the
Government had adequately shown that national security was at
stake by way of Mr Richard Hastie-Smith's supporting affidavit
from the Ministry of Defence. The majority thought national
security had been imperilled, but were generally unimpressed by
the way the Government had presented its case.

There was an air of unreality about these proceedings. As Lord
Diplock put it, an act of 'mental gymnastics' was required to exclude
from the judicial mind all events, and all knowledge gained, since
December 1983 – notably Sarah Tisdall's arrest and conviction. In
fact the Law Lords had to perform two feats of mental gymnastics:
(a) to 'forget' the 'subsequent' revelation that Tisdall had leaked a
second, more security-sensitive document; and (b) to 'forget' that
the Court of Appeal had privately known this (as I have argued)
when delivering judgment.

Here Lord Roskill offered the most revealing comment. Very
properly confining himself to what had been known *at the time* of
the Appeal Court hearing, Roskill referred to the significance of the
second document – though it had never been mentioned during the
judicial proceedings of December 1983: 'Anyone knowing that the
one document had been leaked and that the other might have been
leaked must ask themselves the question, What else? and What
next?' Roskill's 'anyone' could not refer to the Government alone;
in order to uphold the Appeal Court's ruling the Law Lords had
to consider the evidence presented to that court, the information at
its disposal on 16 December 1983. Roskill's comment may therefore
be taken as the first judicial confirmation that the Appeal Court
did know that a second document had been leaked, or 'might have
been', as he discreetly put it. It's possible that Mr Justice Scott had
been unaware of the second document when the case came before
him in the High Court, for he was notably dismissive of the Government's national security arguments. But then, abruptly, the Appeal
Court hurled itself into the arena with an alacrity later ridiculed by

Lord Scarman: 'I am torn between admiration for their speed and apprehension lest in the rush justice suffered. However, there was in the conduct of the Crown nothing to suggest any urgency.'

The conclusion must be that the Government had not regarded the publication of the first document as constituting a major threat to national security – hence, as Lord Scarman pointed out, the leisurely pace of the recovery proceedings, stretching from 31 October (the day of publication) to the beginning of the High Court action on 14 December. The fact that the *Guardian* had published one document but not the other may have allayed suspicion; only when it was confirmed privately, off the record, that the same source had indeed leaked both documents did the proceedings jump into top gear. And if the Government and Appeal Court suddenly knew what had previously been merely suspected; if intense activity abruptly replaced a sedate stroll through the corridors of the law; then how and why did they suddenly know?

Again it was Lord Roskill, speaking ten months later in the Lords, who is most revealing. Once more confining himself to what was known in December 1983, he said: 'The appellants [the *Guardian*] did not, I think with entire propriety, publish it [the second document]. . . .' It was this 'propriety', this sense of patriotic responsibility, that the *Guardian* had wished to impress upon both the Government and the courts.

Following the Appeal Court's ruling, an *ad hoc* emergency meeting of journalists was held in Preston's office. (This meeting was not mentioned in the crisis-report published in the *Guardian* the following day, nor was the existence of the second document.) Preston had already decided to obey the court order and hand over the published document. Whether or not the purpose of the meeting was to compromise the staff by gaining their complicity, that was certainly the outcome; they emerged convinced that compliance with the court's ruling was awful, repulsive – but inevitable. Only Aidan White, Father of the NUJ chapel, kicked against it; the others groaned and swayed like the women of Argos in lament for a royal nemesis. Morally associated with Preston's decision thereafter, the chapel was reduced to searching for scapegoats outside the paper: Lovell, White & King; Rawlinson; the judges; the Government.

His distress palpable, the editor explained that if he were thinking only of himself and his own sense of honour, he would tear up the document there and then; but he had a duty to the paper, our paper, so suddenly profitable and so vulnerable to a Government itching to pluck out this awkward liberal thorn in its flesh.

The journalists were presented with the spectre of huge, escalating, pulverizing fines if the *Guardian* defied the court. It was whispered that lawyers spoke of £100,000 a day. As one of those

113

present later put it to me: 'We would have been subject to mounting fines and the *Guardian* couldn't have stood it. If we'd destroyed the document a judge might have gone crazy.' There was also a strong feeling, perhaps communicated by the deputy editor, David McKie, that no support would be forthcoming from Fleet Street.

According to the legal opinion I have consulted, the destruction of the document (which could preclude escalating penalties) might have resulted in a fine of £50,000 or £100,000 – a negligible forfeit for a company enjoying an annual profit exceeding £3 million, possessing shares in Reuters worth millions, and indeed owning a hunk of Blackpool tower. Had the editor gone to prison circulation would have leapt over the tower.

But, as Preston explained, 'All my working life I have preached respect for the law.' This principle weighed heavily; once the paper had embarked on the legal process surely it must abide by the outcome? But suppose the court had commanded the editor to name, in the interests of national security, a source, a civil servant, whose identity was known to him? The fact is that the assembled journalists took refuge in the vague hope that handing over a piece of paper might be the end of the affair.

The *Guardian*'s respect for the 'law', as we have already noted, has its limits. Section 2 of the Official Secrets Act of 1911 clearly warns:

> If any person receives any . . . document . . . knowing or having reasonable grounds to believe . . . that the . . . document . . . is communicated to him in contravention of this Act, he shall be guilty of a misdemeanour . . . .

And may go to jail for up to two years.

It so happened that the *Guardian*'s respect for the 'law' had in recent weeks assumed a prominent, and highly political, dimension – the SDP dimension. In leader after leader the paper had attacked the printers' union, the NGA, for flouting court injunctions against illegal secondary picketing at Warrington. Such picketing had become illegal under the Tory Employment Act of 1980. The journalists assembled in the editor's office were also aware that the *Guardian*'s management was currently invoking this same Tory legislation by joining eleven other national newspapers in a three-million-pound action for damages against the NGA.[1] Thus the scent

[1] In February 1984 the Fathers of the eight *Guardian* union chapels, including the NUJ, wrote jointly to Peter Gibbings, chairman of the company, urging him to withdraw from the legal action undertaken against the NGA on the basis of the Tory legislation which the paper itself had originally condemned in principle. This was not reported in the paper.

of profits seeped up through the ink of the leader writers. On 14 December, the *Guardian* began its High Court defence in the document case; the following day a *Guardian* leader again warned the NGA to respect the law, advising the union (which had planned a national printers' strike) to 'climb down as best they can'.

So how could the paper urge one principle of action on the NGA while flouting the same principle on its own behalf? But this did not exhaust the arguments for complying with the court's ruling. Enter now the sinister shadow of the second document (which had been seen by about a dozen members of the staff before its reported destruction, and whose full contents, it was hinted, could not be divulged). One *Guardian* journalist commented:

'There were only about six in the know: Preston, Cole, McKie, Ian Wright, Ken Dodd, Fairhall, though a few others had glimpsed the document. They behaved throughout in a secretive way, timid, frightened, engaging in an elaborate dance with the Ministry of Defence. There had been no [wider] consultation and they had bungled.'

Indeed another reporter who had been assigned to write a story incorporating material from the second document told me that he hadn't actually seen it. It was McKie who now introduced the subject into the emergency editorial meeting of 16 December. Peter Cole later (24 March) resumed what had been said:

It wasn't even, as the deputy editor noted, as if the destruction of the [published] document would bring the whole miserable story to a close. If we destroyed the first document now, the attack on the paper was likely to be renewed on the basis of the second document. The Government might well argue that this document had indeed been a direct threat to security ... and our decision not to print it and destroy it constituted our recognition of this.

McKie repeated this argument to a staff meeting held on 29 March, after Sarah Tisdall's trial.

It was of course an absurd piece of pleading: how could the Government punish the *Guardian* for *not* having published the second document? How could the Government bring an action for recovery of a document which had already been destroyed? Yet the quoted passage gives a wider game away. When the meeting convened in Preston's office there was not a word in the official record concerning the existence of a second document; neither the Government nor the Appeal Court had mentioned it. It was only after this meeting – perhaps an hour later – that the deputy Treasury Solicitor asked Preston for the second document when the editor handed him the published one. So what convinced McKie, Cole, Dodd and Preston that the second document constituted so great a danger? The answer is visible, if submerged: the Government (and then the Court of Appeal) had already been told about it in private; to defy the court now – and thus thwart the search for the source of both leaks – might result in a full blast of the Crown's criminal engines. They were doubly trapped; by a foolhardy resort to an uncertain legal process; and by having divulged more than they were asked. So it was *sauve qui peut*.

To quell the natural revulsion of decent journalists at the prospect of betraying a heavily used source, two further ideas were implanted. The first was introduced obliquely: might it not be the case that an unknown source does not merit the same degree of protection as one who takes a journalist into his or her confidence? After all, what do we know of this mysterious and possibly sinister source who immediately vanished into the twilight? When this was first reported to me I was sceptical: given the fact that the *Guardian* had exploited both documents so energetically between 22 October and 1 November, surely no decent man could advance so lousy a proposition. Had there been in the collective memory some confusion between Preston's position and the astonishing one offered in *The Times* leader of 17 December? 'The recipient's obligations towards an informant who does not trust him with his identity can hardly be one of the same kind as those in a genuinely confidential relationship. No explicit or implicit contract exists, and it is almost quixotic to act as if it did.'

But my doubts were misplaced. Far from repudiating this position, Mr Preston later publicly embraced it as his own. The endorsement provided by *The Times* was not only prominently displayed in the *Guardian*'s major 'Tisdall' issue of 24 March, but four days later *The Times* published a letter from Preston gratefully acknowledging the 'sympathetic' leader of 17 December and one sentence in particular: 'No explicit or implicit contract exists, and it is almost quixotic to act as if it did.'

The emergency editorial meeting was treated to one more argument corrosive of inbred journalistic ethics. Perhaps the unknown source of the leaks was 'not so white after all'. What, really, might his or her motive be? A journalist who was not present at this meeting recalls: 'Even before the case came to court we'd been made to feel that the second document was a genuine breach of national security and therefore the *source was a security risk*' (my emphasis).

The meeting broke up. 'There were,' as one of those present recalls, 'many churning stomachs.' All the way to lunch. Preston walked down to Holborn Viaduct, retracing the steps taken by

Sarah Tisdall eight weeks earlier, on another Friday, holding the same document. The deputy Treasury Solicitor was waiting for him.

Sarah Tisdall was now doomed. Preston knew he would face public criticism but was determined to limit it by suppressing any mention of the second document. This required a self-generated D-Notice at 119 Farringdon Road and a rapid intervention at the *Observer*.

On 17 December the *Guardian* published a front-page story and a leader lamenting the great document disaster. No mention was made of the second document. Heseltine had sent '*a* memo' to Thatcher; someone unknown had photostatted '*the* memo' and '*it* was delivered to the *Guardian* that evening'. This use of the relentless singular amounted, of course, to disinformation and to my knowledge not only the public at large but most of the press continued to be deceived by it. Preston had only to lift a Ricardian eyebrow to ensure that young *Guardian* reporters chronicling the case never mentioned the second document. This charade continued for a further ten weeks after Sarah Tisdall signed a confession, on 9 January, to having leaked both documents. 'The truth wasn't going to help anybody,' Preston later told me. Perhaps this motto should replace 'one of the world's great newspapers' on the letterhead.

One man, however, threatened to blow the cover. David Leigh had worked for the *Guardian* until July 1981 when he moved to the *Observer*. Leigh had had his past disagreements with Preston and there was a sharp edge to his interest when he learned from a senior member of the *Guardian*'s editorial staff the contents of the second document.

Preston's attitude towards the truth resembled that of a landlord towards a vacant property – if he chose not to occupy it that didn't give squatters the right to take it over. Learning that Leigh intended to publish the full facts in the *Observer*, Preston telephoned the paper's editor, Donald Trelford, to ask a favour: to kill the story. It was a big favour to ask because Trelford's editorial style is very different from Preston's. Whereas Preston now peers at the world from the dark recesses of the centre-fold with a donnish distaste for 'investigative journalists with their single-track minds', Trelford's style is brash and buccaneering, competing for the ratings with a regular diet of front-page 'exclusives', some of which uncover genuine scandals while others are dead by Monday morning. David Leigh is the quintessential front-page man; his job is to know what he ought not to know.

Neither Preston nor Trelford will disclose what was demanded or granted during the telephone conversation, but it is clear that both Trelford and Leigh preferred to doctor the story rather than

117

bury it. Convinced that the *Guardian* had come clean to the Government behind the scenes, Leigh decided that if Preston didn't want to have received the second document, the *Observer* might as well lay claim to it. Preston was furious; so were Cole and Dodd; the counterfeiter had been robbed of his wallet.

Doctored, the *Observer* story appeared on 18 December under the headline 'New Heseltine secrets leak':

> Details were obtained yesterday by the *Observer* of a secret minute by the Defence Secretary, Mr Michael Heseltine, which outlined for senior colleagues how British troops were to be deployed to stop the political risk of US servicemen opening fire on Greenham Common women. This document is potentially more explosive than the *Guardian* document, also written by Mr Heseltine. . . . The new document's nature explains both Mr Heseltine's fear at what political damage the Whitehall 'mole' might still do, and the manner in which the Defence Secretary behaved in Parliament last month when the issue of shooting the peace protesters came up. The document is a minute on 'contingency security arrangements' at Greenham Common once the US cruise missiles arrive. It was circulated to Ministers and the Chief Whip's office along with the *Guardian* memo of October. . . . During last week's hurried appeal by the *Guardian* against a High Court ruling that it must hand over the document, the Defence Secretary's lawyers emphasised the hypothetical dangers to 'national security' if the mole should leak other documents.

These extracts from Leigh's (unsigned) article would surely lead any reader to conclude that the same mole had leaked both documents. But it would also encourage the conclusion that the two documents had found their way to different newspapers. Thus the doctored story, as it emerged after Preston's intervention with Trelford, protected the *Guardian* but not Sarah Tisdall. Preston would clearly have preferred no story at all. Trelford himself was evidently content not only to impose surgery on Leigh's story, but also to apply bandages to his own editorial in which he subscribed to the accepted fiction that there had been only one *Guardian* document, political rather than military in nature.

The *Observer* story had awkward repercussions, bringing Chief Detective Superintendent Ronald Hardy of the Serious Crimes Squad to the offices of both the *Observer* and the *Guardian*'s solicitors, Lovell, White & King. Hardy wanted the document in his hand, a second nail in the source's coffin.

Eight months later, after I had published my report, Preston wrote a letter to *Granta* magazine further denying any collusion between the *Guardian* or its lawyers and the Government, regarding the second document:

> In the *Observer* episode Caute portrays Detective Superintendent Hardy scurrying round to the paper in search of the second document. But a few pages before he'd had us telling the Government that we'd had it. Had the Government failed to tell Mr Hardy? Or is Caute merely determined to put the worst gloss on every event, irrespective of the fact that they're mutually contradictory?

There is no contradiction. The Government's first attempt to lay hands on the second document took place immediately after the Court of Appeal's judgment – and before the *Observer* article appeared – at the offices of the *Guardian*'s solicitors. It was then that the deputy Treasury Solicitor, Mr Bailey, asked Preston for the second document. When Superintendent Hardy returned to those offices on the same quest, he was clearly convinced that the *Observer* story originated within the *Guardian* – as it did.

Preston invited the editor of *Granta* to scrutinize the record for himself. 'I am entirely happy to go through the written facts or verbal evidence with any member of your editorial board.' The editor, Bill Buford, reports that he promptly telephoned to take up the invitation but was fobbed off.

What Preston told Trelford when urging him to kill David Leigh's story was most probably (neither of them will say) that such a revelation would greatly embarrass the *Guardian*'s lawyers who, *on the face of things*, had been trying to convince the court that the leaker of a single, essentially 'political', non-security-sensitive document would most probably never do anything more dangerous – despite their private knowledge that he or she had already done so. This explanation, of course, is not inconsistent with the *Guardian* side having *privately* tipped off the Government side as to its receipt of the second document.

When Sarah Tisdall was arrested she confessed to having leaked *both* documents; and was eventually charged in court with having done so – yet in a manner which inexplicably minimized the second document while concentrating the whole 'damage assessment' on the (much less damaging) first document. Opening the case for the prosecution, Roy Amlot, QC, merely murmured that the *Guardian* had never formally admitted having received the second document, casually adding: 'Of course the *Guardian* had it.' Amlot then let the second document fall into oblivion; the trial judge seemed hardly aware of it. Why was Preston not subpoenaed to answer the question: 'Did you receive it and did you use it?' Why was the *Guardian* not prosecuted for clear breach of the Official Secrets Act?

The explanation given by the Attorney General on 25 March, after the trial, is out of Alice in Wonderland. I quote from the *Guardian* (26 March): 'Asked why the Government had not prosecuted the *Guardian*, Sir Michael replied that the Act was an "odd" one . . . he claimed at the time there was no evidence as to how the *Guardian* got its information. It could have come from a number of different sources.'

This is nonsense: by 9 January Sarah Tisdall had already fully confessed. On 12 April Havers tried another tack:

> So far as the *Guardian* staff were concerned, in addition to the possible evidential difficulties in establishing a case against them, there was not the same element of breach of trust – there was also the fact that the evidence against them had been obtained by a compulsory civil process. In the circumstances, it was not thought right to prosecute them.

Here again one faces a bizarre mis-reading of the record by Havers. On 31 October the paper had published the first document in full; and soon afterwards confirmed its possession of the document in a solicitor's letter; no 'compulsory civil process' was required to prove anything. The truth of the matter is that Havers, or the DPP, let the *Guardian* off lightly because of the paper's cooperative conduct; and that conduct consisted of two actions: (a) complying with the court order to hand over the published document; (b) privately disclosing that two documents had been received, with the mitigating explanation that the paper had been too patriotic to print verbatim the second, more security-sensitive memorandum about who would do the shooting at Greenham Common.

Unless, of course, one believes that Mrs Thatcher's Attorney General is too sensitive to the freedom of the press to prosecute the daily paper most consistently critical of the Government.

The *Guardian* was spared not only prosecution but also the odium of being subpoenaed to appear in court as a witness for the Crown; spared the public humiliation of betraying Miss Tisdall yet again, in public, under the cool gaze of the young woman in the dock.

FOUR

For years the *Guardian* had prided itself on assessing each situation, rationally and without partisan bias. Speaking in Manchester during the 1958 campaign, Churchill had taken aim at the editor of the *Manchester Guardian*:

> So long as an unending flow of brilliant articles are produced putting everyone in their place and often stating all the arguments on both sides of every question, the editorial duty in the world is done.

To this the incumbent editor, A. P. Wadsworth, replied:

> All common political instinct demands that one choose a side – it makes things wonderfully easy – but, sometimes, perhaps, the wisest course is to try and tell all sides their faults – and suffer the brickbats that always afflict the candid friend.

Contrary to widespread belief, the paper does not have a left-wing tradition. In 1951 Wadsworth concluded: 'For the next few years a Churchill Government is, it seems to us, the lesser evil.' In 1955 Wadsworth again adjudged Labour not yet ready for office. In 1959 and again in 1964 Alastair Hetherington came out for Labour, though calling for increased Liberal representation on both occasions: 'I believed that if Labour's action was tempered by the Liberals it would avoid excesses in public ownership and social policy. . . .'

Preston's immediate predecessor as editor, Hetherington, describes in his book *Guardian Years* the discussions which took place among senior staff at the time of the two general elections of 1974. Some remained loyal to Labour, some preferred a Lib-Lab pact, others, including Hetherington, looked for a consensual coalition of all three parties. Hetherington recalls the final senior staff lunch before polling day in October 1974; enter, here, Peter Preston:

> . . . Peter Preston, while admitting to past adherence sometimes to the Liberals and sometimes to Labour . . . agreed

121

that Wilson ought to be encouraged to come to terms with others. . . . Afterwards, walking back to Gray's Inn Road with John [Cole], I said I thought it was 7–3 in his favour [i.e., pro-Labour]. He disputed this (or so he recalls), reckoning it was 7½–2½, with Peter Preston split between us.'

There is no virtue in iron dogmatism but clearly a ½–½ editor may not do well in a crisis like the Tisdall affair. By the 1983 election the political situation had radically altered with the birth of the SDP-Liberal Alliance; the *Guardian*'s staff was now painfully, almost fratricidally, divided. Finally, on the day before the election, Preston wrote a leader failing to come to any 'broad conclusion'. Conclusions, he said, tended to come 'piecemeal'; and so, 'We would wish to see what comes next.'

The captain procrastinates and trims his sails to keep the crew together. Preston's navigational posture may not have served Sarah Tisdall well but it offers editorial staff a high degree of latitude, allowing each to form an image of the paper's centre of gravity according to his own inclination.

An NUJ chapel meeting was convened at the *Guardian* on 21 December 1983. At the same time Preston issued new guidelines about the destruction of classified documents, the implication being that a system had been at fault rather than individual: structuralism instead of sodomy. 'It has been a horrible blow,' he told his staff. 'But the paper goes on and, I hope and believe, in a way that shows that it can't be squashed or intimidated.' Resentful of an Early Day Motion in the Commons by Brian Sedgemore, MP, calling for Preston's resignation, the chapel meeting expressed its respect for 'the editor's painful decision' and reaffirmed its 'total support for the editorship of the paper'. Grief and wrath were diverted on to the hapless Lovell, White & King; two months later the chapel unanimously passed a motion of no confidence in the Holborn Viaduct solicitors. Subsequently the paper entrusted business involving civil liberties to the law firm which did so well for, by, and out of Clive Ponting.

On 19 January the Father of the NUJ chapel at the *Guardian* wrote to Miss Tisdall offering her £258 towards her initial defence costs and promising further financial help. On 27 January her solicitor, Mr Christopher Murray, of Kingsley, Napley & Co, sent an appreciative reply: 'Having been granted legal aid, her legal costs are, of course, covered. She was nevertheless most touched by the generosity of your members.' The national executive committee of the NUJ, meeting on 3 February, took a less charitable view of what the Hon. General Treasurer described as Preston's 'odious lapse'. The union's president, Eddie Barrett, commented: 'The fact is that the *Guardian* editor has shat on a principle we hold dear, and shat on the informant.' David Thompson, FoC at the *Daily Mirror*, expressed complete disgust: 'I don't know of a case of anyone who cracked like Preston.' Feelings now ran high; Sarah Tisdall had been charged at Bow Street magistrates' court on 11 January. The act of betrayal had yielded its victim, young, female, helpless. Early in April Preston, himself a member of the union, was condemned by the NUJ's annual conference meeting at Loughborough. The motion was passed overwhelmingly after it was moved by the City of London branch, whose Father declared: 'The editor of the *Guardian* did not only betray Sarah Tisdall. He betrayed every one of us here.' The *Guardian*'s FoC, Aidan White, quoted words written about the most illustrious of *Manchester Guardian* editors, C. P. Scott.

> If it came to the point, he was perfectly ready to sacrifice the commercial success of his newspaper to its journalistic integrity . . . better extinction than a failure of principle.

Nevertheless, the feeling was widespread in the union that the highly principled journalists who staffed Britain's leading liberal newspaper had too readily capitulated when the chips were down. This was resented at the *Guardian*. After all, many members of the union earn their bread working for papers with virtually no principles to sacrifice: stories, even interviews, are invented; news is distorted; trade unionists or peace campaigners are smeared; the right of reply is denied; blatant errors go uncorrected. The FoC of the Manchester Chapel, Robin Thornber, wrote to the *Journalist* indignantly rejecting NUJ criticisms of Preston's actions:

> If the *Guardian* had continued to refuse to hand over the memo, the fines for contempt would have been continuing and mounting. If the document had been destroyed the paper would have been fined a massive amount – enough to break the company.

The same month the Group's chairman, Mr Peter Gibbings, announced that profits had risen to £3.4 million compared with £2 million the previous year. Sales were up by 6%, to 480,000, advertising was buoyant, and the *Guardian* was still outrunning its main rival, *The Times*.

In the same issue of the *Journalist*, the deputy FoC of the *Guardian*'s London chapel, Bernie Corbett, also complained about the NUJ Executive Committee's disparaging references to the performance of the chapel:

Coverage of our constructive response to the incident –
approval of guidelines for the future; instigation of a chapel
inquiry; a strong house agreement claim for the chapel's right
to take part in editorial decision-making – would have made
an uplifting lead story.

But when Corbett returned to the subject in the December issue he
seemed rather less uplifted. Although the chapel had originally
voted to collect the princely sum of £10 per head (or 0.05 per cent
of salary) for Sarah Tisdall, this had not materialised in full. The
chapel's demand for representation on the boards of the *Guardian*
and its parent company, and on the Scott Trust, had been turned
down flat. As for policy consultation, Preston 'has written at length
to the chapel', reported Mr Corbett, 'pouring cold water on most
of its ideas'.

The comment that follows was made to me not by some malcon-
tent young Turk, but by a senior department editor at the *Guardian*
who stressed the admirable editorial freedom from management
interference enjoyed by journalists – as when the paper prominently
reported on its front page staff opposition to the selling-off of
Reuters, even though the management had been closely involved
in drawing up the flotation scheme and stood enormously to benefit
from a sale:

There is a strong current of hypocrisy and mealie-mouthed
compromise. This is as apparent in the radicals as in the
middle-of-the-roaders. The paper purports to be centre-left
with a radical tinge. In fact we are a paper of the new establishment – the 35-year-olds who will occupy positions of power in
ten years' time. It's very easy to sound radical when you're
not yourself threatened. Take the paper's policy on private
education: totally against it. Yet almost all of the management
send their kids to private schools. The paper's supposed to be
against company cars but you see lots of them at the *Guardian*.
We behave like reputable, middle-class, Volvo-owning citizens.

Yet it's not impossible to drive a Volvo and keep faith with one's
sources.

What measure of courage is required to protect a source in the
face of legal sanctions? E. D. G. Lewis, of the Manchester *Daily
Despatch*, published an article in 1937 drawing on a confidential
circular issued by the Chief Constable of Southport – who was livid.
Lewis was charged and fined after refusing to identify his source.
In the 1960s two journalists went to prison rather than divulge
confidential information to a tribunal investigating security matters.

In 1980 Granada TV was sued by British Steel after screening a report highly damaging to the Corporation and based on documents leaked by one of its employees. Despite adverse rulings in the High Court, the Court of Appeal and, finally, the House of Lords, Granada made no attempt to persuade its researcher, Laurie Flynn, to disclose the name of his source. Not that Flynn would have done so anyway; as he puts it, 'a man must do what a man must do'.

The *Guardian*'s leader comment on that case, published on 18 August 1980, makes instructive reading. Praising Granada and Mr Flynn for their courage throughout the ordeal, for having stood firm 'at a high cost and considerable personal risk', the leader concluded: 'now there will be no need for disclosure or broken promises'. The editor of the *Guardian* at that time was the same man who, three and a half years later, meekly handed back the Tisdall document to the Government. During the interval, it seems, he had developed his 'respect for the law'.

A source is a person who should enjoy the status, if not the sentiment, of a friend – and this applies equally to unknown sources whose material is exploited. 'If I had to choose between my sources and my country,' E. M. Forster might have said, 'I hope I'd choose my sources.' This was apparently the attitude of Samuel Popkin, a Harvard expert on Asian affairs and Vietnamese village life who found himself suddenly caught up in the investigation into the leak of the 'Pentagon Papers' in 1971. A grand jury wanted to know which US Government officials had helped him in his research. Popkin refused to identify them and was promptly jailed by Judge Arthur Garrity – a verdict upheld on appeal by the Supreme Court.

Despite the First Amendment and the Freedom of Information Act, American reporters have frequently been driven to rub their principles on the whetstone of courage. In 1972 the Supreme Court affirmed the obligation of journalists to testify fully, like other citizens, to courts and grand juries. In one of the cases under review by the court, a *New York Times* reporter, Earl Caldwell, had refused to disclose to a grand jury information about his contacts with Black Panthers. In 1982 a television reporter declined to inform a New York grand jury how he had obtained the jury's own secret report on a case of illegal gun sales. Not until 1984 was New York's 'shield law' upheld in a test case, protecting reporters from contempt charges arising from their refusal to disclose information or sources.

FIVE

'Six months,' said Mr Justice Cantley.

She was driven from the Old Bailey to Holloway prison for women in north London. She had stayed up all the previous night, and the trial had been the worst ninety minutes of her life. Six months – with good conduct, only four. And the lawyers were already lodging an appeal against the sentence. They had advised her not to disclose her offence to the other prisoners, but as soon as she had arrived, been stripped at reception, given a medical, and put in a cell with three other women, the inevitable question came at her: 'What yer in for?' She soon realised the absurdity of the lawyer's cautious advice: her case was all over the radio, TV and papers. The other women vaguely lumped her in with the Greenham lot – nutters but okay – after a demonstration outside Holloway kept them all locked in their cells throughout the weekend. She encountered no hostility: one prison officer whispered, 'I'm with you one hundred per cent – and I didn't say that,' before vanishing.

She was lodged in the best wing in Holloway and kept (she is sure) from visiting the notorious long-term psychiatric wing in the course of her work duties. A prisoner who is immediately visited by MPs is treated warily – and indeed there was a later occasion, in the open prison in Kent, when she informed three Liberal MPs that the prisoners had not received the 'hour of association' accorded by the rule book; next day she was summoned and a double hour of association was granted. Holloway wasn't too bad, apart from being shut in the cell: the baths had locks and the library contained good books.

The day of her appeal she dressed in the clothes she had ironed and was nonplussed to be strip-searched on her way out – and again when she came back, minus the Chief Justice's mercy. In the open prison one could move about more freely, but she shared a room with nine and developed an intimate dislike of the prison officers, bullying authoritarians who enjoyed putting the girls on charges, changing the rules without written notice, levying fines and indulging in arbitrary victimisation against which there was no appeal. One homosexual officer specialised in forcing thin blondes to strip. Starting pay was 90p – by the time she left she was up to

£2 – but you could be fined a pound for filching an apple from the kitchen garden or a half loaf of bread. Even though the prisoners spent a lot of the time working in the kitchen garden, dressed like the old Land Girls, she developed a craving for fresh fruit (and also for chocolate). She spent her prison pay on honey.

Most of the women were in for conspiracy, fraud, stolen cheques and credit cards, and for addiction. The addicts described themselves as such and trembled uncontrollably from deprivation during their first two days inside, then calmed down and grew fatter. The food was bearable, institutional puddings, with the main meal of the day at 11.30 in the morning. Since neither food nor cigarettes could be imported from outside, either by parcel or by visitors (some relatives smuggled in booze, which was hidden in the garden), the women extracted the tobacco from cigarettes into tins and then eked it out as roll-ups. If the cigarette paper ran out, they shredded Tampax. Matches were forbidden so smoking notionally stopped after they were confined to their rooms at 9.00 pm; however one cat burglar made regular night-time forays down to the boiler until she slipped and burnt herself. As a non-smoker, Sarah Tisdall observed these rituals with interest.

More important to her was the writing and receiving of letters. No limit was placed on the number of incoming letters (Sarah Tisdall received mail every morning from relatives, friends and strangers), but only one outward letter a week was provided by the prison, confined to four sides of lined paper. Two more could be purchased. She developed the art of writing to several people in a single envelope, but censorship was strict and no criticism of prison conditions permitted. On one occasion she artfully wrote to her mother in faint mockery of the special treatment she was being accorded: because of the ever-present menace of journalists (at least two penetrated the garden and one took a splendid photo) the prison had taken an unstated decision to refuse her permission to go swimming at Maidstone public baths. Yet they had put her on a domestic science course, the culminating treat of which was to visit a Maidstone supermarket. This letter to her mother was not stopped but it had its effect: she was allowed to visit the swimming baths. The women were instructed to say nothing about their identity but since they all turned up wearing the same clothes and the same swim suits, and changed in a separate room, the lads in the pool soon tacked on: 'Here come the cons.'

She kept a prison diary but destroyed it before she left. She feels they would have confiscated it anyway and it might have incriminated some of the other women, including the cat-burglar desperate for nocturnal smokes. She doesn't find writing easy and notes that Clive Ponting, whom she admires enormously, wrote his book in civil service-ese.

The day she left prison she was driven out of a back entrance in her father's car but the press were wise to it and pursued them as far as Maidstone, where a police car cut off the pursuing hacks. By ill-fortune the Tisdalls later passed a pub and were recognised, the ensuing pursuit by three cars ending only when Sarah and her fiancé dived into the Underground at Piccadilly Circus. The headlines in next day's tabloids were predictable: 'Mole goes to earth'. She spent a week caravanning with her mother and younger sister in Cornwall and wasn't recognised. In fact she has never been recognised: young, soft faces require relentless exposure before they become etched into the public consciousness.

She leads a quiet life, working for a small publisher and suffering agonies when assigned to write a letter of rejection. She isn't tempted to enter the public arena or capitalise on her brief notoriety, though she smilingly reflects that even when sixty she'll still be a 23-year-old mole. She's not an intellectual and is diffident about issues of principle, preferring to talk about her own experiences. No one would suspect that she had been a famous rebel – she can't bring herself to discuss her state of mind at the moment she took the two documents: 'It's too private' – but there are moments when the scorn for authority abused flashes through.

Former Foreign Office colleagues still write to her, but not by diplomatic bag. She had wanted to travel and had spent an engaging six months working in Khartoum, where girls were in short supply and she was never short of an escort. Her job was servicing visa applications, but otherwise she did not meet the natives much: the British club was as exclusive as ever, with the memsahibs still complaining, like the wives of consuls at sunset, that servants were no longer what they had been.

Did prison change her in any way? Make her more cautious, perhaps? She thinks not but may not, as yet, be able to judge: she certainly feels less awe of 'the law' then she did; prison, as she remarks, gets easier the longer you are inside. You learn the ropes. She carries a little of the pride of the graduate; she has seen the other side and done her national service.

While in prison she had a visit from the editor of the *Guardian*. She prefers not to think about it.

SIX

The drama of an individual's principled rebellion against authority, her indictment and harsh punishment, inevitably assumes symbolic proportions; ordinary people whose lives fail to stretch to their dreams invest their beliefs and frustrations in the protagonist. Sarah's mother, Mrs Jennifer Tisdall, commented on the flood of mail that poured into the family home on the outskirts of Plymouth: 'Because many of these people who have written seem to have a tremendous need for someone to have done what she did, to make her into something that she is not, to turn her into a bigger person than she in fact is.'

The mother feared that the daughter might attempt to fulfil people's expectations of her after her release. She quoted a letter from a former wartime RAF pilot who enclosed £5:

> ... to buy your daughter, Sarah, a bottle of drinkable wine or some other small gift to help her through this difficult period .... I have come to believe that if more people were to show your young daughter's courage in standing up to be counted, the manipulations and deceits that lead to wars might be exposed in time to prevent them, a point eloquently expressed by Pastor Niemoller himself: 'When they came for people in the next street I refused to protest. When they came for someone in my street I was afraid to protest. When they came for my neighbour I was still afraid to protest. When they came for me there was nobody left to protest.

Many middle-aged sympathisers were keen to 'adopt' Sarah as a daughter. From the diocese of Manchester Canon A. R. Gawith wrote to the *Guardian*: 'She has earned our respect and admiration for the very qualities of her humanness that remind us how much we need them and how much we have driven them out ... she could easily have been my daughter, or possibly yours.'

The former RAF pilot was not alone in drawing parallels with German resistance to the Nazis. Professor G. R. Edwards, of the University of Bradford, commented: 'At the end of the last war we read moral lectures to the German people on the inadmissibility of

129

pleading that their participation in the holocaust was in obedience to their legitimate government.'

Guardian readers were clearly unhappy with, and sometimes sharply critical of, the paper's decision to hand back the incriminating document to the Government. But the symbolic responses associated with the kitchen stool, muesli packet and earthenware coffee mug were very different from those who (let us imagine) began their day with bacon, eggs and kidneys simmering on the mahogany sideboard before glowering at *The Times* or *Telegraph*. Brigadier P. K. Goozee blasted 'the hand-wringing sentimentality of last Saturday's *Guardian*' and even the 'sanctimonious claptrap of yesterday's *Sunday Times*'. Rear-Admiral A. D. Torlesse blamed much of it on the stupidity of the Foreign Office which had carelessly entrusted such sensitive documents to a 'junior and inexperienced clerk' – though in fairness one must remind the Rear-Admiral that not long after he wrote those words a much more senior civil servant from his 'own' ministry, the MoD, followed along the same awful road. Miss E. L. Smith, however, would hear nothing against the Foreign Office. Sarah Tisdall, she said,

> was at the beginning of her diplomatic career and as such she was not paid to decide what the public should know. "Hers was not the right to reason why – hers was to do or die." . . . She has abused the privilege of working at the Foreign Office – yes, it is a privilege to work there – and the trust that was placed in her . . . . In my book she got what she deserved.

Mr Eric Phillips thought she should have gone to jail for five years.

Sympathy for Peter Preston was notably lacking from correspondents of every ideological hue (a common fate for those who try to occupy the middle ground), but a notable exception was a letter from Mr Des Wilson, the professional publicist and now Secretary of the Campaign for Freedom of Information: 'Do we allow the newspaper and its editor no room for error? Must our friends be faultless? . . . Those who call for the resignation of the Editor of the *Guardian*, or condemn the *Guardian* for betrayal are responsible for a betrayal themselves – a betrayal of the friendship and integrity and loyalty of this newspaper.'

But Ms Gill Emerson, of Gravesend, was not impressed:

> It's all very well for Des Wilson to fawn over the *Guardian* for its 'defence of civil liberties' and 'compassionate policies'. It costs nothing to espouse trendy liberal causes in print. The *Guardian* makes a tidy profit from doing so. However, it is a fat lot of good for all concerned if at the first sign of a fight –

i.e. the Sarah Tisdall case – the *Guardian* proves to be such an ineffectual pushover.

Three days later Mr Wilson followed up with a large advertisement in the paper: 'If the demands of the 1984 Campaign for Freedom of Information are met, people like SARAH TISDALL could not be imprisoned.' Preston himself took up this theme when he argued in a radio interview (see below) that the Tisdall affair had proved indispensable for mobilising political support for a Freedom of Information Act. The *Guardian*'s political columnist, Peter Jenkins, seemed to have his doubts: 'A Freedom of Information Act . . . would certainly not leave the Sarah Tisdalls free to pass confidential memoranda to the *Guardian*. . . . We can be sure that in any list of categories of disclosure, drawn up by any government, at least one – and probably both – of the memoranda she leaked would have remained subject to the sanction of the law.'

In the British context, this may be true; and even under the much more permissive rules governing civil service disclosures in Sweden, Tisdall's action might have involved a police inquiry and judicial sanctions. The lesson to be drawn is not the one proposed by Des Wilson and Peter Preston; the lesson to be drawn is that a principled act of civil disobedience should be *defended* at every stage by both the principal and (where relevant) by the newspaper which published the information.

But was the lesson drawn? On 23 May, two months to the day after Sarah Tisdall went to prison, the Radio 4 programme *Midweek* broadcast an extended and leisurely interview with Peter Preston, the main topic being his decision to hand back to the Government the document which led to Sarah Tisdall's arrest. The interviewer was the earthy Derek Jameson, formerly editor of the *News of the World*. Jameson had recently been involved in a not over-successful libel action against the BBC, a wound which, as we shall see, Preston prodded at every opportunity.

I have cut some of the discursive questions put to the editor of the *Guardian* but have faithfully recorded every syllable of his replies.

DEREK JAMESON: Have you had a good year?

PETER PRESTON: Huh, I've had a good year and a bad year . . . . I think you'd say, I think you'd say that the paper had made a profit for the first time anybody can remember . . . . As far as the bad year, well I mean, I walked into an elephant trap in November, which you will doubtless refer to shortly, and I'm still limping . . . .

JAMESON: . . . How come that the editor of the liberal *Guardian*, the paper of conscience, got himself into such a terrible mess, I mean many people think today you shouldn't be here, you should be in prison.

PRESTON: Oh . . . I mean . . . we're talking about, we haven't mentioned the word, the Tisdall-cruise missile . . . I mean very simply, and if I were, if we were reversing and I was asking you questions, er, it was a terrible mess, I mean, I've said so many times, quite happy to go on saying, er, for ever and a day, er, but just turning it round the other way, Derek, I mean you had a, er, just after about we were having our difficulty you had your difficulty, you had your difficulty with that libel case against the BBC who, we won't, er, say anything about this in the context and you said, afterwards, which stuck in my mind too, that you were talking about the reputation of Fleet Street generally and you had sued because of that. It's always been my feeling for many years now, I mean the press, I mean I agree with what you were saying at the absolute start, we do share an awful lot when we're sitting round and talking and operating, er, that the reputation, whatever Fleet Street says about its reputation in the outside world, its reputation among the people, er, is pretty low –

JAMESON: Let's just go through the Sarah Tisdall affair for those who've forgotten . . .
    . . . and it had nothing to do with security, with secrets or how to handle things, is that right?

PRESTON: Yes, although, I mean, it's like listening to [?unclear?] in terms of sort of producing, er, quick answers. Really one could write a book –

JAMESON: Yes . . . Everyone says why did that bloody fool Peter Preston give the document back? . . . . Would they dare put the editor of the *Guardian* in prison? Why didn't you do those things?

PRESTON: Well, I mean, the answer is, er, that, I mean the question it sounds fine but that wasn't quite the order of events or how things happened. By the time, er, that we realised what was going on, for heaven's sake we've written about this endlessly in the paper, er, one was in a situation where lawyers were involved, and let me just come, sort of, back with the question which I was asking you, I mean you, you went to court, you said, to redeem some of the reputation of Fleet Street, and it was very clear at the time, when we were talking about last November, we're not talking about what we know about Miss Tisdall and we don't even know, as a matter of fact you said it was the writing at the top which identified it, that was what was thought might be the case, it wasn't actually in terms of what happened,[1] but looking at it the other way, I mean you said you went to court to redeem the reputation of Fleet Street as you said and the jury weren't exactly helpful in these contexts,[2] I mean I think the difficulty is, we found ourselves last November, er, defending ourselves in a court against a motion for the return of the document under a piece of the law not that just, that had been foisted upon us, as that we had actually argued for in a defence in these cases, that's, that's your law and my law, I'm sure we both thought it.

JAMESON: I would have said, 'I haven't got the document.' I would have lied. I'd have said, 'No, I haven't got it, sorry old boy, can't help you.' Are you too honest to do a thing like that?

PRESTON: I mean I think that's a case that could be made against me, er, in all these matters, I mean I'm very defensive about this and I'm not sort of, er, bullish at all.

JAMESON: Oh indeed – well I mean, let's make clear. . . .

LIBBY PURVES [programme presenter]: . . . You don't want to pretend anything at all. It seems to me very painful and very admirable.

PRESTON: No, it's, I mean, people said to me a couple of months ago, you must stop saying, er, this is awful and answering questions as frankly as I've been answering the questions that Derek has put, I mean I can't pretend other than that the answers are what I feel. On the other hand, I mean, life does move on, er, a lot of issues have come to the fore as a result of this which frankly would not have been there before, and if you're looking for downsides and upsides, I got the Freedom of Information, er, newsletter – campaign which has been going like a bomb for the last nine months which is filled with statements by the Labour Party and a variety of MPs and unions which are all oriented towards the Tisdall case, all oriented towards the fact that, er, she's there for four months and that we did what we did and the law was what it was and looking at all the arguments through. And what you find there, and I don't think you'd have got it from Neil Kinnock, er, without sort of catalyst, is the sort of commitment to a Freedom of Information bill, for Steel, for the Alliance, for Labour, er, which will be there[3] I hope I shall be around to quote it against them when they're in government and say, 'Hey, you said definitely you'd be doing this, what about it now?'

JAMESON: They'll forget all about it by then, fear not. I must, I must ask you this. I do get the feeling that you yourself take the view that you should have been in the dock with Sarah Tisdall and if Miss Tisdall was going to go to prison, perhaps you should have gone to prison?

PRESTON: Oh, I mean, I felt . . . to be absolutely honest, er, one was stuck with a situation where, I don't know – we didn't know what would happen, but the document – I thought the whole thing, and so many of us thought the whole thing was leaked at such a high level that frankly, to sort of –

JAMESON: Everybody was getting it?

PRESTON: Everybody was getting it[4] and we wouldn't, we weren't necessarily going to reveal anything – as as as it was it was pretty horrific, but that's life.

JAMESON: I suppose I must ask you, though I want to end the subject, but I must ask you on behalf of Fleet Street, why haven't you published the definitive account of the affair by David Caute, which I believe was commissioned by the *Guardian*?

PRESTON: No, that's, that's, that's absolutely untrue –[5]

PURVES: That's a complicated issue, I think, can we not start on that. . . .

NOTES:

1 Preston here gives the false impression that his own action in handing over the document was not forensically decisive in Sarah Tisdall's detection and arrest.
2 There was no parallel between Jameson's libel action, which involved a jury, and the Government's civil action against the *Guardian*, which did not.
3 There may be some truth in this – hence the famous debt owed by Christianity to Judas Iscariot (though Judas stopped short of making the claim).
4 'Everybody' wasn't getting it. By the time the *Guardian* faced an action for recovery of the document, it was clear that no other paper had it. What, in any case, is the relevance?
5 See pp. 135–38.

SEVEN

If we suppose that the passionate attachment to secrecy is confined to governments and bureaucracies, we deceive ourselves. The *Guardian* is, among other qualities, an 'investigative newspaper'; its diligent scouts forage for buried information, for private memoranda and confidential minutes, whose publication will discomfort the powerful, the rich, the corrupt, and the incompetent. Yet to investigate the *Guardian* is not easy. One encounters the standard reflexes of any institution under challenge:

'I can't comment.'

'I didn't personally see a second document.'

'I don't actually know if there was one.'

'No comment. Sorry.'

'You're free to read between the lines.'

'Officially I can tell you there was only one document. Anyone who saw a second document is probably old enough to keep silent about it.'

'What are you talking about? I don't know about any second document . . . and I wouldn't tell you if I did.' (That was managing editor Ken Dodd, at Bow Street magistrates' court; one of his colleagues, with whom I had been talking, said to him: 'You sound like a lawyer.' Yet the colleague, who had been assigned to cover the case, wrote all his reports over a period of three months as if only a single document had been received by the *Guardian*.)

A departmental editor said: 'All knowledge of a second document is surmise. What leads you to imagine two documents arrived in the same envelope? Aren't you aware the police believe that a second document was leaked to the *Observer*, not the *Guardian*?' A few minutes later he said: 'If we *did* receive two documents,' adding: 'I'm trying not to confirm the existence of a second document.'

Investigating the *Guardian* was an instructive experience. When I began the enterprise in January 1984 I had no idea where my research would lead. Not a word had been written, and not a single formal interview granted (I had first approached the deputy editor and news editor) when I received a sharp letter from Peter Preston, dated 21 February. Expressing admiration for my work 'since Oxford' – we are roughly of a generation – and for a recent book

135

of mine about Rhodesia, he went on to rebuke me for preconceived bias, for approaching what he called 'my staff' without his permission ('It would have been nice to have been asked properly'), and for having decided to 'hang, draw and quarter' him.

A second letter, dated 8 March, was more conciliatory. It would, he expected, be possible for us 'to have a reasonable discussion within a few weeks', as soon as the trial, now set down for 23 March, was concluded. 'Meanwhile,' he wrote, 'I would be grateful to know if you have got any specific commission for the article you are intending to write. It's always a help to know where something may be placed. And who knows, being the *Guardian* we might even bid for it ourselves.'

Well, who does know?

The trial of Sarah Tisdall took place ten days later; by midday she had been sent to prison. Preston was not in court. Having heard nothing further, I telephoned David McKie and pressed for an immediate interview. Three days later I met McKie and Peter Cole, the news editor, in McKie's office, having in the meantime absorbed the *Guardian*'s 4,000-word long *mea culpa* in the Saturday edition – a document which – as all my sources within the paper immediately confirmed – left unresolved, or glossed over, certain crucial episodes.

The interview with McKie and Cole fell into two segments; my substantive questions on the events of the past five months; and the small matter of the 'commission'. The former I have already discussed; as for the commission, McKie left his office for a few moments – if he wasn't speaking to Preston down the corridor he must have been consulting the Almighty – and returned to propose that I write 4,000 words for a deadline in mid-April. I took this to be a commission; in 'Fleet Street', as in the stock exchange or any self-respecting Arab bazaar, these things are done on the nod, and do not require written confirmation. I was pleased because there could be no more relevant audience for what I wanted to write than the *Guardian*'s own. But I was naïve.

Preston himself had to be approached by telephone, but only through his secretary. He was playing the grandee. I came back at noon the following Friday. Preston was not alone; close at his side was the gnomish, terrier-like Ken Dodd, the paper's managing editor and general trouble shooter in matters legal. I vaguely assumed Dodd was on hand to keep a record of the proceedings but it soon became apparent that the game was two-against-one; the atmosphere was frosty from the start and rapidly degenerated to the glacial. Obviously McKie and Cole had reported the general direction of my inquiries, which were far from welcome, in particular my knowledge of the telephone call made by Preston on 16 December to Donald Trelford urging him to bury David Leigh's 'second document' story in the *Observer*. I was not then aware that two days after my interview with McKie and Cole, Preston had reacted to this news in the approved Chicago fashion, again telephoning Trelford and urging him to put the screws on my source.

I duly raised this question: was it true that Preston had asked Trelford to suppress an accurate report scheduled for the 18 December issue of the *Observer*, and if so why?

In chorus both Preston and Dodd demanded to know what my source had told me. Preston then inveighed against 'investigative journalists' with their 'single-track minds'. I pressed the question again.

'Why don't you ask Donald Trelford?' Preston retorted.

I had tried, but in vain: two letters and a succession of calls extending over three weeks. In any case it was evidently Preston who had telephoned Trelford on his own behalf; the onus was properly on Preston to explain.

'It's a confidential matter,' he said.

Dodd said: 'He has every right not to answer.'

They both came back to my source: what had he told me? I said I didn't want to discuss my sources.

'Ah! Ah! There you are! You want to preserve your confidentiality but we're not allowed to protect ours.'

Preston said: 'There was no plot. You're dancing on the head of a pin.'

It was clearly a sharp pin.

It seemed almost impossible – as people who knew Preston well had warned me it would be – to nail him down on any point of serious substance. The evasions and circumlocutions, the crablike motions around any point at issue, are difficult to convey, although the transcript of Preston's radio interview with Derek Jameson may provide some indication of the difficulty.

Finally, I raised the question of the commission. Preston shook his head; he'd never heard of McKie's proposal of 4,000 words by mid-April. However, he would delegate the entire decision to his Features Editor, Richard Gott.

On 2 May I sent Gott my article. The letter of rejection came by return. Gott cited four reasons for turning the piece down, although one – old wounds, new wounds – would have sufficed:

(1) I think that if the *Guardian* were to publish it, it would inevitably seem, not necessarily that the *Guardian* endorsed your view (which it obviously doesn't), but that it believed your arguments were interesting and worth discussing. I don't think they are.

(2) I think the piece is wrongheaded from beginning to end.

I don't agree with its argument at all. Of course one often allows batty arguments to appear on the Agenda page – part of its purpose is to stimulate argument and debate – but I don't think the *Guardian* would be doing itself a service by embarking on what would be seen as a further course of self-flagellation.

(3) I can see no good reason to publish something that adversely compares the *Guardian* with the *Observer*.

(4) I think readers' appetites for reading about their newspapers' internal problems are strictly finite, and I have been reinforced in this view by the great splurges that have appeared recently in the *Observer* detailing their Matabeleland difficulties and in the *Sunday Times* on their Oman behaviour. I found both extremely tedious and self-indulgent.

Yours,
Richard Gott

Extra-mural radicalism directed at the evils of capitalism and imperialism, offset by corporate vanity and the closing of ranks when the wound lies in the local gut.

Preston's own response arrived two weeks later in the form of a letter which he distributed to a number of newspapers. It contained some substantive points which I have discussed elsewhere in these pages; but the thrust of the missile lay in its tail:

I'm bound to say that the article is libellous not merely of myself, but of half a dozen others. Long ago I made a private vow never to sue in the rough business of journalism; and I'll try to hold to that view now. Others involved, of course, may have no such hang-ups. But if you would like to sue me on my considered view that (in this instance) you are a devious, sloppy and malevolent operator with a rare disregard for fact and a rare talent for obsessed distortion, then that would be a different matter.

The article was published in the August issue of the Cambridge magazine *Granta*, edited by Bill Buford. In substance the piece was very much as I had submitted it to the *Guardian*, although an over-heated preamble had been subjected to surgery and a number of phrases modified to satisfy the libel lawyer: as far as I can tell, these gentlemen make a living by devising ways of altering the form of wording without changing the content. Not a bad living either: the lawyer was paid twice as much for vetting the piece as I was for writing it.

Preston responded with a letter published in the October issue of *Granta*. I quote:

Can I offer you a malevolent little fairy tale for some future edition? It features – and I can deck it out with Scott Fitzgerald or Budd Schulberg trappings if you wish – a brilliant young academic and writer grown twisted and desperate in the throes of bleak middle age. Twenty-five years ago he was a fellow of All Souls and a young meteor for Harvard and Columbia. His first novel came garlanded in prizes. His energy was legend. He wrote plays and learned treatises in profusion. And then, strangely, the creativity drained away. The thunderclaps came slowly and with diminishing returns. His first marriage crumbled. Over ten years – apart from a couple of trivial, penny-coining novels, he published only two books. And by the winter of 1983 he was reduced to scratching a living doing fill-in work at Bush House where, in three months, colleagues found 'little he wrote that was usable'. Age and disillusion and a burning political rage had laid a career waste. He was a small, podgy man with a crooked smile and a shiny suit, reduced by pursuing random passions and hawking them, fruitlessly, from paper to paper and magazine to magazine. There was some residual reputation; for a time friends helped him out; but the ashes of what might have been lay littered and cold.

Why, you may wonder, am I not first offering this stupendous article to the *Guardian*, the paper I edit? Because I wouldn't touch it with a barge-pole. The facts of David Caute's career, as far as they go, are accurate enough. The quotes are accurate too, by Mr Caute's chop-sentence standards. So are the grin and the suit. But by another test the thesis is pre-ordained hatchet-work and may, for all I know, be utter bunk. I wouldn't print it. So why did you devote so much of your last issue to the much-amended Caute rendition of the Tisdall case, which is precisely the same sort of factional, tawdry, driven exercise?

The facts were scarcely 'accurate enough' but that is a minor point. Clearly, what most gets beneath our skin is behaviour that reminds us of our own unease. The adulterer who uncovers his wife's exasperated, answering infidelity is likely to be more, rather than less indignant. Theatre, film and television critics with a weekly licence to rubbish and perhaps ruin the work of writers, actors and directors, react with hysteria at the first sign of a rejoinder calling their own competence into question. They know about damage. As for Mr Preston, he enjoys the freedom of his own leader columns to

139

lambast or ridicule virtually every public person and institution at home or abroad; and clearly enjoys what he enjoys; and might regard this steady stream of fire as a civic duty or whatever. But members of the damage industry well understand, as I have said, the damage.

The power an editor wields is not confined to the pen. He can suppress as well as express. Not a word about my article, neither report nor review, appeared in the *Guardian* following its publication. It is perhaps not idle to mention that the paper had reviewed virtually everything of substance I had written for the previous twenty-five years.

In October the House of Lords delivered judgment on the Tisdall document case and Preston responded with a leader. I sent a letter for publication. The Letters Editor refused to publish it. When I pressed the point, the Boss intervened. No.

Lacking an Official Secrets Act to invoke in his own defence, the editor of the *Guardian* used the weapons of silence available to him. The Tisdall affair was Preston's *Belgrano*.

EIGHT

The form of 'espionage' practised (albeit in a single, isolated act of rebellion) by Tisdall and Ponting is generally supported, or condemned, along tribal lines; our 'principles' are paid-up partisans. But I hold that the 'espionage' of disclosure is a vital motion of democratic activity, regardless of the government or issue involved. The theory and practice of elective government, in any of the constitutional varieties on display in the shop window of the West, fall far short of genuine participatory democracy.

General elections staged every five years, dominated by party machines, sustained by a non-elected bureaucracy, merely offer to a passive, sceptical electorate a choice of brightly packaged cargoes, aggressively marketed then quietly shelved. At election time the politician is a manifesto man, a policy-and-programme man; in between elections he is the steely executor of 'unforeseen crises', very much in business to make 'hard' decisions whose unpopularity, like the taste of cod liver oil, is the measure of their worth. While out canvassing for votes, you might take him to be a mandatory of the people, his rosette evoking the cockades worn by Jacobin tribunes and *sans culottes*. But no sooner are the votes cast to the advantage of his party than he effects a conjuring trick worthy of the Great Mendoza; in a flash we no longer have a mandatory but rather a 'representative', elected to Parliament to serve our best interests – rather than to heed our wishes. Now a minister (or rehearsing for the part), he groans to his senior civil servants about the constant chore of constituency meetings, of keeping the local faithful sweet, and readily agrees with the bureaucrats that it would be prudent to disclose the bare minimum about plans in the pipeline. It all looks different from the top. People, the press, even Parliament – all cantankerous or frankly hostile impediments to smooth-running government. The great cogs of the machine of state are oiled, it transpires, not by the aggregated herd of individual citizens, but by the powerful corporations and pressure groups which dominate economic performance and financial priorities. What can John Smith know of the awful warnings whispered in Claridge's by the man from the IMF? Of the latest Soviet missile deployments in Eastern Europe? Of Prince Saud's discreet intimation that the Gulf States may cut their oil production by half? When the Argies suddenly run up their flag over Port Stanley then the British electorate is treated as a passive force to be roused, manipulated, mobilised – but consulted? are you serious!

In a crisis the people abdicate to Parliament, the Commons abdicate to the Cabinet, the Cabinet abdicates to the War Cabinet . . . . And what is the practice of governance if not one crisis after another? Are we not for ever a short jab of the button away from war? And what is war, today or tomorrow, if not foresight, secret contingency planning, iron resolution in an emergency? Whatever Rousseau may have said, my dear fellow, debating societies are not notoriously the people to summon to a fire. What we need, damn it, is what our competitors demonstrably possess: good management. In government; in business; in industry; in everywhere. What we must have is leadership.

The anarchists are right: government itself is the evil. Power the enemy. However, Hobbes had hold of a darker truth – we do not know how to survive without it. The conclusion is therefore inescapable: an active democracy (as distinct from the TV-dinner variety) requires a constant subversion of the representative government we defend against dictators, juntas, bomb-throwers, and messengers of the one-party state. This subversion takes the form of non-violent (though not necessarily 'legal') guerrilla harassment of the fat slug institutions of state power; the vast discretionary powers claimed and exercised by government must not be conceded. We were never asked what form of government we wanted; it was simply thrust in our faces, huge and unavoidable, like the great tit greeting the new-born child.

All the metaphors for this subversion are to be found in the guerrilla action of the peace women at Greenham Common, from passive prostration before the wheels of the missile-carriers to fast wire-cutting after dark; from blockades and legal tussles to a telephone-linked network of observers monitoring the cruise convoys. Tisdall and Ponting were, after their fashion, wire-cutters. I suspect that theirs is the spirit of revolt that Camus sanctioned in *L'Homme révolté*.

But wait: is not the purpose of Law to curb the anarchy of a thousand conflicting wills? Is there to be a special dispensation for those who acknowledge themselves as civic saints? Do not judges remind dissenters that 'you cannot take the law into your own hands'? Here again we require a dual posture: to break this or that law in a principled manner is not necessarily to shit on the whole institution of Law – the struggle for democracy, or national independence, in virtually any country reminds us of that. But I do not throw in the phrase 'principled manner' carelessly, or for good effect, and I shall later suggest where Miss Tisdall and Mr Ponting failed in that regard. Civil disobedience, properly conducted, is both a challenge to a law and a surrender to the courts – where a new battle is fought. But wait again: where do we draw the line? If we sanction the unauthorised disclosure of information by Tisdall or Ponting, why should we not take the next step and applaud Alan Nunn May or Klaus Fuchs for passing atomic technology (entirely out of conviction, and not for money) to the Soviet Union? I don't know, because the surface of the floor is too slippery to define the steps: Soviet defectors who spill the Kremlin's beans are lauded while ours are branded as traitors. We can only thrash about in the net of double standards, of Policy masquerading as Principle. Yet it's also clear that the worst argument against desirable reform always has been: 'But where may it not lead? Where do we draw the line?' Enfranchise the small shopkeeper class, and next it will be the workers, then women – and so why not children and babes in arms?

What disturbs about the clarion calls of the Left for freedom of information is that our principles bend like rubber according to convenience. When the Tories are rate-capping or abolishing Labour-controlled councils, the Labour Party Conference discovers – one bellowing speech after another – that true democracy resides in local government. But when a Labour administration is attempting to impose comprehensive schools on recalcitrant Tory boroughs and shires, we equally discover that the will of the people resides in Westminster. Labour councils are the tribunes of the people; Tory councils are composed of blimps, cliques and lackeys of local business. With an almost careless twist of the tongue we put our passionately professed principles into a convenient reverse. As Lenin cynically observed, 'Who, whom?' It all depends who is doing it to whom. The other day one Labour GLC committee chairman was openly challenged by another about some action he had taken. The retort was revealing: 'You're merely giving comfort to the capitalist press.' This is the standard shorthand for the socialist version of secrecy. It means: 'Comrade, let us wash our dirty linen in private. *They* will exploit our disagreements.' But if the 'capitalist press' is not to know, how will the people know?

Imagine a quite plausible scenario. A future Labour Government is laying sensitive (and therefore secret) plans for the removal of nuclear weapons – initially American missiles – from British soil. Given the hostility of the Opposition, of the service chiefs, and of Washington, these plans would be highly classified: the usual rationale. Then come the leaks: to the press, to Tory MPs. What, then, of the Left's professed values? What, then, of the nascent Freedom of Information Act? Far from hailing the 'Tisdalls' and 'Pontings' of that future incarnation as people of principle, the constituency Labour parties and student socialists would call for 'firm action' against a hidebound 'Tory' civil service intent on subverting a socialist government. A *democratically elected* socialist Government.

A prosecution follows. The Official Secrets Act, which we didn't have time to reform, is wheeled out, *faute de mieux*. The culprit, Sir Instant Retaliation, a deputy permanent under-secretary at the MoD or Foreign Office, is arraigned at the Central Criminal Court, amid Tory protests – 'a brazenly political trial!' cries Mr Douglas Hurd, the Shadow Home Secretary – and appears before Mr Justice Deterrent (yes it is he). The defence pins its case on the 'national interest'; it is not in the 'national interest' that Britain should be denuded of nuclear weapons and laid open to Soviet invasion; it is not in the 'national interest' that ministers should lay secret plans unknown to Parliament. The prosecution reminds the jury that under the British constitution the elected (as it happens, Labour) Government of the day is, while it retains the support of Parliament, the sole interpreter of the national interest. Mr Justice Deterrent listens, nods, takes some notes and declares, during the second week of the trial, that Sir Instant Retaliation is clearly a highly principled public servant with an impeccable service record – selflessly devoted to the safety of this island nation (decorated for gallantry beyond the call of duty while serving somewhere), and a firm believer in Parliamentary government.

Mr Justice Deterrent winks at the jury, several times. The Left, incensed, notes that the jury, who are winking back, are not ordinary citizens at all, but stockbroker-types, and their bourgeois wives, all recruited from the Home Counties commuter belt.

Sir Instant's acquittal does not go down well in *Tribune*, *Socialist Review*, *Marxism Today* and the CND organ, *Sanity*. The annual general meeting of the National Council for Civil Liberties detects no civil liberty at stake, other than that of 'the British people to live without terror of nuclear extinction'. In the *New Statesmen* an alert journalist digs up the fact that Sir Instant Retaliation attended the same school and the same Oxford college as Mr Justice Deterrent and was involved in the same notorious boating brawl; belongs to the same St James's clubs; and is indeed the judge's brother-in-law many times over.

But the problem of secrecy in government and society lies deeper than the grim demonstration of hypocrisy and double standards. To open wide our mouths in denunciation of secrecy is mere noise unless we dig to its roots and examine its role in our psychological survival. The fact is, we cannot live without silence and its embattled cousin, secrecy. Secrecy is silence under the stress of two forms of challenge: the Other's demand to know; and the Self's impulsion to confess. The stress arises because of a perception that disclosure will be damaging.

Knowledge is power; it is also a commodity far more valuable than the Patent Office can realise. Silence and secrecy are bank vaults: our security depends on the locks. The breaking of an oath of secrecy – 'telling', in the language of the children's code – touches a sensitive spot. Judas betrayed Jesus by telling. We may admire Sarah Tisdall and Clive Ponting from a distance, but would we employ them?

I used to sit on the executive of the Writers' Guild. We passed a resolution in favour of a Freedom of Information Act. But even as we did so we held a heated debate as to whether full minutes of our Council meetings should be regularly distributed to the members of the Guild. Scriptwriters who brilliantly satirised secretive Whitehall bureaucrats in their television serials now began to frown and groan. Members of the Council, they objected, should feel free to speak and vote 'without fear'; no conceivable minutes could be accurate enough to prevent misunderstandings; and suppose the other side (the TV companies or the Publishers' Association) got hold of our plans, our bargaining positions, our 'bottom lines'? Besides, we often discussed individuals, members whose subscriptions had lapsed, hard-luck cases, all strictly confidential 'between these four walls'.

On another occasion a writer asked the Council to withhold its small annual donation to Amnesty International until that organisation stopped experimenting on hapless animals to test the effects of electric shock torture on human skins. An argument broke out and sprouted like a cactus. The incensed writer threatened to resign; next day a story to that effect surfaced in a newspaper. Almost the whole of the next monthly council meeting was devoted to the question of who had so treacherously leaked the writer's threat to resign and what kind of an inquiry should be set in motion.

Recently I received a copy of a letter written by a colleague, marked 'for information only'. The original letter had been addressed to the ambassador of a foreign power, protesting against certain specific arrests and acts of repression in His Excellency's country. But it was not to be published. On that understanding the ambassador had received my colleague in person and listened most attentively to his complaints; indeed he had hinted that such pressure, from well-informed Englishmen friendly to his country, was really quite welcome to him. But of course a letter sent to the press would immediately indicate that its author was no longer friendly and therefore his complaints would be discounted. And the victims would remain in prison.

This strategy of silence is much more dubious than withholding the names of the victims of an air crash, or even 'embargoing' a press release until a specified hour. As with government secrecy, the visible side of the coin gleams with good intentions while the side close to the palm is tarnished. It would be a severe blow to my colleague to become an 'unfriend' of a country where he is always welcome, always free to pursue his research, and often granted rapid access to the President and his intimate circle.

The safest padlock on the treasury of our knowledge is the invisible one of silence. When we come to the trial of Mr Clive Ponting we shall encounter the crusading investigative MP, Mr Tam Dalyell, camped outside the Ministry of Defence and demanding to know every detail about the sinking of the Argentine cruiser, *General Belgrano*, on 2 May 1982. Confronted by Dalyell's questions (and Dalyell's knowledge), the Secretary of State for Defence, the Rt Hon. Michael Heseltine, must exchange his perfect silence for a riskier commodity, secrecy. In refusing to say, Heseltine must say something; in framing sentences he begins to bleed; the law will not protect him against haemorrhage, such are the clinical risks of saying anything at all.

Marked 'confidential' was a Home Office briefing, dated June 1983, advising a new minister that it was administrative policy to maintain long queues of people claiming the right to enter Britain from the Indian sub-continent. The memo admitted that this policy enjoyed no legislative authority and that if it were *exposed* there would be a risk of legal action in the British courts and under the European Convention on Human Rights.

But just as Mr Heseltine (rightly) feared that even a part of the truth would provide Daylell with what prosecuting counsel, in an excellent metaphor, was to call 'marvellous ammunition', so Clive Ponting inevitably guarded certain awkward episodes with a discreet silence when he came to trial. I later asked him about one such episode. He went 'off the record'. After the interview I sent him a transcript containing my question followed by the words 'Clive Ponting here spoke off the record'. The transcript came back with that sentence excised – and my question deleted as well.

Before we denounce governmental secrecy, we must wonder how easily we can divorce it from those forms of secrecy which, paradoxically, we regard as vital to our identity, our dignity, and indeed to our civil liberties.

In Orwell's *1984* the Inner Party not only keeps the populace – the proles – in ignorance about its own secret deliberations, it also penetrates every facet of a citizen's private behaviour and thoughts. This total scrutiny, this remorseless invigilation, is what we most fear. The ground-floor windows of British homes are customarily veiled in lace; our nightmare, like Orwell's, is the glass cubicles in which the inhabitants of Zamyatin's futuristic dystopia, *We*, were forced to live. The National Council for Civil Liberties, therefore, is constantly reclaiming the invaded terrain of individual secrecy while launching offensives into protected areas of state secrecy. But individual secrecy is not promoted by that dubious name: it's called 'privacy'. Secrecy bad, privacy good. Thus *they* may not:

– bug your home or office, tap your telephone, or open your mail;
– examine your lawyer's files, your doctor's files, your social worker's files, your probation officer's files, or your income tax returns. Nor gain access to the membership lists of the associations you belong to;
– demand to know how you voted in an election;
– publish your name if you are the victim of rape or the luckless child in a contested custody (or surrogate motherhood) case;
– demand to know your identity if you have disclosed information in confidence to a newspaper;
– require you to give evidence in court if you are the defendant.

Some of these 'rights of privacy' are mainly instrumental, strategies against institutional interference or conviction on flimsy, misleading evidence. But behind such demands lies the deeper, psychic need for privacy and silence. The secrets of the bedroom are only half an hour on the underground from the Official Secrets Act and the bewigged strictures of Mr Justice Cantley and Mr

Justice McCowan. It is 'no business of mine' (a phrase as revealing as 'marvellous ammunition') how your wife is in bed. It is no business of yours to reveal what goes on in the great bed of state. 'Six months.'

We need silence like we need sleep (we have a special fear of blurting out the truth when invaded by dreams; of shouting out the other woman's name). Our patterns of speech are bounded by much longer periods of silence. When we are alone or asleep our silence is mechanical and non-significative, like the silence of the switched-off radio, but when we are with others our silence is charged with meaning. It is the language of non-disclosure. We recoil from people who seem compelled to spill out whatever comes into their heads, not merely because a torrent of trivialities is boring, but because we associate verbal incontinence with vulnerability, with 'marvellous ammunition'. Piaget's research has shown how the ability to keep a secret, to padlock thoughts and knowledge, is a vital stage in a child's development. The tap that leaks is flawed or useless.

Knowledge is power. Many students taking public exams grow distraught at the prospect of their parents opening the envelope and discovering the result before they do. What is sought here is the space for adjustment available only within one's own silent monopoly of crucial information – and a cushion against the power that knowledge will give to the Other. In cases of extreme tension we may invert the process into one of total dependence: 'No, you open it, I can't bear to look.' Sartre remarked:

And, for me, knowledge has a magical sense of appropriation. To know is to appropriate. Exactly as, for the primitive, to know a man's secret name is to appropriate that man and reduce him to slavery.

Never mind the 'primitive'! Demand of any officious character in uniform his name and number and you are likely to witness a sudden nakedness, an onrush of vulnerability.

The dialectic of language and silence brings us back to the *instrumental* demands of civil libertarians for 'privacy'. The Hollywood blacklisting hearings before the House Un-American Activities Committee in 1947 demonstrated how 'freedom of speech' also involves 'freedom of silence' – as indeed did the *Guardian's* betrayal of Sarah Tisdall's anonymity, which led to deterrent punishment *pour encourager les autres*. The 'Hollywood Ten' (John Howard Lawson, Ring Lardner, Jr and eight others) pleaded the First Amendment when refusing to disclose to the Committee what they believed and what they had joined. The First Amendment guarantees freedom of speech and association. To confess to membership

147

of the Communist Party, or fellow-travelling support for Communist causes, or sympathy for Henry Wallace, was in those dark days a quick way to lose a job as director, actor or scriptwriter (not to mention teacher or electrical worker). So the Ten pleaded that freedom of speech necessarily involved freedom of silence. The courts were not convinced and the Ten went to prison. Subsequent victims of the purge employed the same strategy but a slightly different tactic; they invoked the Fifth Amendment, which protects a person against self-incrimination. In so doing they were forced to abandon a vital point of principle.

To illustrate this retreat, we may invent a parallel. Because we accept that freedom of the ballot involves secrecy of the ballot, no policeman or prosecutor is allowed to ask a suspect or defendant how he voted: call that the First Amendment. Now imagine altered rules, whereby the question could be asked – 'Did you vote Labour last year?' – but the defendant has the right not to reply because a truthful answer might incriminate him: call that the Fifth. The alteration involves a substantial erosion of civil liberty, because it means that voting Labour has become incriminating. Thus the depth of the silences allowed to us is a crucial measure of our liberties. The crux of a totalitarian 'show trial' is the confession of the accused.

We cannot survive without silence and its cousin secrecy. In travelling from his home to his office the minister or civil servant does not undergo a psychic metamorphosis at Swiss Cottage or Earl's Court. His first motions of the day – bath, covering his body, disposing of soiled undergarments – are secret ones. His project all day long will be to remain inside the whale. At every juncture the civil servant (like the businessman, the stockbroker and the shop steward), is dividing the world into 'I' and 'you', 'us' and 'them'. His necessary inclusion in the larger corporation to which he *belongs* involves a perpetual exclusion of 'outsiders'; if challenged, he calls it 'loyalty'. Just as the programme commands for a computer may be effaced ('suppressed' in the jargon) from the screen or the print-out while remaining operative, so every discussion, draft, memo and decision at the MoD is 'commanded' by suppressed codes signalling the adversarial context. We tend to assume that it is the content of a document which is secret; far more secret, because more vulnerable, is the reason behind the decision to stamp it 'Secret'.

When a Tisdall or Ponting leaps out of the whale in the name of a more abstract loyalty, our civil servant instinctively knows that such conduct, however principled, makes life impossible. He stands naked; the laundry basket is open to the public. The Official Secrets

148

Act, for all its aberrant punitive power, is merely a doodle on the great unwritten code of psychological survivial.

A Freedom of Information Act is fine, but genuine 'freedom of information', a door truly open, must reveal, floor upon floor, corridor after corridor, desk after desk, rows of neon-lit people who can see (and breathe) only in the twilit stomach of the whale. Whatever analytical coherence we impose on our political system – ruling class, power élite, 'establishment' – the 200,000 people who are ingested every day into the offices of Whitehall are conspirators in an entirely different project: survival through obscurity; the comfort of corporate silence; membership of the sealed tank.

During the Ponting trial I was teaching in the Politics Department of Bristol University, a few yards down Woodlands Road, as it happened, from the heavy pile of reddish Victorian stone, decorated with a variety of ugly Gothic and Elizabethan conceits, which is Clive Ponting's old school. I asked my students whether they approved of what Ponting had done. Almost without exception, they approved. But what of the personal dimension, of the oath taken and the freely accepted code broken? The students shrugged: so what? 'Loyalty' struck them as a hypocritical mystification of political chicanery. But ten, twenty years on, won't they have embraced the strategies of silence?

NINE

In March 1984 Clive Ponting was pitched, at the age of thirty-eight, into the higher politics, the higher chicanery. Like nineteenth-century Russian serfs, we tend, indeed need, to believe that corruption is confined to the middle ranks, to hirelings and courtiers; if the incorruptible Tsar only knew about it, all would be instantly rectified. Ponting now discovered otherwise. On any evening of the week after he became head of DS5, a section of the Defence Ministry dealing with naval affairs, he could have entertained a dinner party with reports of blatant jobbery at the top: not only Stanley and Heseltine, but Thatcher as well. Nor was he merely a passive witness to the constant face-lifts and skin-grafts about the sinking of the *Belgrano*; his job was to assist at the operating table.

It proved too much for the young man on the flying trapeze. Leaving Bristol Grammar School with spectacular A-levels, he had gained a first in History at Reading before passing into the fast stream of the civil service in 1970. Soon he was transferred to the largest department in Whitehall, the Ministry of Defence, with a budget of £17 billion: a fortress surrounded by powerful lobbies – the Treasury, the armed services, the defence contractors, the secret services, peaceniks on motor cycles armed with spray guns.

Graduating from the Civil Service College, Ponting was promoted assistant principal in 1974. Here rank is what counts; the only dream is the next rung on the ladder.

In 1979 came Mrs Thatcher, determined to launch an immediate onslaught on waste in the civil service. To cut through red tape and departmental protectionism, she conscripted a super-efficient baron from private industry, Sir Derek Rayner, joint managing director of Marks & Spencer. Each department was instructed to lend him a principal for six months; Ponting was nominated by the MoD.

It was heady stuff. Rayner called his young aides to the Cabinet Office conference room overlooking St James's Park, and impishly distributed copies of *Your Disobedient Servant*, by Leslie Chapman, whose frustrated campaigns against wasteful spending had led him to disclose how Parliamentary committees were regularly misled by the Whitehall bureaucracy. Five years later Ponting, quivering on the narrow ledge, took down this book from his shelves. Chapman had been threatened with the Official Secrets Act, but not prosecuted.

Each of Rayner's young turks was given sixty days to report back. It wasn't glamorous work: touring obscure food depots to discover why the three services maintained separate channels of supply; visiting derelict barracks to find out why the three services maintained separate dental corps; and logging up yet more miles to ponder three independent musical training centres maintained by – again – the three armed services. Ponting produced a sixteen-page report detailing waste, incompetence and dismal lack of coordination. He reckoned £12 million could be saved immediately, and £4 million a year thereafter by eliminating the hoarding of stock.

Sir Derek Rayner was delighted. So was the Prime Minister. Rayner took Ponting and another young man on the flying trapeze to 10, Downing Street; they were led up to the first-floor study where sat Mrs Thatcher flanked by the Cabinet Secretary and her principal private secretary. 'You simply *must* tell the Cabinet all about it,' she declared. Two days later young Ponting found himself at the Cabinet table, spinning yarns about forgotten mountains of frozen pork.

Clive Ponting became one of Mrs Thatcher's blue-eyed boys. When the phone rang, it was the Order of the British Empire; and when she discovered that he was possibly being penalised for disloyalty to the vested interests at the MoD – he was put on 'gardening' leave – she intervened with a sharp order that Ponting be found a suitable job by the end of the week.

Ponting moved into the higher realms of policy-making when he was seconded to help Defence Secretary Francis Pym carry out a major, highly secretive, defence review designed to impose cost-cutting where it really hurt. But Ponting was already disenchanted; Raynerism was never implemented; Ponting's own proposals were shelved with the others; in 1981 he became a founder member of the Social Democratic Party. But this was not a disenchantment that he or his legal advisers cared to stress at his trial; asked what he thought of Government policy towards the civil service, he replied, 'I was completely in tune with it.' Had he experienced any difficulty in separating his own beliefs from his duties as a civil servant? Ponting's chin jutted, his angular profile a silhouette of English good sense.

'No, none at all.'

From time to time he glanced from the witness box towards the judge.

Had he supported the sending of the task force to the Falklands? 'I was all for it.'

'You're a member of the Buddhist Society in London?'

'Yes.'

'Did that affect your attitude towards your work?'

'Definitely not.'

Ponting is everyone's idea of a clean-cut, straight-up-and-down young public servant. Coolly intelligent, his brain chiselled into logical grids, he is neither 'intellectual' nor conspicuously introspective. A gentle Bristol brogue reminds one that this is where middle England is most stable, solid, public-spirited. The chin is lean, the nose a beacon of integrity, and when he smiles it starts in the eyes, as it should.

In March 1984 Clive Ponting was appointed head of the MoD's DS5, which deals with naval affairs: fishery protection, the Gulf war, the Falklands task force. The controversy over the sinking of the Argentine cruiser *General Belgrano* had been rumbling fitfully, undramatically, like a grumbling appendix, for over a year when Ponting sat behind his new desk in the cramped, shabby office allocated to the head of DS5. He had never given the *Belgrano* incident much thought. The name of Tam Dalyell meant little to him. But Ponting rapidly discovered that the Scottish MP, previously derided as the wild man of West Lothian, as an inconsequential maverick disowned by his own party, now haunted the ministerial corridors of the MoD. Dalyell resembled a fireship scattering the serene battle lines of the galleons; for at last he had allies of reputation, notably Arthur Gavshon, co-author of a book which appeared as Ponting took over DS5, *The Sinking of the Belgrano*.

Between Ponting and the Defence Secretary himself there prowled the irate, security-obsessed Minister for the Armed Services, John Stanley, a bullish Thatcherite who had served as Herself's parliamentary private secretary, then as Housing Minister, before moving to the MoD in 1983. Ponting recalls Stanley informing a departmental meeting that: 'Margaret Thatcher is too good for this country. The country does not deserve anybody so outstanding. She is the greatest leader this country has been privileged to have this century and that includes Winston Churchill.'

To paraphrase Bertolt Brecht, when the people lose the confidence of the government, then the government should dissolve the people and elect a new one.

Ponting's first duty as head of DS5 brought him straight to the storm centre. Working on a brief from Stanley, he was required to draft two alternative replies to a letter written by Denzil Davies, MP, on behalf of the Shadow Cabinet. To understand the issues and options, we must first take a short tour through the *Belgrano* incident and its aftermath.

It is not difficult, as I have discovered, to become immersed to the point of obsession in the detailed and conflicting evidence about the sinking of the *Belgrano* – the map references and navigational data, the interception of signals, the discrepancy between South Atlantic and British summer time; who knew what, or may have known, and when, and why – till knowledge and speculation tip into madness. But I shall impose a self-denying ordinance and attempt to identify the bare bones of the matter.

The first hostilities of the Falklands war – leaving aside the original Argentinian invasion – and the first casualties occurred on 1 May 1982, when British planes bombed the airfield at Port Stanley. Round the Falklands the British had imposed (or at least announced) a 200-mile exclusion zone; any Argentinian vessel or plane entering that space would be regarded as hostile. To the south, outside the exclusion zone, a British nuclear submarine, HMS *Conqueror*, was shadowing an old American warship, renamed the *General Belgrano* after she was acquired by the Argentine, plodding through the South Atlantic at 11 knots with her two escorts. At 16.00 local time, 20.00 London time, on Sunday, 2 May, *Conqueror*, acting on orders from British naval headquarters at Northwood in Middlesex, fired three torpedoes, two of which struck the cruiser and sank her. The death toll was 368. It is not in dispute that this action had been authorised by Mrs Thatcher and her War Cabinet, meeting at Chequers around lunch time that Sunday afternoon.

Not only had the *Belgrano* remained consistently outside the British exclusion zone, she had also been sailing due west, away from the task force and towards her home base at Staten Island, for fully eleven hours before she was hit by the *Conqueror*'s torpedoes. We know that the Argentine naval command had sent two signals to its own fleet, at 20.07 (local time) on 1 May and, in confirmation, at 01.19 on 2 May, ordering its ships to head for home. Certainly the first and possibly the second of these signals had been intercepted, de-coded and lodged at Northwood before Admiral Sir Terence Lewin, Chief of the Defence Staff, set out for Chequers to convince fellow members of the War Cabinet that all enemy ships were now a threat, regardless of their temporary course or location, inside or outside the exclusion zone, and should be sunk at the first opportunity. The War Cabinet concurred. It gave the Navy *carte blanche*.

The *Belgrano* was wallowing in waves nine to twelve feet high in freezing temperatures with intermittent fog. The first torpedo hit on the port side, at the operations centre amidships, blasting upwards through four thick steel decks. The second torpedo struck four seconds later, 15 metres from the prow, ripping the bows clean away from the hull. The cruiser's captain later estimated that of the 368 men he lost out of 1,138, probably 338 died instantly. Those who found themselves in the sea suffered rapid hypothermia in an icy wind howling across the waves at 50 kilometres an hour.

Men torn apart, men stiffening into corpses even before they drown. Eight thousand miles away, what Raymond Williams has called 'the culture of distance' – toy ships laid out on pretty models in a television studio. The War Cabinet which gave the Navy *carte blanche* also made sure that we translated the scream of death into a remote board-game; only a small number of hand-picked reporters were allowed to accompany the task force (not a single foreign journalist among them); this number did not include Britain's best war photographer, Don McCullin, whose application was rejected. All despatches were censored by Fleet HQ at Northwood and by vetters in the MoD. When two British ships were calamitously sunk in Fitzroy Bay, the pictures of soldiers turned into human torches were allowed to reach London only after hostilities had ended. Instead of reality the MoD gave us a 'spokesman', a strange Dalek called MacDonald, behind whose robotic communiqués lurked a fiendish joy: as if his whole upbringing and training, his deepest notions of patriotism, were at last fulfilled by *not* disclosing the truth to a huge, national audience.

We gaped at the war like boys peering into the wham-bang

screens in an amusement arcade. When we come to consider how the Government subsequently lied about the sinking of the *Belgrano*, we should not forget that the strategy of disinformation was launched with the task force. The 368 dead crewmen of the Argentine cruiser were instantly translated into a faintly regrettable statistic; they neither choked nor howled – unless we turned to the opening sequence of William Golding's novel, *Pincher Martin* or, less distinguished as literature but true to life and death, Nicholas Monsarrat's *The Cruel Sea*.

And what of Mrs Thatcher? The shooting war was a week old, and the 368 casualties of the *Belgrano* only six days dead, when she told the Scottish Conservative conference:

'What really thrilled me – having spent so much of my lifetime in Parliament talking about things like inflation, social security benefits, housing problems, environmental problems and so on – is that when it really comes to the test what thrilled people weren't these things. What thrilled people was once again being able to serve a great cause, the cause of freedom.'

By means of war. Two months later, celebrating victory before the Tory faithful gathered at Cheltenham race course, she shared her joy with theirs that freedom and the right of self-determination had again been upheld by 'the nation that had built an empire and ruled a quarter of the world'.

Two days after the sinking of the *Belgrano*, the Defence Secretary, Mr John Nott, announced that the Argentine cruiser had been 'closing on elements of the task force'. Nine days later Nott informed the Commons that there had been 'every indication that the *General Belgrano* group was manoeuvring to a position from which to attack our surface vessels'. As the challenge to this version mounted and contrary evidence accumulated, Government spokesmen became more vague and more evasive. On 29 November and again in December, Mr Peter Blaker, Minister for the Armed Forces, replied to Tam Dalyell, MP, that the *Belgrano* and her escorts had been attempting to complete a 'pincer movement' from the south and that the ships' movements had been 'consistent with a threat to the task force'.

As the year passed Tam Dalyell began to accumulate a pile of suppressed information which he regularly shot across the floor of the House. Ministers became irritable. On 24 March 1983 Jerry Wiggin, a junior minister at the MoD, told Dalyell that all his facts and assertions were 'utterly wrong'. During the subsequent election campaign Mrs Thatcher offered hostages to fortune when she declared on 24 May, during the BBC's phone-in programme *On the Spot*, that 'It [the *Belgrano*] was not sailing away from the Falklands' at the time it was attacked.

But the Government's mendacity was not confined to the question of the *Belgrano*'s course and position before she was torpedoed. Also concealed was the fact that HMS *Conqueror* had been shadowing the cruiser for thirty hours without taking action – a fact which does not indicate an overwhelmingly urgent danger in the mind of the submarine's commander. Nott had originally informed the Commons that the sighting and sinking of the *Belgrano* were virtually simultaneous – at 20.00 London time. The Government White Paper of December 1982 repeated this claim. But on 13 July 1983 Lady Young, a Foreign Office Minister, told the Lords that security reasons forbade disclosure as to when the cruiser had first been detected.

Nott's disinformation went even further. He had himself attended the Cabinet meeting which authorised the sinking of the *Belgrano* (and any other Argentine ships found on the high seas). This decision had twice been signalled to *Conqueror* (whose first reaction was to seek confirmation in view of the intended target's course and position). Yet Nott had told the Commons that, 'The actual decision to launch a torpedo was clearly one taken by the submarine commander.' However, in July the commander himself, Captain Christopher Wreford Brown, sailed home to Faslane on the Clyde, and revealed enough of the truth to 'undo the Nott'. It emerged that Wreford Brown himself had not even requested authority to sink the *Belgrano*, although the task force commander, Admiral Sandy Woodward, apparently fearing the 'pincer movement' Mr Blaker later alluded to, had indeed made such a request to Northwood at 02.00 on 2 May.

By the time Clive Ponting took over DS5 in March 1984 the historiographical argument over this single episode was assuming serious political proportions. Arthur Gavshon and Desmond Rice, having submitted a long list of questions to the MoD – the answers to which Mr John Stanley censored or suppressed – published their impressively documented book, *The Sinking of The Belgrano*. Not only was Tam Dalyell, autodidact extraordinary, constantly on the warpath, but the Shadow Cabinet had at last weighed in with questions of their own.

What emerges beyond question is that Lewin and the Royal Navy craved a quick kill. For this there were two main reasons. First, war is war, distances were enormous (8,000 miles), communications intermittent, the risks and perils formidable, anxiety on behalf of the task force acute, and the desire to inflict a pre-emptive blow virtually axiomatic to the naval mind. Lewin (talkative in retirement, as is often the case with men who have enjoyed power) himself has admitted as much in recent interviews. On 2 October 1984 he told the *Guardian* that if the Prime Minister had asked him to delay the attack on the *Belgrano* because of sensitive diplomatic negotiations in progress, he 'would have said yes,' that the Navy would have 'not as good a chance as we have now' of hitting her, 'but a reasonable chance, because once a nuclear sub is hooked into a surface ship, it should be able to tail her'. Lewin had earlier told the *Sunday Mirror*: 'I said we could not wait. Here was an opportunity to knock off a major unit of the Argentine fleet.'

The second reason for the Royal Navy's craving for a quick kill was political rather than operational: paradoxically the admirals were at war with the Prime Minister and the Secretary of State for Defence over the very cost-cutting exercise in which young Clive Ponting had been involved when he worked for Nott's predecessor, Francis Pym, on the draconian and furiously contested naval review. In June 1981 Nott had announced ferocious economies in the naval budget and building programme: one carrier was to be sold, another scrapped, frigates and destroyers were to be mothballed; Chatham and Gibraltar dockyards were to be closed, Portsmouth run down. Too late the Navy discovered, like the white Rhodesians whom Ponting's father admired, that Mrs Thatcher was not, after all, the great white hope. She preferred nuclear missiles and American-built Tridents to the old-fashioned notions of the admirals with 'their fucking floating gin palaces' (in Nott's memorable phrase).

As a result of the naval war in the South Atlantic, which was precipitated by Argentine fury over the sinking of the *Belgrano* outside the British exclusion zone, the sailors got back most of their fucking floating gin palaces. Indeed the more of them they lost, the more they would get. Two days after the *Belgrano* went down the Argentine air force sank HMS *Sheffield* with an Exocet missile. This ship was followed by *Ardent, Antelope, Coventry, Sir Galahad, Atlantic Conveyor* and *Sir Tristram*. By the time Port Stanley was re-taken 255 British servicemen, and many more Argentinians, were dead; 777 British soldiers and sailors were wounded.

It would be grotesque to suggest that Lewin and the incensed admirals wanted to lose a navy in order to regain a navy – or that they rejoiced in these losses. What is clear is that the war meant more to them than the recovery of the Falklands; equally clear is the almost complete dependence of the War Cabinet on Lewin's advice once Mrs Thatcher staked her whole career on recovering the islands by force. As she later put it: 'If ministers had sought to monitor every development in the tactical disposition of forces on both sides and tried to control every engagement in detail from London, the results would have been disastrous.'

That is standard doctrine. But to sink a cruiser with over 1,100 men on board well outside one's own proclaimed exclusion zone, and no declaration of war between the two nations, is a major decision with enormous consequences, political and diplomatic as well as military, for which a Prime Minister must take full responsibility. It was her job to ensure that she was properly briefed and that the latest signals data was at her disposal. In a letter to Dr David Owen, dated 9 October 1984, Mrs Thatcher said she had not known the *Belgrano*'s actual course until November 1982. She should have known. It is beyond challenge that a signal from *Conqueror*, giving her course and position, was sent at 15.00 London time, decoded and understood at Northwood by 15.40, then passed to the Ministry of Defence. That was more than four hours before the submarine fired her torpedoes. Clive Ponting writes: 'What happened next? Nothing. . . . The Royal Navy had been given the political authority for an all-out attack on the Argentine Navy . . . . '

As for the mendacity which finally provoked Ponting to rebel against his upbringing, his training and every consideration of ambition, if Mrs Thatcher knew the truth in November 1982 why did she insist the following May, in the pre-election radio programme, 'It was not sailing away from the Falklands'? The answer does not demonstrably reside in her claim to David Owen in October 1984 that the cruiser 'could have changed course again . . . .'

Ponting was charged by John Stanley with a shoddy assignment: to prepare for the Prime Minister two alternative draft replies to the Shadow Cabinet (Denzil Davies). One draft was to admit that the *Belgrano* had been sighted on 1 May; the other, not. Ponting submitted a draft, dated 16 March 1984, which indicates how deftly the civil service mind separates truth from duty. To admit that the *Belgrano* had been sighted on 1 May, he noted, would merely encourage Tam Dalyell in his allegations that the cruiser had been sunk for political reasons. And, he went on: 'It's a difficult judgment how much information can be released about the sighting on 1 May. An admission made under pressure might only increase the pressure for further disclosures.' Naturally this was read to the jury by the prosecution at Ponting's trial; and subsequently by Defence Secretary Heseltine to the Commons.

Ponting's alternative (and preferred) draft admitted the 1 May sighting but argued that the *Belgrano*'s course was not relevant since she posed an inherent threat to the task force.

On 23 March Heseltine's private secretary informed Ponting in writing that the Secretary of State wanted to study the 'implications of a more forthcoming approach' – would 'the line to be taken' in replying to Denzil Davies affect the 'line to be taken' when answering Tam Dalyell? Heseltine had ordered an in-depth review of the entire episode, fearing that there might be 'a Watergate in this' – or an 'Underwatergate', as Ponting's counsel, Bruce Laughland, later quipped. It became Ponting's task to assemble all the signals and other secret data in a precise chronology of events subsequently known as the 'Crown Jewels'. Their contents were not disclosed in open court and when the Commons Committee on Foreign Affairs was finally allowed to inspect them on 6 March 1985 – solely as a result of Ponting's actions – it was under a vow of secrecy with no notes to be taken. They will now know, as the twelve ordinary men and women who formed the Ponting jury know, that the 'Crown Jewels', marked 'TOP SECRET/UMBRA/HVCCO UK EYES ONLY/' (which refers to signals intercepted and de-coded by GCHQ Cheltenham), provide no evidence of a planned Argentinian naval pincer movement against the British task force.

A top-level meeting took place in the MoD on 30 March 1984, which Ponting attended. Heseltine was lounging on his leather sofa, feet up, flipping through the 'Crown Jewels', a large map of the South Atlantic spread across the floor. Stanley insisted that the whole dossier remained classified and that no information should be disclosed. Ponting pointed out that the commander of the *Conqueror* had long ago spilt the beans; if the material was genuinely classified, ought not the gallant Wreford Brown therefore to be prosecuted? Everyone shuddered: unthinkable. Heseltine remarked that after the Sarah Tisdall case he had no stomach for another Official Secrets Act prosecution (though his stomach later turned over neatly enough after Ponting leaked two documents to Dalyell). Throughout the meeting Tam Dalyell was heard barking outside the door.

The upshot was that the Prime Minister replied to Denzil Davies on 4 April admitting that the *Belgrano* had first been sighted on 1 May (in fact the cruiser had been picked up on *Conqueror*'s sonar on 30 April) but stressing the 'pincer movement' danger and the general danger: so all was explained.

There remained the matter of Dalyell's unanswered letter to Heseltine, dated 19 March. On 12 April, Ponting sent Heseltine an advisory memo, in which he set down the *Belgrano*'s course during the fifteen hours before she was sunk, showing that she had reversed direction eleven hours before being attacked and had held to a course virtually due west thereafter. But it seems that Ponting also advised that although the British Navy had failed to monitor the movements of Argentina's most feared warship, the aircraft carrier *25 de Mayo*, this should not be disclosed in order to protect the 'pincer movement' theory. Heseltine sought to turn this advice against Ponting, after his acquittal, during the Commons debate of 19 February 1985. Ponting, he said, had advised that Dalyell should be told that the other questions in his letter 'all concern operation and intelligence matter on which I [i.e. Heseltine] am not prepared to comment'. Reading this to the packed House, Heseltine remarked: 'These are not my words, they are Mr Ponting's words.'

Obviously this touches Ponting on the raw. In his book he comments: 'The time for analysis was short. The initial draft reply to Tam Dalyell's letter attached to the "Crown Jewels" could not be cleared with intelligence staff in the time before it had to be sent to Heseltine. It was therefore a cautious reply not giving away information.'

One is struck by the fact that Ponting's draft was written three weeks after Heseltine's private secretary alerted him to the need to answer Dalyell. In fact Ponting's break with the MoD's tradition of euphemism and evasion stopped well short of a total commitment to Parliament's full 'Right to Know'.

On 18 April Heseltine sent a stone-waller to Dalyell: he could not usefully add to what the Prime Minister had told Davies. Ponting was indignant; he went to see Heseltine's private secretary about it and learned that John Stanley had again intervened. He was also informed, fairly forcefully, that he was making a nuisance of himself.

It was now, six days later, that Ponting made a move not disclosed by the prosecution during the trial. On 24 April he sent Dalyell on anonymous note in which he told the Member for Lin-lithgow (previously West Lothian) that the answers to his questions were unclassified and that he should press them. 'Dear Mr Dalyell,' Ponting wrote, 'I cannot give you my name but I can tell you that I have full access to exactly what happened to the *Belgrano*.' The letter went on to suggest specific questions that Dalyell should put to Heseltine, including, 'Did the change in the rules of engagement on 2 May [1982] refer only to the *Belgrano*? Did they go wider?' The letter ended: 'You are on the right tack. Keep going.'

Dalyell bounced back with a further letter to Heseltine, dated 1 May, insisting on answers to his questions. The matter was again referred to Ponting, who wrote a strong memo urging that Dalyell be answered 'in accordance with the normal rules for answering PQs [Parliamentary questions] . . . . ' But Stanley warned Heseltine that he would be in deep water if he followed this advice. Ponting comments: 'None of my superiors intervened; I received no support from anybody else in the Ministry.'

On 14 May Heseltine wrote curtly to Dalyell: 'Your purpose in asking the questions you put to me is to pursue your campaign that the *Belgrano* was attacked in order to destroy the prospects for peace negotiations rather than for the military reason that she posed a threat to the Task Force.'

Clearly influenced by Ponting's unsigned note, Dalyell replied on 27 May: 'Was it on the advice of your officials that the questions I posed in my letter have not been answered? I would be surprised if it were so, since I have a high regard for the industry and integrity of Ministry of Defence officials. . . .' It was an indiscreet comment (Heseltine had not sheltered behind his officials) which might have put Dalyell's source in jeopardy. Listening to the Crown's counsel, Roy Amlot, QC, read this passage aloud in court was like watching a cat staring at a saucer of cream beyond the window pane.[1]

On 11 June Heseltine again wrote to Dalyell justifying his refusal to answer questions not only on security grounds but also in terms of the Labour MP's determination to prove that the *Belgrano* had been sunk to sabotage the Peruvian peace proposals of 1–2 May 1982. Later, at the Old Bailey, Mr Amlot was to translate Heseltine's fears of disclosure into an eloquent metaphor: 'Marvellous ammunition for Mr Dalyell.'

But it is an odd doctrine to toss at an MP. May we imagine a Treasury minister withholding unemployment statistics, or bankruptcy figures, or the monthly balance of payments, in these terms: 'No, I'm not giving you any marvellous ammunition with which to attack our general economic strategy.'

The Peruvian peace proposals (of which more later) clearly represent in the *Belgrano* affair the same 'bottom line' as the alleged collusion between the *Guardian* and the Government over the second Tisdall document. Just as Preston would admit virtually everything except that act of collusion, so Her Majesty's Government has been forced into a steady retreat about the events of 2 May 1982 until backed up against the wall of the Peruvian peace proposals. There Mr Heseltine makes his stand.

For a couple of months the sunken wreck of the *Belgrano* receded from Ponting's desk as he busied himself with the danger to shipping from the Gulf war between Iran and Iraq. But early in July the pace was raised again when the MoD received a request from the Commons Foreign Affairs Committee for the full list of changes made in the Rules of Engagement (ROE) during the Falklands war. Ponting says he was convinced that it was perfectly feasible to meet the Committee's request – though he had earlier warned his ministers that full disclosure would reveal: (a) that Britain had issued no public warning about the ROE changes until 7 May, five days after the War Cabinet decided to sink everything in sight; (b) that a note of warning, dated 1 May 1982, from Foreign Secretary Pym and Attorney General Havers about the illegality of such

[1]Dalyell evidently sensed that Ponting's anonymous note to him of 24 April might come to light, for at this juncture of the court proceedings he passed me a note: 'David, if they are suggesting Ponting told me to ask about the RoE it is not so: *I* conceived the idea of asking about RoE. . . .' See p. 182.

action, might now come to light – a warning which had been both ignored and suppressed.

The ministers now sought the advice of two departments, Ponting's DS5, and DS11. On 8 July Michael Legge, head of DS11, wrote the famous minute which Ponting leaked to Dalyell eight days later, thus exposing the MoD's entire strategy and precipitating *l'affaire Ponting*. This grisly document deserves quotation:

> In addition [wrote Legge] a full list of [ROE] changes would provide more information than Ministers have been prepared to reveal so far about the *Belgrano* affair. For instance, the list of changes in the period 2 April – 2 May would show that the engagement of the Argentine aircraft carrier *25 de Mayo* outside the Total Exclusion Zone was permitted from 30 April, and that the change on 2 May was not restricted to *Belgrano* but included all Argentine warships over a large area. It would also reveal that while the public warnings and ROE changes for the MEZ and TEZ[1] were simultaneous there was a delay until 7 May before the appropriate warning was issued for the 2 May change. I therefore recommend that we avoid these difficulties by providing the Committee with a more general narrative . . . .

Every line of which speaks of political calculation rather than security considerations, although in fairness Legge had prefaced his recommendations with the view that the Rules of Engagement remained classified and were drawn 'from the Fleet Operating and Tactical Instructions which is a classified document'.

Clive Ponting believed that the information requested by the Foreign Affairs Committee was not classified and says he indicated as much to his own subordinate in DS5, Nicholas Darms. It seems that neither Darms nor Legge agreed with him. This is an episode to which I shall later return.

In the event Heseltine decided to provide the Foreign Affairs Committee with only a partial, highly selective list of ROE. Alone with his anger, Ponting pitched himself into the void, anonymously posting two documents under plain cover to Tam Dalyell: Legge's minute and a copy of his own earlier draft advising Heseltine to answer Dalyell truthfully. This was later published in the *New Statesman* on 24 August under the title, 'The letter Heseltine never sent'.

In fact Ponting provided Dalyell with only page 1 of his draft

[1]The Maritime Exclusion Zone (declared on 7 April 1982) referred to ships only. The Total Exclusion Zone (declared on 30 April) referred to both ships and aircraft.

advice to the Defence Secretary, answering six of the questions presented by Dalyell. These covered the first detection of the *Belgrano*, the first visual contact, the course the cruiser followed while shadowed by *Conqueror*, her speed when attacked, and why Mark 8 torpedoes had been used instead of Mark 24s. Ponting did not despatch page 2 of his own draft, which contained *refusals* to answer three of Dalyell's questions. These concerned: (a) the timing and nature of signals between naval headquarters at Northwood and the submarine on 2 May; (b) HMS *Splendid*'s search for the aircraft carrier *25 de Mayo*; and (c) the information gleaned from satellite surveillance of the carrier. It seems that Ponting shared the MoD's determination to keep Dalyell in ignorance of the fact that *Splendid* had never found the carrier – a nail in the coffin of the long-serving theory that the British task force was imminently threatened by an Argentine pincer movement from both the north (the carrier) and the south (the *Belgrano*).

On receiving this manna from Heaven, Dalyell made a copy and then passed the two documents to the Tory chairman of the Foreign Affairs Committee, Sir Anthony Kershaw, who, having consulted colleagues, repaid the service by handing back the two documents to Heseltine in person, together with the envelope – but not before the Committee had noted their contents and Kershaw had extracted a promise that Heseltine would appear before the Committee to offer an explanation. Heseltine promptly called in the MoD police.

The perspicacious may detect here a certain overlap between Kershaw's behaviour and Peter Preston's. Admittedly Kershaw went voluntarily to the Defence Secretary, documents in hand, while Preston returned a memorandum written by Heseltine only under legal duress. What joins the two is a willingness to use the revelatory material received while regarding the source of the leak with suspicion; it will be recalled that although the *Guardian* used the content of the second Tisdall document in its pages, the 'kitchen cabinet' also behaved as if the source of such a disclosure might not be 'altruistic', not 'as white as all that' – and possibly a security risk. Dalyell himself was shocked by Kershaw's behaviour, as is Ponting:

> I think it's a strange thing for a Chairman of a select committee which has just been misled to hand back the documents which showed how they had been deceived. It raises questions of the independence of Parliament from the executive.

It does indeed – though Kershaw would no doubt argue that under the law Parliament is not in business to receive classified documents against the wishes of ministers.

Ponting was then detected by forensic deductions similar to those which snared Sarah Tisdall. Eventually he confessed – another subject to which we shall return – to Detective Chief Inspector Hughes and Detective Inspector Broome, of the MoD police. He told them:

I did this because I believe ministers within this department were not prepared to answer legitimate questions from an MP about a matter of public concern, simply in order to protect their position.

Hughes is a florid, balding man who might be on his way to the greyhound races. Broome, the younger of the pair, dapper, less articulate, his feet planted wide in the witness box, offered a dead bat to defence counsel's yorkers. Both officers sat out much of the two-week trial, in smartly pressed suits, at the proverbial taxpayer's expense.

TEN

The decision to prosecute Clive Ponting was a political one. It reflected the present Government's punitive style, its determination to punish dissent, to bludgeon the civil service into obedience. Only one of the documents that Ponting leaked was classified and posed no threat – by the Crown's admission – to that sacred cow, 'national security'. From 1916 to 1979 there had been only 34 prosecutions under section 2 of the Official Secrets Act; hurling himself into the record books, Sir Michael Havers authorised 16 prosecutions during his first five years as Attorney General.

Following Ponting's confession, a senior civil servant in the MoD, Sir Ewen Broadbent, made the journey to Heseltine's Oxfordshire home on 13 August. He told the Secretary of State that Ponting's motive was unclear; that he had recently gone through a 'bad patch' in his private life and had taken up Buddhism; and that grounds for prosecution might be 'somewhat shaky'. On the other hand, given the recent Tisdall case, it might not look good if Ponting, a

163

much more senior civil servant than Sarah Tisdall, were simply allowed to resign.

Heseltine, with or without his feet up on the sofa – we don't know, it not being recorded in the minute of the meeting leaked to Neil Kinnock – commented that the prosecution of Sarah Tisdall had been absolutely right and that the prosecution of Clive Ponting would be equally right. But it was up to the law officers, of course.

Of course: the decision was for the Attorney General to take. Responding to a storm of criticism after Ponting's acquittal, Sir Michael Havers issued a statement:

> I was telephoned on 17 August and I was told the Director of Public Prosecutions and the Solicitor General advised prosecution. I concurred. I did not consult with any other Minister nor was the view of any other Minister conveyed to me before a decision was taken.

Yet Mr John Stanley is known to have telephoned Mrs Thatcher, then holidaying abroad; and not long after the decision to prosecute Ponting was taken – in which she had no part, she says; in which Heseltine had no part, he says – the Prime Minister's press secretary and brillo pad, Mr Bernard Ingham, remarked to colleagues that Ponting deserved a 'hanging judge' in the mould of the great Jeffreys – just a joke, of course, but one for which the Lord Chancellor had to rebuke Mr Ingham.

Nothing stimulates the desire for vengeance so acutely as a sense of betrayal. Clive Ponting was no ordinary civil servant, but one of Mrs Thatcher's blue-eyed-boys, waste-saver extraordinary, OBE: hadn't she intervened on his behalf when the MoD put him on gardening leave?

So Ponting was prosecuted under section 2, the most discredited piece of legislation in the statute book, shredded a decade earlier by the Franks Report, attacked by Havers himself and Leon Brittan when in Opposition, and later dismantled in the Tory Government's own, abortive, Protection of Information Bill (1979), under which only documents marked Top Secret or Secret were to be the subject of criminal prosecution. Yet the Legge minute leaked by Ponting was merely classified 'Confidential'.

No doubt the Attorney General and the DPP expected a repeat of the Tisdall trial: a meek plea of Guilty, no jury in sight, all over in half a day – *pour encourager les autres*. But Ponting, who had been led to believe by MoD officials that a letter of resignation would probably suffice, struck back, devoting all his waking hours during the next five months to the preparation of a devastating counter-attack, invoking in his own defence the entire MoD documentation on the sinking of the *Belgrano* and the subsequent manoeuvres to mask the truth about it.

Late in the day Heseltine decided that the expurgated version of the 'Crown Jewels' requested by the defence would not be acceptable: it must be the full version or nothing. His purpose, we may assume, was twofold. He wanted to pre-empt the argument that a version of the 'Crown Jewels' purged of classified signals data could have been presented to the Foreign Affairs Committee; and he wanted to impress on Ponting's jury that protection of classified military information – the safety of our boys must come first – lay at the heart of the Government's policy of non-disclosure. No doubt he expected any jury to be beguiled by the mumbo-jumbo of the 'UK EYES ONLY' syndrome.

There was a third dividend: part of the trial would now be held *in camera* before a vetted jury, despite an Early Day Motion of protest from more than fifty MPs. Jury selection by the Crown (gerrymandering with common law) goes back to the eighteenth century,[1] while jury-vetting in its modern form has been practised in Britain since at least the early 1940s (although, such is the endemic national tradition of secrecy, the only official admission of the practice related, in deep retrospect, to the trial of the Soviet spy George Blake). In 1980 Havers announced new guidelines for security-sensitive cases, allowing for the weeding out of jurors with 'extreme political beliefs', a term very sagely undefined. The Chartists and suffragettes were all extremists in their time, not to mention Jesus and Gandhi and just about every leader of national resistance to British imperialism. On 21 January 1985 the DPP, assisted by the Special Branch, began sifting potential jurors for the Ponting case. Among those who came through unchallenged was a Labour councillor for the Islington ward of Clerkenwell, even though Islington Council had passed a resolution the previous October fully supporting the borough's own Clive Ponting.

The defence began the trial with some weeding of its own, challenging three ladies no longer young who, Ponting surmised, were 'so clearly of a similar type' that they might form 'a little social group and all vote the same way.' The three ladies sat together in a bemused huddle after being pounced on, victims of a suspicion they could not unravel.

Vetted or not, a modern urban jury is regarded by police, prosecution and judges as a highly unreliable body. Since 1977 every voter has been eligible for jury service (apart from convicts and the medically certified) thus removing the old, dependable image of the juror as a middle-aged householder with a built-in respect for

[1] See various essays in E. P. Thompson's *Writing by Candlelight*, Merlin, 1980.

authority, for 'them'. Jury acquittals have risen from 39 per cent in 1965 to 56 per cent in 1976; on several occasions juries have spectacularly defied the judge's directives, despite the imposing paraphernalia of the court, the wigs, gowns, ponderous entrances, officials bowing to the judge as they back out of the courtroom like lackeys in an eighteenth-century opera – all of which may serve to humble the jury into compliance before the arguments are absorbed. It was therefore a good omen for the defence that some of the younger male jurors at the Ponting trial regularly appeared without jacket and tie – but such speculative type-casting is always idle.

Mr Justice McCowan readily agreed, against defence objections, that part of the proceedings should be held *in camera*; as the week passed it became clear that this was a judge *plus royaliste que la reine*. Thus journalists and public were repeatedly chased from the courtroom, the glass windows in the doors were boarded up, and for twenty-five minutes the chamber was swept for the bugging devices we had thoughtfully secreted in the wigs of the QCs. Meanwhile, back in Islington, Mr Ponting's mail was being opened and his telephone tapped throughout the trial.

The *in camera* strategy is designed not only to keep the public in ignorance of crucial evidence, but also to prevent the press from exposing the arbitary, and often absurd, criteria for classifying documents. It is not the 'secrets' that are secret, but the concealed code of official secrecy. A trial held behind closed doors, moreover, is an *a priori* judicial endorsement of ministerial prerogative. In a trial such as Ponting's two sets of values confront one another: the prevailing mystique of closely guarded knowledge as vital to 'national security'; and the argument that this elaborately woven fabric is merely an altar cloth draped over a pile of chicanery, a blinding of Parliament and people to persistent executive malpractice. By withdrawing behind closed doors Crown and judge structure the proceedings in a theatrical affirmation of the ruling values – rather as if a football referee decided to wear the same coloured shirt as one of the teams and took a few of their free kicks as well. The twelve ordinary citizens of the jury are abducted into two weeks' honorary membership of the inner establishment: Privy Councillors, almost. Summing up for the prosecution in the closing stages of the trial, Mr Roy Amlot, QC, reminded the jurors that they were now privy to secret information known to few of their fellow citizens – the implication being that this privilege entailed a grateful, acquiescent verdict. But a 'privy' is also an old term for an outside lavatory.

Now this – as both prosecution and judge insisted – was not a political trial: there is no such thing in Britain. But no one was fooled, not even the prosecution and judge: the Government was

manifestly appearing dressed as the 'Crown', the invisible Mrs
Thatcher as the invisible 'Regina'. The more Mr Amlot insisted
that politics had nothing to do with it, only the law, only our
constitutional conventions, only a civil servant's absolute duty to
his ministers, the more Mr Amlot plunged, day after day, into a
total justification of everything the Government had done, and not
done, since the task force reached the South Atlantic at the end of
April 1982. Yet there was no sign in court of the politicians and
admirals who had made the decisions: no Thatcher, no Lewin, no
Nott, no Woodward, no Heseltine, no raving Stanley. It was the
civil servants who were despatched to suffer cross-examination.
'Where are the ministers, where are the invisible men?' asked Bruce
Laughland, QC. 'Hardly the spirit of the Falklands.'

ELEVEN

Both Tisdall and Ponting, decent, upright children of solid West
Country homes, failed a vital test of character when they leaked
their documents: they shrank from resigning, from instantly putting
their rebellion on record, from taking the consequences. They lay
low, hoping to escape detection.

This stricture is not universally accepted. 'A prep school moral
issue,' one colleague assured me in the corridors of the Old Bailey.
After all, against a powerful, ruthless state system guerrilla warfare
cannot shackle itself with the arcane morality of *Tom Brown's School-
days* or *Stalky & Co*. And in Sarah Tisdall's case it would have
required remarkable audacity for a very young and junior Foreign
Office clerk to have pitched herself into the headlines. She could
scarcely have called a press conference; and had she presented
herself, anew, at the *Guardian*'s reception desk to offer an interview,
I can think of several gentleman on the first floor who might have
panicked. Nevertheless, Sarah Tisdall should have resigned immediately after she knew what she had done, made a statement to her
employers, and sent a copy to the newspaper.

It is much more than an issue of prep school morality. The
personal conduct of the rebel inevitably affects our view of his cause.
Bruce Laughland's first move in court, before the jury had been

called and sworn, was to urge the judge to rule as inadmissible evidence the whole episode of Ponting's prevarication to the MoD police. 'He did prevaricate,' Laughland admitted, 'and this is not greatly to this credit. But that is not the issue.' In short, he didn't want the jury to know about it. The prosecution did not agree; nor did Mr Justice McCowan. Laughland was left with no alternative but to challenge and discredit the evidence of the two police officers, Hughes and Broome, who interviewed Ponting and extracted his confession.

It would surprise me if Laughland was not acutely aware of how major a role this issue of personal conduct had played in the Tisdall case. 'She didn't confess till the game was up,' chided Mr Justice Cantley. 'In the meantime she put her colleagues under suspicion.' Having passed the documents to the *Guardian* on 21 October, Sarah Tisdall was still prevaricating on 6 January, by which time three colleagues in the Foreign Office Registry were suffering intensive questioning. 'What evidence have you got?' she had challenged Superintendent Hardy, 'others could have done it.' In the Court of Appeal, Lord Chief Justice Lane fastened his moral jaws into this aspect of her conduct as tenaciously as Cantley, quoting another of her remarks to the police: 'If I did know who had done it I would have told you.' Only on 9 January did she 'lift the cloud of suspicion from her colleagues'.

As a result a broad spectrum of the press dubbed her a 'mole'. This is quite wrong and Sarah Tisdall herself resents the term: a 'mole' is an official who systematically works from within on behalf of an outside party or foreign power. Nevertheless, the epithet is not ridiculous when applied to someone who lies low and hopes to keep her job.

Ponting faced the same problem in court. He admitted, with hindsight, that he should have resigned, but under cross-examination his rational, legalistic brain went on grinding out logic-chopping quibbles about the style and timing of his confession, long after he should have turned to the jury and said, 'I was not as courageous as I might have been. I regret it.'

The prosecution claimed that the Government's handling of the *Belgrano* affair was 'not the issue'; Laughland argued that the circumstances of Ponting's detection and confession were 'not the issue'; yet the prosecution had to devote hours in court to defending its record while Laughland's confrontation with the police officers Hughes and Broome seemed at the time a desperate business. Ponting's initial failure to resign created a damaging moral equation.

According to Detective Chief Inspector Hughes, Ponting said to him: 'I can see there is a strong circumstantial case against me but honestly I did not do it.' Laughland challenged Hughes on this, just as he challenged the reality of Ponting's reported exclamation, 'Good God, you don't suspect *me*! . . . honestly I did not do it.' Again we see the formidable force of the logic: if a man can lie about one thing he can lie about everything; if a man reveals lack of principle in his personal conduct how can he claim to defend the 'national interest'? Should we heed Sarah Tisdall's strictures about Heseltine's sneaky, 'back door' manoeuvres if she herself resorted to self-serving secrecy?

Hughes did not claim that Ponting had ever pointed to a colleague as the likely culprit, but he did insist that Ponting had said, 'It may have been someone upstairs before it [the Legge minute] was put away and filed.' Realising how much was at stake, Laughland launched a general attack on Hughes's 'memory' and note-taking procedures, scoring heavily when he asked the police officer why the relevant page of his notebook contained a doodle of a sinking cruiser. Hughes stood pole-axed. One of the jurors then asked to see the notebook but the judge wouldn't allow it.

Ponting argued that he didn't confess when first approached by the MoD police because he wanted to ascertain that the matter would be resolved by administrative means alone. I asked him about this a few weeks after the trial:

Question: If you had gone undetected, did you expect to continue at your post, or in the civil service?

Ponting: I didn't expect to be continuing indefinitely. The reason I didn't resign immediately was that I expected to be moving anyway, within a foreseeable time.

Question: Presumably you were reluctant to throw away your civil service career, or to be forced to leave without a sound letter of reference?

Ponting: Not worried about leaving the civil service, but I felt that if I was to resign it was important to find out what sort of reference I would get.

I am ill at ease with this: you can't say, under interrogation, 'I'll confess if you give me a good letter of reference, but I won't if you don't.' Besides, what sort of a reference could a civil servant who had leaked a classified document expect to get – one omitting all reference to that small event? In short, more self-serving secrecy?

Important moral choices normally involve a conflict of duties or loyalties; an effective act of civil disobedience must recognise this duality. If you decide to withhold a proportion of your income tax in protest against nuclear weapons, it's no use laundering your tax returns and spending the money on a new car. Hard men, scornful of 'prep school morality', may argue that rebel civil servants have a duty to remain inside the machine, to stay and fight another day, rather than abandon the profession to the time-servers, the acrobats of the greasy pole. But if government secrecy is, as Bentham reminds us, corrupting, so is the permanent lie lived by the civil servant leading a double life. Leaking to the newspapers can easily become a titillating habit, each plain brown envelope easier to post than the last, until the civil servant becomes a law unto himself, a self-elected agent of the 'espionage of the saints'. But, as Oliver Cromwell discovered in the 1650s, there are no saints.

As in the Tisdall case, sections of the press seized on Ponting's personal behaviour. I quote from the *Times*'s leader of 28 February 1985:

> He might have made his disclosures openly and then resigned; intead he made them covertly and even sought to escape from being identified by suggesting that even more junior officials might have been responsible.

This allegation was contested by Ponting and Laughland but such strictures could have been avoided entirely if Clive Ponting had written his letter of resignation when he posted the documents to Dalyell.

The distinction which proposes itself is between acts of policy and acts of principle; the former abound, the latter are rare. The man of policy cuts corners in pursuit of his aims like a police car speeding after a criminal in a built-up area; the end, he tells himself (if he even poses the question), necessarily entails the means. The person of principle is more heavily burdened by the duality of ends and means. He may act decisively but in a fashion liable to hurt himself. Of the Labour MPs who broke with the party to form the SDP in 1981, only one, Bruce Douglas-Mann, thought his decision merited a by-election, though he was not likely to win it – and didn't. He is a man of principle. Had Scargill and the executive of the National Union of Mineworkers incurred the very real risks of a national ballot when launching the miners' strike of 1984, theirs would have been an act of principle. But they didn't: in pursuit of policy, they cut corners. Those members of the NCCL who reject the right *not* to strike as a basic civil liberty are children of policy, not of principle. Of Sarah Tisdall and Clive Ponting we can say that their rebellions, morally charged though they were, owed more to policy than to principle.

TWELVE

English judges are not elected, perish the thought. Indisputably they are recruited from a narrow social stratum (a survey of 359 judges, conducted in 1968, found that 292 had attended public schools and 272 had moved on to Oxford or Cambridge), and mainly from the nominal roll of 2,000 barristers. As Lord Goodman, a solicitor among other things, reminded the House of Lords in 1978, if one deducts from this pool those who are too young to be judges, or too foolish, or too successful, as well as those reluctant to confront the rigours of the provincial circuit, then what is one left with?

The point about fees is an important one. Such is the structure of the profession that the top 10 per cent of QCs can expect to earn on average about £140,000 a year – more than three times the salary of a High Court judge. Money is not talent and a brilliant or cunning advocate may not make the wisest, most tolerant judge; yet it's clear that judges are likely to be recruited from ageing men who aren't in most demand.

Enter now the Honourable Mr Justice McCowan and all stand, including Clive Ponting in the dock: The Hon. Sir Anthony James Denys McCowan (club, Hurlingham). He begins by ruling that a faintly dramatised nightly report of the trial scheduled for Channel 4 will not be permitted; he does not want the day's proceedings, and characters, to be re-cast in the jurors' minds late at night by actors whose voices and gestures may generate misleading associations.

McCowan spreads before him a large notebook. Witnesses will have to wait while he scratches doggedly.

For some days McCowan follows the proceedings without hint of bias. But on 6 February the prosecution makes a crucial submission, urging him to rule out the argument known as *mens rea* and insisting that the 'interests of the state' means, simply, 'Government policy'. The defence counters: Laughland's junior, Mr Jonathan Caplan, argues that a civil servant's duty is not confined to his 'official duty' but extends to his moral and civic duty.

McCowan is sarcastic: 'Any old duty will do?' He allows himself to speculate: 'What if secrets were handed over to a foreign power because a civil servant honestly thought we'd all be much better off as a result?'

Mr Caplan tries to explain that such an action would count as espionage and would be prosecuted under section 1 of the Act, not section 2. Attempting to puncture the absolute equation between the 'national interest' and 'Government policy', Caplan quotes two Law Lords in the case of *Chandler v. the DPP* (1962). Lord Reid had said: 'State is not an easy word. It does not mean the Government or the Executive.' But three other Law Lords had disagreed. So does McCowan: 'He's your high spot, isn't he?'

The dominant view within the English judiciary has consistently equated the interests of the state with the policies adopted by the government of the day. When the Thatcher Government outlawed trade unions at GCHQ Cheltenham, the signals intelligence base, the Law Lords refused to intervene. Lord Fraser spoke for the majority: 'The decision whether the requirements of national security outweighed the duty of fairness is for the government and not for the courts. . . .'

This is also McCowan's view. And although Lord Denning later condemned his approach during a debate in the full House of Lords, it's relevant to recall that when Denning was Master of the Rolls he rejected an American journalist's appeal against deportation from Britain on the ground that, 'When the state is in danger, our own cherished freedoms, and even the rules of natural justice, have to take second place'. Yet the 'state' was 'in danger' only because the journalist had discomforted the Government.

Now McCowan makes a move which embarrasses even the prosecution. Speaking in the absence of the jury, the judge brings himself to the conclusion that, 'If the Crown is right, there isn't any scope for an acquittal. . . .' In short, he is going to instruct the jury to convict Ponting. Mr Amlot is at once on his feet: 'There must be some material for the jury to consider. The Crown would be very reluctant to persuade you to direct the jury to convict.'

'But what is the material for the jury?' McCowan asks.

Amlot is forced to back-pedal from his initial submission that the 'interests of the state' fitted the 'policies of the Government' like a glove: 'You have to look at the policy of the Secretary of State to see whether it should be disclosed or not. . . .'

But why? McCowan thinks Amlot is contradicting himself and so do I. At this juncture Amlot, perhaps haunted by the spectre of public uproar – an *in camera* trial followed by an instruction to convict – displays more than a trace of agitation:

'I am very reluctant that in this of all cases you should finish up directing the jury to convict.'

His alarm is shared by the Director of Public Prosecutions, Sir

Thomas Hetherington, who attends most of the trial; as the DPP strides from the court Amlot requests a short adjournment. The political and legal establishments have stumbled into a nightmare of their own devising; the rules of the game have not been understood; the prosecution have merely wished the judge to muzzle the defence by ruling all its arguments inadmissible – not to blow the entire charade of trial by jury. Ten minutes later the court reconvenes and the judge announces that he is now acquainted with recent Appeal Court rulings previously overlooked.

Thus McCowan gives the Crown what it wants: *mens rea* is ruled out as a defence. 'Counsels' speeches will now be geared to my rulings,' he warns. Denied all options but one, the jury will be free to make up its mind.

McCowan provides a taste of what this might mean when the defence calls an expert witness, Henry Wade, Professor of English Law at Cambridge and Master of Gonville & Caius College. According to Wade, author of the classic work, *Administrative Law*, constitutional conventions cannot function properly unless ministers provide truthful information to Parliament. Admittedly these conventions are not 'rules of law', Wade agrees. But: 'The secondary meaning of the rule of law, therefore, is that government should be conducted within a recognised framework of recognised rules and principles which restrict discretionary powers.'

McCowan intervenes: 'This is for me to decide. It may be a matter of law. The jury has to accept my discretion on the law.'

When he finally allows the professor to continue McCowan sits drumming his fingers impatiently on his huge desk. Later he warns the jury that Wade has come 'perilously close' to laying down the law: 'That is my job.' He keeps saying this, like a red-faced boy fuming under an autumn chestnut: 'That's my conker! It's mine!'

Clearly McCowan is tenaciously clinging to the position he has adopted during the mid-week legal arguments – exchanges which have taken place in the absence of the jury, lest they glimpse the uncertain scalps beneath the wigs. They must not know. In 1978 a journalist had broken the rules to reveal that the foreman of the 'ABC' jury had served in the Special Air Service; on Sunday, 18 February 1985, the fourth estate, in the shape of the *Observer*'s David Leigh, again intervenes by publishing a front-page report of the mid-week arguments between counsel and judge. It was Leigh who had first exposed the *Guardian*'s manoeuvres in the Tisdall case; now, on the final day of the trial, he might well have brought a toothbruth in his pocket as both prosecution and judge begin to splutter on all cylinders.

McCowan admits that he had not explicitly forbidden the press to report the legal arguments, but opines that every 'green provincial newspaper reporter' knows the rules. Yet McCowan is not consistent. Earlier in the trial he summoned Tam Dalyell before him after the MP had given a weekend speech in Scotland touching on the behaviour of Mr John Stanley. The jury was sent home. When Mr Dalyell had duly promised to be good in future, Bruce Laughland asked the judge to prohibit reporting of the episode lest it unfairly prejudice the jury against the defence.

'Aren't you a little late?' answered McCowan. 'We raised the matter at the beginning of the day without imposing reporting restrictions. It's now 4.30. . . .'

In other words, when it suits the judge reporting restrictions apply only if he imposes them; when it suits him otherwise, they apply automatically. Furious, he refers the *Observer*'s misdemeanour to the Attorney General, forgetting that section 4 of the 1981 Contempt Act allows all proceedings to be reported unless the judge says no.

Winding up for the defence, Bruce Laughland makes an almost savage preventive strike at the position he knows McCowan will adopt in his summing up:

'My second piece of bias is this; and it is not "soft-soaping" you. It's a prejudice in favour of the role of juries, particularly where the liberty of the subject is at stake. . . . Your verdict will have the special authority which no judge can aspire to. . . .'

McCowan does not like this one bit:

'You have noted Mr Laughland's final remarks to you . . . I say emphatically that would be a wholly wrong approach to your duties and oath. If the case is proved, it is your duty to convict, whatever the consequences. . . .'

He means (and says) that it is no business of the jury's what effect a conviction might have on the future conduct of ministers. As for the British constitution:

'Interest of the state, I direct you, means the policies of the state as they were in July 1984 when he communicated the documents, and not the policies as Ponting, Tam Dalyell, or any of us, think they ought to have been. . . .'

In adhering to the watertight equation between the 'interests of the state' and the policies of the government, McCowan is at least consistent, probably in tune with the majority of the judiciary, and logically responsive to Britain's lack of a written constitution or bill of rights. But he then proceeds a step further, virtually repudiating his promise not to instruct the jury to convict, by insisting that his definition of 'interest of the state' is a question of 'law', not of fact, and thus for the judge alone to decide. 'If I'm wrong, my colleagues will correct me on appeal.'

But in that case, most of the trial has been a waste of time and much of the prosecution's evidence irrelevant. Indeed McCowan is not remotely faithful to his own minimalist advice when summing up. Fastening himself to the prosecution's mast, he launches into an unqualified eulogy of the Falklands campaign: the task force had responded to aggression and fought the good fight thousands of miles from home under perilous conditions. 'You may think, on the face of it, it must have looked as though a pincer movement was developing.' Ministers had shouldered a terrible burden – at the time and ever since. He quotes Admiral Woodward. He also invites the jury to imagine one of the *Belgrano*'s escorting destroyers sinking the British flagship *Hermes* with an Exocet missile.

The judge warns the jury not to consider Ponting's motives, nor entertain any sympathy 'for his comparative youth, his promise, his lost career'. Yet the judge also filters the defence case through layers of scepticism, allowing himself to venture on the (supposedly irrelevant) terrain of motive; 'pique, spite, wounded pride' are held up for the jury to ponder.

Another twist: it would have made no difference in law (McCowan intructs the jury) if Ponting had leaked the documents to the Foreign Affairs Committee rather than to a single MP. But later he tells the jury: 'We are not dealing here with information to Parliament but to one particular member of Parliament.'

And again: it made no difference (advises McCowan) whether Ponting had or had not prevaricated when confessing to police officers Hughes and Broome. But then he adds, as Ponting's wafer-thin frame shakes in mirthless, despairing laughter: 'Isn't it obvious that [the police officers] are liars and tricksters if Mr Ponting is right?'

At no point in his summary does the judge's tone leave any audible gap between the prosecution's position and his own.

McCowan sends the jury out after one last lunge below the belt: if Ponting leaked to Dalyell and the documents found their way into the pages of the *New Statesman* – which drew the conclusion that the *Belgrano* had been sunk to scuttle the Peruvian peace proposals – this surely could come as no surprise to the leaker. Such is the final innuendo of the judge who insisted that motive didn't matter.

'On the morning of the verdict,' Clive Ponting has recalled, 'we had breakfast at the Savoy . . . . We sat at a corner table overlooking the river . . . . So certain was I that I would be going directly from the court to the prison that I had taken the precaution of filling my pockets with things I thought would be helpful "inside" – a toothbrush, toothpaste, shaving kit, and the collected sayings of Buddha.'

His lawyers were gloomy too. Yet the very bias of the judge might backfire. As Ponting later told me: 'On the Wednesday, when he gave his ruling on the law, we felt our best chance would be if he did go over the top in his summing up . . . . When McCowan got to the point of summing up on the "interests of the state", we did actually see some of the jury shaking their heads. Which was interesting.'

Ponting waited for the verdict in a room off the main hall, its seedy chairs and tables all stamped *Domine Dirige Nos*. Turkey sandwiches had been provided but he couldn't eat. I went up through Smithfield Market to the typesetters, convinced that a quick verdict would be the one many of us feared, and handed my copy to the editor of *New Socialist* with the meaningless remark that 'the chances are fifty-fifty'. In mid-afternoon I walked back to the Old Bailey; the place was deserted.

At two o'clock the jury bailiff had called Ponting back into court. Having been allowed to spend the trial at liberty, and seated behind his lawyers, he was now taken into the dock and down into the pit, where he sat alone, facing the cells. Then he was summoned back upstairs. He noticed that the foreman of the jury, a bearded young man, was smiling. It is proverbial that juries smile only when they acquit but at such a moment the best defence against a fate beyond one's control is to banish hope.

The clerk of the court asked the foreman whether the jury had reached a verdict.

'Yes.'

'And is it the verdict of you all?'

'Yes.'

The clerk read out the charge again. 'Do you find the accused Guilty or Not Guilty?'

'Not Guilty.'

Section 2 of the Official Secrets Act was at long last stone dead. It is of course Appeal Court judges, not juries, who create legal precedents. A jury considers only a specific case and every case is different. Nevertheless, within a few weeks of the Ponting verdict the Attorney General and Director of Public Prosecutions acknowledged that the game was up when they refused to respond to an even more radical challenge to governmental secrecy, a televised exposure of MI5. And when the Act was debated in the House of Lords a month later, the Government made no effort to defend it in its present form.

A few days later Ponting, now restored to full pay and accompanied by his solicitor, revisited the Ministry of Defence.

They recognised they couldn't sack me after the acquittal. What they then did was to remove my security clearance to any classified information whatsoever, not just removing my positive vetting giving me access to Top Secret information. I quite accepted that I'd never work in the MoD again. By doing this they meant I couldn't work inside Whitehall. Then they said, 'Whether we can offer you a job is another question, something might come up in one of the fringe bodies at some stage.' But they were attempting – if I'd accepted that then I could not have published the book. I think they were using this as a means of stringing me along and then coming up with no job at all, at a point where the book would no longer have any impact.

Having negotiated a 'preserved' pension plus a lump sum at the age of sixty, Ponting chose to resign and to publish; the MoD police at once struck back by letting it be known they were sending further papers to the DPP. The DPP's office, no doubt stung by Ponting's acquittal, was clearly keen to inform the press about the new allegations, which concerned the unsigned letter that Ponting had sent to Dalyell in April 1984, more than two months before he leaked the Legge memorandum. Ponting's zippy solicitor, Brian Raymond, who must take considerable credit for the fighting tactics adopted by the defence, responded to this new challenge with the memorable words, 'The idea that there is another kettle of fish is a load of absolute rubbish.' Clearly politics and the law are not first cousins to poetry.

The Government responded to Clive Ponting's acquittal by issuing a circular to all departments stressing civil servants' 'lack of constitutional responsibility or role', and their obligation to accord absolute obedience to ministers. Those who experienced crises of conscience could carry their protests to their permanent under-secretary, and through him to the Head of the Civil Service. But nowhere else.

Ponting's permanent under-secretary at the MoD was Sir Clive Whitmore. The Head of the Civil Service was Sir Robert Armstrong. And Ponting's complaint concerned disinformation about the sinking of the *Belgrano*, a crucial episode of the Falklands campaign. It so happened that Armstrong had been a member of the Falklands War Cabinet while Whitmore, then private secretary to Mrs Thatcher, had regularly attended its meetings. So . . . .

I invited Ponting's reaction:

There's got to be a code of ethics, like the First Division Association have proposed, with an appeal outside the department. I mean, it would have been no good for me to go to my permanent under-secretary. He'd been involved in the decisions. He couldn't change Heseltine's mind. There's got to be an appeal outside, maybe to an Ombudsman, maybe a select committee of some sort . . . . The Americans have a much greater distinction between the executive and the legislature. And they have far more research assistants and far more open codes of information . . . . Certainly we need a Bill of Rights, and also the adoption of the European Convention on Human Rights into UK law.

We need it, but we won't get it while Mrs Thatcher's version of 1984 – 'a year of hope and liberty' – lasts.[1]

THIRTEEN

It seems to be the case that when men and women concentrate their energies in a highly contentious action – not least one with traumatic consequences – they experience a need to isolate that action, to sever it from the subconscious and contingent circumstance, to wrap it in pure principle, and to banish the rest of themselves from the ceremony. This is partly because instinct warns that the enemy will swoop upon any chink in the gleaming armour, and strike. 'Pique!' said the prosecution; 'Rancour!' suggested the judge. If St Joan's voices, her Michael and her Catherine, were really generated by sexual frustration, or if that robust girl was really a dyke – then the English have, after all, nothing to be ashamed of, have they? If, as white Rhodesian propaganda claimed, President ———— had suffered the removal of one testicle in a surgical operation, then, ergo, the entire guerrilla movement he was supporting could be exposed as the work of a twisted fanatic. Had

[1]The signs are that ultimate responsibility for vetting civil servants will be assumed by ministers themselves, who will possess authority to suspend anyone connected with 'a subversive group' – defined as one 'whose aims are to undermine or overthrow Parliamentary democracy . . . by political, industrial or violent means'. Ministers will apply the definition, define work 'which is vital to the security of the State' and also define what is 'classified information'. The new guidelines will extend to the UK Atomic Energy Authority, the Civil Aviation Authority, British Telecom, the Post Office, the police and private firms engaged in government contracts.

the British-in-India found Gandhi in bed with a ten-year-old boy . . . .

To forestall such smears, the rebel-on-trial de-louses himself and soaks his armpits in deodorant, transforming himself into a Hamley's Action Man who springs to life only at the trigger-signal, 'Civil liberty in danger!' Like Action Man, he neither dreams nor defecates. But we no longer believe in him.

Clive Ponting is neither a robot nor a cold fish. On the contrary, he is a charming person in the best sense of the word, modest, affable, quick to laugh, and no more reserved than many of his fellow countrymen (we are a tight race). His book, *The Right to Know*, was published a month after his acquittal. The title sets the style, which reinforced the impression I gained in court of an almost disembodied intelligence, rational, principled, Platonic, reacting to events with a meticulous logic, a man apparently relieved of both ego and id, a departmental mind uncomplicated by a subconscious. It is the kind of mind which prospers not only in the civil service but also in politics and the law; you establish a case, then pursue it with chrome-bright assurance. As for the psyche, it belongs to novelists and philosophers – very interesting, no doubt, but not relevant out there in the everyday world of nine-to-five. In Sartre's novel *The Age of Reason*, Marcelle tells her lover Mathieu:

> You are beginning to sterilize yourself a little. Everything is so neat and tidy in your mind: it smells of clean linen; it's as though you had just come out of an airing-cupboard. But there's a want of shade. There's nothing useless, nor hesitant, nor underhand about you. It's all high noon.

When asked about the disembodied quality of his book, Ponting replied: 'I think there were two things. Partly an editorial decision not to have biographical material. And second, just my reluctance to discuss personal things in print.'

Perhaps we distrust light without shade because our own bent souls insist that there must be dirty linen at the bottom of every saint's basket. Whatever the man in the pub confesses to, at the bottom of his pint mug he sees everyone else on one fiddle or another. Yet Sartre's novel carries us to a more interesting conclusion: an excessive display of good faith, both to oneself and to others, is sound cause for suspicion. The soul dies when it declares its redemption. Yet the psychological sources of Clive Ponting's rebellion remain obscure:

Question: Is there anything in your family background or any incident which could have foreshadowed your rebellion against Heseltine and Stanley?

Ponting: I think the short answer to that is no. I had a very conservative background actually, and I think I probably reacted against that rather strongly . . . . One of the most formative influences was reading John Stuart Mill in the sixth form. The politician I most admire is probably F.D.R. . . .

Question: Was there ever an overt clash with your parents about politics?

Ponting: Oh yes, endless arguments. (*Laughs*) For instance my father thought Ian Smith was absolutely right and I thought he was absolutely wrong, so it was pretty . . . much a day-to-day political clash.

Question: But your father was proud of your schooling at Bristol Grammar School?

Ponting: Oh yes, he left school at fourteen, worked his way up through this small company.

Question: Would any close friend have suspected you might one day leap into the headlines?

Ponting: I suspect the answer would be no.

Question: You wouldn't have suspected it yourself?

Ponting: No. I've always been critical of institutions in a funny sort of way, maybe I'm not quite the standard civil servant.

Question: But working in the Ministry of Defence – preparing for war and so on – didn't worry you?

Ponting: No.

Question: If your train is late, do you fume or take it philosophically?

Ponting: The latter. I tend not to get mad about things I can't do anything about.

Question: You don't seek confrontations and rows?

Ponting: No.

It's highly unlikely that Sarah Tisdall ever argued with her parents about Ian Smith (whose long career exactly bridges the fourteen-year gap between Ponting's adolescence and her own).

I have been politically very lazy [explained Dr Jennifer Tisdall]. We were more worried about the next patient or the next meal than what was happening in Parliament. I disliked cruise missiles . . . but had the kind of simple faith that says, 'I suppose the defence chiefs know what they're doing' – one has to trust them.

These are liberal values and they are capable of surprising journeys – to Greenham Common and Molesworth, for example. Or to the audacious act of subversion perpetrated by Cathy Massiter following Clive Ponting's acquittal. The Massiter case, as we shall see, provided a dramatic vindication of Ponting's successful defiance of government mendacity.

It struck me that a conversion to Buddha was a fairly unusual development in a high-flying MoD civil servant and might illuminate Ponting's ultimate rebellion, but here again we did not get far:

I had no religious upbringing at all. I became interested in Buddhism, I suppose, only in the mid-1970s. I just happened to read a couple of books. Someone else who takes one along the same sort of road is Schopenhauer. I got interested in him partly through Wagner. I suppose there may have been a change in attitude. I suppose I've always had a distrust of power, of people in power.

Does Buddhism suggest how a person should live his life?
'Yes. It suggests values that are more important than getting to the top of the tree.'
But still the values seem to float in their own space, touching the man but not seizing him; nothing burns.
It appeared to me likely that Ponting's alienation from Whitehall began much earlier than he indicated in court. During the trial he professed himself 'completely in tune' with Mrs Thatcher's cost-cutting exercise, but in his book he is more critical of the way her ministers went about it. One of his strictures echoes Sarah Tisdall's general criticisms of Government policy during her television interview: 'Cuts in staff numbers were imposed without any consideration of what they would entail in terms of workload or service to the public.' Later he told me that even before he became head of DS5, 'I was disenchanted by the civil service. I was less prepared to accept the dishonesty that was going on – though I hadn't yet seen anything on this scale.'
Clearly Ponting began to break the civil service rules earlier than he implied during the trial. 'I decided to take no action,' he said, referring to Heseltine's rejection of his advice and stone-walling

letter to Dalyell of 18 April. Bruce Laughland asked him whether he had thought of sending the relevant memos to Dalyell after Heseltine's second brush-off letter, of 14 May. 'It briefly crossed my mind,' replied Ponting, but he had buried the idea because at that stage ministers were merely withholding information rather than providing disinformation. ('I gasped when I heard that,' Dalyell later told me.) Indeed Bruce Laughland made much of the fact that Ponting had not stepped from the straight and narrow until the 'watershed' decision taken by ministers in July to misinform the Foreign Affairs Committee.

The reality was different. On 24 April Ponting had sent Dalyell an unsigned letter, encouraging him to pursue his inquiries. That the prosecution knew about this can hardly be doubted; on 19 August 1984, a few days after Ponting's first appearance at Bow Street, the *Observer* ran a front-page story (which must have originated with Dalyell himself) linking the two documents the MP had received in July with an unsigned letter sent to him on 24 April – both communications had arrived in a similar plain envelope. Admittedly this letter had not been attributed to Ponting when published in the *Observer*, a factor which presumably inhibited the prosecution, who did not in any case possess the original letter. It nevertheless baffles me why Amlot didn't ask Ponting whether he had written and sent a letter to Dalyell on 24 April.

Almost offhandedly Ponting disclosed in court that he had already applied to move from DS5 and indeed from the MoD. The prosecution hounds did not pick up the trail. I was puzzled by this at the time but the following exchange during my conversation with Ponting may help to explain Amlot's reticence:

Ponting: I made the decision partly because of Heseltine's replies to Dalyell but partly I wasn't going to spend the rest of my life in the MoD and I might as well move sooner rather than later. I put in the request to move early in May. Absolutely nothing had happened since. It's virtually unheard of to move between departments.

(Thus Ponting's request to leave the MoD followed hard on the heels of his anonymous letter to Dalyell.)

Question: Where did you ask to be transferred to?

Ponting: More or less anywhere. There was no point in being too fussy.

Question: Your request didn't lead them to conclude, 'Ponting is too seriously disaffected to be left in this sensitive post'? That surprises me.

Ponting: That question had been raised, you see. As I said in May, I'd rather move from the Ministry as a whole, but I'd stay in DS5 if it could be done quickly, but if it was going to take some months I'd rather move from DS5. But there was no action on either front.

Question: Yet they didn't move you from your sensitive post?

Ponting: No. In retrospect they obviously wish they had.

Question: You didn't feel you were being bypassed at the time your department was asked to draft advice about the Foreign Affairs Committee's request for a full list of the ROE?

Ponting: No.

This exchange helps to give Ponting's rebellion its necessary human context. His alienation was already radical by late April and they knew it. But the bureaucracy failed to react and left him adrift in his sensitive post, a blunder in terms of 'security' and hence a point not stressed by the prosecution at his trial.

One particular episode – and Ponting's part in it – baffled me during the trial and continued to do so after I had read *The Right to Know*. This concerns the MoD's response to the Foreign Affairs Committee of the Commons. Advice had been sought not only from DS11 but also from Ponting's own department; and it later transpired that on 4 July DS5 had submitted a minute which both anticipated and influenced the Legge memorandum which precipitated Ponting's rebellion. He also explained during his trial that DS5's memo had been drafted and despatched by his subordinate, Nicholas Darms. Ponting insisted that he himself had never discussed or approved the general line to be taken by his own department – he merely held a fifteen-minute conversation with Darms during which he gave his opinion that the ROE were not classified. Quite normal, said Ponting in court, to leave the matter to a subordinate.

Mr Darms, a higher executive officer, and his colleague Margaret Aldred, a principal in DS5, were called as prosecution witnesses. Both claimed that Darms had cleared the general line to be taken with Ponting. It would certainly seem odd if this was not done, given the importance of a response to a select committee of the Commons – and given, also, Ponting's own long-standing involvement in the politics of the *Belgrano*.

Ponting's post-trial narrative, published in the *Observer*, never alluded to the fact that DS5, as well as DS11, had been instructed to draft a reply to the Commons select committee. The same lacuna occurs in Ponting's book where, on page 147, he recalls how the Foreign Affairs Committee's inquiry was passed on to the MoD from the Foreign Office: ' . . . and so it was transferred by the Foreign Office to my colleague, the Head of the division responsible for general policy on operations outside the NATO area.'

He refers to Legge. Not a word about DS5's role, or the discussions he did or did not have with Darms and Aldred; not a word in his general narrative about the conflicting evidence in court until he comes to his day-by-day impressions of the trial. On Thursday 31 January, in the afternoon,

> my two subordinates from DS5, Margaret Aldred and Nick Darms, were hauled in to try and make out that the text of the Legge memorandum . . . had somehow been approved by me first – and therefore was part of my 'plot' to embarrass the Government. . . . It emerged quickly that little more than a passing chat was under discussion – a tiny event which neither could really remember, and which Inspector Broome asked them to put together in identical statements, written jointly, not three weeks ago. Nobody could find a single document initialled by me. I felt sorry for their predicament.

But could one not take it as axiomatic that an official as thorough and clear-sighted as Ponting would have checked on DS5's advice to ministers before leaking Legge's minute to Dalyell? Yet Ponting declares himself to have remained ignorant of DS5's own memorandum until it was introduced into the legal proceedings in a Notice of Additional Evidence in January 1985. You mean, probed prosecution counsel, that even though it was sitting in your float file you never looked it up, despite your claim to have been so outraged by Mr Legge's minute?

Yes, said Ponting.

Mr Roy Amlot displayed heavy scepticism. His thrust seemed to be that Ponting had indeed approved of the very line he later leaked to Dalyell; and had therefore done this not out of principle, as he claimed, but out of 'pique' or – as the judge helpfully suggested – 'rancour'. But pique or rancour provoked by what? This was a riddle the prosecution did not attempt to solve.

When questioned in court by his own counsel, Ponting explained that he had been upset by Legge's minute but had deferred action while waiting to see whether ministers would be so brazen as to adopt its advice that a select committee should be misled. However, when later cross-examined by Mr Amlot, who was implying that it had been less than noble of Ponting to put a fellow civil servant in the public shit, Ponting argued that the Legge minute had *not* annoyed him because his colleague had been bound to follow the mendacious line already established by the ministers, the real culprits. As Ponting put it in his *Observer* article:

This was not a case of the Civil Service freely advising ministers to mislead Parliament, but rather they were simply providing the advice that ministers had already made clear they wanted . . . .

Both versions cannot be advanced simultaneously and I therefore pursued this perplexing conundrum in conversation with Ponting:

Question: Given the importance of the issue, and your own intense interest in it, surely you would have wanted, as head of DS5, to exercise influence on the reply?

Ponting: The impression I got was that the select committee had asked questions about the Rules of Engagement, and I was asked by Darms whether the material was classified, and I said not, so my assumption was that the information would be provided or that it would be put up to ministers that it should be provided. Remember that the select committee's questions were not focussed on the *Belgrano* alone but on the whole war.

Question: Darms just went and wrote his report?

Ponting: Yes. They admitted I'd not seen Darms's minute back to DS11. No doubt he thought his conversation with me had cleared it, it's just one of those things about the way work is done in a busy time.

Question: Isn't it curious that Darms didn't show it to you to clear it? You told your subordinate that the material was not classified yet he wrote a minute proposing it should not be divulged.

Ponting: Yes, it is.

Question: You have said you were not even aware of DS5's recommendations until January this year, even though they were lodged in your float file?

Ponting: I hadn't realised what it was all about and Darms probably thought he'd told me enough and that I'd said something vaguely agreeing with the line.

Question: Perhaps you were being deliberately by-passed because of your opposition to the Heseltine-Stanley line, and because you had already let them know you wanted to move from the MoD?

Ponting: I don't *think* so, though people knew what my views were.

Question: So it was in Darms's head that most of the now famous rationalisation for a continuing cover-up took place?

Ponting: DS11 incorporated his minute into the one Legge sent up to the ministers. When I saw the Legge minute I didn't know it had come from Darms. At the time I had twenty other things going on at the same time. But the Legge minute is simply in line with the policy set by ministers.

Question: But the Legge minute brought you personally to the crisis point. You thought about it deeply before deciding what to do. Yet you didn't look up your departmental float file to see whether Darms's advice had been the same?

Ponting: Even if I had it wouldn't have changed my view anyway. It didn't really matter who was saying this. The advice that was going up to ministers was in line with the policy they'd set in April and May.

Question: . . . were you not by that time so disaffected by the mendacity prevailing throughout the MoD that you washed your hands of DS5's reply and indicated to Darms that he should draft it? But later, when you saw Legge's minute in black-and-white, your cumulative disgust came to the boil?

Ponting: No, it was a question of waiting to see whether ministers would move from refusing to answer Dalyell's questions, to misleading a select committee actually investigating the war.

I detect zig-zags in all this. Contrast in particular the following:

1: '. . . so my assumption was that the information would be provided or that it would be put up to ministers that it should be provided.'
2: It didn't really matter who was saying this. The line that was going up to ministers was in line with the policy they'd set in April and May.

The conclusion seems inescapable that when the Foreign Affairs Committee's request came on the agenda, Ponting was either bypassed – which would explain the otherwise baffling business of his ignorance of Darms's advice to ministers – or, alternatively, sourly washed his hands of one more futile attempt to alter Government policy; then experienced a choking anger when he saw how readily his civil service colleagues played the ministerial game. (I have no doubt that Ponting's rebellion was directed as much against the whole MoD apparatus as against the ministers.) Why did he wait for Heseltine's formal reply to the Foreign Affairs Committee before leaking the Legge minute to Dalyell? Just in case the Secretary for Defence might have second thoughts? Hardly. Or because the leak would carry its full impact only after Heseltine had committed himself in writing?

FOURTEEN

Between Ponting's position and Dalyell's there is a gap partly obscured by the struggle against a common enemy. Ponting had in fact been perfectly content when working in the legal department of the MoD, dealing with the implementation of the Official Secrets Act. Unlike Dalyell, he has never condemned the decision to sink the *Belgrano*, still less the launching of the task force and the recovery of the Falklands by military assault. Paradoxically, he destroyed his brilliant career to expose the cover-up of an action which he is prepared to justify. Suspecting that he maintained this position during his trial in order to buttress his (entirely genuine) image as a sound patriot, I was surprised to find it later confirmed in his book:

> The military case for the sinking of the *General Belgrano* as it appeared to the War Cabinet at lunchtime on 2 May 1982 was strong. It would have been difficult for any Government to reject the clear advice of the Chief of the Defence Staff that he needed action to counter what he believed was a major Argentinian attack. Whether there was *in fact* such an attack under way is another matter.

However, during a subsequent conversation he revealed doubts:

187

This was the major piece of escalation of the whole war and the biggest single loss of life. Were they really determined to keep casualties to a minimum – use minimum force? – in which case they might have held their hand instead of jumping in in twenty minutes . . . I can imagine a different Cabinet might have taken a different decision.

In Ponting's view, when the Government discovered their mistake about the cruiser's true course and position, they should have taken 'a courageous stand . . . that the *General Belgrano* was simply a threat whatever the exact sequence of events'. This, of course, is now, *après* Ponting, the Government's exact stance. But how was the cruiser 'a threat'? The problem is emphasised rather than resolved by what Ponting also said in discussion:

Was it still a threat? you ask. The answer is they may reasonably have thought it was, although in fact it almost certainly wasn't, by then.

Then how could it be a 'courageous stand' to insist that it was a threat?

Well – it might have turned round. We don't know what all the messages may or may not have been.

I had thought that the compiler of the 'Crown Jewels' did know. What about the two signals transmitted by the Argentine naval command to its fleet, the first at 20.07 local time on 1 May, then the confirming order at 01.19 on 2 May, both of which ordered all vessels to turn away from confrontation with the British Navy? Are we to believe that Admiral Sir Terence Lewin and the War Cabinet remained in ignorance of these signals – even if they were treated with caution?
Ponting replied: 'Unfortunately I can't discuss these things.'
The notion that the whole *Belgrano* disaster could have been defended by an honest admission of the actual sequence of events is belied not only by some of the reservations Ponting expressed when advising Heseltine how to reply to Dalyell, but also by the following point he made in conversation:

What they did on 2 May was to say, 'okay, sink any ship anywhere.' That decision isn't compatible with their public line nor was the decision taken two days earlier on 30 April to sink the aircraft carrier *25 de Mayo* outside the exclusion zone.

Too true. To rule the waves, Britannia had waived its own announced rules even though Pym and Havers had warned that such action would be in violation of international law. How could the Government have come clean about the *Belgrano* without opening the whole can of worms?

What has not been understood is that Clive Ponting reached the foot of the Cross as a consequence of a rebellion hedged by caution. Unlike Tam Dalyell, he is not a flamboyant crusader in pursuit of a single, burning truth essential to the redemption of the body politic. It is Dalyell who brandishes the spirit indefatigable, trundling about in a duffle coat, his briefcase bulging with incriminating evidence, the jeers of the pharisees a daily confirmation of his mission. By the thunder of his tongue the Member for Linlithgow knows himself; Ponting's finely edged mind hums discreetly like an electric razor.

Impossible, here, to recover the complete record of Tam Dalyell's singular crusade to reveal the truth about the sinking of the *Belgrano*. From the moment that Parliament convened in emergency session on Saturday 3 April 1982, and launched the task force on a tide of bi-partisan patriotism, Dalyell denounced the whole enterprise as wicked, foolish, and worse. Having predicted disaster – moral, diplomatic and military – the rapid recovery of the Falklands, Mrs Thatcher's triumph, deepened his determination to demonstrate the perfidious and perilous nature of the entire operation. The 368 men who died on the *Belgrano* constitute the crown of thorns he offers to the Prime Minister – but she prefers to wear a different crown.

He has been likened to an eighteenth-century Radical, one of those bloody-minded tribunes who relished persecution, emerging from each trial on the shoulders of the people. One is struck by his patrician demeanour: not the haughty drawl of the English counties, but the quieter self-assurance of the Scottish shire. He went to Eton and King's College, Cambridge; his mother's father was Baron Wheatley and she in her time served as commissioner of the West Lothian Girl Guides. Tam Dalyell himself became a schoolmaster with a knack for managing boys' soccer teams and a love of the sea. Reared on a tradition of decency and public service, on the kind of patriotism which regards jingoism as a jumped-up perversion of national values, Dalyell is at heart a team man (devoted to the Labour Party) with a remarkable capacity for jumping out of line when he sees a foul. The ego, of course, is formidable.

An amateur scientist by vocation, Dalyell revels in the details of weapons technology, and when he whips through the names of our nuclear submarines – *Conqueror*, *Splendid*, *Superb* – he does so with the clipped and intimate affection of a Tory admiral, leaving the Labour Party faithful of Bromley or the Isle of Skye gaping in bemused admiration. Twenty-one degrees west, twelve degrees south, he snaps. Ergo. Were he a Militant MP from Merseyside, the Tories would shrug him off, but his social background excites a familiar anger, a sense of betrayal, and only the other day a Wiltshire man of property told me that Dalyell's national service with BAOR had been a 'disaster – he never got beyond the rank of private'. Ergo again.

Perhaps Tam is a frustrated field-marshal, a roll of leaked documents his baton. He's always on the go, an over-spilling energy, restless, perseverant, relishing the taxing existence of a dedicated MP. Hot from a division bell at 6.10, he hurtles from Westminster to Victoria Station by underground, reaching the train with a minute to spare, his forehead beaded with sweat. ('It's all right, I'm a jogger.') His solemn features are cut out of granite.

Between division bells Dalyell is to address Bromley Labour Party. The journey takes only fifteen minutes and is not renowned for its hazards, yet the train has scarcely gathered speed before there is a deafening crack and the passengers on the other side of the carriage flinch. Instantly alert, Tam departs to make an inspection and soon returns with news of shattered glass.

'A stone through the window. I thought at first it was a shot.'

'You know too much.'

He offers the ghost of a smile, as if evening sunlight had fleetingly touched the granite outcrop. Like other Scots, he is not sure when his leg is being pulled. 'I've been too charitable to John Nott,' he announces.

Dalyell is wearing a smart blue business suit, a tie which looks regimental, and brown shoes which turn up at the toes. Without his briefcase this evening, he clutches a wad of papers on his lap; any one of them could be the Prime Minister's letter of capitulation leaked straight from the Cabinet Office. Dalyell has sources everywhere; some may feed him what he wants to hear, but saintly espionage on this scale is bound to unearth real dirt as well. Beneath the short, wiry hair resides a vast but faintly disordered data-bank. It tends to ingest more rapidly than it digests.

He explains why he has been 'too charitable' to Nott. He also reveals 'something I didn't know until three weeks ago'. The bees buzz in his bonnet: one or two will sting the rounded rumps on the Treasury front bench.

We reach Bromley without further attempts on his life. But will it be prudent to make the return journey with him?

Born in 1932, Dalyell was too young to have served in the war, but likes to toss at warmongers his experiences as a trooper in the Royal Scots Greys with the British Army of the Rhine. Elected to Parliament at the age of thirty with the support of the Scottish mineworkers, two years later he became parliamentary private secretary to Richard Crossman, whose *Diaries of a Cabinet Minister* are full of affectionate praise for young Dalyell as a loyal, devoted friend and assistant with a stubborn and occasionally obtuse streak. The Wilson and Callaghan administrations, however, brought him no advancement; a rebel over British military involvement in Ulster, he won himself no favours by a fierce rearguard against the Callaghan-Foot plan to devolve power to elected Scottish and Welsh assemblies. The beginning of the end of the United Kingdom, warned Dalyell, and quite irrelevant to the needs of the people of Scotland; his book on the subject appeared with a preface by a high Tory Regius Professor, Hugh Trevor-Roper.

Denied a post in government, Dalyell had to be content with the chairmanship of the Parliamentary Labour Party Foreign Affairs group in 1974–76 and again in 1979–80. It was in this capacity that he developed a keen interest in Latin America and was deeply impressed by the almost universal condemnation, from Mexico to Patagonia, of Britain's occupation of the Falklands. He also served as an indirectly elected Member of the European Parliament.

Following Callaghan's resignation in 1979, Dalyell voted for Foot as leader (despite the devolution episode), stood for election to the Shadow Cabinet, and received sixty-six votes, coming fifth among those not elected. Foot appointed him Opposition spokesman on science. Then came the Falklands and a calamitous rupture in the Labour ranks, following hard on the heels of the fratricidal struggle for the deputy leadership. (Dalyell had voted for Benn; he will mention this to Bromley CLP, evoking applause; he will then mention his respect for Denis Healey, evoking none.) Outraged by what he regarded as the myopic jingoism of Foot and John Silkin, Dalyell was one of thirty-three MPs who on 20 May 1982 voted against the continued use of force to solve the Falklands crisis. Foot sacked him.

When Dalyell gets stuck into an issue he employs every available argument and a few more besides. The Falklands campaign was a crime because it was immoral to win it and immoral to lose it – Dalyell deployed a weight of technical knowledge to demonstrate our lack of adequate air cover and claimed from inside sources that the Air Chiefs had warned Mrs Thatcher of the dangers. Dalyell pointed out that he hadn't 'fired live ammunition and inhaled all the fumes in the turret of a Centurion tank' for nothing. Having served on the ship school *Dunera* in the Bay of Biscay, he could also imagine 'what the Roaring Forties would be like in winter in sub-Antarctic conditions.'

Alighting at Bromley, we study the return timetable: another division bell beckons at ten, plus a TV interview – I doubt that

Dalyell needs much sleep. A veteran Bromley socialist is waiting in filthy weather to welcome Dalyell to a no-hope constituency (Tory majority 18,000, Labour candidate lost deposit). We beat up Bromley High Street into the Roaring Forties, making for the H. G. Wells Memorial Hall, which resembles a Methodist chapel and probably was. Our host recalls a recent visit to Moscow where his party were shown Wells's correspondence with Lenin. I anticipate a turn-out of five; the hall is packed. Tam is a crowd-puller.

It was Dalyell who hounded ministers from cocky mendacity into sly evasion and, finally, via Ponting, into grudging confession. When HMS *Conqueror* sailed into the Clyde flying the Jolly Roger, he lost no time in winning the confidence of members of the crew with more respect for the truth they had experienced than for the Official Secrets Act. His greatest prize was the diary kept by the submarine's navigator, Lieutenant Narendra Sethia. By December 1982 Dalyell knew too much. Ministers took refuge in sarcasm: 'The honourable Gentleman's behaviour in these matters begins to cast grave doubt on his mental stability,' said Cranley Onslow, a junior minister at the Foreign Office, on 12 May 1983; yet less than a year later Clive Ponting found the corridors of the MoD haunted by Dalyell's menacingly well-informed questions.

Dalyell is armour-plated but not thick-skinned. He certainly doesn't enjoy isolation and is touchingly grateful for evidence of support from any quarter. He is generous to Labour colleagues who also resisted the patriotic stampede of 1982, and has attempted (unsuccessfully) to prise open the Tory ranks by driving a wedge between the vulgarly bellicose Thatcherites and the decent, moderate, old-soldier squires like Pym and Whitelaw who have known war service and understand what war means. Dalyell is also capable of flagrant appeals to our lost sense of national honour: 'If it had been Harold Macmillan . . . or Alec Douglas-Home or the right honourable Member for Sidcup [Edward Heath]' in 10, Downing Street, such lies would never have been told. (In May 1983 Dalyell was expelled from the Commons for five days after calling Thatcher a liar.) He has also sprayed the Labour benches with the same nostalgia: Crossman, Silverman, Wigg, Gaitskell, Wilson even, would never have let the Prime Minister get away with so many unanswered questions. He means what he says but there is more than a touch of opportunism about such tributes.

He poses with the old-timers of Bromley CLP for a photo-call. It being a socialist camera, the flash has to re-charge between shots, rather like the party itself between elections. The local party secretary is an attractive woman whose forefinger is wrapped in a huge bandage. She has been bitten by her female cat and not (she affectionately recalls) for the first time: 'I made the mistake of giving

192

her fresh meat. I thought it was Eric under my chair but it was Emily.'

The meeting starts twenty minutes late. Some confusion between 7.30 and 8.00, explains the chairman contentedly. He stumbles into an introduction, changes his mind, and declares, 'Tom Die-ell needs no introduction from me.' One heartily agrees.

Dalyell rises. He looks grave. He goes straight for Mrs Thatcher's throat: 'I make the gravest of charges against a British Prime Minister – calculated murder for her own political ends.' (Later an Irishman will ask whether she should therefore be brought to trial; Dalyell will display exemplary caution.) He then points out that the woman who lured Argentina into war and sank the *Belgrano* is the woman with her finger on the nuclear trigger, though his flat, schoolmasterly tone is curiously devoid of emotional charge. It isn't merely that he has said it all many times before, and will continue saying it so long as invitations pour in; what leavens Dalyell's voice is the sober, workmanlike culture of the Lowlands. The *Guardian* writer Alan Rusbridger, followed Dalyell on a speaking tour of Scotland:

> His voice seems to fluctuate between weary impatience and astonishment – astonishment, still, at the nature of things he describes; impatience that what seems so self-evident should need saying all over again.

That's true. But it may also be the case that Dalyell, like other inspired muckrakers, is never sure, from moment to moment, whether he's the only sane man in the world or plain mad.

The hallmark of a Dalyell speech on the *Belgrano* is its astonishing wash of detail and technical jargon: exact dates, times, map references, navigational courses, quotations, sources, weapons capabilities. I can only imagine an audience unfamiliar with the chronology of events as utterly at sea, yet the party faithful in the H. G. Wells Memorial Hall appear totally absorbed by Tam's unfolding narrative of treachery in the highest places. Worse than a crime, a blunder; worse than a blunder, a crime. During the past two years Dalyell has likened the Falklands war to the Duke of Buckingham's expedition to La Rochelle in 1627, to the Jameson Raid against the Transvaal in 1895, to the Russo-Japanese war of 1905, to the Dieppe commando raid of 1942, to Guadalcanal, Iwo Jima and the Solomon Islands – and I doubt whether my research is exhaustive. Yet he seems enthralled by the masculine paraphernalia of warfare. When he speaks of 'razzing' at sea (re-oiling) he enunciates the word with relish, innocent of its suggestion of filthy activities among bored sailors below decks. It's like hearing Colonel Chinstrap denounce the empire.

And where did our ephemeral victory land us? He spells out the financial cost, ramming home the Government's cut-backs in social spending, but this is done on automatic pilot, the standard reflex of a politician. The real story lies in Argentina's menacing re-armament – my notebook cannot keep pace with the list of diabolical ordnance, Rolls Royce engines, French gearboxes, German subs 'with their propeller signals muffled' even, internal machines possessing not only a fighting capacity but a 'formidable loitering capacity' as well. French anti-runway bombs capable of blowing . . . it's no use. But one thing is certain: Dalyell will not mention how military defeat in the Malvinas brought down the junta, led to free civilian elections, the emptying of gaols, and the current trials of the torturers from ex-President Videla down. No, he turns it the other way: if we don't reach a rapid, long-term settlement very soon, then the Argentine military will overthrow the elected civilian government.

As for our victory in 1982, it hung by a hair. If one more capital ship had gone down then Mrs Thatcher was prepared to drop an atomic bomb on the city of Cordoba. Dalyell states this as a fact: he has his sources.

The Ponting case comes up: Tam holds aloft Clive's book. A member of the audience asks whether he believes in completely open government. Dalyell goes back into his shell:

'Not entirely. I'm a cautious man. I believe ministers have a right to confidential information from their civil servants.'

Before this can be absorbed Dalyell has released another bee: 'the murder' of Miss Hilda Murrell, a prominent anti-nuclear campaigner in her eighties, by British Intelligence agents. Dalyell refers darkly to inside sources 'that wild horses won't drag out of me' – though no wild horses are visible in the H. G. Wells Memorial Hall. The murder of Hilda Murrell is viewed by Tam as a logical extension of the Falklands conspiracy and it wouldn't surprise me if he were right.

Dalyell is cut out of one cloth but the fabric is intricately patterned. Generous, open, abstracted, dedicated, shrewd, ideal-istic, ego-centred: all the adjectives apply. The term which to my mind sums him up is the old military one: gallant. Though not always too scrupulous in his use of evidence (he has a remarkable capacity for believing what he wants to believe), he is above all a man of honour. He lacks the sly wolf-look of other Labour MPs who practise journalism; after all, he can make his own stories. If the truth shines he cannot blink: his detractors call it tunnel-vision.

One day during the first week of the Ponting trial (which Dalyell doubly haunted, both in the evidence and in the flesh), he was summoned into the well of the court to face the wrath of Mr Justice McCowan. Dalyell had given a weekend speech in Glasgow which the judge regarded as contempt. Bring counsel with you, McCowan warned, but Dalyell came alone and immediately greeted the judge as a 'member of one high court to another'. (Tam carries a thick wad of House of Commons notepaper in his briefcase.) He then opined that a speech delivered in Scotland was a matter for Scottish courts and, if necessary, for Scottish advocates. McCowan was not impressed and threatened to put the MP 'in a place where you can make no more speeches'. To my surprise Tam knuckled under: he knew the point where the game ends.

A traditionalist, he is at home with the more byzantine aspects of Parliamentary procedure. He is quite capable of intervening during a debate on seat belts to ask the right hon. lady how many of the 368 victims of the *Belgrano* were wearing seat belts when she fired 'her' murderous torpedoes at them. Or to intervene during a debate on child benefits to ask how many of the *Belgrano* widows were expecting babies when their husbands were killed. These two examples are invented, but Dalyell won't rest until *she* falls to her knees in the Commons and tears out her own lacquered hairdo: 'Yes, yes, I lured the dagoes into a war so that I could restore my waning political fortunes by murderous slaughter! Aaagh!' It may not happen.

Dalyell gives the impression that there's nothing personal about his detestation of Mrs Thatcher.

Even now the Parliamentary Labour Party will not travel with him the whole way about the *Belgrano*. This became clear during the post-Ponting debate in the Commons on 19 February 1985. Despite some coruscating wit and rhetorical flourishes from Mr Gerald Kaufman, the Labour front bench – like Ponting himself – was accusing the Government of having shamefully lied about a naval action it shrank from condemning. When it came to the vote, the Opposition abstained on a Government motion describing that action as necessary and legitimate. Kaufman's quip that the Government could now 'drape itself in the White Ensign, though its true colours are the Jolly Roger', was mere flourish. (Indeed the Navy has no aversion to the Jolly Roger, as *Conqueror* showed.)

Nor does the Labour Party go along with the most dramatic quiver in Dalyell's bow – that Mrs Thatcher sank the *Belgrano* to scuttle viable Peruvian peace proposals. Ponting, too, is sceptical. The reader interested in pursuing this question is directed to the appendix at the end of the essay.

FIFTEEN

Secrecy is forgiveable, and in some incarnations inevitable; we need to frame our actions and words in strategic silences, in not-saying, from at least the years preceding adolescence. But, as Orwell reminded us – wrong though Mrs Thatcher declared him to be on the first day of 1984 – governments strive to deny us the secrecy they so jealousy preserve for themselves. The other side of governmental secrecy, in short, is surveillance. Only a few weeks after Ponting's acquittal at the Old Bailey, a woman of the same generation, thirty-seven years old, provided a devastating exposure of the security services' invasions of privacy and relentless assault on basic civil liberties. She did it, moreover, with the highest possible profile – on television – and if she was not guilty of a flagrant breach of the Official Secrets Act (section 2), no one ever was.

But the Government, despite Heseltine's bravado onslaught on Clive Ponting during the Commons debate of 19 February, was cowed; Attorney General Havers meekly announced that he would not prosecute. I spoke to Ponting about this: surely he must take some credit? He nodded modestly: 'Cathy Massiter might well have used the same defence as I did. Yes. It's clear they didn't want another contested section 2 case. They can't face another acquittal. Whether we've finished off section 2 is another matter.' It's not merely another acquittal they can't face; even more damaging is the capacity of a fighting defendant to drag the murky activities of anonymous operatives into the daylight. The Government currently lavishes on the security services almost one thousand million pounds a year, more than ten times the publicly acknowledged sum. Parliament does not know because it does not want to know; the Permanent Secretaries Committee on the Intelligence Services, elected by no one and answerable only to the Prime Minister, can draw on almost limitless funds. The Public Accounts Committee regularly inspects the accounts of all departments without limitation – but not the 'Secret Vote', which is traditionally passed 'on the nod'. The nod (and wink) are the prime gestures of the British establishment. The 'secret vote' presented to Parliament for 1984–85 appropriated a mere £76 million; yet MI5 , with its 2,000 full-time operatives, is reckoned to spend £160 million, while the Special Branch, with about 1,500 members and a £40 million budget, has expanded sixfold since Orwell wrote *1984*.

MI5 was not created by Act of Parliament and no statute defines its role or powers. Its notional guidelines are based on occasional administrative statements, the seminal one being the Home Secretary's directive of 25 September 1952 that 'the Security Services should be kept absolutely free from any political bias or influence'. No inquiry was to be carried out on behalf of any government department unless the 'Defence of the Realm' was at stake.

Let us measure what we know about MI5's current activities against those two admirable criteria (about which Parliament itself was not even informed, quite typically, for eleven years).

The better to 'defend the realm' the security services regularly and systematically 'tap' and 'bug' trade unionists, activists of CND, *Peace News*, the Bertrand Russell Peace Foundation, officials of the National Council for Civil Liberties (NCCL), the Greenpeace environmental pressure group, the El Salvador Human Rights Campaign, Plaid Cymru, Anti-Apartheid, and virtually any group campaigning for a British military withdrawal from Ulster. According to David Norman, general treasurer of the Post Office Engineers' Union, whose members execute phone-tapping directives, 'To our certain knowledge the process of tapping telephones is systematic and widespread.'

In 1984, 423 warrants were authorised – but a single warrant may cover an entire organisation and its staff. The accumulated tapes from the phone lines tapped in the building known as 'Tinker-bell' in Ebury Bridge Road, are relayed to MI5's red-brick headquarters in Curzon Street, where banks of spools located on the fifth floor turn day and night. Meanwhile, intercepted mail is taken from sorting offices to Union House in St Martin's-le-Grand, where the boys are waiting with hot needles, steam and photocopiers. Due to carelessness, nuclear disarmers may discover in their envelopes literature about chemical waste, while citizens concerned about repression in South Africa are faintly surprised to receive appeals on behalf of the 'Bradford Twelve' or the families of striking miners. But this carelessness is also deliberate: the aim of such operations is not only to monitor communications but also to inhibit them.

To be effective, surveillance cannot be confined to the professionals. The most insidious aspect of the operation is the enlistment of one ordinary citizen against his neighbour. As long ago as 1957 Lord Chorley, President of the Association of University Teachers, told the House of Lords that in the London area lecturers were frequently invited by MI5 or Special Branch to report on both colleagues and students, even to act as spies and search filing cabinets. How corrupting this process can be is illustrated by the

197

approach made to MI5 and MI6 in the early 1960s by three leading Labour politicians, Hugh Gaitskell, George Brown and Patrick Gordon-Walker, who handed over the names of some fifty 'suspect' Labour MPs with the request that they be put under total surveillance. No doubt MI5 was delighted to reinforce its power by doing for Her Majesty's Opposition what it was already doing for Her Majesty's Government – in April 1967 Harold Wilson admitted that MPs had been under surveillance and promised to discontinue the practice. But it goes on. According to Chapman Pincher, the *Express* journalist who introduced George Brown to the men in raincoats, the security services regarded fifty-nine Labour MPs in the 1974–79 Parliament as potential threats to the defence of the realm. The files on MPs of all persuasions, we may assume, serve to keep Parliament's head well down.

Mr Tony Benn, citing this evidence in his book *Arguments for Democracy* (1981), offers (as might be anticipated) some remedies. Mr Benn would have Parliament publish annually the true budget and staffing of the security services, the number of political dossiers on file, and an account of what is done with the information therein. But then Mr Benn, as if pulled by the atavism that few Englishmen can quite dispense with (former minister of the Wilson years that he is), slips back into the mystique of the Wise Guardians, proposing

> a special House of Commons select committee, meeting when necessary, in secret, composed exclusively of privy councillors, empowered to question both the responsible ministers and the security chiefs on the whole range of their policy and activities – to report annually to Parliament in a form that can be published.

Who could have imagined that so passionate a champion of freedom of information would offer us a solution containing the words 'in secret'?

Miss Massiter decided to break ranks and to spill the MI5 beans on television. Like Tisdall and Ponting, she belongs solidly to middle England; to reinforce the image, the makers of the television film had her striding across the English countryside in short hair, anorak and gum boots – no wine bars or shady places, no Marxist classics on her shelves for the men in wide-lapelled Austin Reed macs to take down with gloved hands. Her testimony has not been challenged.

The breaking point for Cathy Massiter came after she was assigned, in 1981, to head MI5's investigation of the Campaign for Nuclear Disarmament. Files had been opened on CND's chairperson, Mrs Joan Ruddock, on its general secretary, Monsignor

Bruce Kent, and several of its vice-chairmen. According to Massiter, it was the Home Secretary himself, Mr Leon Brittan (he who appears to have stepped out of the Munsters and the world of Charles Addams), who in August 1983 authorised the telephone tapping of John Cox, a vice-president of CND – and a member of the Communist Party. And this despite Mr Brittan's assurance to Parliament, given in December 1984 and repeated in March 1985, that campaigning for nuclear disarmament is 'an entirely legitimate activity which does not fall within the strict criteria of the 1980 White Paper' defining subversive activites.

Enter now the inevitable Mr Heseltine. It was his memos to the Prime Minister about the installation of cruise missiles that Sarah Tisdall took to the *Guardian*; it was his resolve to deceive Parliament about the *Belgrano* that led Clive Ponting to communicate with Tam Dalyell; and it was his unscrupulous misuse of MI5 in a strictly partisan context that brought Cathy Massiter to the end of the road. Two months after he became Defence Secretary in March 1983, Heseltine set up within the MoD an outfit called DS19, staffed by civil servants, whose sole task was to discredit the nuclear disarmers, even though the 1952 guidelines expressly forbade the security services from 'political bias or influence'. Headed by an official who had been closely involved in security work when serving in the Northern Ireland Office in Belfast, DS19 approached MI5 for hard stuff on CND's most prominent activists. As the general election approached, Heseltine then named fourteen of CND's twenty-six officers and council members as Communists, ex-Communists, socialists or left-wingers. He stopped short of vegetarians and nudists.

'We were violating our own rules,' said Massiter, 'simply because of political pressure. The heat was there for information about CND and we had to have it.'

The most debasing aspect of this kind of invigilation is not the compilation of hearsay and tittle-tattle in dossiers (Thames Valley Police are said to have files on 250,000 people), but the corrupting enlistment of private citizens in the expanding enterprise of surveillance. Ordinary trade unionists are instructed to tap telephones; college lecturers are invited to spy on colleagues and students; and activists completely trusted by their comrades are covertly turned into spies. According to Massiter, the main mole inside CND was Harry Newton, a sixty-six-year-old veteran of left-wing campaigns who had been recruited by MI5 in the 1950s, when still a member of the Communist Party. Treasurer of the Institute for Workers Control, Newton (says Massiter) advised MI5 that Monsignor Bruce Kent might well be a crypto-Communist and volunteered to provide a complete office layout of CND headquarters – doubtless to facilitate a little bit of what the Americans call burglarizing. According to Massiter, illicit breaking and entering is a full-time activity of one (named) section of the guardians of the realm.

Before we draw comfort in a vision of the sallow boys hurling themselves from the windows of Curzon Street in the wake of such revelations, we should take careful note of the confused cries of anguish and disbelief which Massiter's film provoked among CND's long-serving activists. Harry Newton is dead and beyond interrogation; his close friends hated to hear his reputation defamed. E. P. Thompson, who had known Harry Newton 'off and on for thirty years', regarded him as 'an unlikely agent', adding that as an historian he knew that 'agents always are unlikely persons'. Suspending judgment, he demanded an immediate public inquiry: 'We will not get this inquiry.' Pat Arrowsmith, who has probably never suspended judgment in her entire, gallant life, resumed her long knowledge of Harry Newton and concluded emphatically that no way could such a fine man have worked for MI5. In short, confusion and despondency in the ranks of the 'target'.

Maybe the sallow boys are not clearing their desks in Curzon Street but popping champagne corks. Go further and imagine Miss Massiter as MI5's actress-of-the-year, her task to demoralise, to excite suspicion, to foster a corrosive distrust for every colleague, every familiar face at the annual conference, every tent at Greenham Common. Fantasy? Of course.

'The security services are now the rats' nest in the head of the body politic,' writes E. P. Thompson. He urges, by way of remedy, 'every honourable person who knows of illegitimate abuses of our liberties to blow the whistle together.' Quite right. But he goes further, recommending 'citizens' watch committees in every community, like the Polish committees for social self-defence'. By these tactics we may be able 'to survey the surveillers'. Brown rats to combat the grey rats? How does one 'survey the surveillers' without scrutinising everyone in sight, not least all those operatives *they* will plant in our watch committees, Curzon Street's bearded fruit-juice drinkers holding *Sanity* and *Civil Liberty* under their sulphurous armpits? Vigilantism, like violence, becomes a habit; it cannot be nicely confined and the whole proposal reminds me of the standard Falklands cliché, 'We must fight to show them force doesn't pay.' MI5 ran a Jew called White within the National Front; to con the Fronters, he engaged in physical violence against blacks.

So now we see the hideous contours of the conspiracy confronting us. Our duty, clearly, is to surrender to the unthinkable. We can no longer afford to accept at face value the rugged lines of integrity, the reassuring thatch of white hair, the passionately humane oratory of our great dissenting philosophers and historians. Thompson? G.

D. H. Cole? Bertrand Russell? R. H. Tawney? Each of them, it must now be faced, a master-creation of the waxwork modellers whose commissions are shared between Curzon Street and its money-spinning annexe, Madame Tussaud's. Orwell himelf sat there throughout 1984, tobacco and tiny typewriter before him, staring across at Boy George and Geoffrey Boycott. Ah, Orwell! Why did he really change his name from Eric Blair? Who can now doubt that he was recruited while serving with the Imperial police in Burma? Then deep cover (the struggling writer, the 'down-and-out' assignment in Paris and London, an adaptation exercise known in the Circus as 'charades'). Then north to Wigan and Bradford to cover himself in coal dust and report back to Control on the leading troublemakers among the unemployed. Ready now for the master class – Spain! *Homage to Catalonia* was pay day, a stick of dynamite under the Popular Front. Orwell/Blair's bullet in the neck at Huesca was genuine bad luck, so they got him a job in the basement of 200 Oxford Street, working for the 'Indian Section' of BBC External Services (another annexe, but with animated dummies) while he prepared his final coup, a dagger in the gut of the wartime alliance, *Animal Farm.*

Unfortunately, due to the usual rivalries between the departments, they almost cocked it up, the Ministry of Information begging Jonathan Cape not to publish the anti-Soviet satire to such good effect – the same blunderers also got to Gollancz and T. S. Eliot – that the Circus had to pay off a comparatively unknown publisher called Warburg before they could set the cat among the pigeons and get the book into the shops. But too late to thwart Labour's victory in the post-war election – a few heads rolled for that! The war over, they let Orwell go his own way: MI6 regarded *1984* as a bonus, bonded sealing wax on the Cold War, but I'm told MI5 harboured deep misgivings about a novel which cast the security apparatus, the whole spectre of disinformation technology, as a threat to the liberty of the citizen. Visiting the author in hospital soon after its publication, they quietly pulled the plugs. Nonsense?

How patient is Control: they waited all of forty-one years before launching Thompson's 'The Poverty of Theory', another raging quarrel on the Left, splitting the progressive camp between those enamoured of Parisian jargon and those who preferred Blake.

Of course – grotesque nonsense. Yet it is a distinctive feature of the modern Security State that it hauls the real to the frontier of the surreal with the tenacity of soldier ants dragging a paralysed grasshopper home to their queen.

'Orwell was wrong,' declared Mrs Thatcher, happy in the knowledge that her MI5 had the National Council for Civil Liberties under full surveillance, with files on its General Secretary Patricia Hewitt (now assistant to the Labour leader, Neil Kinnock), on its legal officer Harriet Harman (now a Labour MP), on most of the NCCL's staff, its branch secretaries, and lay members of its council. The logic of this is quite simple. Unlike CND and Greenpeace, the NCCL does not engage in demonstrations or disruptive physical action – it simply monitors and analyses and protests against telephone tapping, mail interception, the bugging of trade unionists, the steady extension of police powers. It is therefore a threat to the defence of the realm.

So are Sarah Tisdall, Clive Ponting and Cathy Massiter. But Miss Massiter, despite her meticulously documented exposé of MI5's full range of illegal activities, was careful to name none of her former colleagues, the operatives. Given the Ponting verdict, the Government knew very well what it had to lose if it took her to court – the identification of one Curzon Street boy after another (albeit *in camera*), an intimidating procession of defence witnesses, mayhem among the filing cabinets. Not worth it.

In a vain effort to minimise the damage, Leon Brittan told the Commons that, to come within the guidelines for legitimate surveillance, a person or activity had *both* to threaten 'the safety or wellbeing of the state' *and* to be intended 'to undermine or overthrow parliamentary democracy by political, industrial or violent means.' Considering these two criteria, both necessary preconditions for surveillance, one is baffled beyond measure to understand how they could cover, for example, the National Council for Civil Liberties. But Mr Brittan, in that fine old tradition, would answer no questions concerning specific persons or specific organisations. Silence is the rule.

SIXTEEN

It has often been said that Britain, unlike Germany and Japan, did not suffer during the last war a destruction of her obsolescent industrial plant thorough enough to impose the modernisation of technology and attitudes required of a competitive nation. Indeed the military victory in 1945 may have fertilised an innate smugness, a self-congratulatory insularity, which later landed us in the pea soup of stagnation. No doubt this is a simplification but let us hang on for the moment to what must be at least half-true. The myopic self-confidence which led post-war governments to turn their backs on European integration was also bound up with the confident assumption that our own traditions of liberty and democracy were rooted in more solid foundations than those which had crumbled across the Channel – witness our post-war 'loyalty-security programme' (to borrow the American term) which was on the whole conducted with exemplary restraint.

The Cold War did come to Britain and Attlee did, in 1948, introduce a 'positive vetting' programme. And there were the famous spy cases – the atomic physicists Alan Nunn May and Klaus Fuchs, the diplomats Burgess and MacLean – which generated intermittent hysteria. Nevertheless, American liberals, confronted by the livid paranoia which gripped a whole society from 1948 until the late fifties (commonly mis-termed 'McCarthyism', though the Senator from Wisconsin merely jumped on a bandwagon set in motion by the Truman administration) – the American liberals constantly paid tribute to the 'British way', the innate restraint and good sense of the old island race. No general purge swept the British civil service, the professions, the universities, the labour force; Parliamentary committees did not embark on a dragnet witch-hunt; there was no 'Un-British Activities Committee'.

Times have changed and *The Times* too. One will not find in its leader columns today any echo of these words, published in March 1948 in response to Attlee's announced security programme:

> Rightly these go as far as possible, without imperilling security, to leave a Communist in the enjoyment of his job, even in the Civil Service.

One will not find in the popular right-wing press today any echo of the outraged response of Lord Beaverbrook's *Evening Standard* to the same security programme:

> We are flirting with unwholesome things, strange to our way of thinking, slimy to our touch, monstrous with the possibilities of injustice, oppression and private revenge.

The following morning Beaverbrook's *Daily Express* demanded:

> But who says that Britain is so open to a Communist coup that she is forced to dabble in Communist devices to counteract it?

According to my estimate, during the fifteen years after World War II, some 9,500 American civil servants were fired on loyalty security grounds; a further 15,000 resigned while under investigation; over 2,000 industrial workers and 3,800 seamen were forced out of their jobs; more than 300 producers, actors and writers were blacklisted in films, television and radio; among municipal and state employees, the casualty count exceeded 500; 600 school teachers were fired; and about 500 people were arrested for deportation on account of their real or suspected political convictions. Behind these banal statistics lay the wider, all-encompassing fear of an age of suspicion and paranoia.

Innate good sense was our priceless treasure. The fact that the British loyalty security programme never reached purge proportions, and never allowed itself so manifest a profile as its German counterpart, the *Berufsverbot*, merely reinforced myopic self-congratulation. By 1961, about 163 British civil servants had been suspended, but only an estimated fifty of them were dismissed or forced to resign. While American conscripts in the armed forces suffered a draconian purge on account of their past political affiliations, in 1956 the British Secretary for War revealed that only 27 regular soldiers – and no conscript national servicemen – had been discharged on security grounds.

Among distinguished American scholars who pointed to the British way as a model while fending off local vigilantes, one could mention Grenville Clark of Harvard, the sociologist Robert M. MacIver, the historian Henry Steele Commager, Herman Finer, professor of political science at the University of Chicago, former Attorney General Francis Biddle, and so on. Visiting England while researching a major work on civil liberties sponsored by Columbia University, Eleanor Bontecou reported: 'There appears to be clear recognition . . . that in such a struggle the bludgeon techniques of suppression are valueless. The surrender of traditional values . . . is regarded as not only dangerous . . . but also unnecessary.'

American observers noticed that, paradoxically, the British constitution – unwritten, customary, executive-orientated – appeared at first sight to provide fewer safeguards for civil liberties than the American Bill of Rights and 'separation of powers'. Herman Finer therefore concluded: 'Liberty is more genuinely guaranteed by the spirit of decency, fair-play, self-restraint and concern for the rule of law than by the rigid outlines of procedure.'

And isn't this precisely the form in which we like to congratulate ourselves? Theodore H. White, the journalist-historian of successive presidential campaigns, diagnosed the crucial British asset as a sense of kinship: 'This kinship begins, I think, in the simple ability the British have to associate .... They have somehow acquired a trust in each other that rises tier by tier to their trust in government and willingness to let it lead.'

Professors H. H. Wilson and Harvey Glickman concluded a detailed survey of British internal security procedures with this appreciation: 'There is a characteristic confidence, unspoken and probably deprecated, in the loyalty, devotion and common sense of the ordinary citizen . . . there is present a calm certainty that the "other chap" will play the game and do his part.' Reviewing their book, Professor Thomas I. Emerson, of Yale, commented: 'The British have not succumbed to hysteria . . . They have met the new problems with calmness, without fear, rationally, and with the utmost confidence in the ultimate worth of their tradition.'

Professor Robert K. Carr, of Dartmouth College, found 'an air of calmness and a spirit of assuredness in England that seems to reflect faith in established institutions, trust in the common sense and loyalty of the people, and confidence in the integrity and fairness of public officials.'

Indeed many of these American anglophiles, firm believers in democracy though they were, actually diagnosed the poisonous factor in American society as the demagogic populism of politicians constantly whipping up support among the electorate – whereas by contrast it was the self-assured élitism of the British tradition of *noblesse oblige* which provided an enduring guarantee of civil liberties. As Carr perceived it, the British governing class is swayed by honour, duty and reason rather than by the vagaries of maddened public opinion.

Observing sinister developments in the United States during the 1950s, the British press wallowed in self-congratulation. The *Manchester Guardian* deplored these 'exhibitions of the crude persecuting spirit . . . a spiritual totalitarianism as dangerous in its way as that of Moscow.'

The *News Chronicle* warned its readers that 'Americans themselves are practising those very evils of which they accuse the Kremlin and its satellites.'

Expressing disgust at the latest speech by J. Edgar Hoover, Director of the FBI, to the xenophobic American Legion, *Reynolds News* invited its readers to imagine the unimaginable: 'It would be as though the chief of Scotland Yard climbed down into the ring of sectarian politics in Britain and branded every shade of opinion different from his own as "Communist or Communist-inspired".' *Reynolds News*, alas, was dead before the advent of the new generation of Chief Constables: Mark and McNee of London, Alderton of Manchester.

Applauded by many American libertarians, the British system

205

continued to substitute 'good sense' for 'due process'. We didn't need to codify our civil liberties because they supposedly circulated, like anti-bodies, in our national blood stream. British civil servants and servicemen who came under suspicion had no right to legal representation (until September 1962) and no right of appeal to a tribunal or court. The three-man advisory board (consisting normally of retired civil servants) was worth, in its vast wisdom, any number of shouting attorneys. The advisory board was not obliged to disclose how or why allegations had been made, and if evidence might reveal sources then that, too, could be withheld. Cross-examination of hostile witnesses was not permitted. All very well provided that the Three Wise Men displayed good sense and tolerance for unorthodox opinions; but not so very well once the American infection, a kind of political AIDS, entered the national blood stream. Unknown to the American liberals, the British establishment was rapidly absorbing the tougher postures prevailing across the Atlantic. It was on 14 August 1954 that the *Daily Telegraph* warned that Communists and their allies must be treated not as fellow-citizens but as conspirators against the state on the American model.

In 1956 the Government published the *Findings of a Conference of Privy Councillors on Security*, the prevailing philosophy of which was encapsulated in the following comment: 'it is right to continue the practice of tilting the balance in favour of offering greater protection to the security of the State rather than . . . safeguarding the rights of the individual.' In 1962 followed the Radcliffe Committee Inquiry into internal security and subversion. 'We have followed the common practice,' the Committee subsequently reported, 'of using the phrase "Communist" throughout to include fascists.'

The secret state has been injected into political and industrial disputes by Labour administrations as well as Tory. In the early 1960s MI5 lent its services to right-wing Labour leaders determined to dig dirt on their own colleagues in Parliament. To demonstrate that the 'Left' was no less patriotic, Prime Minister Harold Wilson used, as he proudly recalled in his memoirs, the security apparatus to smash the seamen's strike of 1966. His tactics were those perfected by American Congressional committees against the International Longshoremen, the United Electrical Workers, and Mine, Mill and Smelter Workers: red-baiting. And we have seen how, in 1983, Heseltine's misuse of both MI5 and the MoD's civil service resulted in a smear campaign against CND worthy of the prevailing rhetoric in the age of Truman and Eisenhower.

One assumes that those distinguished American admirers of the British way might have been surprised by some of Cathy Massiter's disclosures: the phone-tapping of David Higgs of the Fire Brigades

Union so that the Department of Employment could know in advance the union's 'bottom line' in wage negotiations; the same tactic, and violation of guidelines, in the case of Sid Harraway, a shop steward during the Ford dispute at Dagenham in 1977-78; the breaking into and bugging of the home of Ken Gill, general secretary of Tass, the white-collar section of the engineering union; the constant bugging and tapping of leaders of the National Union of Mineworkers. 'Scargill,' recalls Massiter, 'would occasionally shout abuse into the phone at the people who were tapping him.'

Now occurred a marked historical reversal. America witnessed a surge of disgust against the epidemic excesses of 'McCarthyism' and the unregulated covert activities of the clandestine agencies, the CIA and the FBI. The lifelong hero of red-blooded Americans, J. Edgar Hoover, was reincarnated in feature films as a scheming dictator. Films can't be wrong. The Supreme Court, no longer crouching dutifully before the altar of the Cold War, rediscovered the Bill of Rights. The scattershot Congressional investigations were curbed, the agencies were subjected to open Congressional scrutiny, while prosecutors and grand juries dug dirt on executive misdemeanours, not stopping short of the President. 'Watergate' would have been impossible in the United Kingdom, not because such executive malpractice is inconceivable here, but because the ensuing investigation would have been smothered by a tribunal of three retired judges reporting directly, and in strict confidence, to Prime Minister 'Nixon' himself.

A Freedom of Information Act was passed in 1966 and reinforced in 1974, and the American tradition of 'due process' was reinforced by the spirit of tolerance, of what Isaiah Berlin has called 'negative liberty', once so admired in Britain. The British, meanwhile, stubbornly rejected due process while expanding their security services and – perhaps more significant – expanding their criteria of what is 'subversive' or a 'threat to the realm'. Parliament didn't want to know. Bitter pill though it may be to swallow, the best defence of our civil liberties is now the European Convention on Human Rights under whose scathing judgments our governments irritably and obstructively writhe.

Our liberals now adopt Truman's criteria for 'subversion' rather than McCarthy's. With a few notable exceptions, to whom all honour, American liberals began to yell about 'McCarthyism' only when the Senator from Wisconsin (aided by Eastland, McCarran and the rest) turned the terms of the post-war purge against the liberal Democrats who had themselves sanctioned a full-scale onslaught not only on the Communist Party but also on supporters of Henry Wallace and anyone who ever belonged to any of the organisations 'listed' by Truman's attorney-generals. What apparently brought Cathy Massiter to crisis point was the flagrant breach of guidelines for the security services, rather than the guidelines themselves. She wanted a line to be drawn between investigating Communists and Trotskyists (legitimate) and extending the trawl to cover uncontaminated liberals and radicals. For this attitude there is an ancient rationale which purports to distinguish between the enemies and friends of our democratic system. But it is a hazy line, unresponsive to the complex, often idiosyncratic, factors determining nominal political allegiance. Not only Senator McCarthy but also Mr Heseltine have demonstrated how easy it is to set up a colour chart of 'disloyalty' where shades of red and pink are subsumed in a single continuum of contamination.

'Guilt by association' was the scourge not only of the McCarthy era but of the Truman era which preceded it. It is still alive and well in Britain where the opposition parties merely cavil over definitions. The legacy of the 'Natopolitan', Cold War culture which came to the ascendant in the 1950s, in the heyday of the Congress for Cultural Freedom, is still with us, now reinforced by a more efficient and ruthless state apparatus.

In the 1980s no less than the 1950s, social democrats and liberals – recoiling from the smelly specimens to their left – have themselves to blame for the evils against which they now, in tragically isolated acts of defiance, rebel. A fastidious rejection of the Left, a subscription to the cosy dichotomy of 'moderates' and 'extremists', a determined ghetto-ising of dubious bedfellows, always reinforces the culture upon which the purgers, surveillance men and secretive governments depend for tacit popular support and tacit Parliamentary acquiescence. The weekly front-page contest between the *Observer* newspaper and the administrative machine is really a game: 'secret' and 'secrecy' are digits in a battle for circulation; the paper catches the bureaucrats by the balls but has no wish to pull them off; wicked Whitehall investigations or purges are flanked on both sides by the *Observer*'s own regular diet of spy scares and inflammatory 'investigations' of left-wing influence in trade unions or anything under the sun. This is our liberal Sunday newspaper.

'Inside the whale' was Orwell's phrase for the place where we curl up, like the foetus in the womb, to rob reality of its terrors by simply submitting to it. The hostile reaction of the fighting liberal to Big Brother's footprints under his nose and across his desk might be termed 'half out of the whale'.

APPENDIX

The *Belgrano* and the Peruvian Peace Proposals

According to the MP for Linlithgow, Mrs Thatcher sank the *Belgrano* precisely in order to torpedo a peace settlement which would have robbed her of the military victory she desperately needed for political survival. On 24 March 1983, he told the House that she had given the order 'in the knowledge that Galtieri had ordered the withdrawal of the army from the Falklands-Malvinas on the evening of Saturday, 1 May, on the basis of the Peruvian-American peace terms.'

This was fantasy; Galtieri gave no such order. On the same day Dalyell ventured into even wilder realms of 'proof'. It was 'inconceivable', he said, that the *Belgrano* and her escorts had not been aware that they were being shadowed by the huge SSN, *Conqueror* – yet most of the cruiser's victims were killed while at leisure in the canteen or sleeping quarters. 'Does not that show that Captain Hector Bonzo of *Belgrano* believed that the war was over?'

No, merely that he was unaware of the shadowing submarine.

In a speech delivered on 12 May 1983 Dalyell asserted that twelve hours before the attack on the *Belgrano*, 'in the early hours of Sunday [2 May], President Belaunde [of Peru] received a call from Galtieri accepting the Peruvian peace plan and promising to put it to the junta that afternoon.'

We shall see that this claim, too, is incorrect.

Dalyell fastened on to a long report by Paul Foot, who had recently visited Peru, published in the *New Statesman* on 13 May. Foot had written:

> By noon US time, 5pm GMT [on 2 May], after all, the seven-point peace plan had been agreed between Belaunde, Haig and Galtieri. Even before he sat down to lunch with Haig, Francis Pym must have known about this, and expressed his own agreement. He must, too, have conveyed it back to Chequers. If the order to sink had in fact been given at lunch-time, there was still time to countermand the order, or to try and countermand it. For the *Belgrano* was not sunk until three hours later.

In fact there was time to countermand the original order when

209

at 15.00 *Conqueror* signalled that the cruiser had been steaming due west for six hours – but that had nothing to do with the alternative drama, the Peruvian peace plan.

Although Dalyell drew heavily on Foot (he himself had not yet made his own pilgrimage to Peru), and although Foot's information was at critical points inaccurate, it is noticeable that Foot did not describe Galtieri's 'acceptance' of the Peruvian proposals in such unqualified terms as Dalyell: 'Galtieri phoned Belaunde in the early morning. The high command, he said, was almost unanimous in approving the terms, though there were a number of small points to be negotiated.'

We will come to those 'small points'.

At this stage (mid-1983), both Dalyell and Foot still believed, quite understandably, that in sinking the *Belgrano* Mrs Thatcher had scuttled not only the Peruvian plan but Foreign Secretary Pym as well. This illusion was strengthened by Pym's remarks at a news conference immediately after he arrived in Washington on 1 May: 'No further military action is envisaged at the moment except to keep the exclusion zone secure.' Decent Squire Pym, the one dove in a War Cabinet of hawks, shamefully betrayed! It is true that Pym was more doveish than his colleagues, but when he made the quoted statement in Washington he already knew that on the previous day the War Cabinet had decided to sink Argentina's most valuable warship, the *25 de Mayo*, wherever she might be found. He had protested but he had not resigned; and the assurance he offered in Washington could not with honour be given in the light of what he knew.

In October 1983 Dalyell flew to Lima (at his own expense, as he tirelessly points out), talked to President Belaunde and other principals, and returned home more than ever convinced that Pym had said yes to Haig and told London that peace was imminent. Not only Pym, indeed, but the British ambassador in Peru, Charles Wallace, had been kept fully informed. Indeed Belaunde had expected that Wallace and the Argentine ambassador to Peru would initial the peace document that very evening, Sunday, 2 May, 1982.

What is the truth of the matter? An objective observer must watch two things closely: the content of the peace proposals; and the clock. British summer time is five hours ahead of East Coast time in the United States, four hours ahead of South Atlantic and Buenos Aires time, six hours ahead of Lima time.

Belaunde's first conversation with Galtieri, by telephone, did not take place until 01.30 on 2 May – a couple of hours after the British task force commander, Admiral Woodward, got through to Northwood to request permission to sink the *Belgrano*. The two Latin American leaders talked, according to Gavshon and Rice, for

210

forty-five minutes. The transcript of the conversation shows that Galtieri was receptive, indeed grateful, for the Peruvian-American initiative. He promised to consult his colleagues and call back.

He did not call back 'in the early hours' of 2 May; in fact it was Belaunde who again called Galtieri. It was now 10.00 in Buenos Aires, 14.00 in London – the decision to sink the *Belgrano* had already been made and the order relayed. Galtieri handed negotiations over to Foreign Minister Costa Mendez, who conveyed two far from minor objections to Balaunde. According to Paul Foot's article: 'The membership of the contact group [of four nations] was left open, though it was suggested that Canada might come in for the US and Venezuela for Peru.' In fact Costa Mendez vetoed the US outright as too pro-British. He also insisted that the wishes of the Falkland islanders should be weighed but not regarded as paramount; and the new, neutral administration of the islands would have to 'replace everything that was British administration'.

When Belaunde telephoned Haig in Washington with this news it was agreed between them that if the US was unacceptable to the Argentinians as a contact nation, then Peru, too, would be vetoed by the British. Hardly encouraging: the two nations sponsoring the entire plan would have to bow out and it was not known who could replace them. As for the substance of Costa Mendez's demands, they would hardly be acceptable to the British Cabinet.

Pym has said that there was nothing firm, 'nothing on paper' that he could convey to London when he lunched with Haig. The facts already cited must corroborate this. Nor was there any guarantee that when the Argentine junta met that evening they would be able to agree a concerted position; the military barons all had separate swords to sharpen; Galtieri's authority was minimal. We shall never know because the news of the *Belgrano* disaster arrived in the middle of that meeting and it was felt that in honour the only possible response could be ferocious retaliation. The junta rejected the plan and Pym made much of this on 4 May, disingenuously omitting the main reason.

What misled opinion across the world was Belaunde's dramatic, but irresponsible, press conference in Lima, announcing an imminent peace – by which time the *Belgrano* was beneath the waves.

The subsequent British peace proposals, and their rejection by Argentina, merely reinforce the conclusion that the Peruvian-American plan could not have bridged the gap between the two protagonists. Presented on 17 May to the General Secretary of the UN, the British proposals coincided in some respects with the earlier plan: an immediate ceasefire, mutual military withdrawal, interim third-party administration of the islands, and negotiations for a settlement. But while the British were prepared to withdraw no further than 150 miles from the Falklands, the junta insisted that both nations must return their armed forces to home base. The main crunch, however, came over the interim administration of the Falklands/Malvinas. The British wanted to restore the *status quo ante* in so far as UN rule was to be 'in conformity with traditional laws and practices and in consultation with the Legislative and Executive Councils, the Islanders' representative institutions. . . .' Such a stipulation was unacceptable to Buenos Aires, which insisted on free access for its nationals with respect to work, residence and property – a claim, incidentally, which brings no comfort to Tam Dalyell's argument that the Argentinians were interested only in nominal sovereignty, not re-colonisation.

Ponting is right about this: 'There were really two irreconcilable positions. Diplomacy could have sorted out interim arrangements but the crucial question at the end was always: Who's going to get the islands? In essence the Argentinians wanted a guarantee that after a short time they'd get them. Thatcher could not sign up to that.' In fact Ponting first said, 'No British Government, particularly not Thatcher. . . .', but then revised his comment.